RUNS IN THE FAMILY

(2nd Edition)

Kevin Ikenberry

Theogony Books
Virginia Beach, VA

Chris Kennedy/Theogony Books
2052 Bierce Dr.
Virginia Beach, VA 23454
https://chriskennedypublishing.com/

Publisher's Note: This is a work of fiction. Names, characters, places, and incidents are a product of the author's imagination. Locales and public names are sometimes used for atmospheric purposes. Any resemblance to actual people, living or dead, or to businesses, companies, events, institutions, or locales is completely coincidental.

Ordering Information:
Quantity sales. Special discounts are available on quantity purchases by corporations, associations, and others. For details, contact the "Special Sales Department" at the address above.

Runs In The Family/ Kevin Ikenberry. – 2nd ed.
ISBN 978-1942936978

For My Girls

Chapter One

An impossibly perky voice bounced through the women's dormitory announcing the dinner trip to a nearby restaurant. "Come on, everyone! Let's go spend our last night on Eden having good food, dancing, and fun!" The cut-stone walls only managed to amplify the annoying pitch of the girl's voice and add a reverberating echo for good measure.

The group's intended plans gave a momentary pause to Mairin's hands as she laid out her linens for the night. Rubbing her throbbing temples, Mairin Shields decided she could definitely eat, and the prospect of a bland meal like lunch in the Civil Cafeteria turned her stomach. She didn't know anybody in this group of women other than Alicia Jones and her entourage. While a disadvantage, the anonymity she had from those she did not know leveled the playing field. Maybe just this once there'd be a little parity. Mairin snorted. The Academy had been nothing more than high school with a four-year academic hangover. Cliques and groups filtering through the halls and buildings in search of their identity, and wanting desperately for the popular groups to notice them, would never change, and it made Mairin sick.

Mairin had endured fourteen years in the Eden Academy flitting from group to group aimlessly, never quite accepted by one, never quite abandoned by another. She played sports, but honestly, did anyone equate golf to a sport anymore? She enjoyed drama, but never found herself cast no matter how hard she worked. She went through the motions as a good student, but not brilliant enough to gain the notice of her peers. Anonymity and mediocrity were her friends, though her teachers plied her for more and often got what they sought from her. The flashes of brilliance died quickly though as the culture of her peers crashed in. Gaining the notice of a teacher tended to write off the rest of the year socially.

Loneliness was a relative term anyway. Her parents lived and worked light-years away, separating themselves by an impressive gulf of two galaxies. Outside of an occasional letter or hologram, the last time the three of them managed to be in the same place at the same time was during the Festival of Holidays three years before. Sure she could talk to them, but when she needed encouragement or support the three-day wait for a reply to her holomails weighed on her. Especially because the other women at school thrived on reminding her that her parents were away, that she was unworthy of their friendship, and an outsider.

Sleepless nights spent sitting in her closet with her sobbing face in a pillow brought no comfort, only a small tight steel band of resilience in her gut. It wasn't much, but she'd made it this far, wherever that was going to take her. Until this morning, that journey wasn't much to be excited about. Colonel Munsen changed all of that.

She glanced at her bunkmate. The short-haired girl said, "Might as well get some real food. Gods, what a day."

Mairin nodded with a shy smile. "Sure." As the group of girls gathered by the barracks room door, she made her way to the rear of the group. Alicia Jones took her position as the ringleader and looked at the expectant faces turned to her. She caught Mairin's eyes for a fleeting second and smiled.

This is a bad idea, Mairin thought, as she followed the group outdoors.

The grass of the Civil Quadrangle shimmered gold in the fading sunlight, the full disc of Adam, the larger of Eden's two moons, rising over the horizon. Selected by the governments of Earth as the first colonization planet, Eden was nearly a perfect copy of the distant Earth. Slightly larger, and with a marginally more severe tilt and similar gravity, it gave the appearance of an abundant world shaped by eons of development. With considerable terraforming efforts, Eden developed its biosphere in the span of only ten years. Just enough time to evacuate a sizable portion of Earth's population to colony ships and make their way across the void seventy light years.

First contact with the Vemeh in 2105 nearly destroyed Earth, a true case of mistaken identity. The Vemeh found Voyager 2, and the Golden Record—meant to portray the diversity of life and culture on Earth—was misinterpreted as a distress call. The Vemeh attacked Earth's major population centers, killing almost exclusively men, with devastating effect. Within a few hours, the Vemeh realized the error they'd made and committed themselves and their allied civilizations to making reparations. The Vemeh gave humanity the keys to the universe. One hundred and seventy-five years later, humanity had spread deep into the void.

Mairin felt the last traces of sunlight warming the side of her face as they walked down the main thoroughfare. More civilians roamed the city's heart now, the unlucky ones who worked the first day of the week's end. Shops and restaurants sprang to life from their afternoon siestas as evening blossomed through the city. A cool dry breeze sifted down through the mountains. Mairin smelled the wind and knew rain would come. Maybe not today, but soon. It wouldn't matter to her; she'd be off the planet in the morning enroute to her training site back on Earth. She'd spend five weeks aboard the *Fleet Battle Platform Yorktown* getting to know her imprint.

The last lingering sensations from the imprint procedure finally abated. A mild headache, and nothing worse than that. When would it manifest itself? And how? She didn't want nightmares, especially ones about things she knew nothing about. The breeze made her shiver a little, but she looked up into the darkening sky and smiled. *Relax*, she reminded herself, *take things one step at a time.*

The group chatted and gossiped about the day of medical tests, examinations, and the cute male nurse in Room Three. Mairin smiled but said nothing. She hadn't set foot in Room Three all day.

After starting the initial exam, a message flashed on her screen to report to Room Six. A trim, stone-faced man in a Terran Defense Force dress uniform stood waiting for her. In his hands was a file with her name on it.

"Let's get down to brass tacks, shall we, Mairin? You're not fit for military service and your administrative specialist track work here at the Academy is sub-par at best. You're headed for a lifetime of menial service."

Mairin lowered her head. His words were everything that her parents said, except theirs came from vmail messages and holotapes from their colonial positions far out on the Rim. She met his eyes and watched a smile come across his face.

"My name is Colonel Munsen, and I'm here to offer you a unique opportunity."

She blinked behind her eyeglasses and smoothed her straight black hair away from her face. "What kind of opportunity, sir?"

Munsen nodded as if her words pleased him. "It's classified, Mairin, but if it works you'll have a genetically perfect body capable of limited increase in human performance and a career in the Terran Defense Forces."

For a moment, she'd stared at him. "What's the catch?"

Munsen laughed and put his hands on his hips. In the dim light of the room, she could see he was older, with gray hair at his temples. He rubbed his face with his left hand, and then flexed his fingers as if looking for something. There was no wedding ring. "You're a genetic match to a soldier who died a long time ago, your great-great-great grandfather. We're hoping to transfer some of his memories to you."

"And if it doesn't work?"

Munsen opened his palms to her. "No harm, no foul. You'll still have the genetic perfection and I'll ensure you can re-test for military service, if you'd like."

Mairin chewed on her lower lip for a second. "And if it does work?"

"You'll go to the front," Munsen said. "We need strong combat leaders, Mairin. It's my hope that is what this procedure will do for you. That and a significant amount of holotraining. What do you say?"

There hadn't been a thing to say except yes. Life in janitorial services or worse was not what she wanted, nor what she felt she deserved. Everyone around her always looked past her. Even the group of women leaving the dormitory had no idea she was there.

They entered the restaurant, Togolth's, and found themselves seated in an almost private room at a table expansive enough to accommodate all of them. Mairin sat along the back of the room, nearest the rear exits and hung her sweater jacket off the back of her chair. A flurry of waiters appeared with towels hung on their arms asking for drink orders.

The popular girls trilled over the wine list, snobbishly commenting on their inferior choices and lavishing praise on vintages they'd probably never been able to afford. A few girls ordered mixed drinks, fruity frozen concoctions only just potable. The mahogany bar was magnificent from polished top to bright brass rails at its feet. Familiar beer taps hung above it and shined in the fading light of the day streaming through the windows. *Out of place*, she thought. It belonged in a dark pub not a faux bistro. Mairin looked at the waiter, her eyes twinkling brightly enough the waiter noticed and smiled.

"For you, miss?"

Mairin hadn't even looked at the menu. She nodded toward the bar. "I'll have a Guinness, please."

"You're drinking *beer*?" Alicia Jones demanded from down the table, bringing conversation to a screeching halt. The smile on her face was the condescending face of damnation.

Mairin blinked. *What was she talking about?* A different waiter placed a perfectly poured stout fresh from the ornate brass taps on the table in front of her and bounced away. She didn't look up at Alicia, she looked at the stout and wrapped her hand around the pint and drank. The foam tickled her upper lip, but she swallowed a good mouthful of the stout and felt a rush of blood in her ears. She licked her lips savoring the dark, sweet, and bitter stout, and drank again. Lowering the glass, she smiled at Alicia and said, "*Slainté*."

"What is *that* supposed to mean?"

Mairin grinned through her shock. *What a trigger!* "It's Irish for health. What do you care?" When Alicia turned away to another conversation in horror, Mairin beamed at her reflection in the mirror and gently touched the metal band on her wrist, activating her neurals. Within a second, she'd sent an acknowledgement of the first physical trigger to Munsen. The first beer of her life tasted like something she'd craved for days. She raised the glass, toasting her reflection silently. *Well, Grandpa, what else are you going to show me?*

Dinner conversation flowed about prospective job assignments and hopeful destinations. Mairin didn't care. She drank two pints of Guinness and picked at her pseudo-Italian neo food. Every other girl raved over it, but it was bland. Mairin knew it wasn't her voice, her taste buds, her stomach or anything else giving her that conclusion. It was the imprint. She wanted something...fresh. Something that didn't taste recycled. Something that came straight from the ground. The group stood to leave and bubbled outside en masse. Mairin retrieved her jacket and followed, but outside the bistro's door, she waited until Alicia and her giggling brood disappeared around the far corner heading in the opposite direction towards the business district. She breathed in the evening air and headed in the direction of the Eden Market. With luck, the local farm stands would still be open, and she could find something to satisfy her taste buds.

An hour later, after a walking meal of fresh bread and mutton with Muenster cheese and two green apples, Mairin returned to the campus. Eve rose in the east as a perfect half circle of bluish light as she made her way back to the empty barracks. She collected her belongings and the linens from her bed and made her way to the elevators. On the top floor, she found the roof access and stepped outside into the lush recycled garden. Mairin didn't know quite how it worked, but every large building held rooftops that repurposed the wastewater produced inside and contributed to the building's electrical power through passive chlorophyll-generated power. How plants producing their sugar interwove with the production of electricity Mairin didn't know. She wasn't a heliobotanist. She'd been trained to handle administrative forms and processes, not the science of this new universe. She settled under the fronds of a stunted palm and laid out her linens into a makeshift bed. She sat cross-legged for a long moment before she chuckled. "Can't say I've ever slept under the stars before."

She lay down, supporting her head with her hands, elbows off to each side and smiled up into the stars. Destiny lay out there in the heavens. Not the one that she'd expected, but her destiny just the same. Familiar scents took on new spicy twinges. A cool breeze raised pimples on her skin.

Goose pimples.

The words came from the depths of her mind and echoed slightly. She looked through the sawgrass lining the roof's edge toward the low mountains. Mists curled in and out of the mountains giving the appearance of purple whales playing in a dark gray sea.

Foxfire, she thought and then said aloud. She didn't understand it, but a quick check of her neurals showed it to be a colloquial term from Appalachia. The back of her neck tingled. She smiled and spoke to the wind, "I can see I have a lot to learn."

Sleep took her without much more thought and brought dreams of horses, sabers, and bugles.

* * *

Early the next morning, Mairin met Colonel Munsen on the steps of the Civil Assignments building. "Good morning, Colonel."

"Miss Shields," he smiled. "Thank you for meeting me this early. I have one simple question for you. Are you willing to serve in the Terran Defense Force?"

Mairin sighed. "I'm afraid, sir, but willing to go."

"What are you scared of?" Munsen leaned toward her.

Dying was the first word that surfaced in her head. She tossed it away. Everyone dies, whether it would be on a battlefield doing something tangible or in a crappy job on a civil colony could be her choice. Fear wasn't the answer either. She'd been alone too long to be afraid of much except not knowing what to do. "I'm afraid I'm not ready to join the TDF, sir."

Munsen took a long slow breath, but did not stop looking at her. "Let me tell you a secret, Shields. None of us are ready when we think we are. It's just something you have to do to the best of your ability. The rest of it will work itself out."

"I understand, sir. And my training?"

"You will immediately enter into the Terran Defense Force in the grade of cadet. You will be transported to Earth for officer training, at the completion of which you will be commissioned as a second lieutenant. You'll start holotraining immediately. Upon completion of your advanced training, you will be reviewed for assimilation to your imprint's last held rank. Are you aware of what that was?"

She thought for a moment. Images of horses and guidon flags, tanks and personnel carriers filled her head. "Captain. And I want the cavalry."

He laughed. "I'll make sure that you are considered for it, but I believe that you'll be accepted. Especially in light of recent events."

"What do you mean, sir?"

"The Greys attacked along the Outer Rim yesterday. Our forces are marshaling for operations, and your life is about to get interesting. Still want this?"

Mairin had expected the outbreak of war to have more of an effect on her, instead of instant acceptance and commitment. She nodded. "Yes, sir. When do we leave?"

He looked down at her bag and smiled. "If you're ready, we can depart right now. The *Forrestal* is in orbit and preparing to debark for Earth. The *Yorktown* headed toward the Rim a few hours ago. With a fold generator, we'll have a five-week journey."

Mairin replied. "What will I do for five weeks?"

"Sleep, mainly. The first portion of your training is a more in-depth imprint and basic training. Some weapons familiarization and how to conduct planning for operations. All standard stuff, really. You'll wake up and proceed directly to field training." Munsen laughed. "The best drill sergeants we have are all virtual now. The best way to ensure the training is perfect."

"We can leave whenever you want, sir."

"No goodbyes?"

Mairin laughed. "Not here."

Munsen nodded. "There's one last thing we have to do. One of the things a commissioned officer holds most dear is their commission. It is a direct appointment from the Executive branch of government. The commission is for life. The oath you are about to take is similar to that, but only extends to your performance and training as a cadet. As a commissioned officer, you will be able to do this as well, commission cadets and eventually officers into the TDF. Are you ready?"

Mairin stood up straight, her imprint putting her at the position of attention. "Yes, sir."

"Then raise your right hand, and repeat after me." Mirroring each other in the dawning sunlight, they recited the oath of office tweaked only slightly from the original oath sworn by the officers of the Continental Army of the United States nearly five hundred years before. Munsen dropped his hand at the end, "Congratulations."

What in the hell have I just done? Mairin tried to smile. "I'm not quite sure what to think. This has happened so quickly."

"I think you will do well based on what I've seen."

"You've been watching me before the whole imprint thing as well?" Mairin shook her head. "I should have known that, sir."

And if you've been watching me, that means I'm more than an experiment, too. Whatever that means.

Munsen laughed, "The new part of you does know about it, and would have suspected it, and is not surprised, you mean."

"Maybe so, sir." Mairin chuckled. She looked around the quiet quadrangle and into the yellow sun of Eden. *I'm never coming back here. And I'm okay with that.*

But I have much to learn. Including just who in the hell you were, Grandpa.

She gazed into the warm morning sunlight. *In for a penny, in for a pound*, she told herself. *Don't look back, no matter what.* And she didn't, not even after the *Forrestal* pushed gently out of orbit and began to spool up its fold engine.

* * * * *

Chapter Two

"It's been three weeks, Thom. You have an explanation for this, I presume?" On the small video screen, the Chairman reclined her chair and reached for a pack of tobacco free cigarettes without meeting Munsen's eyes. He knew she'd be furious, but her breach of etiquette surprised him. Scientists, no matter their stature, didn't talk to Coalition commanders in that tone.

"I fail to see where you need an explanation, Madame Chairman."

She looked over the flickering end of her cigarette and narrowed her eyes. "Colonel, let me be perfectly clear with you. Imprinting, while technically a military procedure, falls under this directorate as my personal responsibility to the Coalition. While I report to you by the letter of the law, the care of the patients is my sole responsibility, and not yours. Are we clear?"

Munsen nodded, but said nothing as they locked eyes for a good ten seconds.

She cleared her throat. "Now. Why are you going to leave her at Libretto and not bring her to Earth, as required by regulation, for indoctrination and training under close supervision? And why did you commission her as a captain?"

"Her imprint took faster than any previous and the depth of the connection seemed worthy of self-development."

"She should have come to Earth for that diagnosis. She could've gone walkabout here and been constantly monitored. Her imprint is one of the best we've ever seen take, but leaving her in Styrahi space, unmonitored and unaccounted for is a security risk! You've jeopardized this program!"

Munsen frowned. "How have I done that, Madame Chairwoman? The Styrahi worked with us to develop the encephalographic hologram readers and integrate DNA to the actual brain scan. They gave us the technology to connect the two; how can this officer's imprint be a goddamn security risk? They helped make her!"

"Have you read the full file of her imprint? Her ancestor?"

Munsen nodded. "Nothing there that's a security risk, either. Good soldier, a little concern with his failed marriage, but he progressed normally through the officer ranks until his death in combat. Decorated for bravery, again nothing that causes any type of concern for security, unless you aren't telling me something."

"The biggest concern I have is far beyond this imprint business. You're taking an untested, barely trained officer into combat. In a division of a type that hasn't been fielded in over a hundred years, I might add." She smoked for a moment. "You're convinced that she's the right person for this operation?"

Munsen folded his hands. "From all of the imprints I've seen, hers has the requisite knowledge."

The chairwoman shook her head. "If this imprint continues to integrate, it could become the most complete imprint ever done. That is a security risk because it would be a perfect integration of memories, instincts, and training from generation to generation."

"And the Greys most likely do not have the need for such technology," Munsen continued. "The Styrahi use imprinting frequently, and are not concerned with perfection in the passing of information. The Vemeh already work from a hive-mind. I do not get why you are protecting this woman."

The chairwoman sighed, "Look, Colonel. We both understand that holding your cards to your vest is often the best course of action. That's what I'm trying to do in this case."

Munsen felt his collar tighten. *Politicians.* "That system worked a few hundred years ago. This world evolved beyond those petty concerns, Madame Chairman. The simple fact we now maintain classified information again could inflame the individual nations within the Terran Coalition. Wave the planetary security flag all you want, but hiding information from the Coalition will come back against our efforts. The Vemeh, Styrahi, and Tueg all demand transparency in our military matters."

"I appreciate your concern, Colonel, but this program remains classified. I intend to protect our assets as much as possible in this conflict and beyond. The Council mandates this."

The Terran Council. God save me. Munsen laughed. "These people were imprinted to fight this conflict, not revive a hundred-year-old dogmatic political process. They are going to war and most likely they will die protecting an Earth that many of them will never lay eyes on again. Those imprints believed in their nations and would fight to defend them. But those governments are gone. Attempting to bring them back will devolve this civilization. It was bad enough when their imprints lived and died."

"This isn't about America, Colonel."

Bullshit. "Then why worry about this particular imprint so much? She's going to a combat force and will have a low life expectancy. Why worry about her in particular?"

The chairman smoked for a moment and met Munsen's eyes slowly. "If her imprint characteristics can be duplicated and refined with other imprints and DNA matches, our efforts to create and deploy an effective combat force multiply by orders of magnitude. If we do that, we push the Greys out of this side of the known galaxy. That gives us the freedom to get our people out of this system."

Munsen grunted. "There's no reason to think that they're coming here."

The chairman nodded. "But we cannot be sure. This program is an effort, whether we like it or not, to continue the human species. We may have our faults and foibles, Colonel, but it's our job to ensure there's a human race to succeed us. Mairin Shields and the other two hundred imprints out there are a critical need. They understand what it means to fight. Look around, Colonel. A vast majority of our citizens have no concept of war. No concept of compromised security. No fear that their lives will continue. Having that fear drove us, Colonel."

"I don't think our imprinted soldiers have those fears," Munsen replied. "On the contrary, I think their success hinges on the peace and coexistence of this world." He stood slowly and straightened his uniform tunic. "Yes, we have fear, Madame Chairman, and it will drive us. But imagine what we could do if we all decided our existence as a species would be a hell of a lot easier if we gave up all of our baggage. This world is the way it is because we screwed it up the first time, and our imprints understand that and will fight not to bring back anything at all, but to keep us from screwing it all up again." He snapped off the video and shook his head. Politicians never change.

He moved out of the room and felt a smile on his face. *Too bad the nationalist bullshit is rearing up again*, he thought. Still, the fact that the governments of Earth were completely aboard the program was promising. Maybe now humanity would get off its collective ass and get out of the solar system once and for all.

* * * * *

Chapter Three

The dreams started like movies and holo programs projected on a dark wall. Mairin was the only person in the theater when the movie played, and she was the star.

Late summer in the mountains of Tennessee, the sun was setting, and the air felt crisp with the coming night. Cicadas screeched, and the smell of honeysuckle surrounded the small knoll that appeared to host more weekend parties than cadet field training exercises. Everyone seemed happy, flushed, after the six-mile march into the mountains. The instructors gave them room to breathe for a change, and voices became excited and animated. Laughter rang out. They were halfway through a short field training exercise, and everyone was excited. *Three more days*, Mairin thought. *Three more days and that shower will feel like heaven.*

She'd learned how to shoot a pulse rifle well enough to qualify as an expert marksman. She'd found her way through the wilderness using only a map and compass, and they'd learned the basics of moving tactically as infantry. *Everyone has to start somewhere*, she thought with a grin. *Might as well start with the infantry.*

They'd walked in, humped they called it. *Or was it rucking? Something like that. Ruck for rucksack, but it's a backpack?* She'd blinked the questions away and simply started walking. They weren't allowed any music, so she'd hummed a song and stepped to the beat to keep up the pace with the others. After the first mile, some of her counterparts lagged behind the group. At the end of the second mile, five or six of the cadets were walking well in front of the rest. Mairin walked proudly with them. No one was leaving her behind.

The last mile was steep and winding. Her legs burned form the exertion, but she kept her pace. The instructors stopped them on the top of a knoll with the top cleared away from the activities of intoxicated locals. The cadets were to make camp in two-man teams underneath ancient canvas tents. Not exactly tactical, but a place where they could begin the next phase of their training.

"Listen up, people. Gather 'round."

Mairin finished pushing the last tent stake into the soft black soil, grabbed her rifle, and walked to the center of the patrol base. It wasn't meant to be a tactical base, not with the tents erected and a small fire pit being tended by one of the sergeants. A real patrol base meant hand-dug firing positions, no fires, and little comfort. Soon, they'd be thrust into that environment. For most of them, it would be the first time. Mairin wandered into the knot of cadets and stood near the middle of the horseshoe forming around Captain McDaniel. She looked around at their faces, her twenty-nine fellow cadets, sensing them. Most of them were too scared of Staff Sergeant Snyder and Captain McDaniel to notice Mairin.

McDaniel scowled at them. On his camouflaged uniform he wore the Ranger tab, jumpmaster wings, and air assault wings. No combat patch, and no combat infantry badge, Mairin noticed for the first time. He made no excuse for hating cadets, and now it was obvious why. He feared the war had moved on without him.

McDaniel growled, "I'm only going to say this once. This training rifle uses blank ammunition. Same kind of thing the army trained with for years. This, as you can see, is a beer can. It's going to show you the effect of blank ammunition if you fail to use the blank firing adapter on this weapon." McDaniel held up a red metal square that slipped over the muzzle and screwed in place. "The sole purpose of this piece of equipment is to maintain gas pressure in the barrel so that the bolt will recoil off the buffer spring and chamber the next round. Without it, this rifle is nearly as dangerous as when its fully locked and loaded with live rounds."

Mairin watched McDaniel unscrew the blank firing adapter and put the muzzle of the rifle into the can, hold it erect and pull the trigger. A third of the platoon recoiled at the sound of the blast. The can erupted in a burst of flame a few inches in diameter. Mairin merely blinked as the can flew across the perimeter like a rocket engine trailing shreds of aluminum on its path.

"All of you make sure, right now, that your blank firing adapter is in place. We will not have any injuries on this field training exercise, am I clear?" McDaniel watched them closely. "Sundown is in thirty minutes; we'll be sending out the first patrol in forty-five minutes. Squad leaders, I'll brief you here in ten minutes. Get your gear stowed, grab some chow, and be ready for operations. Move out."

The group dispersed and Mairin fell into step with her tentmate, Cox, who smiled in his aw-shucks grin and drawled, "Nothing like a little drama, huh?"

Mairin shrugged, "More power than I thought a blank would have." Sometimes it was just easier to go with the crowd.

Cox grinned. "You ain't never been hunting, Shields. I can tell that."

Mairin smiled. "You got me there."

"You okay?" Cox looked at her as they put their sleeping gear into the tent and left their load bearing vests and magazine belts outside to carry on patrol.

"Yeah, sorry." She smiled and pulled out her issued ration for the night. Chicken a la king. *Gross.* Cox had spaghetti. "Wanna trade?"

Cox grinned. "Sure."

Mairin switched meals with him and thought, *no imprint on you either. You'd know that spaghetti is to be coveted. Or maybe you're just being nice to the new cadet.* She scratched her ear, a bad habit from her days wearing eyeglasses, and dug into the ration. "You're going infantry, right?"

"Yeah. Hear you want to be a tanker." Cox shoveled food into his mouth.

Mairin shook her head. "No, cavalry. There's a difference."

"Spare me," Cox said. "This army ain't about horses and guidons and that nonsense. Better think of something different."

They finished eating in near silence, watching the rest of the platoon doing the same thing from their tent positions. The designated squad leaders were in the middle of the perimeter getting an operations order from Captain McDaniel. Mairin covered a smile developing with a spoonful of food. *I'm a goddamn cadet all over again.*

Word came down that her squad would man the perimeter when the first patrols went out. Captain McDaniel personally briefed them before leaving with the first patrol of the night. "All right, when we're ready to return to the patrol base, we're going to approach. Most likely we'll sound like a herd of elephants tromping around. When you hear that, whoever is in the position closest to where we are approaching from will challenge us. Either the patrol or the patrol base uses the challenge and password to establish identity quickly. In a combat situation, failure to answer the challenge correctly results in bullets flying. In this particular case, the patrol will challenge you. We will sound off with the word 'pink.' You will reply with 'stockings.' Do I make myself clear?"

Mairin settled into her position with Cox and looked out across the rapidly darkening mountain valley. In the distance, Cherokee Mountain held the last tendrils of light on its peak for a long moment before finally succumbing to the spread of night. Mairin looked at it for a long moment. There was something about it. Something familiar. Something familial. The warm air began to turn slightly cool as they lay in the fighting position. Mairin rested her chin on one palm and waited.

"Don't fall asleep," Cox chided her.

Mairin nodded and concentrated on watching the woods and underbrush to her front. They lay there quietly until the sun fully set. The sky was clear and moonless. The darkness total. Mairin felt her eyes dragged skyward, wondering where Eden was in that black field of diamonds. Where were her parents in that big black void? From here, what was once the center of humanity, the war seemed so far away. It would return most likely, and the Earth might be scorched again beyond recognition. Mairin sniffed the wind, catching a fresh breeze of honeysuckle and a rush of memory so vivid it took her breath away.

Plunging her hands into the green vines, pulling the white and yellow blossoms out in fistfuls, smelling the honey, tasting the bitter flowers, wiping pollen and sap on her shirt. Dirty little fingers from playing in the fields near the house. They'd been throwing rotten tomatoes at each other, all the neighborhood boys. They sprayed each other with water to get rid of the evidence. Then a drink of cold, rubbery tasting water from the hose.

Mairin blinked a few times to hold the tears in. *A memory?* The images came like waves, crashing into her and tearing at her emotions as they bubbled from the imprint to her. *Is this going to take me over? Erase me? How can I live with this?*

One breath at a time, she told herself, but the voice wasn't quite her own. Settle down. Focus. Be constantly aware of your position and the tactical situation. Fail to do so and good soldiers die. She felt her breathing return to normal and she leaned over the rifle, taking in every sound, every movement.

Mairin looked at her wristwatch, another anachronism of this training environment. They'd have integrated combat helmets with time displays eventually, but for now they worked with simple green plastic watches Mairin believed were almost as old as her imprinted ancestor would have been. Three hours passed. Cox lightly snored, his mouth open against the stock of his rifle. A rustling in the brush down the hill to her right brought Mairin to reality. She nudged Cox with a sharp elbow and gestured down the hill towards what had to be the approaching patrol. Or a herd of elephants.

Cox leaned over. "They'll come in by Geary's position."

Geary would have to take this seriously, Mairin thought. *No, he can't take anything serious.* The rustling sounds came closer and her hands tightened on the rifle. They were too loud. In combat they'd already be dead if the enemy weren't asleep. The rustling stopped. A few seconds later a voice stage whispered from the patrol.

"Silk."

The perimeter did not respond. *Not gonna get us that easily*, Mairin thought with a smile. She'd wondered if the instructors were going to mess with them or test them somehow. *Even on the first night of the exercise*, she thought. Of course they'd do just that.

"Silk." The whisper was louder, more of a screech. It sounded like McDaniel.

Mairin exhaled slowly, remembering to breathe as tension rippled around the perimeter. *What is Captain McDaniel doing? Is he seriously testing us like this?* No one responded for at least thirty seconds, and the voice got louder, more insistent. Almost shrill.

"Silk!"

Shifting her elbows to better see down the hill, Mairin froze as she heard Geary's deep southern drawl. "It's *pink*, dumbass!"

#

Mairin woke laughing surrounded by sweat soaked sheets. Disoriented, she blinked away the vestiges of the incredibly lucid dream. *His memory. It was his memory in my dream, but I was there in his place.* New pieces of information flitted just outside her brain's reach, like a word on her tongue that she could not remember. The memories were there, like ghosts of dreams past. They would be there, for her use, when she needed them.

They were her dreams now. Most of them were serious and disconcerting. Few of them were funny or memorable. They intermixed from familiar images to ones from far away and long ago. There was no panic, no anxiety as she lay there exploring the void. A shrill beep pierced the stillness and the images disappeared. Calm and relaxed, she heard the beep again, much closer and insistent, and pulled a deep breath through her nose. The tinge of antiseptic and a whiff of ozone purifier triggered her mind into action and began the process of awakening. Slowly, more sounds began to pour in. The hushed voices of matronly nurses, the mumble of a doctor speaking the jargon of his trade, and the scuff of boots on the deck of the medical ward confirmed her first coherent thought. *Hospital.* She blinked slowly, willing her eyes to adjust, and moved to sit up. A hammering ache split her head from ear to ear. She winced and slumped back into the pillows.

"Just relax, Captain."

Mairin blinked dumbstruck. *What did she say?* "What?"

"There's not much time to explain. We'll dock at Libretto in an hour." The red-headed lieutenant raised the bed so Mairin sat upright and saw a plasticene bottle of water and a large envelope on the bedside table. "You'll feel like moving around in a few minutes. When you do, your uniforms are in the locker." She tossed her head to indicate the gray cabinet built into the room. "You'll want to pack and be ready to disembark quickly. We're not staying at Libretto long."

Did she call me Captain? Mairin shook her head. "I'm not going to Earth?"

The lieutenant started to turn away, but stopped. "Ma'am, I'm not aware of what your orders are. All I can tell you is that we're prepping to jump to Rayu Four, about a hundred lyes away, for combat operations. We're disembarking you at Libretto; it's a Styrahi colony planet."

It didn't make sense, but it was the military. There was no surprise, and past the initial confusion Mairin understood. *Things change. Be flexible, dammit.* She almost smiled. The thought actually felt...right. "That will be all, Lieutenant. Thank you."

The nurse's eyes widened slightly at the quick change in tone and manner as she stood a little straighter. "Yes, ma'am. Good luck to you."

Mairin smiled, "You, too."

Alone, she sipped from the bottle of water, felt the numbness of hypnosleep fading gently, and life returning to her body. The envelope contained identification tags, a regulation TDF identification card, and five thousand credits. She counted it twice, marveling at the sum of money she held. More than the annual Eden Academy tuition, and yet in her hands it seemed so small.

She activated her bracelet in safe mode and let her cognitive interface warm up slowly. Five weeks, three days, sixteen hours, thirty-two minutes and twenty seconds since she'd gone to sleep. There were fifteen personal messages, fourteen million news articles and another two million breaking alerts. She deleted the news and alerts before blinking the messages away. She opened a search window and queried Rayu-4.

No information available.

Stupid, she thought. *Maintain the element of surprise. Retain the initiative.* The phrases rolled easily through her mind, though she partially understood them. Her headache began to fade slowly as her metabolism boosted and adjusted her biochemical levels appropriate to her genetic map. Mairin instinctively looked for her eyeglasses, then realized she could see clearly across the room. *No more glasses*, she thought with a smile, as she swung her legs over the side of the bed and stood on the cold metal deck. The locker held two sets of combat uniforms—combat vehicle crewman suits, she corrected herself. Attached to them were the sewn-on badges for Combat Action, Parachutist, and Pathfinder. She traced a finger over the captain's bars and wondered how in the world she'd already made captain.

Assimilation wasn't supposed to happen until she finished training, she thought with a smirk. There'd be no extra training. Whatever was happening at Rayu-4 upset that apple cart in a hurry. On the floor of the locker was a green duffle bag open at the top. Inside was her denim bag from Eden. Next to the bag sat a pair of the strangest boots she'd ever laid eyes on.

Mairin chuckled. *Tanker boots*, her mind whispered. The all leather boots had no laces, only two leather straps. Laces got caught in machinery and couldn't be worked out of a boot if they were wet and muddy. The straps were better, at least George Patton thought so. Whoever he was. Her neurals immediately flashed the information for her study, and she blinked it away. The hospital garment came off and she dressed quickly, tugging the leather strapped boots around her feet and ankles last. The spurs weren't there. She'd have to find a set on Libretto. *Surely there is a clothing sales store on the planet?* All the crazy lingo running through her head! She stood up, looked at her reflection, and felt something very different. She felt solidly in control, confident, and while nervous at her core she knew she could be ready for anything. She smiled at her reflection and pulled her shoulders back a little.

"Gotta do something about this hair." She frowned and laughed out loud. *No shaving my head*, she thought at the imprint in her mind and laughed. *Nothing wrong with looking like a lady and fighting like a demon.* She collected her belongings and strode from the room. A sailor told her where the quarterdeck was to depart. She found it quickly, and sat to wait as a message flashed in her neurals.

Captain Shields: Your training cycle has been interrupted. Cannot be helped because of operational needs. You are to remain at Libretto and wait for the Fleet Battle Platform Ticonderoga and no other vessel. There is no timetable for the Ticonderoga's arrival. Check in with the LNO at Libretto daily for updates.

Munsen

Mairin read the message three times. "Sonuvabitch," she said to herself. *What am I going to do on Libretto?* Hadn't Munsen said they needed her at the front? Disbelief turned to a small measure of anger at having her plans changed. Being flexible was necessary and impossible at the same time. Her thoughts turned slowly, coalescing into one distinct, unnerving question.

What in the hell is going on?

The shuttle arrived ten minutes later. Boarding, she sat at a window seat and looked over the smaller horizon of Libretto. Swirling continents of dark green tropical vegetation interspersed the large oceans. Deserts stretched to the polar region, covered a mile or more deep in ice. The shuttle passed within a stone's throw of an immense column curving out of sight in both directions. *A space elevator*, Mairin thought with an impressed grin. She'd suspected that Styrahi engineers long ago managed to crack the code on developing structures that could literally stretch from the surface to geostationary orbit. The space elevator remained an engineering rarity on Earth colonies, but as the Earth strengthened their alliance with the Legion of Planets, such technologies and materials slowly made their way into everyday life. While not life changing, the new technologies paled in comparison to the simple effect that intelligent extra-terrestrial life existed.

The forms it came in, however, caused more of a shock to Earth than the technologies and the war they brought with them. Granted, the Greys were an anti-climax, proving every story, sighting, or interaction reported with tall, gray-limbed aliens with big black eyes actually happened. Many Earth governments nearly folded under the outrage of hidden information. The tabloid-crazed population of Earth collectively clamored for the heads of governments to roll. The insectoid Vemeh by comparison readily assimilated into Earth culture because they were alien enough.

The first day of peaceful contact, when the Vemeh essentially arrived with a universe spanning "wanted" list with the Greys blamed for unwarranted visitations, meddling in galactic affairs and planeticide, Earth jumped on the bandwagon and embraced the Vemeh and their quest for justice. But the two races would be joined by one of the oldest civilizations in the known galaxy, the ones who had given the Vemeh the keys to interstellar travel with the promise of alliance against the evil Greys. When they arrived shortly thereafter, the Styrahi came upon a planet ready to welcome them with open arms.

And to promptly have everything turned on its ear.

Mairin exhaled just before the shuttle's door opened and, as it did, the cramped cabin filled with moist air. She stepped down from the hatchway and smiled at successfully touching down on three planets in her young life. She looked around at the dense vegetation lying off to one side of the landing pad and was reminded of South America. She'd only been a toddler when they left Earth, so the memory clearly wasn't hers and that was just okay. But not really. She caught her reflection on a window and relaxed that it was still her face and her body, even if the thoughts and memories were not. *It's not going to control me. I can handle this.* The strange echoes grew easier to listen to and harder to question at the same time. She wondered if he'd ever been to South America. There was no more to the whisper and it faded from her mind as she walked to Reception.

Maybe I can look him up? She queried her neurals for a complete genealogical chart and left the search running. After her retinal scan identified and cleared her into the Libretto City Reception Center, Mairin knew to report to the TDF Liaison Officer. This far towards the core, a planetary garrison wasn't necessary. The only troops to speak of on the planet would be those on rest and relaxation leave. Mairin consulted a terminal in the Reception area. She quickly found the correct office and rapped the doorframe twice. A muffled voice came from inside. "Enter."

Opening the door, the sweet smell of the planet's atmosphere vanished in a funk of sweat and alcohol. A large, heavy set man sat at the desk, his uniform jacket unbuttoned and a tall glass of amber liquid in his pudgy hand. He looked at Mairin's uniform quickly and met her eyes. "It's after duty hours, Captain. What's the purpose of your visit?"

The man's tunic sat askew enough that Mairin could not see the man's rank. The office walls were bare, without a trace of personalization or even an I'm-so-proud-of-me wall. She looked at the no name officer and checked the local time in her net, 1400 hours. "What are the duty hours of this office then?"

The man sat forward.

Mairin saw the silver oak leaf clusters of a lieutenant colonel on his shoulders and felt her mouth dry quickly. "You report to a senior officer in that tone, Captain?"

She snapped to the position of attention, looked over the fat man's head and saluted crisply. "Sir, Captain Mairin Shields reporting. I'm in transit with instructions to wait for the *Ticonderoga*."

The man returned her salute with a wave nowhere close to his head and spoke. "The *Ticonderoga* isn't even on the schedule for the next two months. We can't have you sitting around doing nothing on this planet for that amount of time." He smiled only with his lips. "You will report to this office as your place of duty every morning at six hundred hours with the coffee made. You will do exactly what I tell you to do," he looked her up and down, "when I tell you to do it. Is that clear?"

Mairin was sure the words wouldn't come. She took a deep breath and felt her mouth open. "With all possible due respect, sir," she emphasized the last word by dropping her eyes from the back wall of the office and looking him in the eye. "You can take that set of orders, and your leering at my body with obvious sexual intent, and shove them where the sun doesn't shine."

The colonel's mouth dropped open as he tried to stand. "How...how dare you!"

"How dare you!" she roared at him. "I will not be objectified and harassed by a rear echelon motherfucker like you!"

The colonel wobbled to his feet, stabbing the air between them with a pudgy finger. "Now see here, you little—" He blinked and paused, his face growing more gaunt with every passing second as his eyes shifted from left to right rapidly. He blinked twice and looked at Mairin for a long moment. "Captain, you are to contact this office every day by twelve hundred hours to see if the *Ticonderoga* appears on the incoming ship log. There are..." he paused, "no billets available for you in our barracks area. You will live on the economy. I am instructed to ask you if you need anything."

What the fuck did he just read?

Mairin thought about that for a moment, wondering how she would pay for anything, and chastised herself in the same breath. The Styrahi invented the economy without currency. She'd be well taken care of and there were credits in her bags. She felt her breathing instantly return to normal, the genetic re-map at work. "No, Colonel. I will not need anything from this office or from you."

The fat colonel slumped to his chair and waved her away with barely a second glance. "Get out."

Outside the office, Mairin leaned against the wall for a moment reeling. Her face flushed, heart thumping away in her chest. She'd never done anything like that before. *What just happened?* She'd torn into a higher-ranking officer and he'd taken it. *What did he read?*

After a long moment, she leaned forward and stood up straight. *What is a rear echelon motherfucker?*

She chuckled and pushed away from the wall. More importantly, what exactly do they expect from me?

She walked down the corridor marked City Centre and found herself in a train station. The maglev train silently accelerated into the underground tube. The flashing lights of the tunnel pulsated at enough of an interval that Mairin closed her eyes to avoid it. Twelve minutes after boarding the train, Mairin opened her eyes as the maglev slowed and stopped. Disembarking into an impossibly clean terminal, Mairin stepped onto a moving sidewalk. Striding quickly and lightly, she noticed the gentle incline of the walkway. *How far was the landing pad from the city?* Ahead, the thick forest parted, and the walkway rose into daylight surrounded by impressive structures standing thousands of meters high stretching in all directions. She turned around and saw, in the distance, the gently curving edge to the city. A dome—an immense dome—covered the city. Its edges appeared to vibrate, like waves of heat rising from hot sand, and explained why she's seen nothing from orbit except something she kept calling a spacedock and the shuttles arriving and departing the ships in orbit.

That's how they hide the city from orbit. A real life cloaking device. Mairin gaped. Amazing.

The walkway came to an end. Mairin stood for a long moment and realized she was staring. She'd seen a Vemeh before, and she could easily pick out the humans amongst the crowd, though it was tougher to discern the females at a distance. The Styrahi were everywhere, as it was their city after all, and every being that looked like a woman above six feet in height was likely no woman at all but a Styrahi.

Sure she knew what they were and what they looked like, but she still gaped. The imprint quiet, Mairin wondered if the shock was too much. Things were much different in his time. The Styrahi were exquisite. Some statuesque, some athletic, some simply gorgeous, though all of them were beautiful, with perfect smiles, bright eyes, and shining healthy hair. *Planet of the goddamn Barbies*, she thought with a laugh.

When the Vemeh made first contact with Earth, humanity panicked, even after hostilities ended. Tensions elevated as every horrifically awful media play of alien attack featuring giant insects caused most of humanity to resist the Vemeh presence.

The Styrahi arrived within a few days and descended from the sky in their gleaming silver-winged vessels. The doors opened and when five tall, incredibly gorgeous women appeared, Earth drew a collective breath. Here was the proof that humanity was not alone in the universe. Humanity was not the perfect occupant for the universe after all.

No one was sure who saw it first, but these new alien friends, such gorgeous visions of human perfection, were a little more than that. They weren't human after all. Not with eighty-two chromosome pairs and their decidedly inhuman and hermaphroditic genitalia. The Styrahi caused a cultural hemorrhage throughout the modern Earth. The fringe cultures of homosexuality, never quite achieving their goal of equality, shouted from the mountaintops for recognition. They deified the Styrahi, even after the realization that they were human only in a degree of appearance. The Styrahi looked upon them with curiosity. What was a partnership when there was no possibility of creating a genetically paired child? Yet through their travels, the Styrahi understood, and they encouraged Earth to fully recognize and integrate all of its people. But they would not integrate humanity themselves.

Their DNA and human DNA would not allow complete compatibility or reproduction. The Styrahi's reproductive system selectively secreted male and female agents during the Styrahi's twenty-ninth and thirty-third Earth year. They took only one partner, and they had their children together in perfectly harmonious relationships. Human and Styrahi relationships were possible, though ultimately short-lived, as the Styrahi breeding cycle required.

Styrahi never married, nor did they divorce. Their partnerships were the perfect blending of love, respect, communication, and adoration. Their beauty and their seemingly perfect lives bred much human discontent, until it was apparent that while the Styrahi were systematically destroying the customs and organized religions of Earth by their sheer presence, they brought much more to the table.

They were swift, efficient and deadly warriors—something more akin to warrior poets or warrior statesmen. They needed help, but understood Earth's unlikely evolution to peaceful coexistence. No matter to them, they knew the truth about war. War could be taught to anyone, but few can apply it. For the Styrahi, they'd planted the seeds for fighting this war within humanity in 1947.

Humanity proved their worth as warriors regardless of who had won or lost World War Two. The accident at Roswell was perfectly executed to keep modern knowledge of extraterrestrial life mere speculation until the time was right. With a captured Grey spacecraft as a gift and technological blueprints for everything from stealth technology to nuclear energy planted aboard, the Styrahi believed correctly that humans would be able to reverse engineer and implement these new gifts. That technology would breed prosperity and peace. And humanity proved them right, to a point.

The Styrahi believed that eventually humanity would stop fighting itself and be a truly equal civilization. When that happened, the Styrahi never planned that humans would successfully forget war. Yet, they brought the imprint process to the Terran Defense Forces, or so Munsen had said. Mairin pushed the thoughts away and tried to enjoy herself.

Mairin moved through the city awash in smells of rich coffees and tantalizing fruits. The markets flowed with all known species represented, all sharing their produce and goods with each other. Mairin stopped in a short line and had a small cup of espresso, relishing it. She saw a hotel in the distance and walked to it quickly with thoughts of a long bath swimming in her head.

The clerk took her information and gave her a large suite on the sixtieth floor overlooking a river with an unpronounceable name the locals called "Little Amazon." A large bed dominated the room and Mairin fell onto it, looking out into the beautiful city, full of beautiful people, and smiled. It felt like a home, something she'd never really known. She closed her eyes and breathed deeply, savoring the smell of the clean linens and the fresh flowers on the bedside table. The smile stayed on her face as a dreamless sleep took her away.

*****

Chapter Four

The chirping comset startled Munsen from his snoring. Feet on his communications console, Munsen didn't bother to sit forward or even open his eyes. He fingered the talk button. "Munsen."

"Sir, this is Major DeWitt. I'm the deputy action officer for Libretto and had instructions to report the arrival of Captain Mairin Shields."

Munsen rubbed his eyes. "Go ahead."

"Sir, Captain Shields arrived at thirteen forty-six hours local time. She reported to the TDF Liaison Officer and has checked into a suite at the Grand Hotel. Room number is six zero zero four seven. Do you require any additional information?"

"What else can you give me?"

"Apparently she had an altercation with Lieutenant Colonel Montgomery at Reception. Basically told him he was a rear echelon motherfucker and that she would not be reporting for duty to make his coffee and let him stare at her all day."

"She said that?" Munsen grinned.

"I don't have the full transcript from the office, sir, but that's the gist of it." DeWitt paused. "Shall I put her on report, sir?"

"You'll do nothing of the sort, is that clear?" Munsen rubbed his chin. "I want to know the minute she leaves the city."

There was a pregnant pause and Munsen knew what DeWitt had to be thinking, *why would she leave the city?*

DeWitt answered. "Yes, sir. We'll report to you if Captain Shields leaves the city. Is that all, sir?"

Munsen smiled. "Very good. Thank you for the report, Major."

"Out here, sir."

The connection clicked off and Munsen leaned forward with a long sigh. Phase one of the plan was complete, and Mairin was now on Libretto unsupervised. Phase two would commence immediately, and, as he typed instructions to his most critical assets for the mission, Munsen knew it was worth the trouble. If they were right about Mairin Shields, then the course of the war could change. Hell, humanity itself could change. Never had one young woman held so much in the palm of her hands.

Munsen could accept moderate risk without batting an eye. There were far too many contingencies he'd not constructed mitigation plans against, but barring something tragic, Captain Mairin Shields would finish her integration and command troops in the field. That was the main purpose of imprinting, wasn't it? To tip the scales in the favor of the TDF and turn back the Greys. Or was it something else entirely?

In the case of Mairin Shields, there was so much more at stake.

Telling himself he needed the sleep, Munsen finished the splash of whiskey in his glass. There would be a time soon enough when sleep would be a precious commodity. He wasn't a man to waste opportunities, or good Tennessee whiskey.

* * * * *

Chapter Five

Hurry up and wait. Bust your ass getting where you're supposed to be only to sit on your ass until someone on the other end is ready for you. What was there to do while she waited for her ship? Probably the same thing everyone who ever waited for a ship did.

"Can you talk to me?" She laughed at herself as soon as she said it. Of course the imprint wasn't capable of talking. No imprint ever communicated out right, not from shreds of memory and instinctual behaviors. *What am I going to do with you?* She looked out the window at the slowly waking city and her stomach rumbled. *Not eating for five weeks will do that*, she thought with a smile and rolled out of the warm sheets.

In her shoulder bag, her clothes from Eden Academy were still neatly folded, but with the ozone smell of a stale spacecraft. Maybe there would be a place to launder them in the hotel. The thought stopped her. Why bother? Something about them was wrong and she tossed them into the garbage can before tugging on a pair of uniform coveralls. She tied her hair up in an almost regulation ponytail and looked at herself in the mirror. A smile began to dawn. Maybe this wasn't going to be so bad after all.

Bouncing out of her room, the trials of Eden Academy seemed ever more distant and, to a certain extent, beneath her. Reunions weren't likely to be in her future. The smells of eggs and bacon came to her well before she reached the Galaxy Dining Room. The massive buffet beckoned Mairin quickly through the food line. After dropping one hundred twenty credits for real Estean eggs, three-year-old ham, and something vaguely akin to potatoes, she walked into a nearly silent dining room. There were no Styrahi in the dining room, only clusters of civilian humans. Tourists. A few pairs of eyes kept on her, but most either quickly looked away or started up languished conversations quickly trying to cover their silence at the appearance of a Terran Defense Force officer. Most failed. Mairin slunk over to a table along the far wall and away from the curving windows. *Why do people always do that?*

It's the uniform, she thought. These are people that cannot fathom warfare and they're seeing someone who they've been brought up to fear. To them you're a butcher, a heathen, and a mindless idiot following orders and killing on sight. Mairin blinked at the thought, and almost immediately understood. This was a truth very unfortunate to most civilians. They looked at every soldier like a poor dumb fighting rooster. Soldiers were to be pitied. They're bred to fight and they claim patriotism in the defense of their country because they're dumb enough not to stand up for their basic entitled rights.

Mairin felt her stomach turn. Looking down at the combat decorations on her chest she felt her skin crawling. Yes, Mairin. In their eyes now you are a combat veteran, and no matter what degrees you obtain, no matter what education you achieve, as long as you wear this uniform, you are a poor dumb idiot to most of society. They don't care one iota about you as a person. They see a uniform and the first emotion they feel is pity.

Well fuck them, she thought and nearly laughed out loud.

She looked across the room and out the window for a long moment. *Am I going crazy, hearing a voice that's not my own?* She waited for an answer, but had none. She finished her breakfast and walked out of the still nearly silent dining room. She could cure at least one part of that just by dressing the part. She didn't have the right clothes for this planet, so she could change that. Hell, she could change the way she looked if she wanted to. There were enough credits in her account to pay for an esoteric body map if she wanted. She didn't realize she was smiling as she walked out of the hotel into the bright morning light of Libretto City.

Not five steps out of the first hotel, Mairin met a Styrahi with long blonde hair who smiled at her warmly. Mairin blurted, "Excuse me, do you speak Standard?"

"Of course."

"Can you tell me where to, um...?" She looked down at her coveralls.

The tall beauty laughed. "Go to the Central Corridor and go down two levels to the Shopping District."

Mairin blushed, but looked up at the woman. "Thank you."

"*Mai eisheend*" she said and walked away. Mairin made a note to add a Styrahi dialect coach to her hypno rotation. Anything would surely be better than topics like field sanitation and mag-tank repulsor systems maintenance.

Daylight washed the sky in a splendid shower as Mairin exited the hotel in a newly purchased sundress and sandals. She smoothed her hair back, jostling the opal earrings she'd found in the massive shopping center. The inner-ringed shopping district held shops of every imaginable fashion, catering to alien species from across the known galaxy. Interwoven through the mostly subterranean district, the artistry of water features brought a peaceful, comforting air to the shopping experience. She'd laughed at the concept of a shopping mall. Knowledge that her ancestor hated shopping but never peeped about the six-hour binge made her giddy.

After a quick return to her room to drop off the mess of packages collected during the trip, Mairin grabbed a thin sweater and slung it over one arm. Stomach grumbling, she decided that unpacking the pile of bags would have to wait. Having a place of her own, unlike her shared apartment on Eden, was something new. Even if it was a simple hotel suite, for the time being it was hers. Shopping without any familiar eyes around liberated her. *No wonder they called it retail therapy*, she thought with a grin as she made her way to the entertainment district.

A Florentine plaza gave way to an immense granite staircase falling down to the water's edge. Mairin bounced down the stairs breathing in the moist air as the first strains of music began to find her ears. Turning a corner, the district spread along the riverside for more than five kilometers. Every breath of wind brought a new scent of cooking food. Music of all kinds and volumes wove together into an ascending symphony. The sight of a closed Irish-themed pub named Seanachie's brought a hint of regret. *No Guinness this evening.* She accepted the thought with little surprise as her imprint continued to emerge.

She saw a sushi bar across the boulevard and walked over, her senses guiding her to a seat at the tip of the bar's peninsula. Soft ambient music played from the ceiling speakers above her as Mairin pulled out a chair and sat. The air was redolent of ginger and wasabi, and her mouth watered.

The Vemeh chef clicked his mandibles in greeting and a uniformed Tueg waiter, blue skin rippling under his yellow serving smock, bounded over. "May I get you something to drink?"

"Sapporo. Draft if you have it."

The waiter smiled, an eerie sight with his protruding lower jaw, but Mairin returned it. A scant moment later, she sipped at the ice-cold beer and smiled again. *You don't seem to steer me wrong, do you?* She ordered a spicy tuna roll for her first course and watched the Vemeh chef work his magic.

Mairin felt the itchy anxiety of being watched as she hefted the first bite of spicy tuna roll to her mouth with the chopsticks. As she looked up across the u-shaped bar and the blur of the Vemeh chef's knives flying through his preparations, she squinted a little in the fading orange light and paused just slightly. Ten feet away the most exquisite green eyes she'd ever seen watched her own eyes. Every Styrahi seemed beautiful beyond reason, but this one's beauty stunned her. The woman smiled and Mairin responded in kind.

Mairin reached for her ice-cold Sapporo and she raised the glass to her lips and drank, eyes holding the Styrahi's gaze. She felt something come alive inside her. As it flowered and blossomed, she relished the recognition of being wanted. The raven-haired Styrahi held her smile, raised a bottled Sapporo to her lips and sipped, but her eyes never left Mairin's. Mairin shuddered. *This really can't be happening,* she thought with a smile. *Not from someone so...beautiful.*

What are you thinking, Mairin? You're a human woman, not a Styrahi. She's not interested in you. And why do you care if she is?

Mairin looked down into her sushi roll for a long moment, dancing her chopsticks through the ritual of separation, a touch of wasabi, and then a dunk in the soy sauce. She fished the piece out of its soy bath and looked up again hoping for another glance of flashing green eyes. Gone. Mairin's heart sank and she sighed.

A blink of movement caught her eye and she glanced left, and into those green eyes. The Styrahi sat, pulling a sweet-smelling breeze of perfume along. Mairin's mouth dried up as she looked up at the taller woman's eyes.

"Mind if I sit?" Her voice trilled like a strummed harp.

Mairin smiled as she somehow found the words. "Please do." *Please do what? Please do me?* She bit the thought back, but her face betrayed her in a flush of crimson. *So much for doing me no wrong. Dammit.*

"And what was that little thought that crossed your mind, *cariad*?"

Mairin cocked her head to the side, her brown curls draping across her dress. "Carry-ad?"

The Styrahi smiled. "It means beloved. In Welsh." She reached out and gently stroked the back of Mairin's shaking hand. "My name is Tallenaara, but my human friends call me Tally."

Mairin blinked. "Welsh? As in Wales? On Earth?"

The Styrahi laughed. "Yes, as in Wales on Earth. I studied architecture at Cardiff. Spent five years on your planet in all. I didn't catch your name."

Mairin blushed a little more. "Mairin Shields."

Tally spoke a traditional greeting in Styrah and smiled. "First night on Libretto?"

Mairin nodded. The will to speak seemed to have evaporated under the green-eyed beauty's gaze. There were a million questions she wanted to ask, and a fevered need to have them answered. She swallowed and spoke slowly. "How did you go about studying on Earth?"

Tally sipped from her beer bottle. "Part of my service here, Mairin. I assisted Hekatarna, Styrah's greatest architect, in building this city. I was sent to your planet to learn all about human beings and to develop an architectural concept to make them feel at home in our ports of call. You are from Earth, aren't you?"

Mairin smiled at the hint of a lilt in Tally's voice. "I was born on Luna, and moved to Eden Two when I was six. Was there all through the Academy. I was going to be an Administrative Technician."

"And what are you now?"

Mairin paused. *Should I tell her that I'm an officer? Is that a security threat?* There was no response, so she answered, "I'm an officer in the TDF now. Awaiting assignment."

The woman's eyebrow raised slightly. "Straight from Civil Consideration to an officer's commission?"

"Um. Yes." Mairin blanched. Did I just say something wrong?

"You must be an imprint."

Mairin looked away. *Oh shit, girl!*

"It's okay, *cariad.* It's not a new thing, nor a military secret, no matter what they told you. The Styrahi have imprinted our offspring for generations. How else would we be able to stabilize our core values and beliefs and avoid cultural shifts and regressions?"

Mairin nodded. "Cultural regressions? As in what happened on Earth?"

Tally laughed and shook her head. "Nothing like the rise of reality entertainment or something like that. When you arrived on this planet, did it resemble Earth?"

"Yes."

"We engineered it that way. By spending time on Earth and learning as much about your cultures as we could, we were able to build a place that allows humans to acclimate to deep space travel. Virtually every core-bound transport comes through Libretto for that reason."

And why Munsen put me here to wait for the Ticonderoga. Mairin looked around as she chewed on her sushi. The quaint restaurants, the shopping district...the shopping malls. The feelings rushed up quickly. "It's too perfect," she said and turned to look at Tally. "You've essentially created what Earth should have continued to be."

Tally smirked, "And why did it fail to do that?"

"America, really. Their citizens all had unalienable rights for life, liberty, and the pursuit of happiness, but as the media portrayed happiness to be a vapid, self and celebrity obsessed, thrill-seeking, camera-loving idiot, that's where most of the world's youth went." She sipped from her beer, expecting a mental chiding but received none. If anything, she felt a little passion burning in her stomach. "And let's talk about celebrities. Before the Hollywood Amendment, male and female actors would make nearly a thousand percent more per feature film than the average family made in a year. Nobody bothered to stand up and say enough is enough. To that end, people with no measurable talent were lauded and showered with attention and money."

Tally nodded. "And the public would love them and pay them more and more, wouldn't they? Such a waste of time and money."

"Just like professional athletes." Mairin shrugged. "It's a shame that First Contact came too late to save America from itself."

"That's where your imprint is from, right?"

Mairin took a breath. "My great-great-great grandfather. Died during the Afghanistan War in two thousand and sixteen. That's all I know."

"No wonder you're quite passionate about it," Tally laughed.

Mairin blushed again, "I didn't really know he was."

"Random memories and emotional responses are part of what imprinting is about. Not that it's an easy process to endure, but over time it gets easier to deal with. The very passionate responses are muted with time and with logic, which increases exponentially the longer you retain the imprint. Perhaps you should look into his history."

Made sense to Mairin. "There are so many emotions, but the physical triggers have been good."

"How many have you had?"

"This is my second," she gestured with her chopsticks as her mouth was full. "Delicious."

"Maybe one more to go," Tally commented. "Most of the time, a physical trigger is something that soothed the imprint and should have the same effect for you. Very rarely are triggers harmful." They sat in silence for a moment, each eating from their plates quietly as the conversation lulled.

Mairin smiled. "So what do you do? I mean, outside of studying architecture on Earth and all?"

"Like most Styrahi I have two vocations, and one is a service vocation. I am an architect part of what you call a year, and for the other part I help to monitor natural resources and planetary ecosystems."

"How do you monitor them?"

Tally smiled. "Like scientists monitor anything and everything. I live outside the dome and monitor about two hundred acres of forest and wetlands. It's quiet, remote, and absolutely beautiful at sunrise and sunset."

Mairin nodded and caught herself hoping to find out just how beautiful it was. "Are you counting birds and bees?"

"No." Tally laughed and Mairin loved the sound of it. "We use technology, but we're more interested in preserving what we have. That's why we developed imprinting and why most of our colony planets strive towards homeostasis. Libretto is almost to that point, especially as we keep the dome separate from most of our resources."

"Sounds like a lot of work."

Tally shrugged. "Not as much as you might think, and being outside the dome allows me greater freedoms than inside. I love a good sushi night, but more often I'm content to be home."

Mairin didn't say anything. Tally's life sounded idyllic and happy, unlike her own life on Eden. The hurt would never truly fade, and Mairin accepted that, but relished the opportunity to dream about something different. Looking at Tally, Mairin wondered how different it could be. She played with another piece of sushi, rolling it in the small bowl of soy and wasabi before putting it into her mouth. Mairin chewed slowly trying to think of something to say. Tally's green eyes sparkled in the light and Mairin felt her heart skip a little.

Tally turned to Mairin. "And do you have plans tonight?"

Oh shit. "Well...I think...I mean I'd planned on wandering the city a little. Most likely I'll go back to the hotel and sleep. Recovering from hypnosleep is difficult, I hear." She smiled.

Tally nodded and folded her napkin across her plate. "Well then, I hope to run into you again, Mairin." She spoke for a long moment to the Vemeh in her native language, nothing that Mairin could catch. As she turned to walk away, she touched Mairin's bare shoulder with a warm soft hand. "*Cariad*," she said softly and walked away.

Mairin sat at the bar and finished her sushi and beer staring into her reflection. What just happened? You were scared to death! Why? When Tally sat down I was thrilled, but I'm suddenly afraid to do anything? Why? Among the thoughts of the beautiful Styrahi, the strange conversation, and all of the confusion the imprint threw at her, she thought idly about how she'd managed to go out looking as bad as she did. Not many human women could look as perfect as a Styrahi, but she could at least do her hair and maybe wear some make-up, right?

And just what in the world has come over me? Mairin popped another sushi piece into her mouth and sipped her beer. *How much of this is your fault, Grandpa?* Snorting back laughter, Mairin noticed her hands shook slightly.

Am I a horny old soldier or a giddy schoolgirl trying to get a date? She tapped her chopsticks on the top of her last bite of sushi. Why can't I be both? What's really stopping me from being who I am?

She thought of her classmates at Eden Academy, partying after commencement and getting ready for their new careers. She'd be out and amongst her new career before most of them completed the first week of their training. And she could likely be dead by then, too. *So why the hell not?* The answer was staring at her reflection in the glass facade of the sushi bar. *I can do whatever I want. Why not be who I want to be? Even if that means I'm....well....it's not gay if it's an alien species, right?*

When Mairin left, the Vemeh chef gestured for her to return soon. She nodded and smiled, then walked straight back to the hotel wondering if the genetic therapy salon was still open. *No sense looking like a hag*, she thought with a grin. Her next thought equally shocked and excited her.

What would Tallenaara like?

* * * * *

Chapter Six

Emerging from foldspace held a litany of side-effects for the novice astronaut no matter the size of the vessel and the power of its fold engine. The manuals said the best course of action was, "to hold one's breath and exhale slowly through the deceleration. Keeping your eyes closed helps as well." None of the suggestions helped Admiral Takeshi Yamato despite more than four hundred folds and nearly a year of service aboard the *Fleet Battle Platform Yokohama.* Holding onto the armrests of his bridge chair, Yamato fought the urge to vomit as the inertial dampeners kicked in and slowed the *Yokohama* to point one five *c* on approach to the Winter colonies.

Opening his eyes, Yamato fingered the 1-MC controls and spoke to the entire vessel, "All hands, this is the Admiral. Battle stations."

The bridge crew began a rapid-fire litany of pre-combat checks as the two thousand-meter-long vessel swung towards the tiny Winter colonies now appearing like a string of bright pearls instead of dull gray asteroids. Through the viewscreen, Yamato saw the running lights of the *Fleet Battle Platform Viraat* right where she should be, trailing six heavy weapons cruisers in her wake. The *Kuznetsov* and her cruisers would arrive in the next few minutes as the fleet accelerated towards Winter Prime. Yamato looked at his communications specialist, "Signal the *Viraat* to come about and put her cruisers on line."

"Shields to maximum, Admiral. We have the debris field of the *Surprise* off our port bow, two points at ten thousand kilometers." Shipboard Systems chimed from Yamato's right.

"Scanning Winter Prime. Showing more than eighteen thousand lifeforms on the surface, Admiral." Weapons and Tactics responded. "Cannot break out species from this range, but it's safe to say the Greys are there. Winter Prime had a population of just under ten thousand prior to invasion."

Yamato nodded and looked at the mission timer. The *Surprise* arrived on station four and a half minutes ago and had already succumbed. Eight hundred souls lost. Yamato calculated roughly six minutes to the first point where his drop squadrons could deliver ground forces to the planet. The plan to fall planetward from the cover of the light of the Winter system's star should let them close further to the planet. Coming out of the sun had worked since Richtoffen's era. Otherwise his drop and recovery squadrons would be at risk on the long journey to the planet's surface and back. More time away from the battlefield left the troops on the ground. Yamato sighed and repressed a shake of his head. *Too many logistical variables just like Telis*, he thought. He looked off the port side and saw the *Kuznetsov* pull into formation. "Prepare all squadrons for drop, main cannon batteries to full power, concentrate shields on the front quarter."

Didn't they hear me? Yamato thought for a split second as he followed the frozen stares of his bridge crew out the main vidscreen. "What the," he managed to blurt before he caught himself, not from shame at his loss of military bearing but as the power of speech failed him. The disc of Winter Prime formed a perfect circle with a circumference of roughly five hundred miles. Silhouetted against the stars, a massive domed ship with seven conical pods ascended. The pods dropped away from the main body and took up positions between the mothership and the *Yokohama's* battle group. Yamato watched the alien ships as they oriented on his vehicles and began to fire.

"Drop all squadrons and engage all available weapon systems," Yamato yelled and spurred his bridge team to action. "Get all of the drop squadrons clear and standby for combat maneuvers. All cruisers engage *heavy*; I say again *heavy*." The *Yokohama* began to buck wildly from side to side as the shields failed under bombardment. The cruisers alongside unleashed a fusillade of nuclear tipped missiles into the collection of alien vessels.

"Drop status!" Yamato barked.

"Seventy-five percent," Weapons and Tactics yelled above the concussion of continuous explosions. "Hull breaches in all forward spaces, Admiral. Forward guns are deadlined."

Yamato slammed a fist down on the armrest of his chair and stood. "Emergency drop all squadron bays now!"

"Admiral, combat maneuvers?" The frightened young Ensign at Helm caught Yamato's eye.

Yamato looked at the bridge, saw the indicators that all squadrons had dropped free, and accepted fate. The *Yokohama* would not survive this engagement. But the soldiers needed time, and they needed a fighting chance. He'd give it to them. "You ever hear of Horatio Nelson, Helm?"

The Ensign shook his head and Yamato chuckled. Another thing this future generation hadn't learned. "Forget the maneuvers, son. Straight at 'em."

Yamato keyed his terminal and sent a distress call Earthward. There wasn't time to figure out where the Greys were headed, Yamato could only hope that time would allow Earth to prepare a successful defense. He blinked away a vision of cherry blossoms blowing in a fierce wind and straightened in his chair. If he could never return to Hokkaido, he would give the Greys one hell of a fight.

* * * * *

Chapter Seven

Mairin kept to the hotel and its luxurious swimming pool and salon while her genetic therapy healed. A few minor adjustments here and there, giving herself a little more of the body, hair, and complexion she'd wanted since she'd played with dolls, but nothing outlandish like an extra breast or a third eye like some people paid dearly to have. She wanted to be different, but not freakishly different. Still, the addition of a stronger, more athletic figure and fuller breasts were very alien at first, but she accepted them easily enough. For the first time in her life, she had a healthy tan. The mirror had been her friend much of the time, as she marveled over how good she looked without her glasses and without her long, straight hair. Cropped so that it hung above the shoulders and draped down across her face with longish bangs, the darker hair shimmered in the light and made her look both older and confident. Her clothes fit much better with more of a woman's figure to pour into them. The feeling thrilled her to the core.

Helios rose over Libretto and dappled the sky with a shimmer of golden highlighted clouds. The streets were quiet, only a few birds squawked and pecked along the broad square. The crisp air made her smile, the dim light of a peaceful morning grounding her. Centering her. She was a new woman in body and mind, leaving her unrecognizable compared to how she'd left Eden. The genetic remapping left no marks, and she hardly had the headache the technicians warned her about. Dressed in tight shorts and an equally tight support bra, Mairin glanced down at her bare feet and chuckled to herself. *Forgot running shoes. Guess we'll see about this enhanced body of mine.*

She began to run in the short awkward strides of gym class while watching every inch of the approaching path for hazards to her feet. Down through the entertainment district she trotted, enjoying the solitude and relishing the feeling of something new. A new start. A new beginning. *It doesn't matter*, she told herself. *It's a second chance.* She smiled at the thought. *Good morning, Grandpa. How are you today?*

She laughed at the thought and relaxed. There was no pain in her feet as she ran. Not even the slightest bit of discomfort. Running barefoot felt amazing and free. She requested some music in her neurals and activated a simple tracking program to see how far she'd run. The training aspect didn't really matter mainly because the exertion just felt good. For the first time in her life, running brought a smile to her face.

She ran the second mile in seven minutes even, without breathing hard. Leaning forward and urging herself onward, her breath got ragged when the third mile passed in a short five minutes. Sweat flowed out of her pores at mile number four. A bridge appeared and she turned around, having run the fifth mile in a little under five minutes. She held the pace easily and winced at the sudden change in music piped to her ears. Her neurals flashed the information and she squinted. *Who is Pat Benatar?* Her pace accelerated. After a few bars of the rock music, Mairin became a fan and kept it playing along as she returned to the hotel, showered, and went for breakfast.

Over a plate of eggs and potatoes, she read a vmail from her parents and replied in simple text. Talking out loud to someone that no one else could see was just rude. The word cellphone bubbled up from her mind and she shrugged it off. Sometimes it was best to let the imprint make the connections on its own. *Definitely much easier*, she thought with a grin.

A new message from Munsen said the *Ticonderoga* was a few weeks away now and that she should begin additional hypnotraining. She spent the morning with her programs and simulations, adding in both the Styrahi dialect and Welsh that she would report as purely recreational reasons, if asked. The afternoon was warm and pleasant, and the rooftop swimming pool beckoned.

As night fell, she made a reservation for the next day at the championship golf course and decided to head out into the entertainment district for dinner. She dressed in a simple flowery sundress that accentuated her remapped figure and hugged her now slightly curvier frame in all the right places. A quick styling session at the salon perfected her look for the evening. The best part was that the technicians really didn't change much at all, just a little enhancement here and there, and she felt like a new woman for the second time in two months. Amazing what a more flattering female shape could do for confidence.

Mairin wandered along the river looking for just the right place to eat when a tobacconist's shop caught her eye. She walked through the open storefront, looking around with wide eyes, when a hand caught her arm.

"Well now. Made a few changes I see."

The voice sent a shiver up her spine and her legs trembled in excitement. She'd hoped for this, dreamed of it, for the last three days. The crushing wanton anticipation, hoping to see those glittering green eyes and black silky hair. The warmth of Tally's hand on her shoulder. The whisper as she'd left, all of it racing up in Mairin's mind.

"Tally." Mairin turned and smiled up into Tallenaara's eyes. "You like?

Tally grinned. "Very much so, especially your hair. Most imprints go a little crazy with genetic remapping the first time. You've restrained it nicely." She laughed. "Then again, most of the nice-looking human females we do get on this planet are remapped males taking every opportunity to explore life as a woman."

"That really happens?"

"Every so often, though it's been a while since I've personally known one." Tally caught Mairin's wandering eyes. "And you? Searching for something?" Tally asked with a toss of her head at the expansive and comfortably appointed store.

Mairin shrugged. "Imprint."

"Another physical trigger," Tally said. Her smile said she very clearly remembered the first time they met.

Mairin blushed. "Now what do I do?"

Tally smiled and pulled her into the store. An hour later they each emerged with a small parcel of cigars, and for Mairin a lighter and cutter that Tally purchased after much argument. Mairin smelled the humid air and exhaled more forcefully than she'd intended, like a desperate sigh. "It smells like rain."

"Time for the *nahalla*, our monsoons," Tally explained. "For the next month it will rain every night or so. After a month, it will start to get cooler as winter approaches."

Mairin looked at Tally's eyes and felt flushed all over. "I was, um, thinking about getting something to eat. Care to join me?"

A warm smile spread across Tally's Styrah features. "Do you like jazz music?"

Whoever Dave Brubeck was, he was a genius. The dark, smoky club thumped and shook with the bass and reverberated with the horns of every song. The holoband played anything requested, though Mairin didn't know any Miles Davis, and though she'd never heard of Brubeck until tonight, she'd already loaded her neurals with everything Brubeck ever recorded. Dining on filet oscar with creamed potatoes and asparagus, they followed the meal with a bottle of Wolcian Malbec and her first cigar. Mairin smiled and swayed side-to-side feeling every bit as good as she'd ever thought possible. *So far, this imprinting business isn't too bad.* She closed her eyes, her senses following the music and the music filling her and soothing her. Her heart swelled as the music faded and she felt the warm touch of Tally's hand on hers.

I should be worried about this. I've never been attracted to anyone like this, much less an alien who was so much more than human, but looked like the most beautiful woman in the universe. She trembled a little, smiling wider to try and shake off the anticipation. Tally's hand squeezed hers and Mairin clasped it, not letting go as her mind rebelled. I really shouldn't be doing this. Why the hell not? She couldn't possibly be thinking about this Styrahi as a lover, could she? What am I thinking?

"What's wrong?" Tally leaned in close, her breath tickling Mairin's ear.

"Nothing."

Tally leaned back and chuckled. "That's not what traveled across your face."

Damn. "What do you mean?"

"You stopped swaying and smiling. You're thinking about something. Most likely what you're doing sitting in this dark, smoky bar holding hands with a Styrahi. That you're going to end up in big trouble. Something like that?"

Mairin blushed, but did not respond for several accelerating heartbeats. "You're right."

"And is it your sense of duty that's causing this?"

"I don't even know what duty is yet, Tally." Mairin drained her wineglass and motioned for a refill. "I'm terrified."

Tally's green eyes glittered in the darkness. "Terrified of what?"

Mairin looked at their clasped hands. "This."

"Why?"

"Because I've never."

Tally smiled. "Never been with a Styrahi?"

"Never been with anyone."

Tally wrapped her other hand around Mairin's. "And if I told you I'd never been with a woman before, would that make a difference?"

"Yes." Mairin smiled nervously. She could feel her heart thumping in her chest, could hear her pulse in her ears, and she felt flushed even above the warmth and sultriness of the jazz club.

"I nearly asked you home with me that first night." Tally grinned. "But I wasn't sure what you would do."

Neither was Mairin. Suddenly tired of it all, Mairin sighed. "I can't do this, Tally."

"What do you mean, *cariad*?"

Mairin frowned across the table. The band launched into another flawless Dave Brubeck song and for the briefest moment, Mairin allowed her thoughts to drift along the beat of "Take Five", so much so that she needed conscious effort to meet Tally's eyes. "I can't keep doing this, Tally. What do you want me to do?"

"I want you to be true to yourself, *cariad*."

Mairin squeezed her eyelids together. "I was scared that first night. Scared to think what would happen if I woke up in the same bed with you panicking that I'd made a huge mistake. Can you understand that?"

"Worrying about your new career in the Terran Defense Force? How quaint. Not a shred of thought for me at all, was there?" Tally snorted. "Don't you think I know your regulations as well as you do?"

"It's not that!"

"Then what, Mairin? What kept you from staying out with me the other night? There was something there. You felt it. I felt it, *cariad*. But you said you had other plans. You ran away. How am I to know that you're not going to run away again?"

Mairin felt tears stinging her eyes. "Because I don't care about stupid regulations. I don't care about anything anymore."

"That's a lie. You want this new path that's been laid out for you."

Mairin thought for a long second. Tally was right. She wanted something much different now that she'd had the imprint. There was an honor that came with it. Looking across the table and into Tally's green eyes, Mairin discovered the most pressing belief of those who stand up to fight for their neighbors. *I will fight with you and for you*, Mairin thought. "I do. And you know that I do, but there's much more to it than that. Until I met you, I didn't know what it meant to stand up for something."

"And you'll do that how? By telling your commanders that you screwed a Styrahi on your leave time?"

Mairin flushed. "No, Tally. By telling them that I fell for one."

They said nothing for a long moment. The music faded until just the piano twinkled through the bridge of "Take Five." Mairin reached across the table for Tally's hand. "I mean that, Tally."

Tally smiled. "And what are you planning on doing about that, Captain?"

"Taking you up on your offer, Tallenaara." Mairin grinned and looked up into Tally's eyes. "I've loved you from the moment we met." There was nothing from the imprint. Maybe it was being quiet, or maybe it knew better. Mairin enjoyed it however it had happened.

"Then I suggest we do something about that."

Mairin leaned close enough to smell Tally's perfume, and as she did, she closed her eyes and hoped that there was a kiss in the warm air. Their lips brushed together, then clasped upon each other tightly. Mairin could taste the wine and cigar on Tally's tongue as they kissed. She flushed again and felt her breath hitching in her chest. The desire so forceful, the need so great, she wanted everything that Tally was as a part of her. The kiss ended, and they smiled at each other for a moment, saying volumes without speaking.

They stood and left the club hand-in-hand, catching an autocar in the rain.

*****

Chapter Eight

Mairin woke as the bus stopped and opened its doors to let in the cold Kentucky darkness. Outside she could see light fog masking a long thin valley. A few buildings and a tall watch tower crowded into the neck of the valley behind a large flat area covered in ankle-twisting gravel. The other officers around her murmured with excitement, and she could see why.

The swinging doors of the bus opened to a gravel parking area and twenty M1A1 Abrams main battle tanks. Weeks of maintenance classes, simulated tank gunnery, and an introduction to tactics would conclude today with the first actual firing range. They clustered in their three-person training crews and waited for their instructors to arrive. The tanks arrived first, driven onto the range by enlisted soldiers who would make up the fourth person of the crew.

Driving a seventy-ton tank on a crowded range is not something lieutenants should do. Mairin snorted at the thought, but realized the truth in the statement. One of the tanks spun almost three hundred and sixty degrees on its tracks and backed into position at the loading dock.

Sergeant First Class Lopez walked up to Mairin's crew and smiled. "Good morning, everyone." There was no saluting on the range, and Lopez's casual demeanor helped to calm some of the nerves she felt.

"Good morning, Sergeant," they responded like trained privates.

Lopez smiled. "All right, we're going to be the first tank on the firing line. We'll have our own driver, Specialist Parks. The three of you will rotate through the loader, gunner, and commander positions. We're going to load two rounds, first one sabot and then one HEAT round, and boresight the tank. While everyone else is boresighting behind us, we'll load our rounds for Table Six."

The Army referred to training scenarios as "tables", primarily in gunnery. Table Six was the simplest qualification table, and depending on the breadth and depth of the training, tank gunnery tables went to Table Twelve. This was the first time the young officers would have the chance to actually fire a tank's main gun in simulated combat conditions. Hours of simulated gunnery training on state-of-the-art computer simulators meant exactly nothing when actual rounds headed downrange.

Lopez looked at the three officers for a long moment and settled his eyes on Mairin. "Shields, you're the commander for boresighting. Murray will be the gunner, and Vrasky is the loader. Let's get your steed ready to ride."

Mairin practically strutted to the tank. Angular and sleek, the massive seventy-ton vehicle looked like it was going forty miles an hour standing perfectly still. Powered by a fifteen hundred horsepower turbine engine, when a tank powered to life it sounded just like it's aircraft brethren with the same engine technology. The Abrams carried a 120mm smoothbore cannon and was accurate to three thousand meters. Longer if she really believed the instructors and their stories from Iraq. Mairin clambered up the right front skirt and onto the front slope. She took a high step and walked across the turret to the tank commander's hatch. She watched as Murray and Vrasky climbed in through the loader's hatch. Murray, the consummate party animal, looked decidedly serious today, and the wise-cracking nasal voice of Vrasky was quiet. *The realization of putting steel downrange sobered many of them, some to the point of quitting.* Mairin wondered how many of her classmates would still be in the Army in five years. Not many, she decided. Her imprint agreed with silence.

Mairin eased into the tight, oblong commander's hatch and felt the back of the seat with her feet. She flipped the seat forward with her toes and slid deftly all the way to a sitting position. Just like the simulators, she thought. The turret and vehicle power switches sat at her right hand, the communications switch just behind them. The Gunner's Primary Sight extension sat in front of her. She connected her dual coils of communications system, her "spaghetti cords," and slipped the heavy combat vehicle crewman's helmet onto her head, positioning the boom microphone so she could talk. She flipped the ear switch to intercom and spoke, "Crew report."

"Driver ready," Specialist Parks called from his position in the vehicle's hull.

"Loader ready." Vrasky's New England accent failed to cover a nervous waver in his voice.

"Gunner ready." Murray sounded almost normal again.

"All right, let's go get some ammo. Driver move out." The tank lurched forward past the other staging tanks and the jealous stares of her classmates. She was going to do something first for a change. Mairin stopped the tank at the ammunition staging point and helped Vrasky get the two boresighting rounds aboard. She watched Vrasky press his knee against the ammunition door switch and slide the first round, then the second, into their holding tubes.

Sergeant Lopez leaned over the loader's hatch and held out a black permanent marker. "Vrasky, label the HEAT round H, and the sabot round S. Makes it much easier to figure out which round is which."

Once the rounds slid into their tubes, the only way to tell them apart was to remove them and look at their warheads. Without the letters scrawled on the firing caps, the likelihood of them taking way too long to load and fire the gun was high. The sabot round looked like a dart, with the exception of its shoes—concave pieces designed to hold the round centered in the gun tube and then separate from the projectile once the round fires. Mairin hadn't won any points with her classmates by pointing out that the name sabot was in fact French for shoes. The sabot round's dart-like appearance wasn't designed to explode, but to kill the enemy vehicle using negative pressure, blowing completely through one side of armor and then through the second fast enough to create a massive low pressure zone. This would create a vacuum force that would pull everything in the turret of the vehicle through a four-inch hole—a gruesome way to die.

The HEAT round looked decidedly different. High Explosive Anti-Tank rounds resembled a soup can with a thinner cylinder sticking up from the centerline. Basically designed as a shaped-charge weapon, the HEAT round killed by explosively tearing armor into bits, which would bounce and ricochet inside the turret like the blades of a food processor.

Mairin watched the ammunition door slide closed and wriggled back into her seat. "Everybody ready? Let's go, Parks." She stood up on the back of the seat, watching as Parks guided them to the range safety point and then onto the firing line. SFC Lopez positioned the tank behind the firing berm in a place where Murray could see the range, but from the front the rest of the tank was hidden by an earthen berm.

"Okay, Shields. You're clear to fire," Lopez spoke through the intercom. She looked over her shoulder and gave him a thumbs-up, wondering how in the world he'd be able to sit there when the main gun fired.

Gulping a breath, Mairin keyed her intercom. "Gunner, index sabot."

Below her, she saw Murray move the ammunition selector switch to sabot. She felt Sergeant Lopez tapping her shoulder. She looked into his smiling face. "You have to stand up for the first one, Shields."

Mairin stood up in the seat, completely clear of the turret above her navel, and looked at the black and white marked board. A chill ran down her spine as she spoke. "Gunner, sabot, boresight board."

The tank rolled forward. Murray leaned over to the gunner's auxiliary sight, mounted alongside the gun tube, and made sure the tube cleared the firing position berm.

"Identified!" Murray yelled. The excitement inside the turret was palpable.

The ammunition door slammed open behind her and she saw Vrasky manhandle the sabot round from its tube and into the breech of the main gun. He slammed the round forward and pulled the arming handle from the safe to fire position. Clear of the main gun's recoil, and plastered against the radio mounts, Vrasky called "Up!"

"Driver move forward, gunner take over," Mairin said.

Parks engaged the throttle and rolled the tank slowly up the berm. Looking through an auxiliary sight, Murray checked to make sure the gun tube was above and clear of the berm. The second it was he called, "Driver stop!"

Mairin rocked forward as the tank stopped. She caught herself with a hand on the base of the M2 machine gun mounted in front of her. "Fire!"

"On the waaaay!" Murray yelled as he squeezed the trigger.

WHAM! Mairin felt the heat from the muzzle as the round fired. Millions of grains of cordite swirled around her, some hitting her smiling face. She saw a cloud of dust from the concussion of the round rising around the tank as she focused on the glowing base of the tracer round punching through the boresight board. *Oh my God!* She yelled at the top of her lungs and heard Murray and Vrasky whooping in the turret.

Mairin directed the tank to back up, and when they stopped, she went through the liturgy of the crew report again. All of them were beaming. "Index HEAT." She tapped Murray on the shoulder.

"Damn straight." Murray grinned, and they got ready to do it again. This time she'd stay in the turret to see how it felt to watch the big gun recoil almost all the way to the rear wall. She wanted to hear it, feel it, taste the cordite in her mouth, smell it on her skin.

As she leaned up to the Gunner's Primary Sight to identify the target, Mairin realized more than anything that she wanted to fire at something more than a board. "Gunner, HEAT, boresight board."

"Identified!"

"Driver move forward, gunner take over."

"Up!" Vrasky screamed and got out of the way again.

"Driver, stop!" Murray yelled and moved to the primary sight.

"Fire!"

"On the waaay!" A flash of light and unearthly sound caught her in the chest.

*****

Chapter Nine

Munsen sighed. "In conclusion, given the staggering losses of three platforms, sixteen vessels, and more than fifteen thousand souls, there are two possible courses of action I see for the Greys advance into our ring of the solar system. The first is both the most likely and most dangerous. Were I the enemy commander, I would feint my forces at the next largest colony. In this case, I would project a major attack on the shipyards of Rayu-Four while deploying the majority of my fleet to Libretto. From there I would control the major lanes to Earth, Styrah, and Vemeh, and could literally put my forces in orbit around any of our core planets within days."

"And your proposed second course of action?" Admiral Chen rubbed a hand through his white hair. At seventy-four, his hawkish nose dominated his weathered and wrinkled face. A singular voice in Naval strategy, Chen relished being widely hailed as the best theorist since Alfred Thayer Mahan.

"In my opinion, the least likely course of action is that the Greys are going to continue to attack the Outer Rim planets and colonies. From Narrob they would proceed to Wolc, and then Eden before making a sweep against Rayu-Four. Either way, they must recognize the threat of our shipyards, but the question of the time the Greys will take to get there is a major contention."

Chen snorted. "What about continuing from Eden straight to Earth? That is a major interstellar passage lane. They could be here in Earth orbit within weeks."

"I sincerely doubt that, sir."

Chen sat forward. Blue eyes blazing, he jabbed the air with a finger. "What do you mean by that?"

"That kind of thinking isn't rational, sir. This is a conflict fought over the last ten thousand years, long before we even thought seriously about spaceflight. To say that the Greys are hell-bent on attacking Earth above Vemeh and Styrah is selfish and ridiculous. The Styrah possess the greatest strategic threat to the Greys and the Vemeh hivemind's technological advantages are staggering by comparison. To say that Earth is their target is foolish and irresponsible. Sir."

Chen sneered. "The Greys have seen by now that we pose the greatest threat. Admiral Yamato saw to that before he died."

"With all due respect to Admiral Yamato, sir, he executed the only course of action he had left. His ground force elements were terribly outnumbered and outgunned, and the firepower of the Grey ships dwarfed the capacity of the three platforms and all of the Fleet vessels mustered. Admiral Yamato dealt the largest blow he could, and that was by ramming the Grey 'mothership' with the *Yokohama*, not by any tactical advantage."

"You will restrain yourself from such accusations, Colonel. As the director of force enhancement, your comments on tactics and strategy are not necessary. I have staffs of people far more qualified than you to give me that information."

Munsen clenched his fists at the position of attention. "Permission to depart, sir?"

Chen shook his head. "Not until I've set you straight. From every indication we have, the Greys have begun to mass their forces to sweep the Outer Rim. I expect them to arrive at Earth in less than three months. We are directing two-thirds of our total Fleet to Earth defense. The other fleet vessels we've parceled out to our allies to appease their concerns and our treaty agreements. No matter what happens, we will defend Earth. If we have to, we will sacrifice all our alliances to do so."

"You are making a catastrophic mistake, sir. The enemy's objective is Libretto. It's the most likely target."

Chen laughed. "I told you, Colonel, I do not need your opinion on enemy tactics. Your job is to give me the best soldiers you can muster."

"So they can be thrown away like cannon fodder? What a novel concept."

Chen stood. "That's enough! One more word and I will court martial you for cowardice in the face of the enemy, and conduct unbecoming an officer. Is that understood?"

"Yes, sir." Munsen dropped the emotion from his voice. This would continue to go nowhere. Chen and the Earth-bound commanders would never be able to see beyond the orbit of their planet. "Permission to depart, sir?"

Chen sat and waved him away. "Dismissed, Colonel. Do not go spouting your theories to my staff. You are supposed to do your job, and no one else's. Write a white paper if you want to, but otherwise stick to your own program of research and leave the fighting to us."

The stateroom door slid closed. Munsen wanted to laugh and punch something at the same time. The truth was simple—when the commanders didn't listen to the troops on the ground, bad things tended to happen. This would be no exception. One third of the Fleet would be defending the main thrust of the Grey attack.

They may hit all of the other colonies first, but Libretto gives them a strategic position. Munsen shook his head. When are we going to start thinking at the level of our enemies?

There was some solace in the fact that he'd hedged his bets, and that more than one hundred sixty of the two hundred active imprints were among that third of the fleet deploying to Libretto. He hoped it would be enough.

* * * * *

Chapter Ten

Mairin woke to a crash of thunder so deep it vibrated her chest. For a moment everything was wrong. The soft sheets were both unfamiliar and comforting. A storm raged beyond the wall of windows. Outside the dome of Libretto City, Tallenaara's home sat on the edge of a small lake that fed into the Little Amazon. The terrain around them dark, only lit by flashes and sheets of lightning, the disorientation was complete and Mairin moved up into a sitting position.

Knees pulled up to her naked chest, Mairin listened to Tally's soft breathing next to her. *Should I even be here? What am I doing? Why shouldn't I be here? And, why can't I love her?* Mairin clutched at the stray thoughts like spiderwebs and brushed them away. She was going to war. All of this might not matter in a few weeks. What mattered was that there was something about Tally that resonated through Mairin. To be near Tally, to hear her melodious laugh, and feel the touch of her hands. Even the thought of six toes didn't bother Mairin. She fought a giggle and won, but barely.

"What's wrong, *cariad*?"

Mairin reached over and put her hand in the small of Tallenaara's back. "Nothing. The storm woke me."

Tally made a sound like a purr and rolled over, raising herself to one elbow. "And what are you sitting here thinking about?"

"About going to war." Mairin turned and frowned. "How all of this might not matter in a few weeks."

Tally rose to a sitting position and wrapped an arm around Mairin. "You have to believe you are coming home, no matter what. That belief will drive you, and protect you. The skills you have, or will learn soon, can get you through the conflict. But without a firm belief in yourself and your loved ones being here for you, you may survive but a part of you will die out there. I don't want that for you, *cariad*."

"What do you want?" Mairin turned and faced her lover. "From this?"

Tally smiled and half-shrugged. "Had you asked me that a week ago, I wouldn't have known how to answer. Now, I'm not sure what I may want, but I know that I want you to be a part of that. Does that make sense?"

Mairin nodded. "I feel the same way."

Lightning flashed outside, but the thunder dulled and faded as the storm rolled over the horizon. They said nothing as the storm grew farther and farther away, just held each other tightly. A short time later, Mairin fell asleep under Tally's protective gaze.

Helios rose several hours later in an eastern sky awash with fiery orange and purple clouds. Mairin opened her eyes to the spectacle and smiled into her pillow.

"Care to join me?"

Mairin rolled over in the plush bed, opened her eyes, and decided it really wasn't a dream. Tallenaara stood over her, dressed in a Cardiff University athletic top and long shorts with hiking shoes. Mairin stretched a little and smiled. "Doing what?"

Tally smiled. "I do have another job, *cariad*. Remember? I thought you might want to join me."

"For what?"

"A long walk in the woods."

Mairin dressed and walked downstairs, tying her hair behind her. Turning into the downstairs sitting room, she fell in love with the wall of windows looking to the north over a small lake and rolling hills. The rich dark wood floors gleamed, and the stone walls called to her. Water streamed down a feature on the wall, and a large fireplace dominated a corner. The couches looked comfortable enough to sleep on. Mairin hoped it wouldn't come to that.

"Something funny?"

Mairin turned and felt her insides tremble. "Hoping I don't have to sleep on the couch."

"Never." Tally smiled and crossed the room to touch Mairin on the shoulders.

It wasn't a dream. Mairin opened her mouth to say something and decided against it. Tally's touch was fire on her skin, and she loved it. They kissed for a moment and Mairin felt like giggling. Just when she wanted more, Tally broke the kiss.

"Ready?"

"What are you planning on showing me?"

Tally smiled and walked toward the door. "The real Libretto."

Outside, Mairin's chin dropped as she looked at the curving clamshell design of Tally's home, with curves in opposite directions and a full wall of windows from the kitchen and living area looking out over a small lake. "Did you design it?"

"Mmhmm." Tally smiled as she tucked some food into a small pack. "What does it remind you of?"

Mairin looked up at the curving roofs and her mind wandered for a moment. There were stairs. A breeze blew up the smell of the lakeshore. The sun shone down and turned the water into a thousand shimmering diamonds. *Circular Quay*. She blinked and said, "Sydney Opera House. The first version."

Tally nodded. "Impressive."

"Imprint." Mairin shrugged.

Tally nodded and finished packing. "Are you hungry?"

"Famished."

They sat and ate a quick meal of mixed grains and nuts. Tally called it mueslei. "Delicious." Mairin grinned around her full mouth.

"I'll teach you how to make it. It's very easy."

Mairin looked up into the windows and caught a brief glimpse of light shifting through the colors of the rainbow. There was no seam. Mairin looked again and moving her head and eyes, she saw it again. "Is there something on the window?"

"In the window." Tally chewed and swallowed before continuing. "The wall faces south, the resin windows contain photovoltaic threads. They're the primary source of power for the cabin, entirely self-sufficient. The entire foundation is built for power storage."

"You live on top of a battery?"

"Not quite." Tally grinned. "The very slight electromagnetic field generated by the foundation does serve as a buffer. The cabin could survive a massive seismic quake with no effort. Just like all of the buildings on Libretto."

Mairin grinned. "Spoken like a proud architect."

"I just design them. We've been building structures like that for four hundred years." Tally touched her shoulder. "Ready?"

Mairin fell into step behind Tally as they entered the forest a few feet above the shoreline. The forest seemed to pull her forward. Like the rooftop garden on Eden, smells bombarded her. The moist soil and bright green plants seemed so alien, and yet so familiar. In the early morning light, strange violet and orange blossoms opened like toothy mouths to take in nourishment. Bees the size of her thumbs buzzed around the flowers. Where sunlight spilled down through the canopy, dew glistened like diamonds. A breeze whistled through the tall, pine-like trees. The sound was nothing that she'd ever heard before and she almost stopped just to listen its beauty.

In the distance, she heard a growling sound to her left and up the hill. Tally did not stop, but the strange sound caused Mairin to hesitate. *Almost all wildlife is more afraid of you than you are of them.* The thought brought some clarity. Her ancestor had done this sort of thing on a regular basis, so much so that his instincts assuaged her fears.

Is that what it's supposed to be? Mairin wondered. I have to know more about you, grandpa. Whatever I can find, including why you loved the woods so much.

Nothing like it, was all that came back to her. The woods erased her anxiety and her fears. All of it called to her to just enjoy and relax. She could get used to such a life, Mairin decided. She walked with a smile on her face until a question came to mind. "So this is part of your job?"

"It's not really a job, *cariad.* It's more of a responsibility. Every Styrah has two vocations, one is our vocation and the other is meant for service to the rest of our culture. This is my service responsibility." She gestured to the lake. "I am responsible for this reservoir and everything within five miles of it. I look out for the flora and fauna, test the water, and monitor some science packages at work here in the forest as well."

"So you're like a game warden?"

Tally looked over her shoulder, her eyebrows furrowed. "We do not allow hunting for sport. There's no purpose to hunting if you're not going to eat and use the animal to the utmost."

Mairin looked down. "I didn't mean—"

Tally turned and looked down at her. "Meet my eyes, *cariad.*"

Mairin looked up. "I'm sorry."

"Do not apologize. Ever." Tally touched Mairin's chin. "Be wise in what you say, apologize only if you are truly at fault for having done something and not having said something."

Before Mairin could nod, or speak, Tally began to walk in long graceful strides. Mairin looked around as they walked. The pine forest seemed vibrant and alive, but devoid of any fauna other than chirping birds. "What kind of creatures are here?"

"Deer mostly, and something like your antelope at the higher places. It's called *smigara*," Tally said over her shoulder. "They sound a lot scarier than they are. We brought a lot of wildlife from Earth as we engineered this planet. There are a great many species of flora from Earth here as well."

"You keep saying engineered. Was this planet not anything like this?"

Tally laughed. "Of course it was. We just wanted to make it feel like home to you humans. Libretto is the hub for all inter-system travel. From here we can fold to Earth, Styrah, or Vemeh in equal time. It's the perfect terminal."

Mairin blinked away a thought about it being a perfect target. She shook her head and looked up at the surrounding hills. Not a defensible position, too many avenues of approach. *Stop it.* She focused on Tally's long legs and slightly broad shoulders. Every movement relaxed and powerful. Was Tally a warrior, too? She seemed too smart, too well read, too perfect to be some type of hardened killing machine. Her touch last night was light and loving, teasing and playful, and then so incredibly passionate.

Mairin smiled to herself. *Not a virgin anymore, girl.*

She shook that thought off, too. For something that seemed so incredibly important as she grew up, her virginity didn't seem that important now. Despite what she'd heard the girls in the Eden Academy locker room gushing over, and it was nothing indecent or risky. Maybe it was the fact her first time was with an alien, and maybe it was the fact that she'd fallen hard for the beautiful woman. Mairin felt her heart flutter as Tally looked around with her green eyes and coal-black hair. She smiled and knew what mattered. Tally mattered, and she wouldn't apologize for that ever again.

They'd walked for nearly an hour before stopping at a small fenced area where a large section of pipe, at least a foot in diameter, came out of the ground abruptly before diving into the soil again. There were monitors attached to the pipe, and what looked to be a valve. Tally opened the fence and walked in. Crouching down, Tally tapped the screen on the monitoring equipment a few times. "All's well with this unit."

"What are you pumping?"

Tally shrugged. "Crude oil."

Mairin blinked. "What?"

"Yes, *cariad.* Believe it or not, oil is still a valued commodity out here in the Rim. Especially for the Greys."

Oil hadn't been drilled for, or refined, for at least fifty years. And longer than that on Earth. "The Greys are interested in oil? Do you sell it to them?"

"No, we don't. Actually we pump it and send it off planet for storage. We want it as far away from us as possible. It keeps the Greys away. If it's not here, they won't come trying to find it." Tally closed the fence. "Now, we've got another ten kilometers until we stop for lunch. You coming with me?"

They kept hiking, Mairin alternately staring at the ground in front of her to place her steps and then staring up into the vistas through the forest at the surrounding mountains. Was Earth like this? What would the planets out there be like?

As they broke out of the forest into a field of tall sun-kissed grasses, Mairin saw several deer across the glade leap to their feet and bound into the woodline. She smiled. At least something here was wild and unpredictable. She looked at Tally walking in strong, powerful strides. *Well, make that two things*, she thought with a smile.

They walked all day, Mairin never tiring. *Perhaps this new enhanced body is a good thing after all*, she'd thought with a smile as the opposing clamshells of Tally's cabin came into view. Helios was low along the western horizon, the bright light of the day giving way to soft grays as the nahalla clouds developed. There would be rain soon, maybe before they even returned to the cabin. There was moisture in the air, a smell both familiar and startling.

She'd never smelled the rain before the imprint, and now she knew that she would always be able to. What kind of man had so many memories? So many thoughts and impressions? Mairin knew that she possessed much of that now, and for some reason that made her special. More special than her classmates at the Eden Academy, and more special than most TDF officers. Her mind flashed to the drunken colonel reading something on his neurals about her. Something powerful enough that he stopped and basically capitulated to her needs and ushered her out of his office quickly.

Why?

She looked back into the wilderness as the path began to widen into the clearing around Tally's cabin. She stopped and looked hard into the fading light of the forest. The dark path in the deep green foliage looked like a path to another world. Somewhere in there was a part of her, it called to her as loud as her love for Tallenaara, and she knew that the forest had a place in her experiences and her destiny. There was so much wonder there. Every second of every day passed in a way that few could understand. Mairin jogged a few steps and began to hike after Tally who looked at her with a question in her eyes.

"I'm okay. There's something about the forest, I suppose."

Tally nodded. "The best two days of my week. You can come with me anytime."

"Okay," Mairin smiled. "New body or not, I need a shower."

Tally grinned. "I wasn't going to say anything, but."

Mairin slapped her lover playfully on the ass and ran into the house. She knew that Tally was following her, and the thought filled her with anxiety and a deep sense of excitement she wished she could bottle and keep with her no matter where she travelled. There was nothing like her lover's arms.

* * * * *

Chapter Eleven

Munsen chuckled. "I agree that a junior officer should not speak to a senior officer in such a tone, but given the circumstances and situation I would attest that her behavior was merited and genuine."

"Not to mention totally out of character if you believe her instructors at Eden Academy."

Munsen nodded. "I think behaviorally we've reached a point of no return, Miles."

"Meaning that your subject has completely integrated the imprint?"

"Among other things." Munsen paused for a sip of scotch, thankful for an audio-only conversation. "Complete integration is something we've seen before on a hundred imprints. She has a new skill set at her fingertips without so much as thinking about it. A month ago she couldn't have pointed an electromagnetic rifle out of a line-up, and now she could perform crew member-level maintenance on it, whether she realizes it or not. We've done what we said we can do, but we've got a high-quality impression and a near perfect-genetic match. There are clearly going to be some anomalies."

"You make it sound like it's a problem."

"Hardly." Munsen smiled. "We're treading new ground. There are at least sixty imprints and officer candidates that have a similar strength of impression criteria. Based on our observations of young Captain Shields, we'll see if this theory is correct. That we can not only capture and pass instincts and skills, but also behaviors and values. If we can do that, we may have a chance."

"We're certain of the Greys intent?"

Munsen frowned. "No, we're not. But we know that they're coming. It's only a matter of time, and the handful of good officers and NCOs we have imprinted and out in the force aren't going to be enough. We need more, and we don't have them. For whatever the Greys want, they are sparing no effort. We're looking at a full-scale attack in a matter of weeks. They've completely plundered the outlying planets of the Outer Rim. For all intents and purposes, they're creating a constant supply route and positioning the logistical elements they'll need for a prolonged conflict, despite the fact that they outnumber us a thousand to one." Munsen snorted at the impossibility of it all. That history could repeat itself so many damned times.

"What was that for?"

"You've done this before." Munsen fingered the glass. "Well, sort of. Position logistics and get our people in place to mass our combat power. We launched a massive air superiority campaign and then attacked. The Iraqis folded like paper. Now, we're back to fighting a war with ungainly warships and untrained ground troops. In World War Two, we got by because of the collective values and beliefs of men who knew the cost of inaction as much as the cost of their actions. Our world has evolved, and with it we lost that sense of cost, that sense of duty to each other. That is what we need most."

"And you think she'll be ready?"

"Yes, I do. From what I've been able to observe through my sources we're seeing a huge jump in confidence, strategic thinking, and tactical knowledge. Hypnosleep has been particularly successful and she is more than ready to command a company of troops now."

"But what else? You're unsure of something."

"You tell me." Munsen shrugged. "In your day, you had a same-sex relationship and the military threw you out on your ass."

"Have you considered that she's not in a same-sex relationship because her lover is not human?"

"Yes. But from the perception—" Munsen started, then stopped.

"Perception is not nine-tenths of the law in this society. You want to bring back old behaviors and values, but you're not clearly thinking about the impact on our society if you do. Captain Shields is doing what she wants to do because of love, and that love will help shape her thinking and her actions. It will broaden her."

"Her relationship with Tallenaara could be detrimental to her command."

"What was that? The Styrahi's name?"

Munsen replied. "Sorry, thought you knew that already. Her name is Tallenaara."

"Oh yes, of course." The voice paused. "How could this relationship be detrimental?"

"Some of those under her command will not understand it, and those above her that are imprinted could cause problems." Munsen paused. "Especially the longer the relationship continues."

"You know that it cannot last very long by the Styrahi standards, and because of that she will bear some emotional weight. I agree with you that it will help her in the long run. As for those above her, I believe that is where you said you would protect her."

Munsen sipped his scotch. "You think this relationship will bring about the same sense of desire, or need to take action?"

"She's already talked herself into action on several occasions. Think about the girl you met at Eden Academy and then take into account your observers watching her walking around Libretto City, watch her hypnosleep sessions, and tell me that she isn't learning the necessity of protecting what she loves and holds dearest. Her parents never taught her that."

"You should have heard their responses to her vmail about joining the TDF." Munsen chuckled. "Mommy could have come straight from Berkeley back in my day. A total peacenik. Daddy took it better, especially with the realization that if we're combing the academies of the Outer Rim for officers, things are really that freaking bad."

"As for her training, has there been any tactical development from the imprint?"

Munsen nodded. "Her sessions have been better than I'd hoped. She is retaining a lot of knowledge in a very short time period. Her memory is almost photographic, and her recall is tremendous. The thing I'm worried about the most is something that I don't think we can ultimately train."

"And what is that?"

"Her heart," Munsen said. "Can she fight against all odds and do what has to be done while losing people and assets all around her? Will she be able to function, but also make the difference I'm counting on her to make? If she stumbles, there is no way to approach Fleet to redesign combat forces. If we don't better address the Greys order of battle, we're going to lose more people than necessary to protect Earth."

"What else do you require of me?"

Munsen drained the glass. "Nothing more, sir. We'll continue to observe and see if she meets the requirements. We don't have much time to play with. *Ticonderoga* is two weeks away, and by then the balloon will have gone up across the Outer Rim. After that happens, everything resides with the commanders on the ground to make things happen and keep this war as far from Earth, Styrah, and Vemeh as possible."

Munsen reached to shut off the communications console to close the private call with his deputy officer on Earth. "If we fail to stop them out here, we will not stop them on Earth. Not without some serious help. I believe they're on the way to Libretto right now. The TDF doesn't agree with me, and they're sending the fleet to Rayu-Four. In two weeks, we'll know for sure."

* * * * *

Chapter Twelve

"Again." Tally menaced over her. "You cannot feint like that and expect a trained opponent will not detect it and counter the maneuver. Always have a backup plan."

Mairin rolled over on the grass and got to her knees. Every fiber of her body hurt through the afternoon combatives workouts, but Mairin knew she was getting better. She was ready when Tally's foot swung in hard toward her exposed ribcage. Mairin caught the foot and twisted, sweeping Tally's other bracing leg away and bringing down the taller Styrahi. Tally rolled immediately to disengage her foot from Mairin's grasp, but Mairin was having none of that.

Tally swung her free leg in an attempt to catch Mairin's neck, but failed. Mairin rolled out and put her foot under Tally's chin and pushed. Tally was just tall enough that Mairin couldn't quite get the extension she wanted on Tally's chin, but she held her position as Tally reached for purchase and found it in the *kmorra*, the Styrahi fighting garment, and pulled. Mairin kept her hold on Tally's leg, but lost her position on Tally's chin.

Now though, Tally was exposed. Mairin dropped the leg and quickly ducked under the arm grabbing the back of her garment. She pinned both of Tally's arms with her knees and put a sharp elbow under Tally's chin.

"Good," Tally grunted. "*Gremmana*."

They separated, stood, and bowed to each other. Mairin smiled. "Better today?"

Tally wiped her brow. "A little." They'd fought each other hand-to-hand for the last six days, for two hours or more in the afternoon sun and stopping only when the clouds of the afternoon nahalla bore down and lightning chased them inside. Mairin learned Styrahi combat discipline firsthand. She pitied anyone that fought them in battle. Tally taught Mairin how to more accurately fire a rifle, how to win a hand-to-hand engagement, and more tactics for defeating an unsuspecting enemy than Mairin ever expected to learn. Tally pushed, and Mairin pushed back to the brink of her mental and physical strength.

Mairin laughed and sat on the grass cross-legged to stretch. "And every day I hurt a little more."

"Discomfort in training means less bloodshed in battle." Tally grinned and sat across from her.

"You're my drill sergeant now, Tallenaara?"

Tally laughed. "Hardly. Just a Styrah proverb."

Mairin leaned into a stretch, focusing solely on her breathing and the warmth of Helios, the Libretto star, on her back. She'd fought well today, putting her frustration and anxiety to use. A message flashed in her neurals, and she sighed. "My ship is ten days out."

Tally sat up and placed her hands in her lap. She frowned. "I'm sorry to hear that, *cariad*."

"Me, too." Mairin looked long into Tally's eyes. "I don't want to go."

"But you have to, and there is a part of you that wants to go. Don't deny that, Mairin."

"I won't. But I mean it. I don't want to go. I don't want to leave you." Tears welled up and she wiped them away. They wouldn't help now.

"You're not saying goodbye now, are you?" Tally smiled.

"No," Mairin said, and after a moment she smiled. She crawled across the grass and snaked an arm around Tally's neck and kissed her. "I'm not saying goodbye at all."

Tally grinned and returned the kiss. "There's no reason to say goodbye."

Their lips touched and Mairin breathed against Tally's cheek. "Just love me."

"I will, *cariad*," Tally said and nuzzled into Mairin's neck.

Later, they washed each other in Tally's expansive tub, and playfully teased each other the way lovers do. Mairin finally went to dress and rifled through her bags for just the right outfit. She'd moved to Tally's home, leaving behind the too-perfect world of Libretto City and its distractions. Her days were spent reading, writing, and getting to know the impulses and instincts her imprint could give. Making friends, really, so that every time she felt a pull or a conscious thought not even close to her own she would recognize and understand it before acting.

Long runs through the forest and long swims in the lake helped to blend Mairin and her imprint into something very different. Looking in a mirror, Mairin could see the physical changes she'd mapped in, but there was a change in her mannerisms, and a look in her eye. Something akin to experience, like she'd seen the universe and wore her journeys well. Mairin liked it, and it made accepting her impending departure a little easier.

Ten days, Mairin thought. *Just enjoy it. You may not have anything like this for the next two years.* She stepped out of the bedroom in a simple blue dress and sandals that clattered against the rich wood floors. Tally was already outside, sitting on the veranda watching the rain with a cigar in her hand. Mairin slipped outside with a smile. "I love a good storm."

Tally nodded, her eyes distant. "Me too."

"What's wrong?"

"Ten days." Tally raised a hand to her cheek and smoothed away a tear that Mairin had not seen. "Ten days and you're going away, and I may never see you again."

Mairin sat on the lounge chair and touched Tally's face. "I'm supposed to be the weak one, love."

Tally snorted. "And I'm not supposed to be in love with a human."

Mairin smiled. "And ten days from now I'll leave here in love with you and wishing I could come back to you every waking moment. Wishing I was here watching the rain and sitting in your arms."

"*Cariad,*" Tally said. "If I'd have known I'd feel this strongly—" She paused and Mairin snuggled into her arms.

After a long moment, Mairin sighed. "I'm scared. I couldn't say it earlier."

"You've no reason to be scared. I will be here."

Mairin chuckled. "I know. I'm just scared of not being here. Not being with you."

"You will be fine, Mairin. You are stronger than you know."

At least I know love, Mairin thought. "At least I have you."

"You do, *cariad.* As long as you'll keep me."

Mairin felt a tear beginning to form. "I love you, Tally."

"And I love you." Tally kissed her cheek tenderly. "Now why don't we just sit here and watch the rain for a little while and forget about starships, duty, being apart. And then I'll pour us some wine and get a fire going, and you can cook dinner tonight."

"You sure you're ready for that?"

Tally laughed. "Of course I am. You had a good teacher."

In more than one way, Mairin thought with a smile. Her anxiety faded as night fell and she sat alone outside. The fire popped and crackled, the smoke smelling sweet and spicy, and Mairin looked into the twinkling sky. She lit a cigar and sat back wondering what it would be like. As dark and cold as space was, there was so much out there waiting for her. New places. New experiences. She looked forward to it, but she knew there was something more. It gnawed at her slowly, like a slow rolling headache. There was a storm coming. Her ship would come, she'd go out to meet it, and all hell would break loose. There was no way to escape it. She'd been imprinted, created really, for this.

She caught sight of Tally walking down from the house to the fire circle carrying another bottle of wine. Mairin smiled. *From nothing to love*, she thought. There was something to focus on, and she decided she needed to do something about it. To make her love a constant reminder, a touchstone, and a reason to come home. She would come back here, to Tally.

Some way, somehow, she would return.

* * * * *

Chapter Thirteen

The pleasantly grim smile of the commanding general filled Thomas Munsen with dread. The reaction never wavered, even after twenty-five years. Breaking up their relationship had been a good move, but one that his former lover still held over him from time to time. One of these days, she'd be in a true position of power as a government civilian. That would be the day he retired. Generals were about as worthwhile as privates in a world where soldiers did only what they were told. "Your efforts are unsuccessful to this point, Colonel?"

Munsen tried not to frown at the all-too-obvious slight. "So far. We're talking about making babies, and there's nothing sure about that, even with two human parents."

General Zhaire nodded. "Time is of the essence, Thom."

"I'm aware of that, but we're down to her last hours on Libretto. Unless you're willing to delay her assignment to a forward unit?"

"No." Zhaire shook her head. "I'm not about to subvert regulations for this experiment, old friend. You had a chance, but she is due a forward assignment. The next time she rotates out of rest and relaxation leave, you can try again. Until she gets pregnant, Mairin Shields belongs to the TDF."

Munsen nodded. "There are exceptions, though."

"Not in this case. We need imprinted leaders out there. Getting our asses handed to us by the Greys, over and over again, is bad press. She reports tomorrow morning as ordered."

"Yes, ma'am." Munsen sighed.

Zhaire grinned. "And you've decided on her first assignment?"

"Yes, ma'am, I have." Munsen met the gray-eyed stare and spoke slowly. "I am assigning her to the Eighth Tank Battalion."

"Under Coffey?" The general blinked in disbelief. "You're putting a woman in a relationship with a Styrahi in a position to lead a tank platoon under a battalion commander who hates the idea of women in combat and who has thoroughly expunged all Styrahi from his command? You must be out of your mind, Colonel."

Munsen replied, "Her ship arrives tomorrow. And she won't get a tank platoon."

"Then what will she lead?"

"Whatever Coffey gives her. There are some extra vehicles aboard that he'd be crazy not to use."

The commanding general reached for her cigarettes, lit one, and blew a long stream of smoke at Munsen. "I'm not happy about this, but I'm not about to request you reassign her. I do trust your judgment, Colonel, but I see her and the progress you've reported as a very critical asset to our efforts to defeat the Greys and protect Earth."

Munsen sighed. "We cannot be sure that Earth is a target, ma'am."

"Earth will always be a target, no matter how many other worlds like it are out there."

Munsen said nothing. That kind of thinking was completely irrational and almost maniacal. Zhaire was a politician at heart, and politicians never change. They only repeat and repeat and repeat the mistakes of those before them. "Whatever the Greys intend, I believe Captain Shields will play a very important role."

"Captain? You've already promoted her?"

"Her imprint was a captain, and the connection is so strong I thought it best. Same responsibility factors and command emphases."

"She's prepared to assume this?"

Munsen nodded. "That being said, we've done all we can. The rest is up to her. If she shows up tomorrow morning in uniform and prepared to do her duty, then we've adequately prepared her to face whatever will be waiting for her."

* * * * *

Chapter Fourteen

The rain stopped early for Mairin's last night on Libretto. She stepped onto the patio and triggered a couch to self-dry before she sat. The warm cushion hugged her body, and she leaned back into it for a long moment to stare at the receding storm and the deep indigo sky of a late Libretto afternoon. She would miss the smell of rain and the crisp breezes as autumn slowly arrived. Would she miss this house and the forests, the trails and the water, and everything about this place? Would she ever return? She didn't know and didn't linger her thoughts on the subject.

Enjoying the moment, especially her last ones here in this personal paradise, was paramount. Mairin sipped from her glass of wine and decided there was time enough before Tallenaara came home to sit, smoke a cigar, and watch the stars come out. Hard to believe there was a time when something as pleasurable as this had such deadly effects. She tried for the millionth time to blow a smoke ring and failed, laughing. Some things she would never get better at, she guessed.

Would it be any different as a soldier? Would she get better at it? She'd not worn a uniform for a month, and only checked her neurals for communications every other day and sometimes not for a few days. The last three days, there'd been no change. *Ticonderoga* would arrive tomorrow around 0900. *Why the 0?* The sarcastic grin faded.

Responsibility tapped her on the shoulder and settled in, like the weight of an ox's yoke. Tomorrow, she would be responsible for soldiers. Tomorrow their lives would be placed with great trust into her hands. Was she truly ready for it? Of course not. *I want to do well,* she thought. *But I'm so scared. Scared of being seen as a mousy little girl from Eden and not some kind of super warrior with a bunch of training I never really went through and the memories of a man dead over two hundred and fifty years. What if I don't make it?*

That was simple. She would return here. Make a life with Tallenaara until the time came for her to take a *shdante*, a mate. There would be time to figure out the rest of her life if that happened. She'd more likely be dead in six months, maybe less. That thought scared her less than being alone. Being alive, but without Tally, would be torture. Would Tally say the same about her?

Mairin smoked for a while and watched the sky deepen to blu-ish-black as the first twinkling stars appeared. She didn't think too much, only to pull the blanket over her legs and shift her weight a little to get more comfortable, if it was even possible. For the moment, there was nothing in the universe as comforting as being in that chair, under those stars, and with Tallenaara due home soon. She could live with that comfort forever and be happy.

She heard the autocar approaching a good minute before it pulled up to the front of the house. Tallenaara walked down the path carrying her for-appearances-only shoes and sat them by the door. "*Cariad.*" She smiled and moved across the patio to kiss Mairin on the lips.

"Thought I was going to have to send out a search party for you. Meeting run late?"

Tally nodded. "Sometimes work never seems to get done." She poured a glass of red wine. "Sorry that you started without me."

"It's okay, Tally." Mairin looked up at the sky. "Just sitting here wondering what it's going to be like out there."

There was nothing to say. Tally raised a hand to her face and smoothed away a tear. "I've been trying to avoid thinking about it. And I didn't want to come home tonight and face the fact that you're leaving tomorrow."

Mairin sat her cigar down and held Tally's hand in hers. "I don't want to go, Tally. I want to be here with you more than anything in the world. But I have to go. I agreed to."

"I know you do, Mairin. And I expect you to. I didn't expect to care for you so deeply, and to love you. Styrah and humans are not a good mix, but you were so different. I wish you didn't have to go, but I know it's for a greater good. One that I hope will bring you back to me."

An emptiness opened in Mairin's chest as she looked into Tally's green eyes. "We said we were not going to do this."

"And we shan't," Tally said. "We're going to dinner, then listen to some jazz music, and then we're going to come home and finish our celebration the right way."

Mairin grinned. "I've been waiting all day, and not so patiently!"

There was a pause, and Tally reached into her gown. "I was going to wait, but seeing you smile is a memory I want to keep. I want you to have something, *cariad*."

"Should I close my eyes?"

"No," Tally said. "I want you to see it first."

The necklace looked like a combination Celtic cross and wreath. The inscription was Old Styrahi and read "Beloved." "*Cariad*, this is my love for you and only you. Will you wear it?"

Mairin choked out a sob as her eyes filled with tears. "Yes."

Tally touched it to her neck and there was a dull rush of heat that faded within seconds. The weight of it fell right between her breasts. "You will carry that for me. I will love you no matter where you go, or how far apart we are."

"I don't have anything to give you."

Tally smiled. "You already have. In ways you may never understand."

Mairin kissed Tallenaara for a long moment, then snaked her arms around the taller Styrahi and pressed herself against her lover. She broke the kiss, not wanting to ruin their plans for the night, and looked up at Tally.

"Let's go inside and get ready then. We have dinner reservations in an hour," Tally said.

"Where?"

"I thought a little sushi was in order." Tally winked.

Mairin wore a black dress and a bracelet of freshwater pearls from the Little Amazon. She tied her hair back as Tally finished slipping into a long dress of red with a white sash that dragged the floor. Outside, the rain began to fall.

"You look stunning," Mairin said and smiled.

"Tomorrow, I wear purple." Tally smiled with a touch of frown. Purple, the Styrahi color of sorrow. "Tonight, I court you."

* * * * *

Chapter Fifteen

Mairin rose before Helios streaked the sky with bright colors. Leaving Tallenaara asleep, she padded down the stairs and poured a steaming cup of *caffe*, the spicy coffee of Libretto. Staring into the sunrise, Mairin sighed. *The next time I get to watch a sunrise*, she thought, *I'll be on some faraway planet and most likely in combat.* The thought of stepping into her boots in a few hours, tying her hair back, and reporting for duty really didn't bother her. All of that was a way of life far different than what she had with Tally. Missing things like sunrises, casual touches, a nice glass of wine, a little jazz music, and the only she person she'd ever loved were things to cherish, but they could not go forward with her. Duty was secondary to life. In a few hours, duty would be all she'd have.

She would lose Tally, too. Eventually, Tally would have to move on—her species demanded it. But would she? Her fingers traced the necklace and lingered there for a long moment. *Would she eventually move on? Couldn't they remain a couple? What was to say that they couldn't, except for the whole Styrah mating cycle? There's an exception to every rule, isn't there?*

Except that there wasn't. Not this time, and not with Tally. From day one, Tally's advice was to enjoy the moment to the utmost. That was all she had.

The ride to the spaceport seemed far too short and silent. They held hands and looked at each other, turning away when tears started to appear. Mairin wore her coveralls and the garrison cap reminiscent of an old Air Force uniform, the gold braid of an officer catching the sun, and her captain's bars polished and ready. She hefted her bags to the walkway and turned to Tallenaara.

There were no words.

Mairin walked to her lover and simply wrapped her arms around Tallenaara. She choked back sobs and tried to tell Tally how much she loved her, but the words wouldn't come. Her mouth opened and closed without a sound. They pulled away gently and looked into each others' eyes.

"Carry my love with you, Mairin."

Mairin nodded. "I love you, Tallenaara."

"I love you." Tally smiled and kissed her one, long, perfect final time.

Mairin stepped away to her bags and picked them up in time to hear the five-minute call for her shuttle to the *Ticonderoga.* She turned and saw Tally walking back to the autocar with her head down, one hand to her face. Mairin felt her tears start and she tried to walk away, but held her spot until Tally looked up at her one last time. She raised her hand and blew a kiss, and Tally smiled through tears. Then Tally stepped into the autocar and was gone.

Stand up straight now. You've been through the toughest part of this; now you're going to walk onto military property, and you have to be ready for it. On cue, she looked up and saw a young staff sergeant walking her way. He was going too fast to be meeting her, but as the soldier walked past, he raised a salute.

"Good morning, ma'am."

She returned the salute reflexively. "Good morning."

The tears stopped. Her back straightened and she walked towards the shuttle bay. *There's nothing about me that's the way I used to be*, Mairin thought with a sense of confidence she'd not had a few weeks ago. Yes, she was leaving her first love, and she wanted nothing more than to stay here on this planet that felt like home, but there was something out there. Something called to her. Needed her. Wanted her to come and share it, make a difference, and serve with others. She did not understand it fully, and part of her knew that she never really would. *Some of us are just wired differently.*

The shuttle had a twenty-six-hour flight to rendezvous with the *Ticonderoga*, and it appeared comfortable enough to maybe sleep some. The thought of red nylon webbed seats strung in a cargo plane brushed past her and she laughed at it. *Soldiers always sleep when they can.* She loaded her bags on the shuttle and stepped aboard, savoring her last breath of moist Libretto air. *I will come back*, she thought. *I will be back, Tally. I love you, cariad.*

The shuttle lifted three minutes later. Mairin faded gently towards sleep, her neurals playing Dave Brubeck and a wistful smile on her face.

* * * * *

Chapter Sixteen

Tallenaara told herself not to cry, that good Styrahi would not behave in such a weak manner in public. But she wasn't in public, now tucked in the back of her autocar and running scared back to her cabin outside the dome. No, she wouldn't cry. She thought of Mairin in her uniform walking away for the last time. The chances they would see each other again were slim and that was the truth.

The tears came.

Tally leaned back against the cushions, smelling the last hint of Mairin's perfume in the air, and wondered what the truth really was in their relationship. *And would it really matter in the end? Especially without Mairin?* The autocar flashed an incoming transmission. Subspace. Tally looked at the console long enough for her retinas to be identified and the transmission connected.

"Tallenaara. Were you successful?" The voice spoke flawless Styrah, with a dialect from the northern tribes. It brought a fleeting memory of wide open prairies and tall trees.

"It doesn't appear so." Tallenaara bit the inside of her lip. "I wasn't able to get an appropriate sample." The lie came easy.

"Without a proper sample, we'll have to find an alternative."

There would always be an alternative. That was the purpose of councils. Planning for such eventualities were seldom simple. Perhaps there would be someone else to carry the burden. Another of her race that could be told that the continuation of their species as a whole rested solely on her shoulders. Tally snorted. That wasn't exactly true. Styrahi would continue to populate the universe. What they wanted, and sought, was a way to make their already fruitful lives longer. A way to extend the very lifetime of the race. One hundred twenty periods were not long enough anymore. Tally did the math in her head. Sixty Earth years. On the seat next to her, a hair glinted in the early morning light. She touched it, and squeezed gently between her fingers until her eyes filled with tears. Tally looked away at the blurring countryside outside the autocar's windows.

The voice came again. "Aren't you wondering what the alternative is?"

Tally knew she'd be pressed for a response. "Is there a replacement identified for me?"

A laugh resonated from the speakers in the autocar. "No, Tallenaara. There will be no replacement. Merely a change in mission."

"I will not attempt to date another TDF officer. Nor will I attempt to get pregnant by one."

"How quickly can you be off planet?"

"Are you listening?" Tally snarled. "I will not do this again."

"You're going to Earth."

Tally felt her mouth drop open. Memories of long rainy months during her time in Wales and friends she'd met along the way came to mind. *Andrew.* Her stomach flipped. "Not him."

"Yes, Tallenaara. Your genetic mutation may allow you to conceive a child with a human, regardless of gender. The probability with a male is lower, yes, but we have options. From your connection to Andrew Cartner during your education, you can get close to him. He is, after all, the Earth's Prelate."

Tally clenched her jaw. They'd been fast friends and he'd not been scared away by her differences. Granted, at Cardiff she was the only Styrahi on the campus, and dealt constantly with the attention and notoriety, until her second year when she finally began to be treated like just another student.

One evening she'd walked down to the Goose's Gander to indulge in a local jazz trio and a bottle of wine. Andrew walked in a half hour behind her and crossed the darkened pub with his eyes on her the entire time, like he'd worked up the courage to approach her. Gesturing to the chair, he asked, "May I sit?"

Tallenaara smiled. "I'm sure there are plenty of other seats available if you'd rather."

"No, I'd like to sit here." He shrugged out of a black overcoat. His school sweater made her chuckle at human emotional connections to things like schools and sports. Andy smiled at her with perfect white teeth and glittering blue eyes. He wiped his wet brown hair back from his forehead and motioned to the waitress. A moment later he had his stout, the lights lowered, and the trio took the small stage again and began to play. He scooted his chair closer to her, to have his eyes on the stage. "Is this acceptable?"

Tallenaara nodded. "If you can deal with the consequences."

"Oh?" He looked shocked but then began to smile. "You don't scare me, Tallenaara, despite your reputation."

She laughed. "Reputation? Oh, it's a little more physical than that. I don't believe I know your name."

"But you know me." He smiled and fighting herself, she returned it.

"I do. I had Concrete Mechanics with you two quarters ago. You hardly ever came to class."

He laughed. "I still earned top marks."

"Laziness on top of potential is still laziness." Tallenaara sipped at her Italian nebbiolo. "Now, what is your name?"

"Andrew. Andrew Cartner."

The pieces fell together. She nodded and turned her attention to the band. The son of Earth's newly appointed Prelate. He'd not been absent from classes because of laziness after all. Security measures often did that, despite their good intentions. The trio finished a song she'd never heard before and then tinkled into "S'wonderful." Andrew reached onto the table, to Tally's free hand, and gently put his hand over it. Her hearts raced at all of the potential things that were wrong with this. But he had a nice smile, and she enjoyed his showing of affection like a note of acceptance. No one in the pub noticed, or even cared to. For a moment, they were just two students, enjoying music in a dark bar, without a care in the world.

He walked her home, all of three hundred feet and up two stories to her flat. He gallantly opened the doors for her and looked up into her face with a rueful grin as they passed other students. His ambivalence to the gawkers made her happy. At her doorstep, he'd merely smiled and nodded. "Thank you for a wonderful evening. I'd very much like to do it again, but I'm afraid I have quite a problem."

Tally squinted. "And what would that be?"

"I was hoping I could ask you to accompany me this weekend. To Scotland."

"For what?" A State dinner or event would require her talking with the Styrahi consulate for permission. She didn't want anything to do with his world despite his smile.

"Some friends of mine are going golfing with their significant others. I'm terribly outnumbered and I believe a fan of good jazz and excellent wine could help me fend off the wolves trying desperately to get me married and copulating like a wild rabbit!"

She laughed. He made it easy. "And I won't scare away your friends?"

He grinned. "Two Canadians, an Irishman, and their dates? Please, although the Irishman you might have to watch. Pour enough Guinness down him and anything with a heartbeat is fair game."

She felt herself smiling wider, if possible, liking the way he was trying to take care of her and defend her from imaginary threats. "And if I say I'll go?"

"I can promise you that I will be the gentleman's gentleman. Dashing, gallant, and chaste, though I cannot promise against the occasional show of affection."

She acted like she was thinking, her decision already made. "I will go."

Andrew smiled. "Then I will see you here tomorrow at noon. We'll autocar up there so Darren can start drinking early. Do you play golf?"

"No." Tallenaara frowned. "I'll be in a dark pub, preferably with jazz music."

"I know those type of places," he grinned. "Then I will see you tomorrow."

He touched her elbow, but made no effort to get closer. A wave of feelings struck her. Sadness, expectation, and excitement all rolled into one. She closed the door, prepared for bed, and slipped between the sheets with a smile on her face. Sooner or later she'd have to let the consulate know of her interaction with the Prelate's son. Until then, she could enjoy his attention and the occasional display of affection. The way she'd felt that night stayed with her for years, until she met Mairin Shields and felt it again, this time stronger and even more natural.

She cleared her belongings from the remote cabin in an afternoon. There wasn't time to waste if her masters on Styrah had their way. The autocar stood waiting, her cases packed and loaded aboard while she walked out to the patio one last time. She'd cleaned the house from top to bottom, as if preparing for a long winter's absence. For a moment she lingered at the lounge chair where Mairin had sat the previous night. Hesitation was weakness, she knew, and cursed the Styrahi proverbs that told her so. Hand in her pocket, she removed the hair she'd plucked from the autocar and held it up to the light. On the back of the chair, so it would catch the light, Tally laid Mairin's strand of hair. Surely they would meet again.

But it would never be the same.

The autocar door closed behind her, and she glanced a final time at her clamshell cabin and set her mind to go to Earth. *Come what may.* There was no point in wishing, no point in prayer. If destiny provided that she and Mairin would meet again, then it would be fine with her. She thought of Shakespeare. Something about meeting again, and smiling.

Julius Caesar and Brutus before battle, she thought. There was certainly something on the horizon. Tally looked out the window of the autocar for a final trip into the dome. She watched the countryside flying by and tried hard not to think of Mairin.

Two days outbound from Libretto, Tallenaara received the first message from Mairin and then spent the next hour dabbing silent tears from her face. Eventually, anger drove out the sadness. There was to be no further contact between her and Mairin. No messages, no actual mail, nothing met the criteria handed down by the Styrahi Council. Disobedience meant excommunication, and while she might enjoy a life with Mairin someplace in a far corner of the galaxy, she would be a non-entity in the eyes of the Legion of Planets. Without medical care, the ability to work, and expressly forbidden from travel, excommunication was not an option. There was far too much in the universe.

And other fish in the sea, she thought and immediately hated herself for doing so.

Deleting Mairin's messages after reading them for the last time, Tallenaara felt no better. Solace came from knowing that Mairin was young. She would find someone else, and the hurt would fade, eventually becoming the kind of memory that causes mental flinches before finally settling into a faded, tinged with regret picture of how their relationship seemed to be. Mairin would be fine. *If she survives the war*, Tallenaara thought.

When she does, I will be there for her. Tallenaara smiled at the thought. They can send me to Earth, but they cannot force me on Andrew. Teaching at Cardiff would be a grand distraction. Putting her every effort into her students and her love of structure would keep her from him. The Prelate of Earth would be far too busy for her. If he couldn't make the time, then Tallenaara would not force the issue.

Clearing her neurals, Tallenaara dimmed the lights and cued music into the room. Losing herself between the wailful jazz of Miles Davis and the soul-scraping vocals of Nina Simone helped to take her mind off Mairin, Andrew, and the rest of the galaxy. For a few hours, nothing mattered. Her hearts hurting, Tallenaara struggled to find the strength she was going to need.

I'm sorry, Mairin.

I'm so very sorry, Tally thought as she drifted to sleep.

* * * * *

Chapter Seventeen

Andrew kept his promise throughout their time in Scotland, only kissing Tally's cheek as they danced in a jazz club in Turnberry. She enjoyed being with his friends and their playful banter. They accepted her immediately, without question, and that alone was worth the trip. Riding home, everyone else asleep but her and Andrew, his warm hand on her exposed leg, they talked in whispers and grins like they'd talked that way for years. Being with him came so easily, filling her smile and lightening her mood. At her flat, Andrew kissed her for the first time, and she responded. Hearts thumping, she pulled him close, but he wouldn't cross her threshold. Holding back, almost teasing, his eyes with their devilish twinkle, she felt love in that moment. Not the prescribed manners and customs of her people partnering to one another, but something completely different and alien. She knew it was love, the way the humans talked about it, made holos about it, and sang about it. Something completely filling, consuming her conscious mind with thoughts of Andrew. She knew there would be nothing to ever replace it. For a year and a half, this was their norm.

There was acceptance in the halls of Cardiff and throughout the Welsh countryside with its lush forests and rolling plains of tall green grass. On campus, she and Andrew were well known now, but the students and faculty kept their secret, driving away the curious and remaining silent. Nearly everyone who saw them together could see the love and laughter in their eyes and couldn't help but accept them. There was something ethereal about them, and even the royals schooling at Cardiff could only stare, smile, and enjoy what they saw.

Andrew refused to talk about the future. "Keep your mind here with me," he said with that grin and squeezed her hand gently. And she did. That he never went farther than kissing her did not bother Tallenaara. Their making love would likely have been awkward and regretful. Andrew was, after all, male, and she suspected that he just wasn't sure about that aspect of their relationship. Perhaps it should have been a warning, she would later think, but her love for him simply reached a level where she respected exactly what he wanted and didn't push the issue any further.

A week before Commencement in a driving summer rain, Andrew came to her apartment with a bottle of nebbiolo and a bouquet of flowers. The joy behind his devilish little smile was gone, and his eyes didn't seem to twinkle.

She knew it was the end.

"We both know we can't continue outside of here." Andrew sighed and sipped the wine. "There would be too much attention on you, and I don't want that."

"This is more about your reputation isn't it?" Tally asked with a bitterness that surprised her. "I have handled attention ever since I came to this planet."

"It's not my reputation," Andrew said but wouldn't meet her eyes. "Diplomatically, we cannot continue our relationship, Tally."

She laughed. "Diplomatically? Politics? Did your father tell you to say that?"

Andrew's chin fell to his chest. That was it precisely. "He told me to say a lot of things, but I'm saying what we both know has to happen, Tally. Your council would react similarly, would they not?"

Tally grabbed Andrew's chin and raised his face to hers. "This isn't about our planets, Andrew. This is about me. Us. Despite your future position over all of Earth's governments, you can make a choice. I believe it's your right. So what's it going to be? A future you've not wanted for the last two years, or me?"

The tears came later, after he'd silently collected his jacket and walked barefoot into the foyer. He didn't say anything until his shoes were on and he'd opened the door. Standing there like the first night he'd taken her home, Andrew smiled with tight lips. "I will never forget you, Tallenaara."

Diploma in hand the next day, Tally went from Commencement to the London platform and caught an old freighter bound for Styrah. Staying on Earth was not an option with the sight of Andrew guaranteed at least every few days in the media. She sat in her smelly rented space aboard the freighter and cried. The freighter limped home, making a twelve-week trip into nearly six months. She sketched and designed with wild abandon, anything to keep from thinking about Andrew, while she put the last four years of her life into cold, hind-sighted perspective. It shouldn't have happened, could not have gone anywhere, or lasted. His father would not have approved and had they consummated their relationship, governments on both planets would have exploded. All was as it should have been, until her arrival at Styrah and quarantine.

Her unique chromosomal mutation opened up an interesting possibility, and a veritable Pandora's Box. Ordered to stay away from humans, the Styrahi Council asked her to help create the ultimate port of call for humans in the Outer Rim. The council originally forbade her to leave Styrah for any reason.

Tally accepted the assignment without question and threw herself into the design of the Terran Embassy and left her mark on Styrah with a sprawling, ecologically sound structure that called to mind comparisons to Frank Lloyd Wright and the Styrahi maestro Heelaani. Within a few months, Tallenaara found herself on a luxury shuttle to Libretto, to first construct a private residence and then to help create a human utopia, the irony thick enough that she could feel it on her skin.

Ten years passed in the blink of an eye, the only bright spot being her liaison with Mairin Shields. Now, Tallenaara found herself headed back to Earth and back to a man who'd meant everything to her, only to lose him because he could not be allowed to feel the same. For fear of his father and the fate of two planets he'd had to walk away. And she had no choice but to let him go. But now? Now what was she about to do?

"If I refuse this assignment?" she'd asked.

"Assignment? This isn't something you have the power to refuse. Under penalty of exile, for life, this is the Council *teitcheen* for you."

Leaning forward, elbows on her knees and head in her hands, she'd wept silently in the cabin. Her destiny decided for her. A destiny she'd wanted ten years ago, but not now. Not for all the water on Earth. Ten years ago, they feared everything about humanity and demanded she stay away from humans. Now, twice in the last six months, she'd been ordered to get involved with humans as part of competing schemes. Take advantage of a young imprinted officer and help her blossom. Rekindle an old relationship that was doomed to fail in the first place. And both times, try like hell to become pregnant. Take advantage of her genetic mutation and see, just see, if she could become pregnant by a human. The possibilities it could bring, they'd told her, were epic. Extend the Styrah lifespan beyond its median sixty Earth years even if the precious genetic chain would be corrupted. Imprinting could surpass most of that, and having a longer lifespan would enable continuation of great initiatives and exploration throughout the rest of the known universe.

Tallenaara understood the reasons. They made perfect sense, but they were playing with her hearts. She loathed her mission, but she understood. She would have to leave Mairin behind. She was a tough girl and would survive just fine. *For now*, Tallenaara told herself, *the weight of a world lies on my shoulders. Like an albatross.*

She resigned herself to the task at hand, promising herself that her culture mattered more than herself.

When the shuttle opened its doors above Geneva, Tallenaara crinkled her nose. *Why did Earth smell like death?* Musty, humid, fossil-fueled death. A scant three hours later, her levtrain shot out from its tunnel under the English Channel and roared into London. Her neural bracelet tingled a message from a waiting autocar outside the Gatwick terminal. An hour later, after the interminable slowness of human customs, she collected her baggage and walked quickly through the vendors and shops to the waiting car. The stretched car bore diplomatic holo markings. She loaded her two simple cases into the trunk and stepped to the open door.

A hand appeared from inside. "Please. Allow me."

Tallenaara took the hand and eased into the rear-facing set of the autocar and caught her breath. The man's accent was unmistakably Irish, and she'd have recognized Darren McMasters anywhere. He smiled with perfect teeth and took both of her hands in his. "My lady Tallenaara, it has been too long."

Tallenaara smiled. He'd called her "my lady" since they'd first met in Andrew's autocar on the way to Turnberry ten years ago. Gone were his oafish student mannerisms, replaced by the sophisticated grace of the practiced diplomat she'd known would be his role. That he would fall into its practice easily given his family lineage was unquestionable. "And how are the peoples of the Republic of Ireland these days?"

McMasters grinned and shrugged at the same time. "A bustling economy, a new spaceport at Shannon, and a dashing single fellow as their Senior Representative to the Prelate's Council? Why, I believe the people of my fair island are in the best of hands."

Tallenaara found herself smiling and laughing. "You haven't changed a bit, Darren McMasters."

He leaned back, releasing her hands and offering her a drink with a nod of his head. "Well, some things have changed obviously, but I try to remain as much Darren McMasters as my position allows. There are times I would give anything to walk into a dark pub for a few stouts without bodyguards or attention. Privacy is something we tend to give up in this sorry business of politics."

Tallenaara nodded and looked out the window. "You both knew that a long time ago." Her insinuation that he and Andrew were still the best of friends met with a fresh smile on McMaster's face.

"Yes, we did. I suppose that's why we did our best to enjoy our university years."

Tallenaara looked out the window. The chances were excellent that Andrew knew of her arrival on planet and had arranged for Darren to meet her. *What else don't I know?* She sipped the offered bourbon and met McMasters's eyes. "Does he know that I'm back on Earth? Is that why you met me? The same old reasons?"

McMasters smiled, but it stopped at his lips. His eyes were bright and ferocious. "Bitterness does not suit you. Actually, he does *not* know you are here, Tallenaara. I haven't decided to tell him about your reappearance on our planet. He was quite upset that you just disappeared after commencement."

"He gave me up for his father and his position. I can't honestly believe he was upset about my departure for too long."

"His father's unexpected passing was difficult. It quite literally took him the better part of a year to re-focus on his duties. He was distracted and forgetful with his mind wondering where you were. Not even your council knew where you were for six months." McMasters' familiar grin returned conspiratorially. "Where were you Tally?"

"Aboard a barely spaceworthy freighter that limped to Styrah by way of Causus."

McMasters said nothing, his familiar eyes bored into her as if looking for a deeper truth. "You look the same as ever." McMasters sipped his drink. "I can imagine he will be pleased to know you are here."

"And just what does that mean?"

"Exactly what I said. He'll be pleased."

Tallenaara snorted. "And that means he'll dismiss me just as easily."

McMasters leaned forward. "I know why you're here. It is only a matter of time before he knows as well."

There was an authority to his voice she hadn't expected. "How do you know what the Council wants of me?"

"As a representative of the Prelate's Council, I am in contact with my counterpart on Styrah. We are in agreement that this is a mutually beneficial arrangement and have given it our support." He paused and smiled again. "Earth is very different these days."

Tallenaara bristled. *How much does he know?* "What's that supposed to mean?"

"Styrah and human relationships are commonplace these days, but there isn't another Styrahi with your genetic mutation."

That she was merely a pawn in a larger drama dawned on her. Tally sighed. "What else do you know?"

McMasters chuckled. "Our representative councils have come to an agreement that this is something both wish to pursue."

"Without Andrew's knowledge?"

"Not at the present time." McMasters leaned back in the seat. "You're aware of the differences between the Styrahi Council of Elders and the Prelate's Council, I assume?"

"That the Prelate is regarded much like a powerless entity, as he speaks for Earth, but the Prelate's Council and the Assembly of Nations are the decision makers. On Styrah, the Styrahi Council is essentially the government and they have the power to direct action on the part of their citizens where the Prelate does not."

"Well put," McMasters smiled. "So you're returning to Cardiff? And as a professor of architecture, no less. I am quite impressed, you know. Your work on Libretto is simply stunning. Like a modern Venice along the Little Amazon, I should say. I wish I could say I've seen it first hand, but my duties keep me Earthside much of the time."

"I can't say I'm familiar with anything on Earth these days."

McMasters chuckled. "It's like riding a bike, Tallenaara. Earth never changes."

Of course nothing ever changed. Humans rarely changed anything over the course of a lifetime. For anything significant to happen on Earth took hundreds, if not thousands, of years. The Pyramids of Giza. The Great Wall of China. How could she expect anything different? Especially from Andrew. "And what about Andrew?"

"He is a very busy man," McMasters started.

"You know what I'm asking, Darren." Tally sipped from her drink.

McMasters chuckled. "He will be surprised and shocked. And I think it will cause him to focus."

"Focus? On what?"

"On what's really important in his life for a change. I think it would do him good." McMasters shifted in his seat. "Tally, Andrew has become increasingly stressed in his position. Even though it is his Council who decides matters of importance, he has begun to take on enormous responsibility for things he doesn't control. His loyalty has become a burden. He wears the yoke when he doesn't have to, Tally. It's affecting his health and frankly, we do not want the hassle of selecting a new prelate, especially as he has no heir."

The words stunned Tally, but she understood. Of course the Prelate's Council would want this for Andrew, and given the Styrahi desire to extend their lifespan, this was the best possible arrangement two planets could make. An heir for Earth and longer life for Styrahi. The walls of the autocar seemed to close in. Tally took a long deep breath, hearts racing, and let it out slowly. She tossed the bourbon back with a flick of her wrist.

I'm so sorry, Mairin.

She sat quietly for a few minutes as a fresh set of feelings bubbled to the surface. She'd just met Mairin and loved her dearly, but this was about Andrew. First love stung deeply. The memory of him standing there at her doorstep as he turned to leave. His heart broken. Maybe hopping that freighter was a bad idea. Maybe if she'd stayed...

She shook her head. McMasters saw it. "Is something wrong, Tallenaara?"

"Wondering what might have happened if I'd stayed on Earth."

"You know that train of thought is irrelevant, my dear." McMasters touched her hand. "You wouldn't be here now if you'd stayed on Earth. And in reality, you know it was most likely for the best anyway."

Tally nodded. "I know that, Darren. But I'm wondering what I'm supposed to do now."

McMasters smiled again and leaned back in the seat, refilling his glass. "All things in good time, my lady Tallenaara. I will ensure that you and Andrew cross paths in the very near future. Until then, you're a professor now, correct? Then live the academic life. First to Cardiff, and then to the rest of your life."

*****

Chapter Eighteen

"You've done what?" Munsen tried to contain his shock. "That was not our arrangement."

The subspace delay of five seconds gave him just enough time to start thinking of his contingency plans before a lilting Styrahi voice came back. "It cannot be helped. We were unable to generate the data we'd looked for and have moved on to a second subject."

"Have you not considered my end of this deal? Success in our experiment with Captain Shields is dependent upon a strong emotional connection! Now you're cutting that off while we were having success! By removing Tallenaara from Mairin's influence, you've destroyed our experiment and put our alliance at risk!"

Munsen told himself to breathe, that he was becoming enraged. It didn't matter. His work was being thrown out the window. The voice returned. "There is likely to be emotional contact for days and weeks to come. That cannot be helped. We have a more critical issue that requires Tallenaara elsewhere. You are aware of the requirements of your service, Colonel. The same holds for the Styrahi Council. When it speaks, it is obeyed."

Wishing for a cigarette for the first time in thirty years, Munsen drummed his fingers on the console. *Think of the bigger picture. There's more at stake than one girl's heart.* "There isn't much time until we're facing a full-scale invasion by the Greys."

"No, I expect we'll see them on the perimeter of our system in the next three months. We are preparing the defense of Styrah. Your battlegroups from the *Constellation*, *Indomitable*, and *Tsien* are in orbit around our homeworld. The Greys will not be successful here."

Munsen nodded. He'd lay his money on the Styrah when it came to the defense of their world. He cleared his throat. "What if Styrah isn't their target?"

"What do you mean?"

"There are at least three other planets I'd take a swing at before marching into your system to take you on. Ashland for one and a host of others. There are planets of strategic importance in a campaign like this. The shipyards at Rayu-Four for example, or Libretto, or Pluto-Charon if they chose to dive towards Sol. To assume they're going to bring everything that they have at Styrah, or any other planet on the Rim, is short-sighted."

The voice chuckled. "This is how they've fought their wars for the last millennia. We will be ready for them, Colonel. Your assistance is appreciated. I am sorry your experiment is now in jeopardy, but this is a matter of our security and cannot be taken lightly."

Munsen nodded, thanked the nameless diplomat, and terminated the conversation. He hit the desktop in frustration. *Of all the times for this to happen!*

"Sir, did you need something?" The speaker in his desk chimed. He'd toggled his assistant's call button in his anger.

"Get me Darren McMasters, Mary. Priority One." Establishing the connection took milliseconds. Getting the familiar voice of the Prelate's Chief of Staff on the line took considerably longer. Fidgeting in his seat, Munsen felt his anger rising. The Styrahi Council trashed his experiment on the first try. They'd known the chances of success were astronomically poor, so why cancel it now?

"Colonel Munsen, what can I do for you?" The video link snapped to life. McMasters sat at his desk, tie undone and hair askew.

Munsen took a breath, chastised himself into calming down, and began. "The Styrahi Council has ordered Tallenaara to a second subject, canceling our experiment."

There was a long pause. "I see. You realize I'm not in a position to sway the Styrahi Council on this matter. The Council has stated they want to explore genetic longevity with human crossbreeding. That Tallenaara has this particular genetic mutation makes her a valued commodity to the Styrahi. They will direct her accordingly."

"We're risking a lot more than their desired longevity."

"And the Stryahi are notorious for taking care of their own, Colonel," McMasters replied. "I'm afraid there is nothing we can do."

"What about Captain Shields? The outcome of this experiment is vital to our global security."

"She is one subject, Colonel. We've imprinted two hundred others to this point. What's your point?"

"Emotional involvement." Munsen sighed. "If we're able to effectively integrate an emotional connection, we can move beyond just imprinting. A true genetic clone, with full memories and experiences, is within our grasp."

"I'm sorry, Colonel. There is simply nothing we can do at this point. From what you've told me, Captain Shields will be just fine."

Munsen nodded and rubbed his temples. "I suppose so. Thank you for your time."

"My pleasure." As the connection faded, McMasters smiled. Munsen could not. There were simply too many variables in play. As much as he wanted to rest, there was more to do.

The work of a staff officer never ended. Real issues already remained incomplete whenever a staff officer rotated to another assignment, and sometimes issues remained after several officers had given the old college try, thrown their hands up in despair, and rotated to another place with the promise of some degree of sanity. Munsen was no different, though he'd learned an important lesson from a good friend and former commander—there is virtually nothing different in the military between doing an outstanding job and doing a shitty one. The fact that there was almost always something left undone became a familiar burden, one shifted and adjusted but never fully released until that glorious new assignment came. The only things that kept successful officers going were often side projects, ideas or long-shot dreams that might actually one day help others make sense of military life. In this case, Munsen's position gave him ample opportunity to let his thoughts play. And in some cases, come to life.

The almost two hundred imprints serving on active duty might actually thank him someday for being given the chance to serve and use their unique talents and instincts. That some of them still had no idea they were imprinted bothered Munsen, but he understood the first rule of research—sometimes the experiment just doesn't work. Sure there are hours to spend investigating and determining the point of failure, but sometimes shit just broke. Flipping through the daily imprint reports for each of the two hundred imprints, Munsen thumbed faster and faster until reading the last report for Captain Mairin Shields. Now en route to the *Ticonderoga* and her first assignment, she appeared to have met all of the criteria for a Class Five imprint. The first of its kind.

A Class One imprint was barely aware that anything was different from their original thought processes and memories. At Class Three, the subject remembered key critical training elements, like how to perform maintenance on a weapon system, or how to navigate using a map and compass. But a Class Five imprint theoretically retained a significant chunk of memory from the original subject, as much relevant training as could be retained, and a connection in likes and dislikes, especially affecting the senses. Like most of the scientists at his command, Munsen had thought this impossible.

The mousy little girl with glasses changed all of that, didn't she? From the moment he'd met her face-to-face, he'd known she was special. The look in her eyes, wide and hurt but with a little core of fire in them, made her different. With an ancestor's imprint, success would be defined as surviving the first assignment. Munsen shut off the neural connection in his retina and sighed. Shields would report to her unit within the hour. With the *Ticonderoga* in foldspace, there would be no report at all.

He put the report tablet down when the chime on his stateroom door sounded. "Come in."

The door opened and a trim woman, standing about five and half feet tall, entered in a crisp Terran Defense Force uniform with the lion insignia of the Intelligence Corps on her epaulets next to the gold leaves of a Major. She wore light makeup, her nails clipped short and perfect, and blonde hair twisted into a bun at the base of her skull. The pretty young officer with the stone face saluted crisply. "Major Conyers reporting, sir."

Munsen returned the salute with a wave near his forehead and gestured to one of the overstuffed chairs in front of his desk. "Good morning. Have a seat, Laura. What do you have for me?"

Conyers folded her hands and looked down for a split second as if nervous. "There isn't much different from my final report. She's sent two messages to Tallenaara, neither have been responded to. Tallenaara is currently off planet to Styrah and will return in a few days before departing for Earth."

"You have the messages?"

"There is nothing of value, sir. Both messages are purely personal."

Munsen frowned. "And you cannot, or will not, share them with me?"

"Personal messages are protected by the Terran Code of Military Justice, sir. To intercept them is legal under certain provisions, but sharing anything that is personal to individuals without the need to know is strictly prohibited."

Munsen said nothing for ten seconds. "There was nothing of any substance to clarify our assertion that she has reached Class Five?"

"No, sir. Without access to the sleep records from her transit vessel, I cannot say. I believe it is safe to say that nothing has changed. I maintain she has reached Class Five, however improbable it is."

"I agree with that, Major. I want to know if there is anything else I should know before finalizing her assignment?"

Conyers paused. "No, sir."

"I'm inclined not to believe you, Major."

Conyers flushed. "Sir, my observations of Captain Shields were complete the moment she stepped into the Integration Center for transport. As soon as she was out of range, I disengaged without detection. From all that I have reported, she is clearly Class Four and exhibits all of the characteristics needed for a Class Five diagnosis. We will not know more until she is placed in a situation requiring those instincts and memory. Most likely that will come only from combat."

Munsen thought her voice broke for a second, but Conyers' face remained impassive. *The responsibility must be tough*, Munsen thought. He couldn't imagine doing what Conyers did. *The emotional connection and toll must be hell.* "You've seen my recommendation for her assignment?"

"I have." Conyers said. "And speaking frankly, sir, I do not agree with it."

Munsen snorted. To a point, he wasn't a fan of the assignment. But, it was a means to an end. "She can handle it. I expect her to."

"Expect?" Conyers raised her eyebrows. "Just how do you expect her to handle it, sir?"

Munsen looked past the young Major. Neural linkage intelligence occupied the top of a list Munsen kept of things to never do. Being linked into a subject's neural network meant intense genetic mapping and emotional chaos. Despite Conyers's emotional connections to Mairin Shields, she determined exactly the same things he had. First, that Mairin Shield's imprint contained a vast amount of training and tactical knowledge that could change the present course of the war with the Greys. The little bastards were rolling over outer territories in a blitzkrieg of mechanized warfare. Their tanks and gun-platforms made quick work of two divisions of reinforcements on the Walker colony, and they obliterated the full Narrob regiment in the span of about eight minutes. Mairin's imprint remembered being taught to act like a true armor officer, with a healthy dose of cavalry. Trained to fight the Soviets coming through the Fulda Gap. A skill-set long forgotten. And second, that she finally had something to fight for in the shitty life she'd been dealt. Now, she would reach her full potential because she had a reason to.

Munsen looked at Conyers for a long moment. He didn't want to know the depth of her connection to Shields. Intelligence operations were far outside his realm of comfort. Something gnawed at his gut, telling him that placing Mairin Shields in this first attempt at an armored division since Operation Iraqi Freedom almost three centuries ago was a huge mistake. That something would happen to her and they would lose the most complete imprint to date. Something also told him that she would be successful, or she would royally mess things up. He blinked away the indecision.

"I expect her to handle it the way she was trained. Nothing more." *Or was there more?*

Conyers paused, pursing her lips, then spoke. "You're afraid if we lose her, we lose any clue to how her imprint took so well. Losing her and anyone else like her was a possibility from the moment this program started, sir. You have to accept that risk."

"And what do you think she's going to do?"

"She will find any way to win the fight, but she will make some rash decisions and undoubtedly fail along the way. How significant that failure will be is anyone's guess."

Munsen thumbed his chin for a moment. "Are you implying something?"

"That it is a matter of time, or the situation, before she acts rashly. There will be consequences."

"You really think that? Almost no one has been closer than you."

Conyers almost smiled. "She's young and in love. You tell me."

Munsen snorted. He'd been there once, too. He'd been in love enough, or stupid enough, to marry a woman he shouldn't have a very long time ago. They'd loved each other, but they had no chance of staying together. *Love turns geniuses into blithering idiots,* he thought. "I'm willing to assume a modest degree of risk here, Laura. Whatever she does, whenever it happens, may have a consequence where we can't even ask her about it."

Conyers looked away. "I understand that, sir."

He knew he shouldn't have gone there. He bit the inside of his lower lip for a second and shook his head. "I'm not completely oblivious to your emotional connection, Major Conyers. I apologize."

"It's not necessary, sir. In my line of work, being emotionally connected for a time to a subject is normal. It will pass."

Munsen looked at the trim young officer and doubted her. The trouble was, he was beginning to doubt himself as well. What if Mairin Shields could not handle her assignment? What then? Start all over? The chances that they could find a perfect genetic match combined with the type of imprint—commissioned officer, combat veteran, single, good family values—were impossible. This imprint, and Mairin Shields, had to work. It wasn't as if the fate of the universe rode the project's back. But with an imprint of this quality and ability, the tides could be turned in their favor despite the myriad of obstacles to overcome. Her first assignment being one of them.

"When she reports to the *Ticonderoga*, you will have full access again?"

Conyers nodded. "There will be a five-day break in our data, sir. Real time transfer is not possible on Fleet vessels. I'll get data every time she sleeps."

Five days in a transit vessel didn't bother him. He checked the neural display again. Forty-six minutes to her arrival at the *Ticonderoga. How soon after that would she report to Lieutenant Colonel Bob Coffey?* The image made Munsen's stomach turn. How long after that would Mairin throw in the towel, or do something stupid?

"I suppose we'll know soon enough." The words didn't make him feel any better. He hardly believed them himself.

* * * * *

Chapter Nineteen

Mairin woke when the transport vessel's bell chimed to life. The announcement to make ready to dock with the *Ticonderoga* came next, and by the time the captain finished the sentence, Mairin was already tugging her coveralls on and flipping her hair into a ponytail as minimally required by regulation. She waited in her quarters for the ship to brake and dock with the *Ticonderoga.* The two vessels came together without so much as a whisper. Mairin expected something much louder and even a little more violent considering the size of the vessels involved. Her transport vessel was the size of a twenty-first century aircraft carrier, over three quarters of a mile in length and with a mass that Mairin would never have guessed. Compared to the *Ticonderoga*, her present vessel resembled a flea on a Great Dane.

Moving with ease through the ship, Mairin found the quarterdeck and thanked the captain, a blue-skinned Tueg named Qaur, for his assistance during the trip. He wished her well, kissing her palms in the Tueg way. She blushed and made her way to the main docking port. Inside the tight passageway, the air was already different. The stale scent of lubricants and spaceflight gave way to something she could only call fresh air. There was a floral quality to the air that reminded Mairin of her first moments on Libretto. She smiled at the thought and fired up her neurals to search for the *Ticonderoga's* mainframe and hopefully a message from Tally.

She found one at the top of her six hundred messages and read it quickly. *Missing you,* cariad. *Tally.*

That's it? Mairin skimmed the messages while gawking at the inside of the *Ticonderoga* and promptly ran into an immaculately dressed lieutenant.

"I'm sorry." Mairin blushed and smoothed a strand of hair behind her ear.

The lieutenant stared at her. His lips were a thin line, almost white. Blue eyes that were cold and distant sat under a short blond flat-top haircut that seemed oddly archaic. He looked enraged. "Are you Captain Mairin Shields?"

Mairin raised an eyebrow. "Yes."

"Follow me." The lieutenant stomped away in long quick strides. Mairin struggled to keep up with her bag slung over her shoulders. The lieutenant's demeanor set off warning bells and the faster he walked, the more Mairin found herself getting both amused and angry. *Chickenshit.* The word came up from nowhere and she looked it up in her neurals, and found herself almost laughing as she walked along. *Behavior that makes military life worse doesn't say much for the command climate.* Her smile faded as they walked into what had to be the training and operational bays for the regiment. The bay was full of soldiers working diligently under the watchful eyes of non-commissioned officers, but what she didn't see began to gnaw at Mairin. There was no bantering, no smiling. Nobody was standing at the center of a group telling stories that started with "there I was," or "this is no shit."

A second glance at the non-commissioned officers, the backbone of any successful unit, and Mairin felt her stomach turn. They were all over the place, supervising as they should by doctrine. But they stood stone-faced with arms crossed, and at least two of them carried riding crops. *Really? We do this sort of thing these days?*

Not we. Not ever.

The lieutenant stopped short of a doorway and stared at Mairin. "Wait here."

Mairin blinked. "Excuse me?"

"I said, wait here."

"Ma'am." Mairin felt her spine stiffen. "I think you meant ma'am, Lieutenant."

Crimson erupted up from the lieutenant's collar and began to creep into his face. "That's only for people I respect or combat veterans. You're neither."

Mairin raised a hand to her coverall jacket, unfastened it, and pointed to her decorations. "The fact that I have these, Lieutenant, doesn't matter one bit. You respect the rank, Lieutenant. Everything else above that is your prerogative."

The lieutenant grunted. "Yes, ma'am."

The door opened, and a very short, very bald man looked up at Mairin. "I said I was not to be bothered."

The lieutenant hesitated, so Mairin extended her hand. "Sir, are you Lieutenant Colonel Coffey?"

"Yeah." He posed against the doorframe, looking annoyed.

"Captain Mairin Shields." Her hand hung in the air for five seconds before Coffey took it briefly.

He dismissed her almost immediately. "I don't have a slot for you right now, Shields. Until we reconstitute at Rayu-Four, I don't have anything for you to do. We'll add you to the rolls, but don't plan on having much to do for the next couple of weeks." He looked at the Lieutenant. "Secure Captain Shields some quarters, ensure she's added to the battle roster."

That's it? Mairin nodded, "Thank you, sir."

"Make yourself at home. Check in with me at Rayu-Four. I'll summon you if I need you." He turned and shut the door in Mairin's face.

Summon? Mairin looked at the impassive lieutenant and forced herself to smile. These assholes weren't going to remove her sense of humor by dismissing her. "I believe you're going to secure some quarters for me. Preferably something far away?"

The lieutenant almost allowed his tight-lipped grimace to crack. A sign of life most likely beaten from the rest of the regiment. "Right this way, ma'am."

Her quarters were almost stately compared to the transit vessel. She could stand, move around, and even do exercises if she wanted. The private sink was an added bonus, but she'd still share her shower and toilet facilities with the rest of the females in her section. Nothing unexpected, yet it was all new. The constant noise struck her the most. Even in the dead of night, when at least two-thirds of the ship would be asleep, there was still the clanging of tools, the occasional shudder of the reaction control system firing, and always the sounds of people all around her. Unlike other captains, Mairin found herself in a room by herself, and while the privacy was welcome in her newly discovered officership, she found she would have liked a roommate, just to have somebody to talk to.

She spent her days in the common areas of the ship, the wardroom for her meals and the dayroom for general activity. Nobody from the regiment gave her any recognition, and while she enjoyed the anonymity, her annoyance with the behavior grew with every day. Wandering the ship became the chosen activity of the day. She fell in love with the hangar deck, ducking under wings and caressing the sleek fuselages of exocraft that looked like they were flying while standing still. Hurricanes, Ospreys, Raptors, and Tornadoes all rested with their wings folded in the tight space. She found the drop bays of the Rhinos and Hammers, capable of holding companies and battalions of TDF vehicles in their racks. Past the drop bays, along the keel of the ship, she found the Heinlein Tubes. *What must it be like to drop through the atmosphere of a planet with just a small shell of protection? The audacity!* She touched a protective shell, inspecting it closely.

"Can I help you, Captain?"

Mairin startled. She turned to a chief warrant officer with a bad haircut and a perpetual scowl. A sporadic and borderline unkempt mustache crossed his upper lip. "Sorry, Chief. Just looking around."

The chief nodded, his eyes on the badges sewn onto her coveralls and then back up to her eyes. "New officers shouldn't be wandering operational spaces. You have no idea what you're doing."

How did he know? Could he really see it? Mairin wanted to scowl, look more experienced, appear more soldierly all in one breath. Instead she smiled. "I suppose you're right, Chief. But when the shit hits the fan, I'd like to know where to go and what to do."

The chief snorted, but his cheeks almost rose in a smile. "You know what these are?"

"Heinlein Tubes." Mairin looked over her shoulder at the launching tubes. "How do they work?"

"Sheer velocity. You strap into the cocoon, or your vehicle, and get shot into the atmosphere. Just like in the holos. That Heinlein guy was a genius. When we don't have to launch a Rhino or Hammer, we can fire troops and vehicles just about anywhere on a planet."

'Something about infantry and everlasting glory, right?" Mairin smiled at the chief, who to Mairin's surprise, chuckled. *Heinlein just theorized them. He had no idea they'd work, did he?* "Why wouldn't we deploy a Rhino or Hammer?"

The chief smiled. "Why use a heavy asset when you don't have to? Some planets atmospheres, say like Earth or Libretto, can accept tubes. If the planet's atmosphere is too thick or nonexistent, it makes more sense to use a Rhino or Hammer."

Mairin nodded. "What kind of vehicles can you drop?"

"Right now, we can drop everything including the new Slammer assault tanks. We're the first platform to be able to do that."

Mairin flashed her neurals. "Do we have any onboard? The Slammers?"

The chief nodded. "We're carrying six. We're supposed to deliver them to the *Hornet* in a few days. They have a full regiment on board, but need six spares. Have you seen them?"

"No. Where are the ones onboard?"

"Storage. Access the ship infonet and you can find them. Someone with your background will appreciate them."

Mairin smiled at the stress he placed on background. "I didn't catch your name, Chief."

"Chief Casey," he almost smiled. "Engineering Senior Warrant."

They shook hands, Mairin meeting his firm grip. "Nice to meet you, Chief. I'll get out of your hair. Thanks for showing me around."

The chief nodded. "Anytime, ma'am."

Mairin walked away for the first time in uniform without feeling like there were contemptuous eyes on her back. She flashed the *Ticonderoga's* infonet and found the Slammers. She also realized she knew everything about them without ever having laid eyes on them. Powered by repulsors with traditional tracks as a backup, the tanks could move at eighty kilometers per hour on the ground, and with repulsors hovering them, more than one hundred thirty kilometers per hour. They carried a 200mm electromagnetic rail gun capable of flinging a sixty-pound projectile more than ten-thousand meters. Slammers also integrated with Fleet-deployed position systems capable of determining targets and directing gunfire to them beyond visual range (BVR). With a crew of four, and a vehicle interface capable of monitoring crew systems and loading the main gun, the sleek machines looked to be a very capable combat vehicle. *Of course, capability depends on the ability of those operating it,* she thought.

Slammers weighed in at a hefty one hundred and thirty tons, nearly twice what her imprint mounted. *Mounted*, she chuckled as she walked. Some things seemed very natural to say and think, and others were just funny. Instead of heading for the storage compartments, she headed for the wardroom and a late breakfast.

Mairin enjoyed shipboard life, except for the coffee. She looked at the brown sludge coating the bottom of her plasticene coffee mug and tried not to gag. She'd reported to the *Ticonderoga* and immediately found herself in administrative no-mans-land. No one knew what to do with her, as her unit was not aboard the *Ticonderoga.* All of the TDF crew positions were fully manned, so she wasn't assigned a specific duty. She checked in twice per day with the TDF adjutant, and spent time wandering the ship and hypnotraining. The morning of this third day, she'd tried to choke down a second mug of coffee in the platform's mess hall, or wardroom, whatever it was called, when a loud whistle hushed the crewmembers around her.

"All hands, this is the captain," the ship-wide loudspeaker known as the 1-MC sounded off and the ship quieted. Mairin looked up from the remnants of her coffee and thought about going for more until she noticed everyone around her frozen in place, staring at the ceiling.

"I'm afraid I must inform you of a change in our mission. The command crew has been aware for the past six hours that we are not headed to Rayu-Four. We have been ordered to Wolc." Smiles and punches in shoulders met the announcement. "There is no liberty or shore leave. In fact, there may never be again. The recent attacks on our outposts along the Outer Rim by the Greys and our subsequent movements in defense of our territory have opened a hole in our defenses. The Greys have launched a large-scale attack in our sector. I don't have to tell you of the strategic importance of the Rayu-Four shipyards. *Ticonderoga* herself was commissioned there three years ago. However, a coordinated Grey attack on Wolc is imminent.

"We are the closest Fleet Battle Platform to Wolc. We will arrive there at our maximum fold speed in just over an hour. I expect that our arrival will be hostile. We are now at Battle Stations.

All crews to your combat stations. Maneuver assets standby for drop, exo-squadrons are placed in Alert Five status.

"We will be completely unsupported for at least seven hours. There has been no contact with the Fleet Battle Group or the Regiment on the ground in the last three hours. We are it, people. We are the last chance to hold Wolc. Let's give them hell.

"God be with us." The speaker clicked off and the crew stayed silent until the klaxons sounded a second later. In a matter of seconds, the wardroom emptied, leaving Mairin and a few cooks in the room. Her bracelet tingled an incoming message.

Report to Charlie Deck, Space Four Forward.

She moved from the room quickly, breaking into a jog as she entered the organized chaos of the passageways. Mairin swung down the ladders to Charlie Deck near Four Forward. She'd been down here before, touring and looking at some of the hardware she'd learned about in hypno. She pushed open the door on a group of seventeen young men, soldiers. No one over the rank of Specialist except for the slight boyish man in the middle wearing the gold bar of a second lieutenant. *God save me from lieutenants.* "Who's in charge here?"

The lieutenant rubbed his buzzed red hair and smiled behind his glasses. Mairin knew what that smile was. The relieved smile of getting off the hook. "Ma'am, I believe you are."

Mairin looked at the lieutenant for a moment, and then over the group to the equipment along the back wall. Six Slammer magtanks with electromagnetic guntubes raised automatically from their mounts to the drop bays. The heavy vehicles hung at a thirty-degree angle in their drop positions. "Those vehicles combat loaded?"

The lieutenant shrugged. "We just got here, too."

Mairin swore under her breath. *What the fuck do they expect me to do?* "How many of you are trained on those vehicles?"

They all raised their hands. "Most of these guys are just trained drivers, but they did get familiarization training as part of their basic hypno," the lieutenant said. "I've identified those freshest out of hypno, there is one per vehicle. I say we load them as gunners, ma'am."

Mairin nodded. "Who says we're going someplace, Lieutenant? Do you know what our orders are?"

The lieutenant shook his head, "Be prepared to drop and take commands from the ground assault commander. That's all."

"It's a start." Mairin smirked. "Okay, Lieutenant crew the vehicles. Who's the senior enlisted person here?"

A tall thin kid raised his hand. "That would be me, Captain." He smiled again and Mairin answered it with a tight grin. *Always wanted to go to Jamaica*, she thought and blinked it away. *Dammit.*

"Livingston? You're now the First Sergeant. Pick the next two seniors to be the platoon sergeants. Get started on pre-combat checks and inspections of those vehicles. Lieutenant, I need to speak with you. Make it happen, people."

The men took a long second and started to move slowly to the vehicles. Mairin raised her voice, "I said *move*, goddamnit!" She caught Livingston's eye and nodded at him. He immediately echoed her commands and volume and the men sprang to action.

The lieutenant's uniform nameplate said Ulson. "What's your first name?"

"Alex, ma'am."

She held out her hand and shook his firmly. "Mairin."

Ulson looked at the badges sewn to her coveralls and re-met her gaze. "Those really yours, ma'am?"

"Yes, but it's a long story."

Ulson nodded, but said nothing for a long moment. "Hope I get to hear it someday."

Mairin gestured with her fingers. "We'll organize as two elements, both with platoon sergeants reporting to you. You'll move with one element always, and I'll be with the other. Make sure they get the vehicles ready and select good crews. Stay out of Livingston's way. Let him really try and be a first sergeant. How long have you been commissioned?"

"Six weeks, ma'am."

"TDF Academy?"

Ulson shook his head. "Officer Training University."

That's better, Mairin thought. Save me from Academy shitheads.

"What's your specialty?"

"Strategic Air Defense, ma'am. Armor was my secondary."

"Not anymore. Just do what I ask you to and we'll do well. All right?"

"Yes, ma'am."

"No sweat," Mairin nodded. "And no lectures from me. I expect you to do what you're trained to do. You'll get the same from me, get me?"

"Yes, ma'am."

"We've got about thirty minutes. I'm going to try and get some answers from our battalion commander. Be ready for drop when I get back."

Ulson swallowed. "Ma'am? Are drops as bad as they say?"

Mairin smiled and shook her head. "You tell me when we get down to Wolc." She jerked her head toward the vehicles, giving Ulson the hint, and went to the comm station, touching her bracelet to it. The maneuver commander responded in fifteen seconds.

"Captain Shields. I trust you've taken charge of those spare vehicles?"

"Yes, sir." In the videolink she watched him fidgeting and felt her stomach curl inward. *Distracted, belligerent. Holy shit, was the man drunk?*

"Okay. Looks like we'll drop about two hundred klicks southwest of Waters City in thirty minutes. Rolling plains and forests. I've got four companies and you. Stay out of their way and be ready for action if I call on you. I'll keep you...uh...informed."

Mairin stared at a darkened screen. Not much in the way of orders. She moved to the center of the space and looked through the collection of papers and map sheets there. Nothing usable. There were eyes on her. Her men were working feverishly around the vehicles while she was standing still. *Never let someone do something you wouldn't do*, she chided herself. She called to Ulson about which vehicle was hers. He pointed to the center vehicle and Mairin strode up to it, climbed up the front repulsor's fender and scrambled up to the turret. Laying a palm on the composite armor as she passed the gun tube, Mairin said, "Hello, gorgeous."

Atop the tank, the standard two hatches dominated the space. The larger hatch for reloading the depleted uranium tipped sabot rounds and the smaller hatch with the fifty-caliber machine gun mount for her. The smaller commander's hatch sat ringed with presumed vision blocks, allowing her to see without leaving the inside of the vehicle. Her hands trembled slightly as she worked the hatch and swung her legs into the vehicle. The commander's information center dominated the right side of her space. The turret controls and sight extensions felt familiar. She flipped down the footpad and kneed her gunner in the lower back. "Sorry."

The gunner looked over his shoulder. "Specialist Lee," he said and extended a hand over his shoulder, which Mairin took. "Nice to meet you."

Mairin nodded. "Lee, nice to meet you as well. You comfortable with this beast?"

"Yes, ma'am. I got it." He turned back to the computer interface and worked the panel through diagnostics. Another figure dropped into the main hatch on the far side of the tank and smiled.

"Ma'am, I'm Private Conner." The bespectacled kid with a cherub's face said. "I'm the commo specialist. Who do you want to talk to?"

Mairin squinted for a moment at the radio. "Ground Force Commander, Air Force Commander, the Combat Information Center for the *Ticonderoga* and all of our vehicles."

Conner smiled. "Too easy." He began a sequence of keystrokes and flip-switches in the communications area that Mairin watched with a grin.

So far so good, she thought. "Do we have an interface yet?"

Lee shook his head. "Still in diagnostics. About ten minutes."

Mairin nodded and let her hypnotraining and instincts take over. She initialized the autoloader without a second thought, then climbed up out of the hatch and looked over at Ulson doing the same. "Stand to in ten minutes. When everyone's up, I'll brief our plan."

Ulson nodded and called down into his tank, and then across to Livingston. "Stand to, ten minutes!"

This would be the easy part, Mairin knew. Make sure the things you really need are present and serviceable, ensure your people have ample time to do the same thing, and most importantly have a plan. Mairin frowned as she traced her fingers on the top of the commander's cupola. The TDF didn't seem to be much on tactics. Most of the training she'd had in hypno simply didn't apply to this situation.

They had no cavalry.

Cavalry.

That's it! Mairin smiled. *Six vehicles. One scout platoon plus two vehicles. Be the eyes of the commander, fix the enemy, recon the battlefield*, Mairin thought. Not that being the regimental reserve would be bad, but without a clear picture of the battlefield, what would the commander be thinking?

All six magtanks came online at the precise moment Mairin specified. She slipped the crewman's helmet in place. She keyed the microphone with her lip and chose their assigned frequency with her neurals. "Okay, troopers, this is how we're gonna do business."

"Lieutenant Ulson is One. The vehicle to his right is Two. The vehicle to his left is Three." She paused. "The vehicle to my right is Four, and the left is Five. I'm Six. Let's see if you got it. This is a guidons call, when you hear it every vehicle chimes in with their number only. Got it? Guidons, this is Six."

"One."

"Two."

"Three."

"Four."

"Five."

Mairin smiled. "Okay troopers, welcome to the cavalry. Standby for drop information." She dropped into the vehicle and keyed the intercom. "Interface?"

<<Yes, Captain?>> The computer's toneless female voice chimed.

"Download drop information from the regimental commander," Mairin ordered as she fastened her drop harness.

<<There is no drop information available. The battalion commander has already dropped.>>

Mairin bit back an epithet and chose another frequency, "*Ticonderoga*, this is Saber Six, Charlie Deck Four Forward ready for drop."

After what felt like an eternity, a voice finally answered. "We have no Saber Six on the signal board. This is the Officer of the Deck. Identify yourself."

"Captain Mairin Shields, in command of six vehicles, Charlie Deck, Space Four Forward. We were given no orders other than to prepare for drop from...," she scanned for Coffey's callsign, "Bullet Six."

Another long pause. "Standby, Captain."

Mairin tried to key in the planetary information for Wolc. "Conner, get me all planetary data aboard. Full download from CIC."

"I'm being blocked, ma'am."

Mairin buckled her drop harness as the CIC called. "Saber Six, this is Thunder Six, Lieutenant Commander Garrett. I'm to understand you've been left behind?"

"That's correct, sir. My troopers and I are ready for drop."

"Well then, let's get you on your way. Standby for attitude correction and max G load deployment. Orbital parameters downloaded. Wish I could spare you a Rhino, but this will have to do. Full data download commencing. We're going to put you down ten kilometers behind the regiment about center mass of the forces. Good luck, Captain."

Mairin smiled. "Scouts out, sir." She leaned back in the harness and felt it lock automatically. She glanced at Conner. "Got our data?"

Conner replied, "Already pushed out. Ready for drop."

Why haven't we dropped? Mairin was about to ask when the entire world vibrated violently.

* * * * *

Chapter Twenty

Munsen leaned back for a moment, allowing the situation to develop in his mind. Like any good staff officer, he was already working on three potential courses of action. The most dangerous course of action was simple; Coffey would do something catastrophically stupid and jeopardize the mission. The most likely course of action was that Coffey and his regiment would perform admirably, but that the mission would not be accomplished without a combined effort of fleet aerial and ground forces. In his mind, there was simply no other way that the Greys could be defeated.

For little grey men, the kind Munsen remembered seeing as a boy in that movie about Devil's Tower or something, the Greys developed and executed a blitzkrieg of combined ground and artillery forces. With their fire power matched with overwhelming numbers of ground assets, the Greys were apt to be a difficult enemy. A concentrated effort with a twentieth century mindset for combined arms warfare would be the best to combat the Greys. The only problem being that as humanity forgot how to conduct the business of war, they tactically regressed.

Munsen shook his head as he watched the drop status. Most likely, Coffey would get onto the ground and deploy his forces in a Napoleonic formation and attempt a full frontal assault. *Nevermind that the enemy is dug in, on higher ground, and fighting from behind every rock and tree. This must be how the Americans watched the British during the Revolutionary War. Are they really going to march up in formation?* The powers that be chose a man full of bravado and ego to lead a regiment of fine troops, and four of his imprints, to certain annihilation.

There was a chime from the armrest of his chair. He touched a button and a familiar voice asked, "They've dropped already?"

Munsen rubbed his chin. There was stubble from a very early morning already on his face. "Just now. How is the situation on the ground?"

"The Greys are dug in on the objective. They outnumber the regiment two and a half to one. They have a better standoff weapon in their particle beam technology, and the only thing going for us is the weather. But, we have to assume that the Greys are equally able to shoot, move, and communicate in heavy rain and fog."

"Or they are better," Munsen snorted. "Did we even think to determine their capabilities before we charged into this?"

The voice replied, "This is the Terran Defense Force, Colonel. We are the best-trained, best-equipped fighting force on the planet Earth. Surely nothing this universe has can defeat us?" The Supreme Commanding General of the TDF chuckled.

Munsen felt a smile form on his lips and let the laugh it held escape. He felt better knowing that there were others, much higher ranking, that agreed with him. As quickly as the laugh came, the icy feeling of letting soldiers down crept from his stomach. "We're going to lose a lot of good troops."

"You've led me to believe that we will lose less by making Coffey activate those six vehicles and deploy them."

Munsen sighed. "He's ordered them to assume a position as the reserve element. Completely away from contact and action. By all appearances, he's left those vehicles without the proper communications keys and crypto to determine their situation and how they can assist the main effort. They're out there in the breeze."

There was a pause. "My notes from our last conversation state that you feel, based on observation, that Captain Shields will not remain complacent, and she will develop any situation, tactical or not, to her advantage. Do you really see her sitting still with six of our newest combat vehicles? Especially when she knows she could be making a difference?"

"Combat does funny things to people."

"And you and I have never seen that, have we? It's easy for us to armchair the war effort, but despite the lack of combat experience, we can't stop trying to take care of soldiers, especially those out there fighting, Colonel." The voice paused for a moment. "Don't ever forget that."

"I feel like the only guy in the armed forces without combat experience right now."

"That's your gut talking, Thom."

Munsen nodded. "I know that. It doesn't mean that I have to like it."

Nothing came from the speaker for a few seconds, enough time for Munsen to wonder if he was about to be replaced. "How long until they reach the surface?"

Munsen glanced at his display. "A little over ten minutes based on their trajectory."

"In that time, what can you do to influence the battle given what you've told me, Colonel?"

"We have to tie in the air assets." Munsen tapped his fingers on the chair idly. "If we allow Coffey to fight this battle his way, the entire regiment won't get within a kilometer of the objective."

There was a heavy sigh. "How are you going to get Shields to that objective?"

"I'm hoping she does that for herself."

"And if she doesn't?"

Munsen gave it a second thought. She would. Everything pointed to the fact that she would respond. How she'd do so was unknown. They would know in a few hours, wouldn't they? "She's going to find her way to the objective. Our job is to make sure she gets the support she needs. God knows that Coffey isn't going to ask for it."

"Then what do you want me to do, Colonel?"

Munsen thought for a moment. He looked across the room at his silent partner. Conyers sat with her hands in her lap, waiting for him or the Supreme Commanding General to speak to her. It was time to up the ante. "I think Mairin Shields needs a roommate."

* * * * *

Chapter Twenty-One

As the drop bay fell through twenty thousand feet above ground level, carbon impregnated parachutes deployed and pulled each of the six magtanks from their racks. With repulsors switched on and in the landing configuration, the vehicles would essentially glide to the planet's surface and come to rest at their mission programmed altitude of four feet. The magtanks would then drop into combat configurations and be ready for tactical movement.

Mairin opened the commander's hatch at ten thousand feet as the one hundred fifty-ton tank fell towards Wolc. Mairin didn't like the terrain. Too much rainforest. Too dense. Not enough open space for maneuver. "Conner, we got solid comms with everyone?"

"Yes, ma'am."

"Get me Bullet Six."

"You're not gonna like it, ma'am." Conner shrugged and plugged the command frequency into her helmet.

"-- is Bullet Six. Who authorized that drop?"

"Bullet Six, Saber Six," Mairin called. "Drop order came from you, over."

Ten seconds of silence. "Saber Six," he screeched, "take up a position as the battalion reserve. Maintain radio silence. Stay put. Is that clear?"

Mairin looked at the grid coordinates fed into her system. The reserve position now some thirty kilometers behind the advancing force. Stagnant. "Understood, Saber Six out."

She chinned the frequency for her vehicles, "Okay people, you heard those orders. We're soldiers and supposed to follow orders. Those are the rules. Well, I'm not gonna sit us where we can't do some good. We'll sit down, run a pre-combat check and move out. I'll send you a plan when we hit the dirt. Six out."

The tactical situation favored the Greys. Coffey had moved the regiment into a wide valley and pressed downhill toward a communications node. Most likely, a heavily defended communications node. The only real avenue of approach into the site was the valley Coffey now advanced his one hundred magtanks into side-by-side, like a parade formation. Mairin looked at the terrain surrounding the objective. *They'll have guns up there on the high ground, and if they've got any type of indirect fire, the regiment will be hammered well outside of their engagement range.*

Crest the ridgeline to the east, maneuver up the military crest on the backside of the hill. Screen the force and attempt to get to the eastern edge of the objective before Coffey does. It's the only thing that can save them. But what about us? A flight of exocraft streaked the atmosphere above her. We've got to be on our guard. Guard. Holy shit! "Conner, punch up the GUARD frequency."

"The what?"

"The GUARD frequency. All aircraft monitor it. We might be able to get some help that way."

Conner worked the computers for a moment. "Located it. Are you sure about this? It's UHF!" His dumbfounded voice made Mairin chuckle.

"Do it," Mairin said. *How are we gonna do this?* Mairin drew symbols from memory not her own, and it took her a minute to understand them as she made them. *Just like scratching out football plays in the dirt. Whatever, Grandpa. We're here, and the regiment is here. What the hell are they doing?* She punched the send button, transmitting the situation to her vehicles. "We got the intel yet?"

"On your screen now," Conner replied.

Mairin studied for a moment. The screen would work. She transmitted the graphics to her vehicles and keyed her radio.

"Guidons, Saber Six. You've got the ground situation. We're going to screen the regiment to the east. We're going to have to haul ass. As soon as we're in repulsor range, engage at gear five and push hard. One has the lead, wedge formation. How copy?"

They checked in, Ulson with a loud "Roger that!"

Mairin allowed herself a smile. She chinned over to the GUARD frequency. "*Ticonderoga*, Saber Six. Flash traffic for Thunder Six."

Ten seconds later, Garrett's voice came back. "Saber Six, new freq package uploading now. Five seconds."

She saw Conner work the frequency into the radio and she chinned to the frequency five seconds later. She heard, "Saber Six, GUARD is for aircraft emergencies only, not tactical vehicles. What can I do for you?"

Mairin frowned. "Thunder Six, roger. I have no support from TDF forces. Apologize for GUARD. Break." She unkeyed the microphone for a moment and then squeezed it again. "Relaying a SITREP to you now." She pushed the transmit button and her situation report went out. "I need full intel on the tactical situation. I do not have access to the Oscar and India net." The operations and intelligence network was reserved for conversations about the current situation only. Without information from the prescribed TDF network, she was essentially blind. Not to mention being all alone.

"Saber Six, you are not where your commander said you would be. Is there something you want to tell me?"

Mairin frowned. "I'm not going to sit here and watch, Thunder Six."

"Saber Six, Thunder Six. Roger, all. Be advised the admiral concurs. We have no contact with Bullet Six. Got your SITREP. Intel download coming in sixty seconds. I've got a squadron of exos I'll give to you for close air. Frequency inbound now. Good hunting. Thunder Six out."

Conner gave a thumbs-up. "Got that freq. Button three."

Mairin nodded. The repulsors spun up quickly. The vehicle leveled out and began to glide forward at over two hundred kilometers per hour. The thickening atmosphere would slow them down to the maximum one hundred thirty. With ground effect at the surface, they'd be down to one hundred five klicks per hour. At the surface, the magtanks slid quickly into position and spread out as much as the terrain allowed. The thicker the vegetation, the closer the tanks would have to be to each other. Definitely not a tactical advantage. She glanced at the situation display and frowned. Not only was Coffey still in a line abreast formation, they were sitting still in the valley and trying to engage the Greys with their weapons at standoff distances. Not smart.

Mairin partially opened her hatch, allowing moist, flowery air to roar into the cramped turret. After weeks of shipboard life, there was nothing finer. She took a deep breath and considered the situation. *A numerically superior force in the defense on dominating terrain. Our weapons are more effective than theirs, but we can still run out of ammunition, and they have particle beams. Christ, they are sitting there baiting us.* She pushed the tactical display aside. The plan to screen the regiment was toast, but they could at least move up the ridge and overwatch the battle. Mairin bit her lip and stood up in the hatch to look out over the terrain. Trees rose up into the sky, making it more difficult to see her tanks as they slowed down.

"Guidons, Saber Six. Repulsors to treetop level. Spread the formation."

Seconds later they were cruising the treetops at eighty kilometers per hour. The sensation of speed and the wind in her face brought a smile. *Almost like flying,* she thought. Approaching a connecting ridgeline, Mairin had an idea. *Forget the screen, we can come in behind them.*

"Driver, hard right. Follow that ridgeline, but don't get anywhere near the crest."

The magtank swung hard to the right and the rest of her vehicles followed. Mairin looked into the tank and realized something was wrong. *Know your troops!* She didn't even know the driver's name! "Driver, what's your name?"

Over the noise of the vehicle, she heard him chuckle. "Ma'am, I'm Private Booker. Nice to meet you."

"You too," Mairin said and shook her head. "Anybody want to tell me what else I'm missing?"

She saw Conner and Lee turn to her and grin. They both shook their heads. The interface's computer-synth voice responded. <<We are being scanned by an unknown orbiting sensor. I have relayed its coordinates to the *Ticonderoga* for targeting.>>

* * * * *

Chapter Twenty-Two

On the bridge of the *Ticonderoga*, Lieutenant Commander Donovan Garrett struggled to maintain his temper. Acting as the fleet aviation battle captain was much more difficult than flying his beloved Rhino. Cursing his luck and the necessity of "broadening assignments," Garrett listened with more patience than he felt possible as a Fleet Signal Commander lectured him on the structure of command frequencies and their proper usage. Bucking for promotion was not something Garrett regularly tried to do. He'd rather be flying. As the battle captain, Garrett held a position where his authority could only be challenged by Admiral Nather, the group commander. In this case, Garrett knew the "Old Man" well enough that losing his composure on a senior officer would be justified.

"Did you hear what I said, Lieutenant Commander?" the man asked. Condescension dripped from the fat man's frown. The full use of Garrett's rank was unnecessary by protocol. In his fifteen years of service with the Fleet, Garrett knew the real reason was to put him in his place as a junior officer.

Well, fuck that.

"I don't give a damn, sir. I know that GUARD is a protected frequency, but those are our soldiers down there, regardless of their fucking chain of command. As long as I'm the battle captain, if they need help, we will give it to them. When this is over, you can take it up with the admiral. For now, please exit the combat operations center, sir." Garrett unclenched his jaw and moved back to the command chair. *Another policy that does us absolutely no good.* "Let me have your attention, everyone. Until you hear from someone with higher rank and greater authority than me that we don't talk to TDF forces on the ground, give any request from Saber Six whatever you can. If you've got a problem with that, note it in your station logs right now. We don't have time for chickenshit."

Sitting in a comfortable chair in the Combat Information Center was not for Garrett. Driving a Rhino, the feeling of combat was detached and focused on one little piece of the battle around his squadron. With the command of a full air group at his fingertips, Garrett felt his brain racing to keep up with the rapid-fire transmissions and communications. Across the planet the Grey forces were being engaged by TDF troops. Garrett looked down on the dayside of Wolc and couldn't see nearly as much action as he could above the nightside. Nightside was a cauldron of raging fires. For now, the space around *Ticonderoga* was secure. Her troops dropped and her defenses at the ready, *Ticonderoga* sat at battle stations above the battlefield. Waiting.

"Sir, we have an Interface report from Saber Six. Orbital platform scanning. The platform is not on our veedars or sensors. I have an orbital element set."

Garrett nodded to the operations officer and reviewed the parameters of the unknown platform's orbit. *It's above and behind us in a geostationary orbit. They've got an idea of how we're deployed.* "Weapons free. Get that thing out of my sky," Garrett snapped and picked up the private circuit to the admiral.

"Don? What's up?"

"Sir, we're taking out an unknown orbital platform that's scanning our forces. Recommend redeployment of the group."

Nather cleared his throat. "Okay, Don. Get your units to Alert Five-"

Garrett flinched from a massive explosion out the port viewscreen. A cloud of molten debris hung in space where the frigate

Oxford had been a moment before. "Launch all fighters! Launch all fighters!"

The klaxons of the *Ticonderoga* went off and Garrett heard the admiral on the 1-MC ordering evasive action. Garrett's seat lurched to starboard and he reached instinctively for an inertial dampening switch on a Rhino, and there was nothing even close to his command chair. Embarrassed, Garrett bit his lip and turned to the tactical display. "Give me all sensors, three-sixty spread."

The display board winked to life and Garrett felt an expletive on his lips. Conscious of his new environment and of every eye in the room watching him, he merely nodded. Three full wings, almost sixty Grey exofighters, were approaching from over Wolc's north pole. *Honor the threat, but be prepared for the threat you don't see.* He blinked in shock. *Both poles. Sucker punching bastards.*

"Give me the Fifty-second, the Sixty-third, and One Five Seventh squadrons on vectors to the north pole. I want the Forty-third and Thirty-fourth on the south pole. The Eighty-seventh on low CAP, and the Seventy-ninth on high CAP. Now!"

No one in the CIC hesitated. Garrett saw orders being passed, icons on the map changing positions, and felt a degree of satisfaction. *Focus. They know you're here now. What are you going to do about it?*

The *Ticonderoga's* guns began to fire as they crossed the terminator into nightside. Streaks of red and blue tracers and small wattage particle beams pierced the darkness. *The hounds upon them, the fox turns ready to strike.*

"Engage at first opportunity. BVR is authorized. Hit 'em hard, hit 'em fast, and keep right on hitting." Wishing he could see his fighters locking on to incoming targets from beyond visual range and firing, Garrett absently attached the restraining belt on his command chair.

Gonna be a rocky day.

* * * * *

Chapter Twenty-Three

The battalion attack stalled five thousand meters from their landing zone with orders to engage the Grey emplacements with standoff weapons. The Greys swarmed on the regiment's objective, a long west to east ridgeline Lieutenant Colonel Coffey codenamed Seminary Ridge. Nearly impassable terrain fenced the narrow sloping valley where Command Sergeant Major Jack Trevayne sat with the rest of the regiment, trying to target and hit vehicles fifteen thousand meters away. Not that the Marauder's weren't capable of it; their electromagnetic railguns were easily able to fling projectiles twice that distance. Short-sighted targeting systems made it impossible to guarantee an accurate shot beyond ten thousand meters. Trevayne spat off the side of the Marauder. They'd opened their hatches to breathe in the wet Wolcian atmosphere, a rarity given most of the deployment zones TDF units found themselves in. Fifteen minutes of sporadic firing into the objective gave no indication that there was any change to the Greys' combat strength. The regiment would have to move closer. Trevayne keyed the private channel to the commander for the fourth time.

"Sir, we've got to move closer. We aren't having any effect. We're the center of the division attack corridor. If we don't start moving soon we're going to leave a massive hole in our lines."

Coffey came back five seconds later. "Denied."

Trevayne felt his vision narrowing. "Sir, we have no choice! Look at your tactical display. We're two minutes from leaving holes on both our flanks. If the Greys see that, they'll roll up our entire attack. Do you understand?"

"Goddamnit Sergeant Major, I got it!" Coffey screamed. "I fucking know what we're supposed to be doing. The situation favors a standoff engagement! I will not attack a superior tactical position!"

You're the one who named it Seminary Ridge, asshole. Trevayne wanted to find something, anything, that would trigger Coffey to order the regiment forward. When the radio clicked over to Command frequencies, he smiled, knowing he wouldn't need to.

"Bullet Six, this is Command Six. Get your ass moving now."

Coffey didn't respond for five seconds. Admiral Nather's voice growled into Trevayne's ears. "That's a direct order, Bullet Six. Move out."

There was still no response from Coffey, but the center of the regimental line began to move forward slowly. *About goddamned time,* Trevayne thought. "Driver, move out. Take us to the right flank. Gear Two."

Almost immediately the volley of fire from the Greys increased. Rounds began to impact all around the vehicle, but Trevayne gave them little thought as he buttoned up and dropped into the commander's chair. "SITREP, Dossett."

His communications specialist, a woman he'd have thought pretty in any other circumstance than sharing the turret of a combat tank, replied quickly. "Red elements are taking the beating in the center. White elements on the left flank are in the clear but do not have contact with the Seventy-third. Blue elements are not in contact with the Ninety-first. We're about sixteen hundred meters behind them right now. We're not going to close that gap at Gear Two."

Trevayne nodded, feeling powerless. He'd been ordered not to communicate with any of the regiment's vehicles without the commander's knowledge. *Pure unadulterated horseshit. Sonuvabitch thinks he's Napoleon!* He punched the controls to zoom out his view of the battlefield and selected icons only. Rectangles and diamonds filled the screen. The rectangles were blue, his forces, and the red diamonds were the Greys. The display was a nearly solid red blob on top of the objective. "Interface, estimated number of Grey vehicles on objective?"

<<One thousand five hundred fifty, plus or minus fifty.>>

"Jesus," he heard Dossett whisper.

"More for us to kill," his gunner replied.

"Shut up," Trevayne snapped. "We're outnumbered at least twenty to one. That kinda bravado bullshit isn't gonna work."

He kept zooming out, seeing a singular blue rectangle, a scout platoon, on the far side of the ridgeline to the east and moving quickly. "Interface, locate the frequency of that platoon at grid eight six four five."

<<I have no frequency on record for that unit.>>

Trevayne dismissed it. "Probably a glitch in the command feed."

<<Blue elements taking increased fire. Distance to the Ninety-first is fourteen hundred meters. Terrain is becoming constrictive,>> the interface said.

Trevayne chinned over to the frequency for Third Company, "Blue Six, this is Black Nine, I'm in route to your position now."

"Roger, Black Nine. We're taking increased fire. I'm down one vehicle," Captain Gibbs replied. A good officer, most likely an imprint but there'd never been the private opportunity to ask. Imprints and Styrahi were taboo subjects in Coffey's Regiment. Their illustrious commander transferred as many of them out as possible, until learning that Trevayne had an imprint. There couldn't be many left in the TDF with more commanders like Coffey being afraid of them.

Trevayne stood in the open hatch and let the wind hit his face. The fresh air was redolent with the sticky smell of pine sap as they rolled into a decimated forest. Rounds impacted the trees above them, showering the vehicle with branches and shrapnel. "Are they airbursting rounds on us?"

<<Affirmative,>> the Interface replied.

"Relay that to command. If these assholes have embedded artillery, our day could be damned short." Trevayne spat again and closed the hatch as a large branch fell to the side of the moving tank. "We've got to have some intel on those bastards!"

Dossett replied quickly. "We're getting nothing on all known communications channels. The Greys are firing a steady ten rounds per minute from every vehicle. No smart weapons, no particle beams."

"Driver, Gear Four. Dossett, relay that to Blue Six," Trevayne clenched his jaw. *Orders be damned. Somebody has to close that gap.* If they didn't, the Greys would surely attack from their defensive positions. *Wouldn't they?*

*****

Chapter Twenty-Four

"Okay people, listen up." Mairin spoke quickly with excitement in her voice. "What we're doing is setting a screen. The idea is that we're out here making the enemy think the regiment is a feint or something. I'm hoping we can open up something in their defense. Maybe even get them to commit forces off the objective. It's a long shot, but worth it. If they do nothing, we'll get up on the ridgeline between them and the Eighty-Seventh regiment and make things interesting." She paused. "Everybody good with that?"

Only Ulson responded. "How about we sound the fucking charge, ma'am?"

Mairin grinned. "Lock and load, you've got firing authority on anything that ain't ours."

A last look at the tactical display confirmed that there was some change on the objective. *Stay fluid. Use the terrain.* Mairin toggled the switches to the display and tried to really see what lay around them. *Fuck it.* She opened the hatch and stood up, the force of the wind nearly ripping her helmet off. Holding on to the trusty M2 machine gun mount—*how many hundreds of years are we gonna use this beast*, she thought—she could see very clearly. The enemy lay ahead and just over the ridgeline. A last spiraling hilltop gave way to a long sloping saddle between the joining ridges. That would be the soft point, where the enemy would expect a counter attack. Attacking from the east along the ridgeline gave a better advantage, mainly from speed and surprise. *How long would that surprise last? Will we be too exposed?*

Heavy gray clouds hung low around the mountains, the humidity palpable. Mairin thought of the rain and touched the reassuring clump of the necklace at her throat. *Not now, Tally. I love you.*

<<There is a detachment of enemy forces to our northeast at seven kilometers. They are well concealed. I count two vehicles and approximately four lifeforms,>> the Interface chimed again. "Now six point five kilometers."

Mairin dropped into the turret and allowed the hatch to close. "Speculation?"

Conner shrugged. "Maybe reconnaissance?"

The Interface replied, <<Grey forces have not employed reconnaissance in any major battle over the last fifty years, according to Styrahi intelligence reports.>>

"Can we engage at closer range?"

<<Not without endangering friendly forces.>>

"What?" Mairin keyed her display. "There's nothing out there."

<<A pathfinder team is on the ground approximately two thousand meters from the Grey vehicles. No record of the mission is present on the regiment's tasking order.>> The Interface fell silent. Mairin waited for more, but there was none. This was going to be up to her. *If they've got a weapon of some kind, or are trying to get behind the line--.*

She flicked the transmit button. "Guidons, Six. Down to Gear One. Standby for FRAGO."

Conner replied, "What's a FRAGO?"

Mairin looked at him dumbfounded. "A Fragmentary Order. A change to an Operations Order."

Conner blinked. "Like an action plan?"

Oh God help me. "Yes, an action plan. Relay that so everyone understands." And when we're done here there's going to be a lot of instruction, she thought. Who trained these people?

"Interface, get me in touch with that pathfinder team. I want to know what the hell is going on."

Mairin halted the formation in a grove of pine-like trees that concealed their position nicely. Two minutes later, a whispered voice filled Mairin's ears.

"Whoever you are, do not compromise my mission," the voice said in Styrah. A dialect that Mairin didn't recognize, but a Stryahi nonetheless. Her heart bounced slightly at the thought of Tally.

"Pathfinder, this is Saber Six. I have six magtanks two point six kilometers from your position. There are two Grey combat vehicles and four lifeforms in front of you," Mairin replied in what she hoped was passable Styrah.

A chuckle in the static. "I am watching them."

"Understood. Do you require assistance?"

"No. Please continue your mission and leave mine alone, *eschessa.*"

Mairin flushed. *Bitch.* "False alarm people. Ulson, get us back on course, Gear Three."

Styrahi can be very prideful, Mairin. The voice was Tally's with the hint of her imprint. Don't take it personal. Get back on your horse, girl.

They emerged from the pine grove and spread the formation to engage repulsors. For a long moment, nothing happened. When Mairin raised the hatch to look outside, she heard Ulson screaming.

"Contact left! Contact left! There's a bunch of 'em!"

*****

Chapter Twenty-Five

Tallenaara sat with her lunch of Dunleavy's fish and chips on the steps of the Glamoragan Building watching the Cardiff students making their way to and from classes. Only a few brave souls shared the steps on the unseasonably cool day, and the lack of sunshine made the cold penetrating despite the layers of clothing she wore. Still, she'd had this tradition during her time as a student, and wanted to sit amongst the statues and see how it felt. The human adage that a person couldn't go home again was very poignant. While the statues were the same honorifics to coal mining and navigation, the warmth of the spot she'd eaten so many lunches on was at once familiar and distant, like a vivid dream that fades over time.

She unrolled a thin flexi reader and the latest issue of Architectural Digest to spend the time, but the passing students distracted and fascinated her. She realized she was looking for recognition in them. A girl with pretty brown hair brought thoughts of Mairin, while the boys in the cardigans made her think of Andrew on those chilly afternoons when he'd walk her across campus because he had a free period and wanted to see her. Coeds holding hands brought a wistful smile, and she remembered the first time, after their trip to Scotland, that Andrew took her hand. There were a thousand eyes on them as they walked, but Andrew's head was erect and his shoulders back. He smiled and almost dared anyone to tell him that he shouldn't hold her hand. She'd drawn strength from him in that moment and knew that he dearly cared for her, and most troubling, she knew that he would be a great Prelate like his father.

Perhaps that first display of affection should have given her clues, and it probably did. Love was like that. In the moment, lovers rarely focused on anything but each other, eschewing advice from friends and warnings from loved ones. For Tally, she could only surmise that Andrew's decision was political in nature. She had not bothered to find out, nor was it worth any effort ten years later.

Tally put away the magazine, collected the paper basket and newspaper that wrapped her lunch, and tossed them into a refuse canister. She picked up her tall cup of coffee and walked slowly to the architecture building. Tomorrow would be her first lecture, and she'd already given the College of Architecture quite a start. Famous alien students who returned to prestigious faculty postings was not something that happened every day.

Walking into a lecture hall a dozen years ago had been a frightening experience. Conversation stopped, and every eye fell upon her. A few of the students whispered and a few laughed out loud. The first of her species to attend the school, Tallenaara promised to do exceedingly well at Cardiff and that she would find a way to fit in. Ten years later, the chiseled teak doors of the auditorium squealed as she opened them and caused a familiar twinge in her abdomen before she stepped inside. She wasn't sure where it started, but there was applause when she walked in, and most everyone in the room made it a point to come and speak to her.

Dr. Winston Mathers, the Dean of the College of Engineering, embraced her and kissed her cheeks in the European manner before looking up at her. "Welcome home, Tallenaara. Cardiff is thrilled to have you walk our halls again and enlighten our students."

She blushed as red as a Styrahi could before looking down into her mentor's eyes and smiling. "I wouldn't be here without you, Doctor Mathers."

He grinned. "You're a faculty member, Tallenaara. And you hold a doctorate from our college. That means you call me Winston."

She smiled, felt the heat in her cheeks, and then laughed. This was a moment every academician experienced. The realization that they are no longer the student. "Thank you, Winston. I am thrilled to be here."

Now, she had an office that overlooked the quadrangle, and shelves filled with the collected works of Frank Lloyd Wright and her other idols. Tomorrow, she would give a lecture on Styrahi architecture to the freshmen of Cardiff, two of whom were Styrahi. Two of the four Styrahi at Cardiff were studying architecture. Things certainly came full circle. *How things change but stay the same*, Tally thought to herself and smiled.

Ahead on the path, a young man walked arm in arm with a tall redheaded Styrahi. The urge to hesitate and stare passed as quickly as it came along. Things were different now. Fresh young faces, the world still ahead of them and no challenge seeming too great. The pleasure of being young. Everything in front of them. The way they smiled at each other, the young Styrahi pulling tightly on the boy's arm, her head drooping to rest on his shoulder. The picture of love. There wasn't a care as to whether it would last or not, nor if it were right and proper for them to be in love. No one else on the quadrangle gave them a second glance.

They passed Tally and the young Styrahi nodded, "*Echeerra, loonta dai.*"

Tally smiled. "*Mi trodanna.*"

The boy looked perplexed at the exchange and then merely smiled.

Tally fought a chuckle. The title was unexpected and thrilling. *Honored teacher, no less.* Tally grinned to herself. Despite the pretense of her return to Earth, the joy and sense of accomplishment she felt in the opportunity she'd been given to teach her craft surprised her in its intensity. No matter the success of her "mission," she relished the chance to teach and mold young students like Dr. Mathers...Winston...had mentored her ten years before.

Lucky girl, she'd said to the young Styrahi. For a moment, she could remember the feeling of hugging onto Andrew's arm, the bright sunlight on her face and the feeling of complete and utter love for him. Knowing that he felt the same was intoxicating. What would it be like to see him again?

How long would she have to wait?

* * * * *

Chapter Twenty-Six

"Bullet Six, Bullet Two, possible counterattack in progress at Objective Seminary Ridge. Could be a flanking maneuver. Unknown number of vehicles heading southeast at high speed. Over."

Trevayne looked out onto the battlefield. Sure enough. At least someone from the battalion staff had their game face on. The command net was much too quiet for a unit involved in a high-speed assault. Trevayne keyed his microphone. "Bullet Six, Bullet Nine, over."

He waited five seconds and then tried again. No response.

"Blue Six, Bullet Nine, no contact with Six element. Echelon to the right and stagger out. Give yourself some space in case they come flanking in."

"Belay that action!" Coffey screamed in Trevayne's ears. "Blue Six, you will disregard that order immediately. Bullet Nine on private channel now!"

Trevayne shook his head and chinned over to their private channel to hear Coffey already deep into a screaming fit. "Now, see here, Sergeant Major! Last time I checked, I'm in command of this fucking regiment. That means I tell people where to go and what to do, not you! You could've given away our flank, Sergeant Major!"

Trevayne felt his face warming. "By what? Securing our movement forward?"

"Don't argue with me! Stay off the command net unless you hear me calling for you. You got that?"

Trevayne tapped a few buttons on his panel. "Roger, Bullet Six, this is Bullet Nine. Understand your order to stay off the command net, but I cannot comply with it. This is an unlawful order."

"Are you fucking kidding me? Goddamnit Sergeant Major, I'm telling you to get off my net! Stay off of it! If you're such a coward that you can't see the enemy is feinting in the hopes we'll turn broadside to them, then I don't want you in my regiment!"

Turn broadside? A feint? "Six, are you saying you believe the enemy action to be a feint? We have units in the path of the enemy. Are we going to leave them behind?"

"They're somebody else's problem. Now stay off my net!"

The channel clicked dead and Trevayne resisted the urge to punch the command panel. Barely. He would need the recording.

"Stephens, send a copy of that conversation to the dump." Like every tactical mission, all recordings from all vehicles were stored automatically in an audio dump file aboard the *Ticonderoga.* Since their earliest use during the Apollo missions of the 1960s, audio dumps were essential to operations, especially when determining where things went wrong. Maybe when this clusterfuck was over, Trevayne hoped, somebody would figure it out.

"Roger, Sergeant Major. File is uploaded."

"Interface, dispatch emergency support request for air cover to the eastern sector. Do it now and without telling me it's against regulation. Driver, make for the far right of the line. Get us up off the ground if you have to."

Trevayne activated his display and saw the lone unit icon behind the ridgeline to the east flashing. Taking fire. "Interface, get those people air cover. And somebody get me a damned frequency to talk to air support."

Who the hell fights a war without talking to the guys overhead? We're right back to World War II!

<<No frequency available,>> the Interface replied.

Wonderful. Trevayne watched the swollen stream of Grey tanks bursting down the ridgeline and ever so briefly cresting the adjacent ridge before descending down the other side. Whoever the unit on the other side of the ridge was, they were going to get annihilated if nothing was done.

Coffey's voice broke over the radio. "All units attack. I say again; all units full frontal attack! Gear five! Do it now!"

What in the name of God? Around him, magtanks lifted up onto their repulsors and began to charge up the hillside at maximum power. The swirling Grey vehicles stopped their assault and hesitated for a moment. With astonishing speed, the vehicles gathered into three lines and began to swing down the ridge, taking up the perfect position for a high-speed flanking maneuver.

Not on my watch.

"Blue Six, Black Nine. Give me two of your platoons. We're gonna hold that flank."

"Roger, Black Nine, you've got Red and White elements standing by."

Trevayne chuckled. His commander wasn't going to like it. Tough shit. "Interface, plot the fastest route to Red and White elements and get me their frequencies. We don't have a lot of time."

He looked at the tactical display one last time, seeing the flashing icon slowly moving backward into the hills on the other side of the ridge. Hopefully, they'd find some good terrain and could hold their own. He wished them luck, and then turned his mind to holding an impossible flank.

*****

Chapter Twenty-Seven

Neither Buckingham Palace nor Number 10 Downing Street were the proper residence of the Prelate of Earth. There were compounds for the Prelate and his Council on every continent to conduct the business of the planet, but the actual residence of the Prelate away from the perils of his job was a remote retreat along the coast of Ireland near Shannon. The first Prelate, Andrew's grandfather, constructed the retreat in the manner of Camp David, the retreat for the President of the United States from the Eisenhower administration to the reintroduction of the Continental Congress and the restructuring of the American government in 2076. Cozy, remote, but very closely guarded and protected, the six cabins and conference hall could easily hold the Prelate's Council if necessary, but with its minimal support staff, the Prelate's Retreat was simply that. No one relished it more than Andrew Cartner. The retreat was the only place in the world he could call his own.

The setting sun barely warmed his chair as he propped his feet on the railing and lit a cigar. A glass of Narrobian red at his side, Andrew avoided looking at his tablet. The duty day, as his father would have said, was complete. For a moment in the waning twilight, the emerging war was far from his mind, as were the usual spate of domestic issues. Rescue teams were already in Bangladesh to save tsunami victims for the second time in five years, and it appeared that the Russian Federation's elections were complete without customary rioting.

What would my father have thought? Andrew sipped the wine and let the thought go. Before his father succumbed to his horrifying sudden aortic aneurysm ten years ago, Andrew wouldn't have cared what his father thought about anything. The lectures and constant teaching and tutelage that Andrew resented so often became the constant want in his life. His father's advice would help him navigate the treacherous world of Earth's political structure. Not that he was doing badly—quite the contrary—but he wanted the counsel of his father. Someone who loved him unconditionally, someone who believed in him, and most importantly, someone he loved.

The last outbound exocraft from Shannon carried his latest fling, an American movie star who clearly worked solely based on her looks, and was as "ignorant as a bag of hammers", as Darren was fond of saying. Andrew smiled at the thought and checked his Omega wristwatch. Darren McMasters was due any time, and they could enjoy the evening together as only lifelong friends could. Nothing would matter, and they'd not talk of work in any manner. Maybe catch a holo, preferably something from America that they could make fun of and compare hopelessly to the golden days of cinema. He'd probably drink too much and smoke more than one cigar, which always gave him headaches, but he needed the diversion. There were times being the spokesman for nine billion human beings was simply impossible. Being a planet at war with a race no one knew much about made it worse.

Darren would bring news of the war, of the latest advancement of the Greys against the best forces stationed in the Outer Rim. Surely there would be some measure of success by now? How long could the Terran Defense Forces continue to have their collective asses handed to them and still keep wanting a fight?

"You look decidedly unhappy."

Andrew smiled and looked over his shoulder. "Grab a glass."

"Already ahead of you." Darren McMasters smiled and poured a liberal glass of the exquisite red wine. "*Slainté.*"

"*Prost,*" Andrew replied as they clinked glasses. "I suppose you're going to brief me on today's war efforts?" The words came out with an almost loathing quality. The briefing would not be good news. Again.

McMasters shook his head and rustled into a chair. "We've dropped two divisions of armored forces on Wolc. They will likely make contact with the Greys in the next twelve hours. The Greys outnumber us two to one, but there is some optimism from the command. Atrocious weather across the planet right now, and given what we know about the Grey vehicles, there is the thought we will have better maneuverability for a change. The next transmission window is in two hours. We'll know then."

Andrew nodded. "We could use a bit of good news."

McMasters grinned and leaned back. "And so could you, by the look of it."

"You have something good to tell me today?" Andrew chuckled. "That would be a change."

"Hardly," McMasters snorted, then paused for a moment. "Tallenaara is back at Cardiff."

A palpable shock ran through Andrew. "What did you say?"

"I said that Tallenaara has returned to Cardiff. She is a visiting professor of architecture now."

The emotions crashed over Andrew. There was shock that she'd returned. Happiness that he might see her again. Anger she'd run away in the first place. Understanding why she did so. Loss. Hope. All of them were rapidly fading save for a sense of excitement. "When does my schedule take me to Wales?"

"Two weeks."

Andrew shook his head. "That's too long."

"I don't think you should rush into this. She's quite busy getting settled."

Andrew shot McMasters a glance. "How would you know, Darren?"

"I took my unstated position as your personal advisor and friend to investigate her presence."

"You went to see her?" Andrew let his mouth drop open. "When?"

McMasters sipped his wine. The pregnant pause almost caused Andrew to impatiently ask again. "Day before yesterday. I was in London and the personal alert you gave me for her rang off at precisely thirteen hundred hours. I went immediately to the maglev station and was waiting for her. I gave her a lift to Cardiff."

"How does...?"

"Amazing. She is as beautiful as ever." McMasters smiled. "She hopes to see you soon."

Andrew shook his head. "I'm half-tempted to make her wait ten years."

They both chuckled and fell silent. McMasters picked up a cigar and deftly trimmed it. Lighting it, he looked at Andrew. "You know why she did what she did, Andy."

My father. And this damned office. "I know," Andrew said. "It was much different then."

"Yes, it was," McMasters smiled. "And yet you handled it with grace and dignity. If you chose to again, I have no doubt you would do the same thing."

"Maybe I would." Andrew looked at the setting sun wondering if his outlook on life was setting as well. Maybe that was why his father never remarried. There was simply not time for a Prelate to live. But what if there was?

"You look like you're wondering about your future for a change."

Andrew glanced at McMasters. "What's that supposed to mean?"

"You took office ten years ago, barely six months out of university! You've not had a chance to live at all, and you refuse to, except for the odd nights when you come here and relax, tell dirty jokes, and watch movies. I think you need to, pardon the phrase, 'live a little.' Prelate or not, you're no good to anyone on the planet if you work like a zombie all the time."

Andrew laughed. "I suppose not."

"Then what are you going to do about it?"

Andrew smiled. "I think I'll visit Cardiff very soon."

"Tomorrow?"

Andrew laughed and looked at his watch. "Could we leave right now?"

"And miss my monthly time with my friend when he's not busy being the Prelate?" McMasters chuckled. "You wouldn't dare."

Andrew chuckled. He thought of Tally's long dark hair on his shoulder and the warmth of her hand in his, easy smiles, and his pain at the sight of her tears. The only thing that replaced her was his duty as Prelate. Now that she was back on Earth, what would it mean for him? For them? He brushed away the thought with practiced ease. The needs of the people of Earth outweighed his own needs. Except this time, it felt a little different, like there was a silver lining to his nebulous world. He'd maintained in all things that hope always existed.

For the first time in ten years, Andrew Cartner felt his heart leap at the hope that Tallenaara would see him again and smile. That he could tell her everything in his heart. That she would let him hold her close. That she would forgive him.

"My trip is in two weeks? To Cardiff?"

McMasters smiled. "Yes."

"Move it up a week," Andrew smiled. "And I trust you have a way to contact her?"

"Of course I do. Tell me why I should give it to you," McMasters grinned.

Andrew smiled, really smiled, for the first time in ages. He gestured with his wine glass. "You can think of a million reasons not to, I'm sure."

"You want it?"

Andrew nodded. "Of course I do."

*****

Chapter Twenty-Eight

Withdrawal by fire was a catchy way to say retreating while still shooting. Mairin stood in the hatch and guided Booker through the trees as the soft green meadows gave way to an increasingly dense pine forest. The small hill in front of them could be defended for a little while, but they wouldn't have much time.

"The Styrahi pathfinder team has taken a position on top of this knoll," the Slammer's interface said in Mairin's ears. "They are broadcasting via direct laser."

"Button three," Conner said with a grin.

"I don't know you, but you're compromising my team's position."

Mairin smirked. "In case you haven't noticed, you've got about a hundred Grey vehicles streaming down the valley. What's so important that they're attacking us? What are you observing?"

"*Echessa*, you need to get off this hill."

Mairin bit her tongue for a moment and then spoke in perfect Stryahi. "Then come down here and make me."

"This is the best firing position within five hundred meters. Five of six vehicles are prepared to fire," the Interface chimed.

Mairin checked the tactical display in her helmet for the trailing vehicle. *Two. Behind about three hundred meters.* She swung around and looked over her shoulder. She keyed a private channel. "One, Six. You have eyes on Two?"

"Roger. They took a hit to the right rear repulsor. We're covering them."

WHUMP!

Mairin looked back and saw a tremendous secondary explosion at the edge of the treeline. The beautiful green grass burned around the hulk of a Slammer. Her stomach knotted. Down four good troopers.

<<Two is down. No survivors. You are now eighty-three percent combat effective.>>

"Interface, disengage combat reporting protocols. You bring that shit up to me again and the vehicle goes under manual control. Understand?" She felt the ice on her words as she said them. Detached and serious.

<<Perfectly, Captain Shields.>>

"Guidons, this is Six. Take defensive positions and engage when the enemy gets close enough." She chinned over to the aviation frequency. "SITREP follows. In defensive positions at vicinity Tango Hotel five six seven six five seven. I've got a 100 Grey tanks barreling down a valley at me. Need CAS immediately."

"Saber Six, Thunder Six. Air support en route. ETA is six minutes. You might want to keep your heads down."

Mairin slid down into the hatch. Three minutes to contact and six minutes to air support. Going to be a long three minutes. "Interface, institute high-pressure procedures for all vehicles. Stand by for a nuke."

<<There is a single life form approaching from the rear.>>

Mairin looked through the rear vision block and saw the approaching Styrahi warrior. She keyed the intercom. "Be right back."

"Helluva time to hit the latrine, ma'am," Conner smiled.

Mairin opened the hatch and climbed onto the rear deck as the Styrahi leapt to it. She towered over Mairin by at least a foot and a half. Tally would have been small compared to the woman standing in front of Mairin.

"I said get off this hill. You are threatening my mission, *echessa*."

Mairin raised her finger and spoke again in lilting Styrah. "And you're threatening my troops. I've got close air support inbound with nukes."

"I am supposed to meet up with Lieutenant Colonel Coffey and his regiment! They will be here any moment."

"They are on the other side of that ridge," Mairin pointed at the craggy peaks to the west. "He's not coming."

The fury on the Styrahi's face faded. "Are you part of his regiment?"

"Yes," Mairin felt a smile coming. "Well, probably not for much longer. I was supposed to be the reserve, sitting behind his line about thirty kilometers. I'm Captain Shields."

The Styrahi nodded. "My name is Tillokara. My team was observing a recon element. The Greys are looking for something."

"Any idea what?"

Tillokara shrugged and looked away. "I think they're drilling for water."

Mairin felt a click in her head. "Or something else."

Tillokara squinted at her. The lines at the corners of her eyes surprised Mairin. The Styrahi must have been in her fifties, by Earth standards. "What are you suggesting? And how do you speak Styrahi so well?"

Mairin almost answered, but didn't.

"Oh, you're a *keerchaca*, then?"

Keerchaca, a casual fling. A one-night stand. Something like a human whore who played with Styrahi. The word had no real human equivalent. Mairin flushed. "Fuck you, Tillokara."

Tillokara said nothing for a moment. Mairin felt the taller woman's eyes boring through her, taking in every detail until her eyes softened, almost piteous. "Not that." She looked at Mairin for a moment but said no more.

"You better get out of here. Keep your head down when the exos roll in."

Tillokara nodded. "There are too many of them. Without assistance, you realize your position is hopeless. Right?"

"I do. Help is on the way. Then we're going to haul ass up this valley and give the Greys something to think about." Mairin said.

Tillokara smiled, "Valtranya, iruhrer." Good luck, warrior.

"And you as well." Mairin replied. She watched Tillokara leap down to the ground and sprint towards her team. For everything that Tally was, Tillokara was clearly not. So very different. Her heart ached as she heard the first sonic boom of the exocraft entering the atmosphere. She climbed up onto the turret and slid into the hatch. Closing it, she felt the tank jerk as the first round went downrange. She heard Lee whooping as a Grey tank disintegrated ten thousand meters away. The countdown timer said thirty seconds.

"Guidons, Six. Button up and hold fast." She looked out the vision blocks at the swirling black mass of vehicles heading their direction. "Kill anything that moves!"

* * * * *

Chapter Twenty-Nine

In exospheric combat aviation, there were two distinct schools of thought. Exospheric interception should involve light, fast, and highly maneuverable vehicles to patrol the heights, or that vehicles that worked in the lower atmosphere had to be heavily armored, and therefore slower than Christmas. Of the fighter pilots, though, there were some who braved the lower atmosphere of planets more than required of their station. Of that merry few, none had a better reputation with the grunts of the Terran Defense Force than Captain Tony Richards. An imprint, Richards carried with him the experiences and memories of a very distant uncle, who'd survived the Battle of Britain as a decorated Spitfire pilot. Every measure of bravado, survival instinct, and seat-of-the-pants flying ability he brought to the fight amplified his own innate ability to something almost otherworldly. And Richards did it all with the grace and humility expected of an English gentleman.

Leading a section of four Hurricanes, the swept-wing twin-tailed exospheric interceptors of the *Indomitable*, Richards swung the sleek vehicle to his right and dove towards the surface of Wolc. "Right, gents. We've got interceptors on the way and our close-air needs to get in there. Spread formation, inbound bandits at mark two, ten kilometers."

A bright flash of light, the implosion of the frigate *Perkins*, reflected ever so briefly on the Greys' dart-like fighters. *Three of them. At least we have the advantage.*

Richards licked his lips. "Visual contact. Two, stay on my wing. Three, split for the hunt."

Richards spun hard to the right, his wingman hugging close to his left wing as the other two fighters broke up and into a wide circle to the left with the intent of flanking the incoming Greys. Richards shot the departing fighters a glance. The maneuver played out perfectly. The targets swung into his reticle as planned. He smiled grimly and flicked the master arm switch for his weapon systems to active. "Fangs out. Let's make things interesting, shall we?"

Richards pivoted the Hurricane and met the approaching Greys in a head-on approach. Immediately, the Greys began to fire. Richards smiled. *Neutral passes are for school*, he thought, and swung the heavy exocraft into a tight descending turn before pulling hard for the vertical and engaging his main thrusters. The maneuver perfect, he slid into position on the rear of the Grey formation and immediately fingered his weapons release switch.

"Fox One," he called, like he was ordering a pint. Assured, calm, and business as usual. The ion-powered Battleaxe missile dropped from its weapons bay and accelerated to Mach Sixteen in the blink of an eye, impacting the far right Grey fighter in a spectacular explosion. "Splash one," he confirmed the kill and the location of the radioactive debris.

The Grey fighters hung together, pursuing Jenkins in Lancer Four by the looks of it. The lad had missed the turn timing again, just like in training. Richards nudged the fighter forward and cycled the weapons system. The Greys jinked and matched Jenkins' every move like they were in the cockpit with the poor lad. He was not shaking them, and Richards nodded in morbid, detached admiration. Staying together made them a more lethal combination. Strength in numbers. Tactically perfect.

"Two, tighten it up," Richards said and saw his wingman pull in to within a few meters. "Now stay with me."

Richards pushed the throttle forward and targeted the trailing Grey fighter. The weapon system locked on, but before he could squeeze the trigger, the Grey fighters separated in opposite directions. *What Delta vee!* Richards thought. *Bloody hell, they're fast.*

As he swung the Hurricane to the left instinctively following the trailing Grey fighter, Jenkins' Hurricane exploded in a blue cloud. "What the hell?"

Lancer Four destroyed by convergent particle beams fired from both Grey fighters. The words flashed across his heads-up display. Listening to the computer would've been easier, but it only served to annoy the rakishly old-fashioned pilot.

Richards blinked at the visual display. *They both shot him, did they?* "Three, where the bloody hell are you?"

"Lead, Three, your six o'clock high at twenty miles. The lead Grey fighter is swinging to your six. I'm on my way."

Richards didn't bother to look behind. "Two, defensive weapon engagement. Fire at will." *Bet you wish you'd had these, Uncle Max.* Richard grinned as he saw the flashes from his wingman's rear-mounted missiles and guns begin to fire. The Grey fighter exploded a millisecond later.

"Splash two," Richards' wingman yelped into the radio.

Richards yanked the Hurricane into a high-scissor engagement as the remaining Grey fighter began to juke away. Thumbing the EM cannon into operation, he waited until the Grey pilot found his rhythm, meaning that he was making the same swinging moves to throw off Richards. The problem was that a good pilot could also time the maneuver. Richards was an exceptional pilot, and by the end of the Grey fighter's third juke Richard walked sixty electromagnetic kinetic rounds through the middle of his opponent's aircraft.

"Splash three," Richards said with a smile. "Three, join up and scan for incoming fighters."

Richards looked to his displays. The *Hokkaido* is gone, *Viraat* hurting. "*Indomitable*, Lancer One vectors to mother."

"Be advised, Lancer One, you are clear to mother at mark five, distance three six zero."

Richards looked down on the swarming surface of Wolc. He checked his weapons stores and smiled. "Roger, *Indomitable.* We'll be along shortly." Punching the squadron frequency, he said, "Lads, I've got a better idea. How about some fish in a barrel?"

* * * * *

Chapter Thirty

Don't over think. Don't over think. Alex Ulson watched the advancing Grey vehicles as he forced himself to breathe and not get lost in the moment. He looked down the line at the other four vehicles left in their little unit and wondered what Captain Shields was thinking. *Stop it!* Shaking his head to clear it, he went back to watching the advancing Greys. *Think, Alex. What should you be doing?*

"Sir, lead Grey vehicle is ten thousand out, permission to fire?" His gunner asked.

Beyond the vision blocks, he could see pine-like trees and more pine-like trees. A thin line of fire gave him sight of the valley, but it was at best ten meters wide. Why couldn't this battle be fought at home? At least on the Llano Estacado of New Mexico he would not need a computer to see the enemy coming for miles and could engage them before they got close enough to use their weapons. The cover and concealment was better up here, though. They'd have a chance. "You heard the boss, Jefferson. She said kill everything that moves."

"What about the trees?"

Ulson looked outside. The worst thing that could happen was they'd lose some of the concealment by knocking the massive conifers down. "Can't be helped. Shoot what you can."

The main gun slewed to the right and Ulson heard Jefferson announce he had a target locked. There was a huge pine tree fifty meters from the end of the main gun. "You're locked on the tree..."

"On the way!" Jefferson yelled as he pulled the trigger. The round flung out of the tube, swerved around the trunk of the tree, tore out a cloud of branches, and continued down range to impact one of the lead vehicles about nine thousand meters away.

"What the fuck?" Ulson asked quietly as he watched Jefferson slew the gun to another tank and fire, only to see the round correct itself slightly in mid-air. "Interface, we're carrying maneuverable rounds?"

"Yes, Lieutenant. We are combat loaded with T540 sabot rounds. Every round onboard is capable of self-guided movement based on calculations from the targeting computer."

Ulson used his chin to select a frequency. "Six, this is One, over."

"Go ahead, One." Captain Shields sounded like she was ordering coffee.

"Um, ma'am, are we on secure comms?"

Three seconds later, Shields answered. "Laser comm, Alex. What's on your mind?"

"Have your gunner lock on a target with the gun tube behind a tree and fire your main gun."

Shields snorted. "That's the silliest…."

"Do it, ma'am," Ulson snapped. "You need to see this."

He turned in his seat and looked down the line. Slowly, Six's main gun slewed behind a tree and fired. The connection was quiet for five seconds before he heard Shields in his ear again. "What in the hell? Did you know about this?"

"About ten seconds before I called you, ma'am. What do we do now?"

He looked through the vision blocks and could almost feel her eyes on him a full three hundred meters away. "Find better cover and protect those pathfinders."

Ulson looked at the mapping function on his station. "I've got a good-sized rock formation at two six three from my position at three hundred meters. It's good cover."

"Stay put, Alex."

From the rock formation, he'd have a decent view of a majority of the valley. The protective cover of the rocks, as well as the built-in camouflage of the trees and rocks would break up the outlines of the Slammers and make them more difficult to hit. The downslope rocks would keep the Greys away, too. Ulson saw branches and bark flying through the air now. Their position lay within weapons range of the Grey vehicles.

PING!

"What the-"

PING! PING! The entire vehicle vibrated. More impacts followed and Ulson grabbed at his harness to steady himself. "Interface report."

"We have been hit by fourteen rounds so far, Lieutenant. Three of which hit the front slope of the turret and did not penetrate. That was the cause of the harmonic vibrations."

"Damage report?"

"Negligible."

In front of his knees, Jefferson sat in the gunner's position laying down an impressive rate of fire. Slew turret, settle the gun, range the target, and then engage the target. "Jefferson, how many rounds we got left?"

"Enough for the whole Grey regiment, sir."

Doubt that, Ulson thought. The beauty of an electromagnetic rail gun was that the massive quantities of explosive propellant to fling projectiles were not necessary. As such, carrying dart-like penetrators alone made it possible to carry much more ammunition than the Slammers predecessors. "Lay back a little bit. We're gonna be moving soon."

"What?"

Ulson realized the voice was Private First Class Ashby, his communications specialist who hadn't said a word since the drop. "I said, we'll be moving soon, Ashby."

"But Captain Shields told you…us to stay put." Ashby clutched the frame of the communications console so tightly his gloves creaked. "You're not thinking of moving, sir?"

Ulson grinned. "That's exactly what I'm thinking, Ashby. Get me Three on a private channel."

"Button two, sir." Ashby seemed to sink into the comm seat and attempt to become one with the wall of the turret.

"Three this is One, you read me Sullivan?"

It took a moment, but Three's commander answered. "Sir?"

"We're going to move in a minute. There's a rock outcropping about three hundred meters from my position where we can suppress the whole flank of those Greys. When I move, you follow. Got it?"

"Roger," Sullivan answered just as Ulson flipped frequencies.

"Six, this is One."

"One, Six, over." Captain Shields snapped.

"Six, request covering fire."

"You're not moving, Alex. I told you to stay put."

Ulson licked his lips. "Ma'am, I've got a position about three hundred meters away that will give me and Three cover and concealment and a view of the whole Grey attack. We can open up their flank."

Shields didn't respond for a moment. He knew she was checking his report, confirming it for herself and weighing the possibilities. "One, Six. Let me know when you get in position. Good hunting."

* * * * *

Chapter Thirty-One

"You're not coming?"

Tallenaara looked up from her glass-topped computer desk and waved her light pen to change the orientation of the building elevation she'd been toying with. Teaching brought her immense satisfaction and more than ample time to explore her own creativity. "Is it required?"

"Not at all," Winston Mathers said. "I thought you might be interested to hear what the Prelate has to say."

Tally looked down again. "I'm very busy."

"Doodling the afternoon away, yes, you are quite busy." Mathers' smile faded. "I don't want to sound old and jaded, but I remember watching the two of you on campus years ago. There was something about you. Something that transcended everything around us. Like we were watching two cultures finally starting to intersect. That our world was changing right before our very eyes."

Tally closed her eyes and felt her teeth pinching her bottom lip. "It was a long time ago, Winston. And I'm not ready to see him."

"I understand." Mathers leaned away from the door frame. "I'll let you know if anything interesting comes up." She heard him whistling his same four bars of Jack Benny down the hallway before the surreal quiet of the building gradually surrounded her. Classes were cancelled for the afternoon with the Prelate...Andrew on campus.

You are ready to see him; you're just avoiding him. She chided herself as she sipped the strong Earl Grey tea. *Why shouldn't I avoid him?*

Out of spite, or am I playing hard to get? She shook her head and turned the elevation on her desk to a new angle and began to draw. Melding the lines from idea to reality, her mind in complete control of her hand as the vision took form in her imagination. A vision that she could see made into reality someday.

"Is that why you're studying architecture?" Andrew had asked one summer day while sitting on the long green grass of the inner quadrangle. "You're talented enough to be an artist, Tally. What brought you to architecture?"

"What I draw can be made into reality." She'd not even looked up from the paper.

"So what does a sculptor do? Or a carpenter? Or a painter? Aren't they making something real?"

"I suppose so."

"Then why architecture?" Andrew leaned in close enough that she felt his breath on her cheek.

"Because it's what I love." She looked up into his smiling face. "And it makes me happy."

"You make me happy," Andrew said as he'd leaned in to kiss her gently on the lips. His eyes traced her face, and his hand was warm against her shoulder as they kissed. She lowered the sketchbook to the grass and kissed him gently in return. She was as happy as she could ever remember being. The sun warm on her back, the grass tickling her feet, and Andrew lying next to her. The memory was almost perfect.

"I hope I'm not interrupting."

She startled and spilled hot tea across the desk. "*Mereete*!"

Leaning against the door and dressed in a tailored black suit with a pale blue necktie, Andrew Cartner's eyes glittered, though he did not smile. "I didn't mean to startle you."

Tally made no move to clean up the spill. She set the mug down gently and looked at him. Her hearts thumped loudly in her ears and she thought how handsome he looked. More like his father now than ever. "You look like your father."

He smiled a little. "It's a shame you weren't here to see me age gracefully. You are as beautiful as ever."

"I thought it was what you wanted," Tally flared. "You said it would never work between us. That your father wouldn't allow it. And that it was not good for either of our planets to continue our relationship."

"I did what I thought was right."

"For whom, Andy?" Tally felt herself flush. "For your father?"

"No," his voice almost a whisper. "For you, Tally."

The sound of his name from her lips almost made her shiver. Tally shook her head. "How could you think that being away from you was good for me?"

"I thought I was right." Andrew shrugged. "I know now that it was wrong. I came to say I'm sorry."

"Don't you think it's a little late for that, Andy? You've waited ten years to tell me?"

"I'd have told you the next day if you hadn't run away. If I could have found you. Where did you go, by the way?"

"Back to Styrah," Tally said. "I hopped a rickety freighter that made the hop in six months. Completely 'off the grid,' as you'd say."

"Obviously." He paused and looked out the window towards downtown. "I stopped looking after a few weeks. I figured you didn't want to be found. Not a day went by that I didn't think about you."

"That's supposed to make me feel better, Andy? You could have found me when I got back to Styrah. And when I went to Libretto, you had to know that I was there. It was a joint initiative between our species!"

"I knew," Andrew sighed. "But my father had died, and I'd become Prelate then. You can imagine my life from that point on."

"I really can't," Tally said. "I have a hard time believing that you have any life whatsoever outside of your work."

"It's tougher than most people can imagine."

For a moment, Andrew's suit didn't seem to fit. His eyes were not clear and bright and his personality not engaged like it always seemed to be. He was pensive and quiet, drawn into himself. There was pain in his voice and something Tally couldn't quite understand that made her sympathize with him despite her wounds. "Why are you here, Andy?"

"I'm not really sure."

Tally laughed. "Something brought you here."

His eyes met hers and he grinned. "Hope, I suppose. Darren told me you were here, Tally. I'd told him to let me know if you ever came back to Earth."

"Why?"

"So I could apologize." Andrew smiled. "So I could see you again."

Tally returned the smile and nodded in the direction of the auditorium as words failed her. She paused and smiled at him, almost saying something else, that she'd missed him for ten years. "Don't you have a speech to give?"

Andrew shrugged. "Remember how we used to give professors fifteen minutes to start class or we'd leave?"

"You get twenty?" Tally laughed.

"I believe that being Prelate means the world waits for me." Andrew grinned. "Are you coming?"

"I hadn't planned to. I'm not one for speeches, Andy."

Andrew nodded. "I understand if you don't want to come to my speech. I'm not a fan of them myself. But I was wondering what you were doing this weekend."

Tally felt her hearts skip a little. "I'm preparing my lesson plans."

"As one of the benefits of being Prelate, I have a retreat in Ireland. Would you care to join me tomorrow evening?"

Tally looked away for the first time. Ten years. "I'm not really sure that I should, Andy. Can you understand why?"

"I can," Andrew said. "I wouldn't be here if I didn't understand that. I've waited ten years for you, Tallenaara. The world has changed so much since then. I've changed so much. I just want a chance to make things right."

Tally nodded. *Wants of the Council be damned*, she thought. Going with him even for one night seemed far better than not. "I'll come to Ireland. As long as you promise to be gentlemanly and chaste."

"Some things are beyond even the promise of a Prelate."

*****

Chapter Thirty-Two

"Will you look at this," Richards said to himself. Below him a regiment of tanks accelerated in a line formation up a tight valley nearly devoid of vegetation. As the senior flight leader, Richards shook his head at the standard tactical package. *Bloody suicide*, he thought as he toggled the master arm switch and chinned the ground commander's frequency. "Bullet Six, this is Lancer One with a flight of three. Do you require assistance?"

Richards waited five seconds before he keyed the microphone again. "Bullet Six, Lancer One, do you require assistance?"

"Get off this frequency and get your ass out of this valley!" Richards toggled the secure connection and identified the voice as Lieutenant Colonel Coffey, the regimental commander.

Richards blinked and swung the nose of the fighter up over the ridgeline to his right. Immediately he saw a flood of Grey vehicles. Icons appeared on his tactical screen and he scanned the frequencies. "Saber Six, this is Lancer One with a flight of three do you need assistance?"

The response was immediate, and to Richards surprise very feminine. "Lancer One, hit those bastards and turn them west into the ridgeline. I've got a section of vehicles up there and we can give them some serious hell. Call down retrieval for the Pathfinder team to my six, acknowledge."

Richards felt himself smile. *Nothing like being told exactly what to do.* "Saber Six, roger all. Lancer One rolling in."

At sixty thousand feet, Richards nosed the Hurricane over and selected his targets. "Two and Three, hit the eastern flank. Give me a thirty second interval before you roll in." Both of his wingmen clicked their microphones twice, acknowledging the transmission. Richards rolled off the flight and made a descent towards the forward elements of the Greys. He saw tank rounds flying from both sides and a great many more Grey tanks than friendlies.

"Weapons system to active," he spoke clearly. "Wide dispersion, tactical nuke. Clearance is," he glanced at the written note board strapped to his leg, "Alpha Sierra Tango Niner Five Two."

<<Weapons systems active, tactical small-yield nuclear weapon delivery confirmed.>>

Targeting icons appeared, and he pushed the exospheric ramjets to full military power. Distance to target ticked off his clock in the blink of an eye. "Lancer One, nuke release." Internal bomb bay doors slid open and ejected sixteen maneuvering warheads. Counting to two, Richards whipped the Hurricane skyward as the first of the small nuclear explosions ripped into the front of the advancing Greys. Rising clouds of rock and soil fell among the Grey vehicles not disabled by the blasts. Right on schedule, Two and Three broadsided the confused formation and laid thirty-two single kiloton warheads into the formation. Richards scanned the ground with a quick sweep of synthetic aperture radar. More than four hundred Grey vehicles were destroyed, and the five Slammers continued their impressive rate of fire.

With a thought, Richards relayed the request to retrieve the Pathfinders and turned in his seat to watch all of his aircraft pulling up from the target. Across the weapons status board, he could see they still had more than a few rounds to expend.

"Good show, gents," Richards called over the squadron frequency. "Join on me for round two."

"Lancer One, this is Saber Six."

Richards chinned to the frequency. "Go Saber Six."

"Lancer One. How about next time you actually hit the targets I request? I don't need a head-on pass! I need you to channelize the enemy towards the west! Acknowledge!"

Richards felt a smile on his face. Someone knew how to fight without having their back against a wall. "Roger, Saber Six. Lancer One rolling in." Richards flipped on his forward looking infrared viewer. Dirt and rock swirled around the Grey vehicles in intense vortices. "Three and Four, on my wing. Spread it out and let's give the lady exactly what she wants."

* * * * *

Chapter Thirty-Three

Darren McMasters joined the applause as the Prelate ascended the stairs to the podium to the ovation of the faculty and students of Cardiff. Andrew bounced onto the stage and smiled widely, waving to the crowd with an energy McMasters recognized immediately. He and Andrew used to watch the videos of iconic past politicians and laugh at what had to obviously be false charisma. Surely back when politicians were actually elected rather than chosen there were a few leaders with that charisma. The world sorely lacked the likes of Kennedy, Thatcher, and Gorbachev for most of the twentieth century and all of the twenty-first. Andrew laughed that those with false smiles and low morals were not qualified to lead anyone out of a wet paper bag. Fortunately, First Contact destroyed much of electoral governments.

Yet as Andrew gestured for the crowd to quiet and sit, his smile remained wide, energized, and genuine. Like he was truly happy. McMasters looked out from the wings of the darkened auditorium as Andrew began to speak. Even his voice sounded more confident, more...well, Andy.

McMasters scanned the crowd, looking for the tall Styrahi with the long dark hair. He strained around the curtains to no avail. Andrew's mood and sudden charisma could only have one catalyst. He'd been to see Tallenaara on one of his usual "I'm going to clear my head" walks.

Satisfied, he actually paid attention to Andrew's words, feeling a swell of emotion in his own soul as his best friend, and the representative leader of the planet, spoke in a voice long absent.

"Friends, I am thrilled to be back here at the finest university in the solar system." The crowd exploded in applause and Andrew smiled, sipped some water, and gestured them quiet again. "I'm here to discuss the future of Cardiff and the future of institutions of higher learning across our planet. Before I do, I wanted to share with you some good news. As you are undoubtedly aware, our efforts at war with the aliens known only as the Greys continue across the outer rim of our galaxy today. In recent weeks, the Greys have advanced over our toughest, bravest forces throughout the rim territories. Tonight, our forces are engaged in the third day of battle at Wolc. I don't need to remind you of the tactical importance of the Wolc colony. Without access to the resources for creating Fleet Battle Platforms and other vessels necessary to this fight, our abilities to survive this war remain in question.

"Tonight, after weeks of bitter losses and overwhelming defeats, we are on the brink of victory. Our newest Fleet Battle Platform, the *Ticonderoga*, arrived at Wolc today and her forces are single-handedly turning the battle for Wolc to our favor. Tonight, we stand on the edge of a declaration of the spirit not just of humanity, but the cultures of our galaxy who have said, 'This is enough! This war goes no farther! We shall not bow to anyone!'"

Applause roared through the auditorium. The power and delivery of his words, far deviating from the prepared speech, caught McMasters by surprise. The smile on his face grew. His neurals showed ten incoming calls, all from the Prelate's Council, who were undoubtedly watching the spectacle Andrew was creating and wondering what had possessed him. McMasters knew the answer and the fact his friend radiated the hope he'd carried for the last ten years made McMasters smile. All was going according to plan.

"And should they come for us? Friends, we will give them nothing! If it takes every last breath of life from our bodies, we will stand firm!"

McMasters clapped his hands along with the crowd. Andy's charisma, long dormant, flashed brilliantly. Turning away, a very satisfied smile on his face, he looked up into the backstage wings and saw Tallenaara. Her eyes flitted from Andrew to him and she smiled with the slightest hint of a shrug. McMasters beamed and winked at her.

McMasters wondered about the power of love, and whether or not it would handle the storm about to happen. His neurals flashed, interrupting his reverie. Terran Defense Forces were about to take the field at Wolc and Grey ships were seen in retreat from the planet, but not on a trajectory that would take them anywhere near Earth's sector. Finding them would now become the most important thing McMasters could influence.

He glanced at Tallenaara, smiling as she watched Andrew, now calmer and on to his prepared remarks with a warm smile, holding court with the audience eating out of his hands. Tallenaara could change everything, he knew, but hated himself for the doubt. His concerns came with the territory. Seeing Andrew happy was one thing. His best friend had been looking for himself for a decade. Tallenaara would not only complete Andy, but unite their two species, if all went well.

* * * * *

Chapter Thirty-Four

The unmistakable flash of a nuclear device cooking off caught Trevayne by surprise. Thank God he hadn't been looking in the direction of the ridgeline or he'd be at least temporarily blind. His mind demanded he find cover, call in a detonation report, and pray. All hit his mind at the same time. He looked in the direction where the flashes appeared and saw three exocraft climbing high over the mountains, swinging in a wide turn, and descending again. The sky flashed again with nukes and Trevayne dropped into the turret. "Dossett, get me in touch with those aircraft."

"Sergeant Major, I'm not able to lock out their frequency."

"Then figure out who is talking to them."

"What the-?" Dossett blurted. "They're transmitting in UHF."

Trevayne squinted. "Then get us on their frequency, Dossett! Jesus Christ!"

He watched Dossett key the correct frequency and she held up three fingers. He chinned his microphone to button three and heard, "Saber Six, Lancer One, one last pass and they're all yours."

Trevayne keyed the frequency. "Saber Six, this is Bullet Nine, over." He waited ten seconds for a response and transmitted again with no response. *How can I hear them and not talk to them?* Fighting with one hand behind tied behind his back would get nowhere. Fast. Gripping the sides of his seat tight enough to make his hands cramp, Trevayne let out a long slow breath. He could hear the exocraft, not the ground forces. "Dossett, let me guess, we have to have line of sight to talk to them, right?"

"Roger, Sergeant Major."

Trevayne keyed the microphone again. "Lancer One, this is Bullet Nine, over."

"I'm a little busy right now, Bullet Nine." The clipped, stilted accent rang in Trevayne's ears. "Call you back in a minute or two."

Trevayne slammed his fist into the turret wall. "Goddamnit! Driver, break to the east and get up on that goddamned ridge! Stand on that gas pedal!" He paused for a second and looked at Dossett. "Get me Bullet Six."

Dossett frowned. "He said to stay off the net, Sergeant Major."

"You and I both know that would never hold water." Trevayne frowned.

Dossett worked the panel. "We're blocked from the frequency."

"Then I hired the wrong goddamn comm specialist."

Thirty seconds passed. "Got it. Button Two."

Trevayne chinned the button and heard Coffey screaming incomprehensibly into the microphone. "Get that...who authorized that nuke...where in the hell are you people? Goddamn it! I said charge! Sons of bitches on that hill!"

Trevayne shook his head. This was going to end badly. The only commander on the ground that seemed to be doing anything about the threat was on the far side of the ridgeline with close air support tied in. From the satellite information he could see, Trevayne approved of the fight taking place. They were effectively neutralizing a full frontal attack with just five...five!... ground vehicles.

Dossett called to him as their vehicle started up the ridgeline. "Lancer One is calling for you. Button three."

"This is Bullet Nine, you in command of those exos to my east?"

"That's an interesting way of putting it, yes." The British voice toyed with him.

"I need everything you've got on the main Grey position, about two miles northwest of your last targets."

The radio crackled for a moment. "I'm afraid we're tapped out, Bullet Nine. But I'm relaying your request as we speak to Thunder Six. Keep the faith, over."

Trevayne popped back up in the hatch and looked around. Amidst the sour smells of burning rubber and hydraulic fluid, the scent of redolent pines filled his nostrils. For a split second, he wanted to tear off his helmet and listen to the field. All of the technology at his disposal could not replace the senses of his eyes and ears. The ridgeline loomed above him, while behind he could see the strung out lines of the regiment taking an astonishing amount of fire from the Grey position. The Grey attack across the ridgeline into the valley seemed to have stalled. Most likely as a result of the nuclear air support. The satellite download still read five vehicles in operation, though one appeared to have suffered massive failures. The vehicles were moving now, albeit very slowly in the thick woodland.

"Bullet Nine, this is Thunder Six. Authenticate Charlie Sierra Six."

Trevayne looked at Dossett who transmitted it directly to his helmet display. "Tango Five Charlie, Thunder Six."

"Bullet Nine, Thunder Six. I've been trying to reach Bullet Six. Can you update his status?"

Trevayne thought for a split second. "Unknown, Thunder Six."

"Are you in command, Bullet Nine?"

"Unknown, Thunder Six." Trevayne licked his lips. "I'm just trying to give my troops a chance with any air support you can give me, over."

The ten seconds passed like eternity, Trevayne's blood pulsing in his eardrums. "Bullet Nine, this is Thunder Six. I have a squadron of exos inbound with nuclear authority. I suggest your people button up and hunker down."

"Roger, Thunder Six, thanks for your support."

There was a laugh on the radio. Trevayne felt a smile on his face as he wondered if the voice on the other end connected the same shred of memory to what he'd said. The voice answered, "Roger, Bullet Nine. We'll leave the light on for you."

* * * * *

Chapter Thirty-Five

Systems check complete, Ulson saw that his wingman wasn't moving any time soon. Both repulsor drives were failing, and the wounded tank's main gun was nearly overheated. They continued to lay down fire on the advancing Grey vehicles, though there were significantly less than before. Ammunition status read amber, about forty percent of the basic load remaining. *How much longer can we sit here and pound on the Greys that are stupid enough to crest the ridgeline?* Whatever the Grey vehicles earlier were looking for was important enough to launch a huge counterattack.

"Alex, you still with me over there?"

"Roger, ma'am." Ulson watched another Grey vehicle erupt. "What kind of vehicles are those? They look familiar."

"They're supposed to be T-55s, tanks used by the Soviets back on Earth a long time ago. The bore evacuator on the end of the tube is a dead giveaway. Plus, the tracks on the T-55 sagged, something called Christie suspension—the Grey ones don't. The original ones were cheaply made and inexpensive to build, and the Greys studied that tactic. Sheer numbers versus better weapons. The Greys can use these as throwaways simply because of numbers." She stopped talking for a moment. "Alex?"

"Yes ma'am?"

"Get ready to charge."

Ulson blinked. "Say again?"

"You heard me, Alex. Look out there and tell me what you see."

Ulson did as he was told. "Lots of Grey vehicles. They're still firing." That was true, but their movement seemed different.

Scattered. Reactive. Almost as if no one was in charge. "They look confused."

"That's precisely why we're going to charge right through them. Get your repulsors up and running. Thirty seconds."

Ulson flipped over to the crew intercom. "Crew report?"

"Driver ready."

"Comms ready."

"Gunner ready."

<<Interface online.>>

He keyed the microphone. "Standby to charge. Gunner fire and adjust. Comms, keep us in constant contact with Six and relay everything you have to orbit. Driver, you'll see the other tanks out on the flank to our right charge. Wait for them to pass us, then pull out with a hard left and get alongside them. Everybody ready?"

There wasn't much response. Charging seemed like a bad idea, but sitting in their rudimentary defensive positions was worse. Hands shaking, Ulson reached up and opened the main hatch of the Slammer. He checked the firing mechanism of the fifty-caliber machine gun without raising himself up. The gun appeared to be in working order. He test-fired it, a chugging five round burst, and settled into the seat. Before he could question what was taking so long, Captain Shields transmitted in his ears.

"Guidons, this is Six. Repulsors to five feet, charge!"

Four hundred meters away, three Slammers rose up on their repulsor treads and began to move through the vegetation. They picked up speed moving downhill and kept up an impressive rate of fire. Ulson watched them break the treeline with all of their weapon systems blazing. The Grey vehicles almost completely stopped firing and then inexplicably turned towards Ulson's position. He chinned the frequency, "Three. You guys hunker down and kill anything that moves. One is on the roll!"

Ulson stood up on the back of the seat, felt the wind tear at him from all sides and grasped the fifty-caliber machine gun firing handle in his hands. "Driver, move out. All weapons active."

The main gun chuffed out a round as the tank rose to five feet. A fresh burst of pungent cordite filled the turret. Ulson could taste it on his lips as he watched the round arc through the sky. The Grey vehicle that had been the target simply shattered with the impact. The fifty-caliber jumped in his hands as he worked it over another Grey vehicle, stopping it cold. There was another target, and then another, and a third. Exceptional clarity filled his mind. Every action was simple and without thought. Unconscious, yet fully aware of what he was doing at the same time. Rounds passing over his head didn't make him flinch, though it was like he could see them spinning as they passed. The main gun slowed its rate of fire as he finished a thousand-round belt of ammunition. Ulson dropped into the tank to get another can of ammunition and realized that none of the Slammers weapons were firing.

"What's going on? Why aren't you firing?"

The gunner turned over his shoulder. "We're through the Greys, sir. About twelve hundred meters to the Greys position across the ridgeline."

Standing up, the first thing he noticed was that his machine gun was oriented over the back deck. Whispers from his former instructors circled around his head. "Target fixation is a killer," he heard his instructors say in his head from just weeks before. Ulson shook the thought away and took a deep breath.

He changed the frequency. "Six, this is One. Orders?"

"Alex, thought I'd lost you for a moment. You're lucky you didn't take out one of your antennas." Captain Shields answered on a private channel. The laser feeds were as clear as if she was sitting next to him.

Ulson felt his face flush. "Sorry, ma'am. It won't happen again."

His headset squelched on the command frequency. "One, there's an airstrike inbound on the Grey's position. ETA is three minutes. We'll be on the reverse slope of the ridge above their position when the airstrike drops. As soon as we can see, we can shoot. That means we'll roll down the hill guns blazing and see what happens."

"What about the friendlies over there?"

"Let me worry about them. Stay ready and reload. Six out."

Ulson keyed over the command frequency and put the remaining vehicles in a three hundred sixty-degree perimeter with their main guns facing out. The Greys behind them appeared motionless on the smoke draped battlefield. The tactical display showed his wingman, Three, was still operational with four life signs on board, and it appeared they weren't firing.

Fingers tapping, Ulson saw that Three's gun was still active with seventy-two rounds remaining. Both repulsors failed and the vehicle had taken a hit in the main gear sprocket, disabling the auxiliary tracks. No wonder they weren't going anywhere.

His own vehicle was in much better shape. One hundred seventeen rounds remained for the main gun and both repulsors were operational. The vehicle reported seventy-six percent combat effective overall.

The satisfaction melted away as he watched the tactical display. Greys swarmed over the ridgeline. Flashing lines indicating the firing of rounds took up the entire center of the screen. No telling how many of the regiment's vehicles remained. He leaned forward and looked outside. "Standby all weapons. Get ready for...."

A blinding white flash exploded to Ulson's front. *Shit!* He blinked and tried to rub his eyes resulting in banging his fingers off the faceplate. Ulson chinned his private channel to Shields. "Ma'am, I'm flashblind."

"Okay." She paused. "Alex, calm down. Close your eyes for a minute. Let your interface handle the move."

The Mandelbrot shapes and exploding patterns of lights on the inside of his eyelids slowly began to fade. He could see the tactical display now. The fringes of his vision were slightly fuzzy. The faceplate of his crewman's helmet had taken the brunt of the flash and saved his eyesight.

"Guidons, this is Six. Prepare to move."

Ulson chinned the crew intercom. "Interface, make the move until I get my eyesight back."

<<Acknowledged.>>

"You okay, sir?" his gunner asked. Ulson didn't know his name yet.

"I will be in a minute. Just make sure we stay with Six."

"Yes, sir."

Finally, he could see again. A few afterimages dotted his eyes like the protein deposits that shackled him to eyeglasses. Adjusting his seat, Ulson looked outside again just as Captain Shields came over the frequency.

"Guidons, Six. Move out!"

* * * * *

Chapter Thirty-Six

The gentle mist turned to a cold British rain as Tally rode to meet Andrew and what might lie ahead. Mairin Shields danced through Tally's mind like raindrops swept away by the wind from the autocar's windows. All of that was behind her, as much as she could tell herself believably. At the end of this trip, what would her future be? What about Mairin's? Mairin would likely not survive. She was probably dead in the action at Wolc. Tally pushed the thought from her mind. There'd been nothing from her for several days now. Of course, she'd been ordered to delete any communications from Mairin, but there should have been something. Until there was, she refused to think more about her.

What is waiting for me out there?

The first time that thought crossed her mind, she'd boarded a small, leaky freighter bound for Styrah to leave Andrew Cartner and his father behind. *Ten years*, she thought. Ten years and right back where she'd started. Gripping a handhold, Tallenaara shifted in her seat as the private airfield came into view. Three minutes and she would be taking the step that had haunted her for a decade. In his smile there was love. In his arms, there would be hope.

But for what?

Being able to prolong the Styrahi genome would be a legacy that even her works could not surpass. Buildings rose, and they would come down eventually. Architects were only truly remembered by students. But was it about love, living the life she'd so desperately wanted, or leaving a legacy?

The autocar began to coast downhill towards the terminal. Tally wished for a different music package for the third time in the last hour, and looked into the falling rain. In the droplets arcing across the window, she saw Mairin sitting in the bay window of the cabin watching the rain. Tally closed her eyes, the power of the memory vivid enough she could smell the skin of Mairin's neck against her face. Tears came, and she forced them back until one threatened to streak down her face.

At the terminal, Andrew waited outside. Alone. From a hundred meters away, she knew she loved him. Perhaps that was all that mattered? She'd loved Mairin, but Mairin wasn't Andrew. His power and status meant nothing to Styrahi, except that he'd fallen in love with a Styrahi who might, just might, be able to have his child. *What would it be like*, she thought. She'd have a child soon enough by Styrahi custom, but what if that child were Andrew's?

She flushed at the thought and smiled. The autocar coasted to a stop. When the door opened, cool evening air poured inside. Tally breathed deeply and leaned forward. Andrew's hand appeared, the Prelate's signet ring glinting in the light of the autocar station. She did not hesitate.

"Thank you."

Andrew held her hand as she exited the car then cradled it to his chest. "I was afraid you wouldn't come. I cancelled all outgoing hyperbolics bound for Styrah just in case."

She smiled at the joke, though the glint in his eyes could have meant he was serious. *Surely not.* "I was thinking about Narrob. There are some fabulous vineyards there."

"Indeed." His voice was barely above a whisper. "I am glad you are here."

Tally nodded. "What does this mean for us, Andy?"

"I'm not sure." His eyes never left hers. "Does it matter?"

Tally smiled. "Can we get out of the rain while we figure that out?"

Andrew laughed and led her into the hangar. A sleek twin-tailed Cirrus exocraft waited. The cabin door was open, and there was no one in the spacious hangar but the two of them. "Privacy is hard to come by in this job, Tally."

"I was afraid there would be press."

Andrew laughed. "They think I was flying out of Heathrow bound for Cape Town tonight before heading back to Ireland."

"So we're heading to Cape Town?" Tally tightened her grip on his arm.

"No." Andrew replied and gestured for her to climb the boarding stairs. "Darren can take care of the business in Cape Town tonight. I have approximately two days of rest built into my schedule before leaving for Tuegor."

"And how long will you be gone?

"A week, maybe ten days depending on negotiations and diplomacy." He laughed. "Apparently, they're quite put off by the fact that I continually shy away from their state dinners, and that I've never engaged in sexual congress with their provided hostesses."

Tally laughed and ducked into the cabin. A trim, blue-uniformed flight attendant with Irish red hair curtsied. "Welcome aboard, Lady Tallenaara."

Heat crept to her face. *Damn you, Darren!* "Thank you." She moved into the cabin. A rich mahogany desk bordered the front of the ten-foot-wide and twenty-foot-long cabin. Two plush chairs dominated the interior space with a table and media station between them. A long, sleek sofa covered the back wall of the aircraft. There was art on the walls—Da Vinci and Ford mainly. A posterized sketch of Edison's lightbulb hung above Andrew's desk next to a scowling photograph of Nikola Tesla. All of it classic Andy. The elevation sketch of Frank Lloyd Wright's Fallingwater house surprised her.

"Look familiar?"

Tally nodded. "Like you transformed this vehicle into your dorm room. I like the Fallingwater print."

"Somebody I knew once said I should go and see it. That it was worth my time, effort, and money. You might remember her."

Tally smiled. "You needed a little culture at that point in your life, Andy. Glad to see that a hardcore engineer like you could find it."

Andrew laughed and sat heavily in one of the recliners. He patted the adjacent cushion. "If I have to spend a lot of time in something like this, I expect to feel at home. Besides, this is my personal aircraft. The one I travel in for state functions is ten times the size, and nowhere near as comfortable."

Tally sat, sighed, and turned her head enough to see Andy smiling at her. "What am I doing here, Andy?"

Andy's smile evaporated, and concern broke across his forehead. "What do you mean?"

"I saw you for the first time in ten years less than twelve hours ago, you've asked me to Ireland with you, and against my better judgment, I'm here, wondering what I'm doing. Does that make sense?"

"Perfectly." Andrew leaned back as the aircraft began to taxi. "If you want me to stop the plane...."

Tally shook her head. "No. I want to be here. With you. I'm just wondering what's going to happen in all of this."

Andrew nodded. "I don't know, Tally. But what I can tell you is that since I've learned you were here on Earth, my heart has been lighter, the burden of my work is easier, and I feel like I have a chance at making a difference again. That might be hard to explain, but even a Prelate can be replaced. There's always someone looking for another family to speak for our planet."

Tally squinted. "They were talking of replacing you?"

"I'm sure in some backroom somewhere that conversation has happened a hundred times. From everything I'm hearing now, they're wondering if I've gone mad or suddenly been possessed by the ghost of my father."

"With some obvious differences, I hope?"

"Tally," Andrew reached across and grasped her hand. "In ten years, society has moved from keeping your race at arm's length with idle curiosity to full-blown inclusion. That's faster than any social or cultural group in history. Ten years ago, we were written off as a dalliance, a flight of fancy by two star-crossed young lovers. Now, if we come together again, there are serious ramifications for both of our species. I am aware of that as much as you."

Tally nodded. Both Stryah and Earth needed this union of effort. Duty meant doing things not necessarily pleasant to uphold what is right. Except when duty meant a second chance at something as important as love. She wanted this chance. Meeting Andrew's eyes she squeezed his hand. "I'm not here for my planet, Andy."

"Nor am I," he said. "But I am here for you, and as such I wanted to show you something spectacular tonight."

Tally smiled. "I was hoping for jazz music and good wine like old times."

"I can do that." Andrew laughed as the plane lifted off the runway and began to climb. "We'll turn down the lights; I have the whole catalog of Dave Brubeck, Benny Goodman, Glenn Miller and all of the others you made me listen to onboard. A glass of red wine will arrive momentarily. For now, tell me about Libretto."

So she did, leaving out the last couple of months and Mairin altogether. "It's as close to Earth as any planet you've been to. It's the best work I've ever been involved with. And I built a cabin there...." She paused and pushed a last thought of Mairin from her mind. "I'd love to go back there one day."

"It sounds heavenly in a way, and the right place for our men and women in uniform to seek as sanctuary when they can't get here." Andrew gestured to the hostess for their wine. "Are you all right?"

"I've just met so many of them headed to war. It's hard sometimes to think about."

Andrew nodded, but said nothing. After a long pause and several sips of wine, he squeezed her hand lightly. "We just try to do our best for them."

Tally nodded. Her voice was thick with emotion, and she hated herself for the thoughts in her head. "They deserve that little piece of home."

"Of course they do." Andrew looked out the window for a moment. "Ah, yes! We're climbing up over the Pole right now. The aurora borealis should be visible any second." Andrew dimmed the cabin lights and "String of Pearls" played softly from the speakers as the ethereal sheets of green and yellow rippled across the sky. "This is my favorite accessory." Andrew grinned as he pushed a button on his console and the cabin disappeared slowly, the illusion perfectly removing the very chairs they remained belted to.

Tally gasped and smiled. "Almost like flying."

"Technically, we are flying," Andrew quipped, and she chuckled. So little had really changed. "I like to think of it as near-space-walking."

The curtains of energy pulsated to the music as Tally sipped the rich wine and felt a wide smile developing on her face. Andrew's warm hand caressed her own. He'd wanted to share this with her. She'd wanted to share so much with him. A lifetime ago and yet today. Awash in the wonders of Earth, Tally fell into Andrew's arms.

They kissed slowly, as if searching each other's desire. She could feel Andrew's cheeks wet against her own. Her tears came to mingle with his and she hated herself for wondering if she were really, truly happy with Andrew, or if she was crying for the love she'd undoubtedly lost to the horrors of war.

Alone with her thoughts in the shimmering aurora, Tallenaara fell asleep in Andrew's arms.

* * * * *

Chapter Thirty-Seven

Night fell as they'd assaulted the objective. The Greys didn't put up much of a fight when Mairin's vehicles shot over the hill and into the main position. A few hundred rounds of ammunition and then it was quiet. Rolling into the enemy position, what had been thousands of vehicles, avatars of Earthly tanks from history, sat burning slowly into the ground. Some showed the scars of battle damage, while others appeared to have melted in place. Looking around, Mairin saw no bodies, only burning and melted metal.

"Alex, are you seeing this?" Mairin chinned her direct frequency. "What do you make of it?"

Ulson came back a few seconds later. "No bodies at all. Their vehicles slagged the moment we gained the advantage. Who fights like this?"

"Slagged?"

"They look like slag piles, don't they? They self-destruct. God, they smell, too."

Mairin blinked at the reality of it even as she wrinkled her nose to the stench of burning shit, the smell of the Greys molten slag piles. *Who fights like this?* "What's our status?"

Slammer Four had lost a repulsor, and One's secondary machine gun was shot off by a Grey tank round before they slagged. Rumors flew over the intelligence nets that the regiment was vulnerable, and the Greys were pulled back and preparing a counterattack. Mairin put her vehicles into a defensive perimeter and sat down to wait. By the time the regiment arrived to replace Mairin's five vehicles, a Grey counterattack was reported to be imminent. Mairin and her command were sent away from the position and told to guard the flank where they'd assaulted. In sheer boredom, she'd allowed Ulson to fetch the disabled Slammer Three. A little bribery to the regimental maintenance team and Three was at least moving now, albeit slowly.

By the time Wolc's star—a reddish-yellow monster some one hundred and thirty million miles away—rose in the sky, the entire regiment was so silent that Mairin suspected they'd collectively fallen asleep. If the Greys were to attack, it could be a slaughter. But they weren't coming. At first light, Mairin stared at the slag piles where the thousands of Grey tanks once stood. They hadn't retreated at all; they'd terminated themselves at the first sign of weakness. The retreat was their transport ship, or mother ship or whatever its tactical designation was, and Mairin wondered for a moment where they might be headed. *Not your concern*, she told herself silently.

When she could see the horizon to the east, Mairin dismounted the tank and walked around her vehicles slowly. Meeting her weary soldiers gave her a pleasant, satisfied feeling. She asked them how they felt, when they'd eaten, if they'd been able to sleep. Soldierly things. She did so on autopilot, almost like someone else was talking. While not the truth, she knew that genuinely caring for her troops would earn her greater respect than anything else. A light breeze touched her face, clearing away the smoke for a moment and replacing it with the sweet smell of blooming flowers in the distance. She shook away visions of the clamshell cabin on Libretto, and breathed deeply. The stench of burning Grey vehicles returned strong enough that she almost covered her mouth with her sleeve.

Staring back down the valley she'd attacked through, her eyes came to rest on a smoldering wreck. What could she do about that? She didn't even know them, and they'd died under her command! Instead of walking back to her track, Mairin unslung her pulse rifle and held it at the ready, barrel down, and made her way down the hill.

Walking felt different with the weight of her combat coveralls, helmet, and the reassuring heft of the pulse rifle, yet instead of clunking her way through the thick forest, there was a grace to her movement. Every impact of her feet nearly silent as she moved, her eyes up and alert to all of the sounds and movement around her as she crept down the hill towards Slammer Two. The breeze freshened, and she could smell the burning rubber and fluids from the tank. The Grey slagpiles were cold, dead, and stagnant. One moment breathing fire and moving like mosquitos, and the next unrecognizable and simply there.

The putridness of the smell turned her stomach. *Was this the smell of death?* Mairin shook her head to clear the thought as she emerged from the treeline, now just four hundred meters away from the remains of Slammer Two. She stopped abruptly and knelt as her vision blurred a little. Light-headed, she placed a gloved hand on the soil to steady herself. Fingers on her throbbing temple, Mairin felt herself falling backwards into a sitting position.

What have I done? Four men she'd barely met, and didn't know their names, were dead because of her! She wasn't a leader, much less a cavalryman! *What am I doing here*? The tears came, and she hated herself for letting them roll over her burning cheeks, but she did. For a minute or so, that's all she did. *Breathe, Mairin. Just breathe.*

Okay, she thought. You're still alive and that counts for something. She blinked and nodded to herself. That's right. Yes, I lost one vehicle, but five others survived, and we counterattacked a superior force and won. Don't.... She sniffled and said it aloud. "Don't get ahead of yourself, Mairin. There's quite a bit of luck in what you did."

That's a better way of thinking about this. You did good with what you had, but there's a lot here that's out of your control. Don't ever forget that. Combat is about the random. Take it in and center yourself. This is the reality of your situation. Understand where you are, and doing the rest is easy. They were the coherent thoughts in the back of her addled mind, but she grabbed onto them with both hands and held on tight. The whispers guided her. Place the humane things into a compartment and seal it until later. For now, there was a mission, and there were people to take care of. That was what mattered. She looked at the smoldering tank and rose to her feet slowly. It's also about doing your duty. There wasn't anything that she could do. The simple fact of the matter was that she was the commander and needed to fully destroy the vehicle. There would be no recovery of remains. Standing orders were to destroy all equipment and remains wherever they lie. Helluva way to care for your brothers.

She stayed upwind of the Slammer as she approached. Removing two thermite grenades, she carefully slid one down the relatively pristine gun barrel of the Slammer. She didn't hear the grenade cook off inside the breech as she went to the rear deck of the tank and rigged a thermite grenade above the repulsor drive system. She pulled the grenade and dismounted quickly, jogging back a good hundred meters to watch the thermite take hold and begin melting the composite armor and components into an unrecognizable mass.

The hum of an approaching vehicle floated on the wind. Over her shoulder, she confirmed it was a friendly tank and turned her attention back to the smoldering Slammer and its crew. The first time she heard her name, she ignored it. Her mourning was too important for the orders and regimentation of the Terran Defense Forces. When she heard her name screamed a second time, her stomach tightened and sweat stung the corners of her eyes.

"Goddamn it, Captain! Get over here and report to me!"

Mairin turned and walked toward the command track, shoulders back and head erect as she took her time. At the front left slope of the track she yelled, "Permission to come aboard, sir?"

"Get your ass up here!" Coffey screamed. His tank began to shut down as he did, and she could hear his voice echoing through the trees.

Mairin did as she was told, assuming the position of attention at the edge of the sloping turret. Coffey jumped up out of the commander's hatch and stood on the front slope. Even with the extra twenty-four inches of height, he didn't exactly tower over her. And she could smell alcohol permeating the air between them. "Sir?"

"I told you to report to me!" Coffey screamed. Veins bulged on his neck and his eyes squinted.

Mairin saluted. *Sniper check*, she thought and nearly laughed out loud. "Sir, Captain Shields reports to the regimental commander."

"Who the fuck ordered you into this valley?" Coffey snapped a precise salute and crossed his arms.

Mairin swallowed. "No one did, sir. I attempted to gain the initiative."

"I don't want you to gain the initiative, Shields! Do you read me? I told you to stay put! Be the goddamn reserve. You almost cost us the whole fucking battle!"

Mairin felt her face getting warm. "Cost you the battle, sir? I think what we did here changed the outcome of the battle."

"For them!" Coffey sneered. "Your little grandstanding attempt may have gained the notice of the powers that be, but you disobeyed my orders! I'll see to it that you're out of this command by nightfall."

"Disobeyed your orders, sir? Just exactly how drunk are you?" Mairin asked and immediately bit her lip. "You cut me off, put me in a position where my troopers were exactly worthless with six of the best combat vehicles in our command. You cut me off from the Operations and Intelligence nets! I had to plead with the air wings for support because I couldn't contact you! So don't sit there, sir, and tell me that I disobeyed orders. You left my troopers out there to rot, and if it wasn't for us, you'd still be in a goddamn line abreast formation getting your ass handed to you by a superior enemy force with better standoff weapons!" Mairin stopped, seeing that Coffey looked absolutely purple. *You've done it now, Grandpa!*

Coffey looked out over the horizon and then back at Mairin. His eyes locked onto the combat action badge and airborne wings on her chest. "Oh fuck! You're one of those imprints! No fucking wonder you think you're Jane Wayne!" He grabbed the collar of her tunic and stopped. His gaze narrowed on her necklace. "The next time I see you, that shit better be gone. I will not have a herm-lover in this unit."

Mairin blinked. After what I said, he's worried about that? What the hell am I going to do now? "Your orders, sir?"

Coffey stepped back and looked at her. "This discussion stays between us. One word to a higher officer, Shields, and I will have you drummed out of this regiment within the hour. Do you understand?"

Mairin nodded. "You realize this skirmish will be reviewed, sir."

"I'll worry about that." Coffey stepped into her face. The stench was enough that she was sure he'd fought most of the battle blind drunk. "You do anything like you did here, even if you win the whole fucking war, and I'll kill you myself for insubordination. Is that clear?"

"Perfectly," Mairin answered. *Not to mention perfectly illegal.* Mairin wished she'd engaged her neural recording, even if it was against TDF regulations. "Permission to rejoin my troopers, sir?"

"Troopers? You think you're the fucking cavalry or something?"

Mairin met his gaze. "We're the regimental cavalry troop, sir. I suggest you man us appropriately before the next battle."

Coffey snorted and then nodded. "I can make that work, Shields. Get the fuck off my tank."

What did I just do? Hell, what the fuck just happened? She climbed down the tank and glanced at the driver who smiled through a grimy face and goggles. He gave her a thumbs-up as the command track turned and headed back up the ridgeline at high speed. *Oh God,* she thought as cold sweat ran down her back. She knelt on the ground as nausea reared in her stomach and she vomited last night's rations into the tall grass. She felt her chest hitch and let the sob come. She knew why she was crying, yet at the same time, she didn't know why. Enormity crashed on her shoulders and she retched again. All of it was too much. Too much.

Oh, God, oh, God, she thought and realized that on top of everything, she'd likely lost Tally. Scanning her neurals, there was nothing from Tally in the last week. Knowing that it was over brought a new sob, but she did not vomit. No, she would get control of it all. This, this was all she really had now. And she knew that she'd done well. She removed Tally's necklace and laid it on the ground by Slammer Two. There was no way it would ever be the way it was again. *I love you, Tally, but we're not meant to be.*

It was probably for the best anyway. She'd likely be dead before her term of service would expire and where would that leave Tally? Alone and pining for a love she'd had and lost somewhere along the way. Maybe they'd meet again someday. Maybe Tally would be proud of her. Maybe Tally would remember her. Wiping her nose on the sleeve of her coveralls, Mairin looked at Slammer Two and set her jaw. This wouldn't happen again. Any of it. Her troopers would have a fighting chance next time.

But what about me?

Next time, she'd know that love was fleeting. No, there would not be a next time. Her stomach felt a little better as she stood and saluted the burning remnants of Slammer Two. *Goodbye,* cariad. Mairin whispered it to the wind and felt a little better. *You're not a soldier until you've been heartbroken*, she thought with a grimace. *Welcome to the club, Mairin.*

"Shut up, Grandpa." She spat into the dirt and turned to walk away. The sun punched through the low clouds and fog for a moment and warmed her face. She'd once hoped that she could honorably serve, but now knew that honorable service wasn't enough. Leading her troops and keeping them safe from harm would have to be enough. That was all that mattered in this stupid war.

Walking through the woodline, hearing the sounds of creatures in the trees and catching the occasional scent of pine as she ducked under limbs, Mairin realized even here and now, there were small things to celebrate. She was alive, as were most of her troopers. They'd fought a superior force and won, with effort and a little good luck. She saw a small purple flower and stopped to finger it softly. Cordite in her nostrils and blood on her hands, she stopped on the battlefield to smell the flowers and squashed the laugh that threatened to erupt from her tight throat.

She thought of her troopers, and Tally, and whatever else awaited them. Maybe it would be like a flower on the battlefield—a singular spot of beautiful precision in a field of chaos and destruction.

There's always hope, she thought.

* * * * *

Chapter Thirty-Eight

Six months later...

The Greys advanced inside the Outer Rim, but the attack on Rayu-4 never materialized. Losses at the Wolc, Radin, and Narrob colonies revealed obvious failures in the TDF strategic campaign. Though Mairin proved that simple tactics and smart maneuvering could be employed on a small scale, the TDF knew when the Greys left the field, they were still superior in force and capable of holding the TDF at bay. There was hope, though.

Coordinated defensive strategies and dedicated close air support proved deadly. Now it was time to bring the Greys back to the fight. Drawing them in, to a time and place of the defenders choosing, dated to Sun Tzu and his predecessors. Historically, the tactic continued to work in human conflict throughout the twenty-first century. There was no indication that, against a superiorly numbered force like the Greys, the tactic would not work as advertised again.

The idea of playing defense and then attacking struck Mairin as being stupid. The enemy was superior in numbers but seemingly slow to react to counteroffensive operations. Maneuver challenged the Greys as it had for anyone not raised in the Spartan army throughout history. *Terrain, the plan itself, or some other unplanned for contingency slowed down the plan*, she told herself. *Be it a soldier, an element, a platoon, or a division there will always be a hole in the line.* There would always be an opportunity for success, and because of that the probability for a counterattack at that precise point was statistically significant no matter how many times she ran the numbers. In the defense, there were too many things that could go wrong when trying to produce a counterattack, especially with poor leadership.

Mairin studied the battle plan for the defense of the colony planet Ashland and looked at her four platoon leaders. She could smell the academy on the three new ones. *Bright-eyed, bushy-tailed and ready to follow every order to completion without fully understanding it*, she thought wryly. *One will get lost, one will forget to shower and shave daily, and one will find every last nerve when it comes to asking "Why?" like a toddler.* She looked across at Ulson and noticed for the hundredth time his change from boy to man. He'd "seen the elephant" so to speak, and in his calm, experienced eyes Mairin saw leadership. She felt a little surer of the forces at her fingertips, and fortunately for the lieutenants under her leadership, a little more patient.

"So, what's the plan, Captain?"

Mairin met the walleyed gaze of Lieutenant Thornton. "You went to the Academy, isn't that right, Thornton?"

"Yes, ma'am." He grinned showing imperfect teeth. Combined with his heavy eyebrows and bulging eyes, he looked like a sideshow attraction. "Graduated in April, but didn't get selected for pilot training."

Five months. Sonuvabitch. Probably rushed through officer training in a hurry by the TDF to fill gaps. Mairin sighed and raised her gaze to the group. "Everyone has seen this, right?" Heads nodded. She blinked the mission timer in her neurals. "We have fourteen hours until we drop on Ashland. You've all given warning orders to your platoons and, based on what we discuss here, my expectation is that you will go back to your platoons and brief an operations order that will detail the plan as we know it. You're going to do that by something called the one-thirds, two-thirds rule. Anybody know what that is?"

Ulson was the only one who raised his hand. "I develop my plan in one-third of the time remaining to the mission and give my sergeants the other time to do what they need to do to have the soldiers and vehicles ready."

"Correct." Mairin smiled. "Lieutenant Ulson is the executive officer of the company as well as being the first platoon leader. He'll help watch over supplies, logistics, and personnel. If you need something, see him." Mairin laid out a printed map of their mission corridor. "Now, nobody get this dirty. I had to bribe the supply officer for the paper to actually print this out instead of trying to do this over your video screens. I'm old-fashioned."

The group chuckled as Mairin began to speak. She'd just finished laying out their first halt position after the drop when Ulson got her attention. "Down the passageway. It's him."

Mairin nodded, her lips tight as she wondered what possible damage Lieutenant Colonel Coffey could do now. When Coffey hit the unit area, she heard newly-promoted First Sergeant Livingston call the troop to attention. Mairin left the Lieutenants at the table and marched up to the commander. As she did, she realized that Coffey hadn't told the company to "carry on" or "relax" or anything. *Chickenshit*, she thought as she stopped three paces away. "Sir, welcome to Alpha Troop. What can I do for you today?"

Coffey scowled as she saluted and took his time returning it. "You know why I'm here, Shields?"

Mairin heard his echo off the bulkheads. This was starting well. Usually he had the presence of mind to chew her out in private and not in front of her troops. At least there wasn't a smell of alcohol on his breath. Maybe he was drinking vodka now. "Sir, I'd assume to discuss our concept of the operation?"

"You assume wrong!" Coffey snarled. "I'm here because for the fourth time in the past week, you've completely ignored a directive on my behalf from the regimental training officer that all of your soldiers must complete the mandatory briefing on consideration of other species! How dare you flaunt my directive? Are you stupid or just soft in the head?"

Mairin flushed. "Consideration of other species training is hardly something I'd call mandatory in the middle of war, sir."

"Goddamnit, Shields! I'm the commander and I make the fucking rules! You and the rest of your unit will stand-down all operations and complete this training! Is that clear?"

"Stand down? Sir, we're fourteen hours from drop." Mairin bit her tongue for wanting to tell Coffey that if he ever referred to her troopers as a unit with that tone of voice again, he'd eat from a straw for a month.

"Not until you finish that training!"

Mairin shook her head. "You'll have no eyes, sir. Without some cavalry in front of you—"

"I don't give a shit!" Coffey fumed. "I won Wolc without your assistance and I can win this fight too! You will not, and I mean absolutely will not, destroy my readiness reporting numbers for any reason! Your unit will be locked in this ship until you complete that mandatory training! Do you hear me?"

The man is delusional! "Loud and clear." Mairin paused deliberately, staring at the smaller man. "Sir."

Coffey spun on his heels. "What the fuck are you people staring at? Get your asses into that training module! Now!"

Mairin watched him go. Her clenched fists began to ache as Livingston approached her. "First Sergeant?"

"Yes, ma'am?"

A thought came and Mairin grinned. "You ever heard of checking the block?"

"No, ma'am I haven't. Should I have?" He broke into a slight smile.

Mairin lowered her voice. "Find out what we have to do for this stupid training. Most likely we have to review a presentation of some type on an individual basis. Set up a rotation so we conduct pre-combat checks and inspections while we're conducting the training. Get us to one hundred percent complete as fast as possible with the least amount of bullshit. You see what I mean?"

"Ma'am, we'll be one hundred percent complete in the next six hours." Livingston yelled for the platoon sergeants to assemble.

"Top, don't get me wrong on this. All training has importance, but in the middle of a war we shouldn't be doing stupid bullshit training like this. In these situations, we do what good soldiers do. Conduct the training, but do not waste any unnecessary time on it. How you get it done is your business."

Livingston nodded, "I understand. That's what good sergeants do."

Mairin smiled and walked away. Not bad for a very newly minted first sergeant. He might actually end up being a true first sergeant before this war was over. Walking back to her lieutenants, Mairin felt at once disappointed in the Terran Defense Forces and happy that at least her unit wasn't chickenshit. The trouble was that every unit turned chickenshit at some point. Commanders who concentrated on the minutia of training and operations usually had rough, ready troops. Those who fostered garrison princesses with spit-polished boots and perfect filing systems had soft, unreliable bunkhouse lawyers for troops, able to talk their way out of anything because being a soldier first simply wasn't their job. Striking a balance between the two was the ultimate challenge for military leaders throughout history. The most successful ones were not always the most balanced.

What would Patton have thought about me? She almost laughed.

Surrounded by her officers, Mairin laid out her guidance to the first sergeant. "It's really simple, folks. We do the training that is prescribed for us, but not in a way that will affect our readiness. Send your troopers to the range, to the conduct of fire trainer, and every other training aid we have. Complete the mandatory shit when we have to."

"Seems awfully reactionary to me, ma'am," Thornton said. "Why don't we just lay out a plan to conduct all of the mandatory training ahead of time?"

Mairin sighed. "Proactivity is a great thing, Thornton. The problem is that in the Army being proactive tends to mean you end up doing things twice because inevitably what you do is not what someone at headquarters wants you to do, therefore you have to repeat everything. The success of command is simple—do the important things quickly, the critical things immediately, and the rest when somebody tells you to and not before."

Thornton and the rest of the lieutenants laughed. Mairin smiled. "Now let me get off my soapbox and back to work." She paused for a moment, showing her game face and then spoke. "Ashland is a smaller planet than Wolc and the terrain is much more open. We're talking lava flows and small hills. Not going to be any real cover or concealment. We've been ordered into a defensive posture, which means that right now combat engineers are down there trying to dig positions for us while the orbital gun platforms attempt to keep the Greys from attacking Port Selkirk. Intelligence suggests the Greys want to take out the port."

One of the other lieutenants, a sandy-haired boy named MacDougal asked, "What's so special about the port, Captain?"

"Natural resources." Mairin gestured at the map. "Primarily precious metals and the like. Remember, this is a volcanically active planet, much more so than Earth but not nearly as bad as Io. Molten ores and precious metals are what brought miners here during the colonization push. Given what we know about the Greys and their vehicles, this is a place where they can get an almost infinite supply of resources."

MacDougal nodded, "Are the Grey vehicles really Russian T-55s?"

Ulson replied. "No, they only look like T-55s. Why the Greys chose the T-55 design is beyond anyone, but what matters is the Grey version has a much better gun, uses repulsors for primary movement, and in the open it's fast." He pointed to the map. "On terrain like this, maneuver has a serious advantage."

He even sounds like a professional soldier, Mairin thought with something she recognized as pride. As strange as it felt, she enjoyed it. "He's right." Mairin pointed at the map. "We're supposed to be here, in a defensive line along the eastern flank. I've recommended we perform a screen mission, essentially keeping the enemy at least partially focused on us. We'll move across the sector about five thousand meters from the regiment. This is important because, given the size of Ashland, we'll be essentially operating at the very edge of the visible limit to the regiment. When the Greys decide to light us up, the regiment will know. We'll withdraw back towards our position and, if the Greys follow that path, the obstacles and mines being laid by the engineers will take some of them out before they become a threat to the regiment."

"We'll have a path through those obstacles?" Thornton asked.

Mairin nodded. "That's your job, Lieutenant. You're going to have to liaise with the engineer company and get the path marked for us. From what we know, the Greys don't employ scouts, so they won't really see what we're doing out there. We just have to be in position and cause the Greys to give away their dispersion and strategy in advance. We relay that information to regiment and then get out of Dodge."

"So we're expecting to get hit?" Lieutenant Mayers asked quietly. "I'm not sure I like that approach, ma'am."

Mairin looked at him for a long second. The soft-spoken kid from Indiana seemed scared, but Mairin sensed there was an intelligence weighing the risks and looking carefully at the odds for survival. "Understand, Mayers, that getting hit is not sitting there and firing weapons at standoff distances at one another until we die in place. We're going to defend ourselves enough to let them know we're there, and then withdraw by fire, getting them to follow us. We'll take some fire, and we'll give some, but we're not going to sit there and duke it out with them."

Mayers nodded. "I'd assume that, as we withdraw, we'll try to alternate movements?"

"Bounding. You got it." Mairin nodded at him. "That's your job, Mayers. You and MacDougal will bound back providing cover for Thornton and Ulson to lead us out the path. Ulson will take care of aerial overwatch. I'm expecting the Greys to have realized the importance of air support." Mairin looked at them. "Okay, that's what I have for you now. Any questions?"

There were none. "Be back here in an hour, and we'll review the plan and do a map rehearsal. Thornton and Ulson, make your coordinations with the engineers and the flyboys. We've got a lot of work to do. Get your plans done and get some sleep."

Thornton squinted. "Where are you headed, ma'am?"

"To do exactly what I told you to do, Thornton. You may be up for twenty-four hours this mission. Good soldiers sleep any time and any place they can. I suggest you do the same."

* * * * *

Chapter Thirty-Nine

The media firestorm fizzled out after only a few weeks, much to Tallenaara's delight. Though the circumstances of a horrific tsunami that engulfed the main islands of the Philippine Free State peeled the cameras away from her new apartment, adjusting to the attention was difficult. With her required security detail, resuming a more normal daily life of teaching and mentoring fit her like a proverbial glove, and she relished the opportunity to be just another professor instead of the next Prelate Consort of Earth.

The afternoon clouds parted for a bit as the breeze freshened. Spring arrived with warmth and less rain than the typical British winter season. Office windows open to the cool air, she sat twiddling a light pen above her desk at the unfinished building design she'd started two hours ago before her attention wandered. She stared at the two-carat diamond ring on her finger, a silly, beautiful tradition of Earth, and watched the light explode in rainbow shimmers and mirrored reflections.

Andrew had asked her to marry him on the golden coast of Australia after a day diving the Great Barrier Reef. The sun setting to the west, the sound of kookaburras in the coastal trees, and his warm hand on the small of her back as they walked along the deserted beach. She'd slipped into a sundress, something vaguely like the ceremonial robes of Styrah but functionally better for humans. Andrew had rolled up his khaki pants and the sleeves of his dark blue shirt without a word. He'd been distracted and nervous all day. Even to the point she'd had to remind him, with a persistent tugging of his wetsuit, that he needed to relax and decompress before surfacing from their last dive. Neither spoke for a long time as they walked.

"What's been on your mind all day?"

Andrew smiled with a touch of color in his cheeks. "Have I seemed distracted?"

"Very much so," Tallenaara replied. "Is something worrying you?"

"Besides the fifty million problems I seem to have inherited and deal with on a daily basis?" Andrew looked out to sea. "Yes, something is worrying me."

They stopped walking and Tallenaara stepped in front of him. "Then tell me."

Andrew took her hands in his and sighed. "I've been thinking a lot about my father recently. What he would have said about us as the world changed. I wish he could see how happy I am."

"I think he wanted you to be happy, Andy."

"He did." Andrew curled his upper lip slightly. "And I think when he died, he knew I realized I'd made a mistake and should have stood up to him."

Tallenaara shrugged. "You can't take back those years, Andy. You have to lay that burden down."

Andrew chuckled. "I have laid it down, Tally. Never to pick it up again."

"Then what's on your mind, love?"

"It's quite hard to describe actually." Andrew smiled. "There's really not a good way to put it with words." He stepped away but held her hands tightly. "I'd planned to take you to a fabulous restaurant in Beijing tonight, but somehow this is better."

"What are you talking about, Andrew?" Tallenaara smiled and cocked her head to one side.

Andrew looked in her eyes for a few seconds, sighed, and knelt in the sand. He pulled a hand back and reached into his pocket. "I'm not meaning to surprise you, Tally. I know we've talked about this a little."

Gods, Tally thought and bit her bottom lip slightly. "Andy, are you...."

He pulled out the ring and held it up on a line between their eyes. "Will you marry me, Tallenaara?"

There were doubts, concerns, and reasons not to. She'd played them over in her mind the first time he'd mentioned her as the Prelate Consort to be. Staring at the ring and Andy's hopeful eyes, she knew the doubts, concerns and reasons not to simply didn't matter. Her hearts thumped with such force that she barely heard herself respond. "Yes. Yes, I'll marry you Andy."

"You know what this will mean?" Andy asked.

Tallenaara nodded. "I do. And I won't like it."

"But," Andrew coaxed.

"I'll have you," she answered with a smile. And it had felt perfect and right.

Yet, sitting in the afternoon sun and smiling at her gorgeous ring, her thoughts turned to Mairin. What would she say? Would she be happy or sad? Did she bother to think about them and their time on Libretto? What would she think when she saw the press coverage? All of her efforts to contact Mairin were unanswered, and while she was capable of getting the information from a variety of sources close to Andrew, she hadn't asked anyone for Mairin's sake.

Without news to the contrary, it was just as likely that Mairin had died along with the thirty thousand soldiers on Wolc. That's when the messages stopped. The casualty lists gave her no definitive information. Without that contact, she knew it was possible that she'd died in the ferocious battle. Andrew called it a pyrrhic victory, a victory at great cost. *He has no idea how great*, Tallenaara thought. *I wish I could have given you something so beautiful, Mairin. I hope your soul rests well on the fields of Elysium, or Valhalla, wherever you will go.* Time for grieving would soon be over, though it was private and borne alone. She sighed. Her fiancé needed her, and she realized with equal importance that she needed him. For that she was thankful to the Council for sending her here. Somehow, they'd known what was best for her.

The vidphone sounded off, announcing a subspace call on Andrew's private line. "Hello?"

"Lady Tallenaara!" Darren McMasters.

"Hello, Darren. What's going on?"

McMasters smiled. "One of my official jobs seems to be messenger for the Prelate's Consort to be." He nodded. "Andrew asked me to call you. He's still in conference with the Tueg delegation. Frankly, I'm not sure how much longer he may be in there."

"Are things going badly?"

McMasters grin became tight. "They're not going as well as we'd hoped, no. Obviously I can't speak to it now on this connection. Just know that Andrew will be in touch as soon as he can be. I have about ten seconds before this connection ends. Any message?"

"Just my love and we'll talk soon." The connection faded to an image of the Prelate's sigil and then a blank screen. Tallenaara frowned and wondered just how bad it could be. Were the Tuegs really considering a withdrawal from the Legion? Absently, she cued her desk to review Tuegan architectural designs. For all their diplomatic prowess and ethics, they were not the most artistic species.

She'd never been to Tueg, and had never really even thought of going. The amount of genetic remapping needed to breathe the Tueg atmosphere was substantial, for one thing, and the climate was less than desirable, absolutely hell on everything but the soil. Still, the impressive architecture the Tuegs created out of their version of adobe bricks gave many species, particularly equatorial dwellings humans, new ideas about ecologically sound and temperate lodging. A majority of Tueg cities resembled massive cliff dwellings, and in their close quarters they developed the ability to make lasting peace.

As a result, they'd been a reluctant partner in the war effort for the last couple of years, and as the Greys continued to advance through the galaxy, the Tuegs clamored more and more for diplomacy. When the first Tueg colony, a small watery planet named Ghratanon in the Vega sector, was attacked by Grey skirmishers, the Tuegs agreed to muster their militias in support of Legion objectives, and they'd fought honorably to this point. And now they were wanting to step away?

Tally's brow furrowed. There was much about Andrew's position he did not share with her, and rightly so. *Those in charge of anything often carry burdens they wish no one else to bear*, one of her teachers had said long ago. Still, with the first victory against the Greys secured despite heavy losses by the forces at Wolc six months ago still ringing across the galaxy, a sudden departure from the Legion seemed strange, if not suspicious. *There must be a reason for this.* She frowned. Andrew would have to go there, a diplomatic visit. At least three months, counting fold time. The semester would end in four weeks. Maybe she'd go along with him? Her first state visit as the Prelate Consort.

She snorted softly. For all of the happiness the thought gave her, the weight and attention of the position were maddeningly disconcerting. Long days at the cabin on Libretto, the long walks, and quiet days working, were of a peacefulness she would never know again. Now, there would be requests, interviews, duties, and responsibilities that, while challenging and engaging, were not the same as being able to simply be. But what if her being was being with Andrew? Would that truly make everything all right? And what if...what if she did have his child? Would that change anything? Or everything?

Maybe what they needed was a diplomatic vacation to Tueg? She laughed. *What else would they do for a month in foldspace?* At least Andrew's ship would be guaranteed to be under gravity the entire trip, unlike that nasty freighter she'd ridden to Styrah.

The vidphone rang again. She picked it up at once and Andrew smiled at her. "Andy."

"I have about a minute, Tally. Do you miss me?"

She grinned. "You know I do."

"Then come out here. To the moon." Andrew grinned again. "I'm in the Presidential Suite at Armstrong. There's a flight from London in an hour."

"I have classes, Andy."

"One tomorrow, and I've already got it covered for you. You can message the exams to yourself and grade them here over the weekend." His smile softened a little. "I really miss you."

Tally smiled. *Oh dammit. That was too easy.* "Of course I'll be there."

"In about eight hours." Andrew grinned again. "I'll be expecting you. And I have your luggage. I love you."

The words made her tingle. "I love you." She blew a kiss like a little child as the connection terminated. Collecting her things took barely a minute, and she left her academic office. She'd make the afternoon maglev easily. And it would figure that he'd taken a bag for her. Was it thoughtful or devious? She smiled. Knowing Andrew, it was a bit of both.

* * * * *

Chapter Forty

Lieutenant Commander Donovan Garrett checked for lint on his Fleet blue tunic, rapped twice on the admiral's stateroom door, and waited. After a few seconds of silence, the door opened and he heard the admiral rasp, "Get in here, Garrett."

The stateroom lighting, dimmed to near non-existence, emphasized the heavily shielded window looking out along the *Ticonderoga's* frame. Moving at seventeen *c*, every once in a while a star appeared to blur into the thin streak of light that Hollywood still used in its movies to show faster than light travel. The Admiral sat facing the window, sipping from his coffee mug. "Pull up a chair, Don."

"Thank you, sir." Garrett sat and relaxed. He ran a hand across his slightly longer than regulation black hair and pointed at the coffee tumbler. "May I?"

"Always. Get a dose of the good stuff for us both, too." Admiral Nather handed his mug to Garrett.

Garrett found the Bushmill's hidden under the coffee urn and poured a generous shot into both fresh mugs of coffee. They stared into the starfield for a good two minutes before the Admiral spoke again. "I could sit and watch this all day. Makes me forget the shitstorm I seem to have inherited."

Garrett smiled and nodded. "I feel the same way some days."

"You don't have to deal with that idiot Coffey on a regular basis."

Garrett understood. The fact that the Terran Defense Council forced Nather to accept the role of carrying a regiment of ground forces added fuel to the Admiral's slow-burning temper. Coffey's constant diversion of resources to create his own special operations forces, seemingly endless personnel issues requiring flag-rank initiated transfers, and Coffey's attitude grated on most of the *Ticonderoga's* senior staff. "What would you like me to do, sir?"

Nather looked at Garrett for a moment as if studying him for the first time. "For the moment, nothing. Nothing at all."

Garrett blinked. "I assumed you'd want my help in looking over him. You know they're going to promote him soon, right?"

Nather shook his head. "He's Terran Defense Force and his chain of command doesn't run through this stateroom. He's a loose cannon we're going to haul and drop into combat operations. This little experiment is not something I'm comfortable with at all. Put an eagle on his collar and it legitimizes his antics."

"This isn't any different than hauling Marines back in the day."

Nather glared. "Marines listened to the Navy in transit and fell under the chain of command of the Navy. This dichotomy between ground forces and aerospace forces is the single biggest reason I think we'll have our asses handed to us. You can bet Coffey will not stand for or allow any type of cooperation that might dim his reputation."

Garrett sipped his spiked coffee. Truth was, the admiral was right. Despite the intention of the TDC, the commanders of the ground and space forces clearly believed their force was the choice for winning this war. Both of them had clearly told their subordinate commanders to keep their cards close to the vest and not allow the other force too much insight. The tactic wasn't a successful way to fight a war. "We'll be alongside the *Moskva* in a week. That will be a welcome respite."

Nather nodded. "The Russians at least give us a ground force we can actually count on. The problem is whatever happens on the surface, Coffey assumes command and then takes credit or places blame. "

"What would you like me to do?"

"Your job, Don. Let your interceptors and bombers deliver the mail and keep this ship protected. Work with Coffey as you have to, and support Colonel Manakov. I expect by the time we reach Rayu-4 we'll have a good idea of what to expect from Coffey, and a better idea of how we'll perform in combat from Manakov."

Garrett shook his head and chuckled. "They always told us history repeated itself. I can't remember any clusterfuck like this situation in our history, sir. Can you? I mean bad intelligence, mule-headed commanders." He paused. "At least we have some good allies."

Nather smiled. "I'd take a battalion of Styrahi over Coffey's ragtag regiment any day. There are way too many newly hatched officers and not enough non-coms to do their jobs."

"Coffey's problems don't stop there."

"I'm aware of the drinking on duty, and I've reported it to TDF headquarters. There's been no response. I'm learning more and more about his anti-Styrahi attitudes with every personnel transfer. There are no more in his regiment now. He's effectively signed his own death warrant."

Garrett snorted. "That's assuming he'll even honor the threat, sir."

Nather nodded, but said nothing.

Garrett turned his eyes back to the passing starfield. A bright streak of light caught his eye in the distance and, for the briefest of moments, he pictured the bridge of a ship in an old movie—or was it a holoshow—and frowned. He finished his coffee, setting the mug on the table between their chairs. "Anything else for me, sir?"

"I'm promoting you to CAG, effective immediately."

"I beg your pardon, sir?" *Commander Air Group?*

Nather smiled. "I'm bringing you up to CAG for a reason, Don. I know you have something for me, and I want to hear it."

"It's really not a perfect plan."

The admiral cleared his throat loudly. "You ever hear what George Patton said about perfect plans?"

"I don't recall anything."

"Something along the lines of a good plan executed now being better than a perfect plan executed in a week. That make sense to you?"

Garrett nodded, "My first request then is to promote Captain Tony Richards to Major. I want him in command of a squadron of exobirds."

"He's the guy that did close air support on Wolc, right?"

"He really pulled Captain Shields' chestnuts out of the fire. So to speak." Garrett licked his lips. *Why did this seem so difficult to explain?* "He's an imprint, too. World War Two Spitfire pilot. Without him, that counterattack would have failed. I was glad to see him down among 'em."

"And you concur with that strategy?"

Garrett folded his hands. "We're too standoff. We're developing weapon systems that take us farther and farther away from the soldiers who are taking and holding the ground vital to war. I think we can do better."

Nather was quiet for a long moment. "Coffey won't work with you. He's caught up in his own career."

"Then we find someone who will."

"Yeah, she led that counterattack on Wolc." Nather shook his head. Their frustration that Shields was just a captain in an army that didn't recognize merit at all was mutual. Not much had changed over the last two hundred years. "That man's going to kill a lot of capable soldiers and there's almost nothing we can do about it."

"You said his chain of command doesn't come through Fleet, sir. What can we possibly do to prevent him losing his regiment?"

"Nothing. Maybe something. We have to act when the time comes. And it will. Stay in constant contact with Shields and her sergeant major. You have to be ready to support them when it happens. If we miss that opportunity, we might not get another one."

Garrett rubbed his eyes. "We'll be ready, sir."

"I know you will, Don. Somehow I don't think you'll let me down."

"Thank you, sir."

Nather stood abruptly and walked across the room to his desk. "There's one little thing, though. I hope you don't mind discussing it with an old man and another cup of Irish coffee."

"What would that be, sir?"

"This." Nather held up the silver eagle of a Fleet Captain. A promotion two full grades higher. "I pulled every string in the book to get you assigned as my CAG and to have the rank you've clearly earned. So I'm going to give you one piece of advice—you and Major Richards take that fight down to the enemy and make every life count."

* * * * *

Chapter Forty-One

Surprisingly, there wasn't a message from the waste management computer, as Mairin let her shower run for a good ten minutes instead of the traditional fleet shower of get wet, turn off the water, lather up, water on, rinse, and get out. With the water near scalding, she turned her back to the spray and let it cascade over her neck and shoulders in an attempt to wash the stress and tightness away. She'd grown past thinking solely about the mission at hand. Her mind drifted over her family, somewhere safe out beyond the Outer Rim on whatever colony they were on. She'd lost track of how many, and hadn't heard a thing from them for three months after Wolc. Only then had they seemed to wonder if she was okay. Of course she'd lied to them. She wasn't in a combat unit. That she was working in an office somewhere and not commanding a cavalry troop. Truth was stranger than fiction after all.

She lathered slowly with the last of her soap from Libretto. The sweet wildflower smell brought the visual of Tally's cabin and the lake in the monsoonal evenings. Only her dreams brought sadness and regret. There was nothing more either of them could have done. And now. She smirked as she rinsed off. Tally was on Earth as the Prelate Consort, or something like that, looking happy and fulfilled. Clearly, Tally's thoughts would be elsewhere now. As should hers.

Her favorite furry towel wrapped around her body like a toga, she walked through the empty showers. Nineteen hundred to twenty hundred ship time was her favorite hour of the day. All of the showers were mixed gender, but men and women had separate hours of privacy if they so chose. And with this shower so far into "green-suit land" that none of the Fleet women would venture to it, Mairin usually had it exclusively to herself.

The door to her stateroom was open with a large green flight bag resting against it. *Dammit*, she frowned. *There goes my private space.* At the door, she nearly ran into a blonde woman in a tight nomex flight suit. "Excuse me?"

The woman turned and smiled. "You must be Captain Shields." She extended a hand. "I'm Lieutenant Conyers. Laura Conyers. Three eighteenth squadron heavy. Your new Rhino driver and roommate."

They shook hands. Conyers was a good two inches shorter than Mairin, with bright hazel eyes and a hint of a drawl. A few wrinkles at the corners of her eyes belied age and experience. Fleet tended to promote more slowly than the TDF, so if she was older than Mairin, it made sense. "You're from Earth."

"How'd you guess?" Conyers smiled.

"That's about the only place you get a good southern accent like that."

Conyers laughed. "You're good, but how good are you?"

"What do you mean?" Mairin squinted.

"Where d'ya think I'm from?"

Mairin bit her lower lip. How could she possibly know? "Southern Virginia?"

"Damn! I'm impressed, ma'am!" Conyers grinned.

Mairin shrugged. "Lucky guess." *Grandpa strikes again.* She stepped into the room as Conyers closed the door and dragged her flight bag into the center of the small room.

"What about you, ma'am?"

"Born on Luna, raised on Eden."

Conyers sighed. "I always wanted to get out that way, just not...you know...this way, ma'am."

Mairin nodded and raised a finger. "I just have one rule, if you don't mind?"

Conyers looked surprised. "Yes, ma'am?"

"In here, my name is Mairin." She smiled. "Understood?"

"Sure!" Conyers practically squealed. "I'm so glad you said that...Mairin. I'm going to pin on soon, and being that I'll be flying your Rhino from here on out...I mean…I'd hoped."

I think we're going to get along well, she thought. "And it's nice to have another female down here in greensuit land."

"I have to admit, I was worried somethin' terrible." Conyers sat on her bunk and began to unpack her things. "How long you been down here by yourself?"

"Six months or so. When I first got here, I didn't even have a room. I slept in my vehicle bay for three nights before Sergeant Major Trevayne got me a place to sleep." She grinned and remembered that, despite her discomfort, sleeping with her tanks was like wrapping up in a gigantic safety blanket.

Conyers unpacked methodically folded clothes and belongings in an endless stream. *Where was Conyers going to put all of that stuff?* "Don't worry. Most of this stuff I'll store in my flight locker. It's a quantum storage unit. One of these days I'm going to get one of them keychain rooms, too."

"Keychain room? What is that?"

Conyers held up her fingers about three inches apart. "Looks like a tube of lipstick, but you plug it into a special slot that all of the experimental Fleet vessels are carrying and it's like an apartment. All of your stuff is shrunk to the quantum level and repositioned based on the amount of space you have allocated to you. When you get one, you get to set it up exactly like you want. I've heard that just about anything is possible, like having an original Van Gogh or customized breezes and ocean views! I can't wait to see one." She held out her hand over her bags. "I mean; it has to beat living out of a bag."

Mairin nodded. "Sounds like a home you'd carry with you wherever you're posted."

"I know!" Conyers smiled. "Who'da thunk it?"

Mairin laughed. *Earthlings*, she thought with a grin. *No, Americans.* The rumors about them being bumpkins appeared true. "How long have you been in?"

"Five years. You?"

"Less than that." Conyers let the question die as she finished unpacking a normal store of clothes and uniforms before returning the rest of her gear to the flight bags. Mairin quickly dressed in her flight suit and boots.

"What kind of boots are those?"

"Tanker boots," Mairin grinned. "Best idea George S. Patton ever had." She twisted her foot so that Conyers could see the shiny black boots with leather straps that wound around her foot in lieu of laces. The concept was a little sketchy to Mairin. Were leather straps really less likely to be drawn into a twentieth century turret ring? Would they flatten or cut where a nylon lace would not? It just didn't seem right.

"Patton, huh?" Conyers chuckled.

"So the story goes." Mairin nodded. "You going into crew rest soon?"

Conyers nodded. "Yeah, I'll be ready to drop you."

"Why do you pilot types get all the perks? I mean, you have to have guaranteed sleep before you fly."

Conyers shook her head. "Not all the time. And we're just as likely as you guys to get after it on a few hours of rest or less. We just don't stay up all the time like you guys do. I mean, twenty-some hours at a time? How in the hell do you do that without stim tabs?"

"Coffee." Mairin snorted and they laughed for a moment. "It's just like patrol aircraft. We take turns so the others can eat or sleep. So we do get a little sleep. Besides, even the Greys can't fight for more than about eighteen hours without a break. It overheats their repulsors and gun tubes."

Conyers sighed. "Seriously. I can't imagine doing what you're doing, Mairin. Leading a cavalry troop has got to be tons harder than flying!"

"I doubt that," Mairin said. "I barely passed differential equations. I can't imagine piloting a few thousand tons of vehicle through various atmospheres and not smacking into the ground. I'd love to try, though."

"I bet you could do just about anything you wanted to."

Mairin actually felt a blush in her cheeks. "Well, right now I need to go make sure my lieutenants are earning their keep, coming up with a plan that's at least half decent and has a chance of surviving contact." She paused and smiled at her new roommate. "I'll try not to wake you when I come back. I'll need some shut-eye too."

"You won't wake me," Conyers said. "Flight tabs. Guaranteed to knock me out for precisely eight hours with the best sleep possible. Sometimes being a pilot does have its perks, I guess. See you in the morning."

"Sleep well," Mairin smiled and walked out of her room. The smile faded as she passed the wardroom and the regiment headquarters area. The conference room door was open.

"Shields!" The nasal voice bounced off the bulkheads.

Shit, Mairin thought. *What now?* She walked into the room. Obviously it was a commander's call. All of the other commanders and their first sergeants were present. She glanced to her spot at the table and saw that Livingston wasn't there either. She met Coffey's eyes. "Yes, sir?"

He smirked. "Forgot about commander's call?"

Mairin shook her head. "Never knew there was one, sir. When did the notification go out?"

"It's SOP." He grinned at her. "Would be nice if you followed it once in a while."

"Begging your pardon, sir. In order for SOP to be followed it cannot be a secret little document known only to a few."

"Shut your mouth and sit down, Shields. Send for your first sergeant, too."

Mairin felt the blood in her face as she moved through the room. Droves of laughing eyes followed her. She moved to her position at the table, withdrew a small notepad and pen from her coveralls and leaned forward feigning rapt attention.

Coffey leaned back in his chair, raised his arms over his head and yawned. "All right, people. Now, we're gonna talk about my plan for this defensive mission. Planet Gonad, as I've taken to calling Ashland, is like fighting on the Moon. Earth's moon. You following me? Good."

He leaned back and put his boots on the table. "Now, the way I see this. Well, the way I see it is totally different from headquarters but that's not important right now, is that we'll dig in with two companies facing the enemy and two on the obliques to defend against the flanking maneuver. We know the Greys are gonna come with a million vehicles and the best place to meet them is on ground we choose.

"Now, we'll have orbital gunfire hitting all of the potential avenues of approach. That's what we call the ways the enemy might come and fight against us, Shields. Pay attention.

"So, I'm gonna have the engineers mine all of the other ways the enemy might try and move against us. How's that for starters?"

The group of officers nodded and smiled. Mairin did her best not to shake her head. Obstacles should be used in a defense to channelize the enemy into exactly where a defender wanted them to go, like an actual kill zone or something to that effect. Without at least attempting to plan where he wanted to put the enemy, Coffey was surrendering the initiative to them. Defending against the flank was one thing, but not determining a place to really fight the enemy was a cardinal sin.

No one seemed to be disagreeing with Coffey, and she knew that raising her hand or opinion would result in derision and laughter. She glanced at Sergeant Major Trevayne who sat stone-faced and would not return her gaze. *What were these assholes thinking?*

The whole lot of them sat with mouthfuls of imitation tobacco and spit into cups and bottles like buffoons. The room stank of tobacco spit, and they all occasionally stuffed more of the disgusting mix into their already full lips. Did they really think they looked like cowboys? Just because their commander did it, was it really necessary? Carcinogen free or not, it was disgusting. A part of Mairin almost missed cancer. She wanted to gag as the lieutenant next to her stuffed his lip to the breaking point with tobacco and turned to smile at her with black-stained teeth, spit leaking from the corner of his mouth.

She looked at her notepad for a moment. And what would the cavalry be doing this time? Sitting in the reserve? Performing a screen ten miles away from the objective? *I wish he'd try and use us correctly just once!*

"Shields!"

"Sir?"

"Glad you're awake down there. I want you and your worthless bunch of sissies to go out and....um....take a look at a big ditch that winds up to the east of our position. The Greys might try and exploit it."

Mairin glanced at the holo map in the center of the room. There it was. A wadi. She blinked. An area reconnaissance mission. Figure out how to get there and back, how to keep the enemy from using it, and how to fight from it if necessary. Easy, in theory.

The wadi was a good three hundred meters wide in most places and looked to be about ten kilometers long. At its closest point it was roughly fifteen kilometers from the regiment's position. Beyond the range of their direct fire support. He was doing it again. Just like Wolc. And Waters City. And Hoffman Colony.

Leave her and her unit out in the middle of nowhere without support. Or worse, expecting that she and her troopers would die sitting still like good little soldiers.

"And Shields," Coffey leaned forward and spat into a cup. "I don't want you yelling and screaming for air cover or fire support or anything else. Your whining and complaining directs assets from this regiment and leaves my people naked."

Mairin saw her vision redden. She made no attempt to stop her mouth. "Left your people naked? With all due respect, sir, you never even thought of using air support until Hoffman Colony. And we used it at Wolc because you saw to it that I was cut off from the intelligence net and had no tactical information! Don't sit there and tell me that I whine about shit!"

Coffey stood and lashed out with a finger. "One more word and I'll court-martial you for insubordination!"

I'd like to see you try. Mairin met his stare but said nothing.

"We'll talk about this later, Shields! Anybody else want to subvert my authority?" He glared at the room. Hands on his hips, he sneered like a satisfied pig and sat back down. "Now. We're going to go around the room and you're going to backbrief me on your plan. You first, Shields."

Mairin took a long breath through her nose and spoke slowly. "Sir, the troop will..."

"Company." Coffey said. "This is a tank regiment. You are a company sized element. I'm through with the cavalry bullshit you and your 'troopers' are selling. You read me?"

"Yes, sir." Mairin said. "My company will perform a passage of lines at H-hour minus three to allow for—"

"What's your mission?"

"Recon and defend that wadi if necessary, sir."

"That's all I need to know. Your details are boring and stupid. I want to know if you can do the mission I've assigned to you, or whether or not I should court-martial you for incompetence." Coffey stared at her. "You done?"

"Yes, sir." Mairin felt alternately amused and pissed off. Like laughing and hitting something at the same time. She imagined it was how insanity might feel. She knew Coffey was continuing to talk and get his glad-handed briefbacks from officers who thought he was some kind of hero. How the man had ever made colonel was beyond her, though she knew the answer lay on the backs of those he'd served with. They'd made him look good through their own competence and devotion to duty, and by proxy he came out smelling like a rose despite his incompetence.

That's how generals are made, she wrote on her pad and drew a smiling face next to it. *Keep your perspective, Mairin.*

The meeting droned into a second hour before Coffey stood and pointed wildly around the room. "We drop in ten hours! Get your shit straight and don't make me look like an idiot!" He stomped out of the room like a mad hornet leaving most of them to smile, slap each other on the back, and bullshit like they were the greatest things since sliced bread. Mairin left without talking to any one and not giving a damn what they thought of her. At the end of this battle, God willing, she'd be standing here again. She couldn't say the same for many of her fellow officers.

Her neurals flashed. Ulson. I took the operations order briefs from the platoons. Not too bad. They'll brief you in six hours. I told Livingston to stay away from the commander's call, too. No sense both of you losing time. Alex.

Mairin smiled. At least something was going well. Without another thought, she walked to her room and stepped in quietly. She undressed in the darkness and smiled at the gentle snoring emanating from the other bunk. Her own sheets were warm and soft. Her head swam for a moment and her stomach lurched with more unwarranted nausea, but Mairin Shields was asleep a minute later, her own light snoring in perfect time with her new roommate.

* * * * *

Chapter Forty-Two

"What are we going to do about the Tuegs?"

Munsen rubbed his scratchy chin. He'd not been to sleep for twenty-six hours. Strategic thought was mostly beyond his tired mind, but he looked up over the mug of coffee. "They will withdraw all forces from the coalition in three weeks. They are starting to encourage their people to return home from across the galaxy."

The delayed response came a few seconds later, the wonders of Vemehian technology. They called it something unpronounceable to humans, who took it and applied popular culture to something fantastical, the way they always did. So they called it an ansible. Across great distances, man could talk in real time with the other sentient races. General Zhaire leaned towards her screen on Earth and said, "What's that mean for our efforts?"

"The Tuegs are executing a homeworld defense. They feel that occupation is imminent, and they are making plans to defend Tueg at all costs." Munsen leaned back slowly. "They've requested the Prelate come to a private conference in two weeks."

"A product of the negotiations on Luna?"

"Yes, but classified to the *n*th degree." Munsen sighed. "I wish I knew what they were up to."

"Suspicions?"

Munsen sipped his coffee. *How to put this?* "I'm not entirely sure. The Tuegs are particularly distrustful of the Styrahi, and I think they feel remaining neutral is the lesser of two evils. I don't like their chances against the Greys, and frankly I'm wondering if the defense of the homeworld is an all-out attempt to take their society en masse to another galaxy. They certainly have the technological ability."

"But how could they accomplish such a thing?"

Munsen shrugged. "I'd suspect a Dyson shell or an equivalent of some type. We know they've encapsulated moons and asteroids before, so it wouldn't surprise me. But that's not to say something else couldn't be possible. Generation ships at sublight speeds? Who knows?"

"How likely do you think it is they would attempt such a thing?"

"Not very. I'm certain it's a homeworld defense. As for what they want to negotiate with the Prelate about, I have no idea." Munsen gritted his teeth against the thought of failure.

"Let me repeat myself. What are we going to do about the Tuegs? Their defection from the coalition will raise doubts among the Legion and could undermine our war effort. The Greys must be stopped at all costs." Zhaire stared at him.

Munsen shook his head. "The Tuegs know that, but are no longer willing to fight alongside us, because the threat to their homeworld is too great. We'll face the same thing if Styrah is attacked. It's customary for them to defend their homeworld. You'd have a mass exodus there as well. No, the Tuegs are afraid and there's no one in the Legion that would tell them not to be. Their concern is obviously one that encompasses Earth, but to what degree I don't know."

"Have you considered speaking directly to the Prelate? Or what about McMasters?"

Munsen bristled. "No, we only talk about the imprinting experiments." Which was a major sticking point, Munsen didn't say aloud. Once McMasters found out Tallenaara had been the Styrahi subject, he'd manipulated the situation to get her back with her college sweetheart. That much was clear, but the reasoning as to why was not.

"What about his consort? I believe you are familiar with her?"

Munsen flared. "Absolutely not! I will not interfere with her again." Finding calm was impossible now. Of all the things to suggest. Tallenaara had been through enough, hadn't she? Interference now would smack of conspiracy to the Styrahi Council. No, she would be left alone at all costs. There had to be other possibilities within the Prelate's inner circle. "I will find some other conduit."

"We have to know what the Tuegs want, and more importantly, what the Prelate will agree to."

"Who knows what he will discuss with them! Until we actually learn something, speculation will get us nowhere." Munsen yawned. "I'm afraid I have to end this call now before I fall asleep."

"How can you sleep at a time like this? I need your advice and counsel, Colonel."

Munsen smiled at the monitor. "And without sleep, you'll get neither from me. Out." He turned off the monitor and disconnected the subspace service completely for the night. He lay on his single bunk within the bowels of a freighter and listened to the sounds of the ship for a long time.

What would the Tuegs want with Andrew Cartner? The Prelate was merely a mouthpiece of Earth. A mouthpiece engaged to be married to a Styrah. A Styrah with a certain genetic mutation that could allow for cross-breeding of their species. Is that why Styrah became involved with Earth in the first place? Surely there had to be more to it than that.

Alone with his doubts, Munsen fell asleep somewhere near Tueg without an answer.

* * * * *

Chapter Forty-Three

Sweaty retracting sheets held Tally to Andrew's chest as Luna fell away. The transport's crew made preparations to enter foldspace, and Andrew's entourage collected and archived his speeches and negotiations from their time on Luna, before ramping themselves into a frenzy. Tally often watched them scurrying like ants from one stressful project to another and wondered why anyone in their right mind would do such a thing. Laying against Andrew's chest, the sweat of their lovemaking still warm on their skins, Tally pushed aside her wonderings about everyone else but Andrew. His breathing wasn't shallow or rhythmic. Without moving her head, she knew his eyes were open and staring into the ceiling. Waiting for her to sleep so that he could get up, watch her for a moment, and then go back to work.

"What are you thinking about?" she asked.

A snort. "I thought you'd gone to sleep."

"And you were just about to get out of bed and work on something." Tally squeezed his chest. "What if I'm not ready for you to go?"

Andrew took a deep breath and let it out. "Then I stay here."

"That's a first."

Andrew laughed. "Come on, Tally. You know—"

"I do." She raised her chin and looked up to his face. "Now tell me what's bothering you. Everything you've told me suggests your negotiations were successful enough to keep the Tueg supporting the war effort. Right? Transports and foldspace support?"

Andrew nodded. "Yes."

Tally was quiet for a moment as she stifled the thought she finally brought herself to say. "What are you not telling me?"

There wasn't a response for a minute. Andrew sighed. "There's another phase of the negotiation they feel can only be conducted on Libretto, with representatives from the Styrahi Council. That's where we're headed."

"You told the press corps—"

"Yes, I lied to them. We'll have an announcement made on Earth soon enough. Darren already recorded it and it will be broadcast in a couple of hours when we enter foldspace." Andrew licked his lips. "Is there something about Libretto I need to know about?"

Tally rolled up onto an elbow, resting partially on Andrew's chest. "What are you talking about?"

"I'm not sure. The whole discussion about getting me to Libretto. And having the Styrahi present. Something doesn't fit." Andrew rolled his head to look at her. "What's so special about Libretto?"

"It's the most like Earth in the known galaxy. The atmosphere is an almost complete replicant. Similar core structure. A little smaller and only about forty percent water." Tally paused. "Similar flora and fauna. Gods, Andrew. I don't know what you're asking!"

Andrew smiled thinly. "I don't either."

Tally blinked. "What gave you the impression about Libretto? That there's something there? Maybe the Tuegs want to meet on neutral ground. Libretto doesn't belong to anyone, Andy. Have you considered that?"

"I have." He sighed. "I'm not comfortable with this. I feel like there I'm going to walk into that room and everyone knows something but me."

"What does Darren think?" Tally ran a fingernail across his chest.

"That I'm worrying unnecessarily." Andrew chuckled. "That I'm reading too much into this negotiation. Just like I did with the Vemeh a few years ago."

Tally squinted. "When the Vemeh wanted to mine Mars?"

"Yeah," Andrew said. "I almost freaked out the entire scientific community by repeatedly asking what was so important about Mars to the Vemeh. In the end, they were looking for a specific element. Scanned the whole planet and never found it. We all breathed a sigh of relief when they wanted Io instead. Of course, we let them have that hellhole without question."

Tally nodded. "It's different when there's something you think you want involved."

"What do you mean?"

"With Mars," Tally said, "you already had a colony presence there and had been successful in determining the presence of life and water. Those are important things. Having the Vemeh ask permission raised a million doubts. It would have been easier if they'd taken it by force."

Andrew flared. "That wouldn't have made things easier."

"It would have erased the doubts in your mind." Tally looked at him for a moment. "Do you see what I'm saying, Andrew?"

"That if there's something we really want, and covet, we tend to get defensive. And usually for all the wrong reasons."

"And you're concerned that because Libretto is so similar to Earth, that if there is something the Greys or the Tueg or the Styrahi want, they're going to want it from Earth next."

Andrew chuckled. "More or less."

"And for all you know, the Tueg want you to meet with them and the Styrahi to discuss their own homeworld defense. All you know is they want to talk to you and the Styrahi Council at the same time. How many times have you done that in the past ten years?"

"A few." Andrew laughed.

"So, stop worrying about all of the possible reasons. You have a staff of people scurrying around downstairs who want to do that for you, for some strange reason. Let them worry about the possibilities."

Andrew pulled her onto his chest. "And I should just be worrying about you?"

"It is two weeks to Libretto after all, right?" She grinned and stroked his chin. Her grin faded. There was already gray in the hair at his temples, like his father. He would die young if he kept up this pace, this worry, this consuming behavior. Leadership, real leadership, tended to be like that. Long hours, little appreciation, and constant unwavering demand for higher and higher production. There was no difference between civilian and military leadership and it was a game for the young that aged them before their time. "Slow down, Andrew. If not for me, then for yourself."

Andrew nodded. "I'll try, Tally. You can't imagine how hard this is."

"Yes, I can, Andy." She smiled with one corner of her mouth. "I see it written in your face, these little gray hairs, and when you sleep. You hardly relax at all unless I make you."

"You do that well," Andrew quipped. "Of course you make me do other things, as well." He shifted under her and his intentions were evident against her thigh.

Tally grinned and moved up to kiss him. "I love you."

"I love you, Tally," he said between kisses. Their tongues danced together for a moment as they warmed into their lovemaking. His strong hands traced her shoulders and cradled her face. His fingers plunged into her thick, dark hair.

She wrapped him in her arms, pulling at him gently. Answering his body with her own intentions and need. Not even the sensory distortion of the transport slipping into foldspace interrupted them. Tally gasped as Andrew entered her. Nothing else mattered as they moved in perfect synchronization against each other. Against the surreal golds and greens of foldspace, the cares of their world faded as they focused solely on each other.

* * * * *

Chapter Forty-Four

What had Coffey said? Fighting on Ashland would be like fighting on the moon? Kilometer after kilometer of dull gray regolith, the occasional boulder and random craters stretched across the horizon. Through the gunner's sight, Mairin centered her sector of fire to cover the two vehicles guarding the closest exit point of the "Big Ditch" so aptly named by the newly promoted Colonel Coffey. First Sergeant Livingston and a tank from third platoon sat in relative concealment, but there'd been no time to adequately update the camouflage patterns, and the green vehicles stuck out like proverbial sore thumbs. *Couldn't be helped*, Mairin snorted. No plan survived contact with the enemy, and their entire planning process had amounted to a serious wargaming exercise, because the moment they'd dropped, Coffey had changed the mission. Now, instead of a simple area reconnaissance mission, Mairin's troop sat waiting to conduct the greatest exercise in futility designed by the brass—the passage of lines.

Somewhere to their front, a Styrahi intelligence team crept through the wadi looking for anything of value. If the Greys were watching the wadi, and Mairin was certain they had to be, at some point an attack would be launched and the intelligence team would come running back through the passage point. Well beyond the direct fire support of the regiment snugly dug in on the high ground, and without dedicated indirect fire and artillery support, the only asset available beyond her own gun tubes were the inaccurate carpet-bombing idiots of the orbital gun platforms.

For the fifteenth time, Mairin wished for a peaceful return of the intel team. Her troops could handle the challenge and password exchanges, the verifications and authentications, and the slow business of peacefully bringing another unit into their lines and passing them to the unit behind. If they came out of the wadi under fire, they had two chances for survival—slim and none. And Coffey had ensured they couldn't talk to the close air support assets. The man'd had the audacity to jam his own units. Only he would have access to the close air frequencies. Finite control he'd taken to calling it. A prescription for disaster.

No air cover. Mairin fought smiling at the memory of Coffey strutting around the briefing room like a scalded rooster. *Screw him. "We will find a way, or make one." Where did that come from, grandpa? Any other pearls of wisdom?* Her communications console buzzed, a direct laser message from Coffey.

The characters appeared across her screen. (You missed your hourly report. SITREP now.)

Mairin bit her lip savagely and typed (Under radio listening silence to include laser emittance.)

(I'll tell you what you can and cannot do. Is that clear?)

"Goddamnit," Mairin swore in her helmet. There was no atmosphere, no flora, no good terrain to protect against the enemy gaining access to their line of sight communications. She typed again. (Negative report at this time.)

(Negative as in what? No enemy? No report? Or are you trying to fuck me over, Captain?)

Mairin stared at the flashing cursor for an eternity knowing that she'd eventually have to answer the bastard, no matter what. A new message opened from Livingston. (Four vehicles sighted bearing zero nine eight at ten kilometers. Appear friendly. Will advise.)

Let's see how you like that, sir. Mairin said to herself in the closed comfort of her pressure helmet, as she forwarded the message to

Coffey and sat forward in her seat, eyes pressed to the gunner's sight extension and magnified as high as possible.

(Engage at earliest opportunity), Coffey sent. Mairin reread the message with her mouth open. The man was insane. She was about to answer when he sent another message. (Close air confirms vehicles are enemy. Engage.)

Mairin looked over at Conner. "Any exocraft activity in the area?"

"No, ma'am. There's a combat air patrol circling at forty kilometers, but nothing close."

"Can an exocraft at that distance make out individual targets on the ground well enough to identify them?" she asked rhetorically. No one answered her. Her stomach tumbled again, and she blinked against the nausea. *Focus! Develop the situation a little more. It's not hesitation if you're ready to act. Get everyone ready, just don't do it in the clear.*

Working quickly, she keyed her console over to the vehicle status screen and ensured that all vehicles showed up. The program would allow her to send reminders to all of her vehicles for maintenance and services to be conducted, and would allow her to see what everyone's status was without a clear broadcast. All of the inter-vehicle communications were secure and encrypted, and linked by optical systems. The system read good on all vehicles. Mairin figured it would have to work.

"Driver, repulsors to standby. Gunner, lock and load battle carry sabot. Press targeting to cannons." Mairin looked at Conner. "Maintain radio silence."

One by one, the other vehicles in the troop followed their commander's example. Repulsors online and guns loaded, Mairin waited for the last two vehicles, the passage point team, to cycle over. Nothing happened. A minute passed, and then two. Mairin began to type the message to Livingston—

"SHELLREP! Twelve rounds vicinity four hundred meters east from passage point," Ulson called in the clear. From the far end of their position, he was the only one who could see into the wadi as much as Livingston. "Horizon obscured!"

So much for listening silence, Mairin thought and engaged her radio.

"Roger, Red One. Black Nine, get your repulsors online and guns loaded. Sitrep in one mike, over." Mairin flipped frequencies and relayed the shell report to Coffey before re-engaging the troop frequency.

"Six, this is Nine. Four vehicles approaching now firing over their back decks. Horizon obscured by smoke. Negative contact with enemy. Confirm vehicles appear to be friendly. I say again, vehicles have proper markings and following procedures for passage of lines under fire."

Mairin keyed the radio on the regimental frequency. "Bullet Six, Saber Six. Vehicles inbound to passage point are friendlies. They appear to be under fire, over."

"Goddamn it, I said take them out!" Coffey roared. "Destroy them now!"

She flipped back to the company frequency. "Black Nine, distance to vehicles? Do you have a visual on enemy?"

"Six, they are two hundred meters and picking up speed. No visual contact. There are rounds falling around the vehicles but cannot determine origin or type," Livingston replied.

This doesn't make sense. There's no way those vehicles could be identified from an exocraft twenty miles away. Coffey had to be wrong. Drunk again. Or were they? "Guidons, Six. Stand by to fire."

"Negative, Six. I have interface lock with one of the—" The connection hissed and Mairin saw a flash of light. Through the sight extension she saw the turret of Livingston's Slammer and the turret of his wingman both tumbling in long arcs away from the exploding hulls.

Sonuvabitch!

"Standby to fire," Mairin called over the squadron frequency. On the horizon, she saw the first vehicle begin to crest the hill. "Gunner, sabot, vehicle in the open."

"Identified."

"Up!"

"Driver, move out, gunner secure the tube."

"Driver, stop."

The Slammer hadn't even rocked to a stop when Mairin called "Fire!"

"On the way!"

<<Negative firing confirmation. Confirmed friendly.>> The Interface chimed.

"Command override!" Mairin screamed. "Kill that sonuvabitch!"

<<Negative firing confirmation. Confirmed friendly,>> the Interface stopped, and the interior light went red. <<Trailing three vehicles are firing at the leader.>>

Mairin looked at Conner. "Is that vehicle broadcasting in the clear?"

"Yes, ma'am. One twelve decimal five seven."

"Punch that freq, Conner."

The connection hissed. "Taking fire, taking fire! Trailing vehicles are not friendly. Stop firing at us! Hit everything behind us!"

The vehicle status report showed Ulson's tank engaging with the coaxially mounted rail gun outside of Interface control. Mairin mashed the radio button. "Cease fire on the leader! Cease fire on the leader! Kill the other—"

The friendly vehicle erupted in a shower of sparks that died before hitting the regolith. Mairin slammed a fist into her thigh. More Grey vehicles crested the slope. Hundreds of them.

"Open fire!" Mairin screamed into the radio and unleashed hell. She watched the Grey vehicles explode in rapid succession. *All detonated after one precise hit*, she thought with agony.

"Saber six, this is Bullet Six. SITREP on those vehicles!"

Her mouth tasted like metal. She wanted to spit. "Bullet Six, I am in contact. Engaged and destroyed unknown number enemy vehicles and one friendly vehicle. I need close air support, now!"

"What?"

She keyed the radio again. "Bullet Six, engaged and destroyed an unknown number of enemy vehicles and one friendly vehicle. All vehicles were not targets. Repeat all vehicles were not targets. Positive interface lock from friendly vehicle." Tears stung her eyes but a steady thumping rain of artillery on their position snapped her to reality. "Guidons, Six. Supplemental positions, move now!"

Her private channel to Ulson chimed. "Why didn't you tell us, ma'am?"

"I tried as soon as I knew, Alex." Mairin held tightly to the chair and the Slammer accelerated over a boulder and dove to the right. "Now's not the time for this. We'll sort this out later!"

Mairin slammed her fist into her tender thigh again and again until hot tears ran down her cheeks. *Stop it, Mairin. Stop it right now.* She tried to run a sleeve under her nose and realized that she was only scratching her faceplate. *How long to the supplemental position?* The thought sobered her. "Conner, time to supplemental position?"

"At this speed, three minutes. We're clear of the artillery for now."

Don't stop. Keep pushing. "Guidons, Six. Push hard to the supplemental positions." She flipped over to the regimental frequency. "Saber Six taking heavy indirect fire. Moving to supplemental positions. Time now, out."

Think, Mairin. Get to the supplemental position and reorganize. You're down two vehicles and eight personnel. Don't make it worse than it is. She took a deep breath and let it out slowly. Her headset buzzed.

"You happy now, Shields?" Coffey gloated. "You got an intelligence team killed because you hesitated."

"You told me to kill them all, sir."

Coffey laughed. "You sure did, Shields. You sure did."

The connection clicked off. She rolled through the regimental line to her supplemental position and grounded the vehicle in defilade with only the optics package on the top of the tank visible. Five hundred meters behind the regimental line in overwatch, Mairin thought about climbing off the track and going to talk to her vehicles. *Not the best idea, given*, she thought as heavy artillery fire began to pound the regiment. She looked at the position of her vehicles and realized that Livingston's first responsibility was always the priorities of work in a position. Security emplacement, range card generation, rest and maintenance plans all being critical aspects of the fight. Without Livingston, they weren't getting done. Even her own crew sat listless in the seats.

"All right, crew." Mairin snapped, an edge to her voice. "Ammunition counts and gun tube verifications, Lee. Conner, I want our precise position within one meter, relay it to all vehicles, and find a way for me to talk to the close air support."

"Ma'am, that frequency is blocked."

"Is that going to stop you, Conner?" Mairin narrowed her eyes slightly. "I'll find a communications specialist that can unblock it."

Conner grinned. "Not in this unit, ma'am. I'm on it."

Mairin called down to Booker. "I want a full vehicle status report in five minutes, Booker. No sleeping." The driver lay reclined on his back in the style of the old Abrams battle tanks. Given no movement, a warm vehicle, and that position, it was easy to sleep even in the midst of a mission. Mairin toggled her console to operational mode. "Interface, encryption keys beta sigma on my mark. Mark."

Mairin thought for a second and then spoke with as much of a normal voice as she could. "Troopers, this is Captain Shields. We made a mistake back there, and while we had the best of intentions, that friendly vehicle didn't have much of a chance anyway. That's cold comfort to the fact we committed fratricide. The bad part is things happen in war, and neither training nor technology will help when the cards are stacked against you like that. We lost—" She paused and made sure her voice was steady. "We lost a great leader and great troopers out there today. Look out your vision blocks at the regimental position. They're taking a beating right now, and that means the Greys are going to come rolling up for a fight. We're going to give them one. For First Sergeant Livingston and our troopers. And if we don't, we'll meet them in Fiddler's Green for a drink tonight.

"Keep your chins up, focus on your duties. Red One, contact me on private channel. Six out."

Five seconds later she heard Ulson's voice. "Ma'am?"

"Alex, not a word or a thought about what happened back there. You understand?"

"Yes, ma'am." She heard him sniff. "The interface let me fire. I'm sorry—"

"I said not a word! Now get it together, Alex. I want your recommendation for a First Sergeant and I need it now." *Give him a task. Show him you still trust him. Bringing him back to the fight will be the best thing you can do.*

Nothing came back for ten long seconds. "Sergeant Dao. He's the best we've got now."

"I concur." Mairin nodded. By the sound of his voice, Ulson was back and ready to get to work. For now. They'd have to talk more later. "I want you to tell him. Will be good for him to hear it from you. I'll contact him later. I want him on priorities of work. Get our people ready for a fight."

"How long do you think we have?"

Mairin looked at Conner frantically working his console. "I don't know, but I'm hoping to have some answers soon. You all right?"

"Yes, ma'am."

Mairin nodded but didn't speak. *How do you tell someone they're doing a great job when they knew they'd just fucked up royally?* "Stay alert out there. I'll be in touch. Six out." Not the best motivational speech ever, but unfortunately it would have to do.

Routine activity brought solace. The actions of her crew, the banter and checklists called out, answered, and finished brought a palpable relief she hadn't believed possible. The activity stilled her brain. The mistake was terrible. But given the communications issues across the regiment and seemingly all the way to TDF Command, the loss, while awful, was really not that bad. *God help me for thinking like the brass*, she chided herself. Her command console danced a jig of green and yellow as vehicles updated their status automatically and with actual human input. *Busy making ready for war*, she thought.

"Ma'am, I've got a *Ticonderoga* CIC private channel off a DCS." The concept of rapidly deployable communications satellites, with onboard Global Positioning Systems, allowed for a combat operation on any planet.

Mairin looked at her board. "Anybody on it?"

"It's monitored. No current traffic." Conner glanced over his shoulder. "I've got it for another two hundred seconds. It's highly secure. You want it?"

Highly secure? Whatever. "Give it to me."

The connection chirped and Mairin heard, "You have accessed a nuclear delivery frequency. You have ten seconds to change frequency without retaliation."

"Saber Six for Thunder Six. Flash traffic. Push frequency to one two one seven five decimal five. Saber Six out." Mairin shut off the connection, fearing a microwave burst would fry the Slammer's communication architecture. "Jesus, Conner! You could have warned me!"

Conner shrugged. "All I saw was that it was monitored and open, ma'am. I opened it." He put a hand to his ear and Mairin's mind flashed to a million old science fiction scenes. Conner was the wrong sex and the wrong skin tone from the memory whispered to her. "Incoming from Thunder Six. Button two."

Mairin chinned over. "Thunder Six, Saber Six, over."

"Your nickel, Saber Six. What's your traffic, over."

"Sir, I need freqs for the close air support near my position."

"Saber Six, you have no close air support tasked by order of your regimental commander." Mairin's blood froze. "Is it true your soldiers killed a friendly vehicle?"

There were a million things she wanted to say, but none mattered. "Roger, Thunder Six."

"Understand, Saber Six. Push all combat data to me now."

She met Conner's eyes. After a few seconds, he gave her a thumbs up. "On the way, sir."

"Sit tight until this one's over, Saber Six. There's not going to be a need for close air on your position and orbital gunfire is finally working as advertised. Not much moving on the battlefield right now."

Mairin relayed the feed from Coffey's gunsight and nodded with a grim smile on her face. The regolith downslope from the regiment's positions was ripped and torn asunder by round after round of orbital gunfire. Massive plumes of rock and debris shot out of each new impact crater. There were no Grey vehicles moving anywhere in the regiment's section. "Confirmed, sir."

"Saber Six, Thunder Six. Keep the faith. Thunder Six out."

Keep the faith? What faith? There wasn't a place for God or faith in any of this. If there was a god, she'd have Tally to come home to. Stupid thought, she shook her head violently enough to pop her neck. There was about a one percent chance that she'd have gone home to Tallenaara. Most likely she would never see that cabin or Tallenaara ever again. Tally was engaged to the Prelate of Earth now, and Mairin was stuck on a godforsaken little world, staring at an enemy that seemed to be losing their advantages, and facing the more dangerous righteousness of her commander's intent to place the blame anywhere other than on himself. Or themselves, she thought. They're all the same. Stuffing their faces full of chewing tobacco and swaggering like dime store cowboys.

The tremors from impacting artillery rounds slackened to nothing over the course of several minutes. The adrenaline coursing through her system began to fade and exhaustion reared its ugly head. Eyes closed, head against the sight extension she nearly fell asleep listening to the hum of the vehicle systems in her earphones and the silence of the regimental net. Silence. Her eyes snapped open. "Conner, are we in the regimental net?"

"Shit!" Conner spun to the console and began to work. "We're cut out of all regimental feeds. The regiment is moving away from our position."

"How long have they been gone?" Mairin's stomach tightened.

"Three minutes, maybe four." Conner squinted. "What are you thinking?"

Mairin pushed the troop frequency. "Guidons, this is Six. Incoming! I say again incoming! All critical systems to standby! All systems—"

WHUMP! WHUMP!

Master caution sirens sounded as the vehicle rocked side to side under the stupendous nuclear detonations. The impact threw Mairin to the floor of the turret where Conner joined her as the vehicle rocked to the other side. Her head ached from the impact and she couldn't hear anything. The main hydraulic housing above the main gun ruptured, sending highly pressurized flammable liquid into the atmosphere. Mairin watched the droplets beginning to coalesce on the floor as she rolled away from Conner and floundered for the plug-in for her helmet. She snapped the connection together and heard the vehicle Interface reading a list of cautions and warnings a mile long.

"Interface, that's enough. Combat readiness report."

<<This vehicle is sixty-two percent combat effective. The unit's vehicles are all in a similar state with an average readiness percentage of fifty-two percent."

Fifty-two percent. "Casualties."

<<Many injuries. No fatalities reported at the present time. Life support systems on six vehicles are approaching danger limits.>>

"Push all data to Thunder Six. Execute emergency action plan Charlie." Mairin looked at her display with bleary eyes. A flat plain lay about a thousand meters behind them. She selected the target and transmitted it to her troop. "Rally point selected. Conner, get me a dustoff. Now."

"A dustoff?"

Mairin shook her head. *C'mon, Mairin!* "A ride! A drop vehicle! Something to get us off this fucking rock!"

"On it." Conner replied like a scalded dog. "Button four, Lieutenant Conyers enroute with Rhinos four-two, four-three, and four-five.

Mairin pushed over. "Rhino Four-Zero, Saber Six. Need a combat load at this rally point." She transmitted the location and waited for the message to bounce to the orbiting recovery vehicles.

"Saber Six, roger. ETA is one-seven mikes."

<<Red Two and White Three have less than ten minutes of air remaining.>>

"That's not gonna work, Four Zero. Need you in ten mikes or less." Mairin watched her vehicles beginning to move with all possible speed to the rally point. "You're gonna have to stand on it, Four Zero."

The frequency clicked twice and Mairin kneed Lee in the back. "Okay, Sergeant Lee. You're the best person I've got that knows these beasts inside and out. How do we conserve everything we've got and get our troopers recovered without dying in place?"

Lee chuckled. "Shut down everything but comms and repulsors."

"We won't have weapons if the Grey horde comes rolling through the gap," Mairin replied.

"We're going to need air cover, ma'am."

Mairin shook her head. "We've been told no. Remember?"

"That was before we took a nuke barrage. We're under protocol for rescue at all costs."

Sonuvabitch! Mairin chinned over to the nuclear release frequency. "*Ticonderoga*, this is Saber Six. Two nukes dropped on my position, origin unknown. Fifty-two percent combat effective needing medevac and close air support now! Acknowledge!" Seconds felt like days. Her limping vehicles now showed more red than green in their life support status markers. *Confirm the impacts from the orbital sensors, people! They'd find it and with any luck they'd tell her that Coffey and the rest of those assholes were taken out by nukes, too.*

"Saber Six, this is Titan Six. Recovery protocol engaged. Help is on the way."

Mairin leaned back a little bit at hearing the Admiral's call sign. "At least we got somebody's attention."

Conner looked at her for a long moment and finally spoke. "What happened to the regiment, ma'am?"

Mairin shook her head. Somehow they'd moved without any one in the troop knowing it. Like they'd planned for it. Rehearsed it. "Were our optical links hacked?"

"No, all of the links from the regiment were live the entire time."

"Then why didn't we see them moving out, Conner?" Mairin said. "How did they move out without our knowledge?"

"I don't know, ma'am."

"Goddamnit," she snapped. The concept of fighting a war where units couldn't talk to one another and technology didn't mesh into a singular effort made no sense. War never changed.

Why? Why do we continually make shit up as we go along? One day she'd ask that question to someone in charge. If she lived that long in this lunatic war.

Watching the approaching Rhinos change their vectors, decelerate and drop to the surface of Ashland with barely a registered impact, Mairin wondered if she'd gone into the wrong service. A shred of jealousy rippled through her. Wanting to cruise through the clouds and feel the acceleration pushing her back into her seat was as palpable as craving Tally's touch. She trembled at the thought of Tally, but felt like she was flying herself. Maybe she could learn?

She pushed the thought away and made sure her platoons were loaded before she ordered Booker to position the tank for pick-up. She linked to the forward visual system of the Rhino and secured her helmet communications by protocol.

She watched the curving horizon of Ashland falling away and imagined wind in her face. *What would it be like?* A scrap of memory surfaced. Riding in the back of a sailplane with long white wings. The sailplane shuddering as it punched into thermals and turned to ride the swelling wind higher and higher. The absolute silence of the cockpit. There was the barest sensation of movement in the sky, except for small windows allowing air into the cockpit for comfort. The ride was forty dollars for an hour and it was money well spent. *Doing it again never panned out, did it, Grandpa?*

Mairin closed her eyes and leaned back against the seat rest. Maybe she could find a way to fly like a bird. Fly away from all of this craziness. *Just be.*

Just be.

* * * * *

Chapter Forty-Five

The officer of the watch announced the arrival of Captain Mubutai to the deck of the interstellar colony transport *Haven*. At the navigational console, the freshly washed face of Alicia Jones smiled a private smile and made her greetings along with the rest of the crew. He didn't meet her eyes and there was no slight to it. She'd relished the taste of her captain not more than six hours prior in the privacy of his dark, humid cabin. She stood and waited until the captain was seated on his dais, aware she was staring not at the powerful man who'd been her lover, but at the lush chair that would hold his frame. One day that chair, or one very much like it, would be hers. All she'd have to do is her job like her apprenticeship mentors told her, or she could fuck her way to the top. Without meaning to, she'd chosen the latter, and rather than falter in the face of adversity, she'd skipped right past the completely flustered and unhandsome first officer and went straight for the captain. He'd said during her interview that he was "old school," whatever that'd meant, his wandering eyes telling her everything that really mattered to him. She might be the best navigator in the colony fleet, but she'd have far more opportunities as a navigation engineer based on who she would bed. All that mattered was that chair. Her chair. The end would justify the means.

Graduation from the Academy seemed to be a lifetime ago. She watched the captain going through his rehearsed motions about the bridge and allowed herself a second of introspection. She'd been rated as the first watch navigation engineer for two reasons. There were not many people in the Eden Academy better than her at third order differential equation theory, and there weren't many people of this day and age that truly realized how the human existence is based on sexual desire. To hunt for that conquest, thrive for it, had dire social consequences two or three hundred years before. In this time, without the teachings of war and the constant conflict of the last two centuries, those who could distinguish themselves either through beauty or through sexuality were the ones who moved ahead. There were no ugly crewmembers for colony ships. If they'd all been blonde-haired and blue-eyed, someone might have raised an eyebrow, but everyone knew that colonies became more and more aware of the potential contamination of their gene pool. Colonies were determined to weed out the irregularities of the human condition. Alicia Jones knew to her core that she was perfect and every experience she'd had to this point confirmed it to her psyche.

The crew sat by protocol and began a litany of rehearsed checklists and reports. Alicia had no part, so she verified her flight profile for the third time in the last hour. Her mathematics were flawless, and verified by the navigational computer aboard the Haven and the colony corporation mainframes planet-side on Eden Two. Her fingers trembled as she adjusted the thruster profiles slightly, accounting for more gravity than reported on the way past a red giant star known as Maneater. As good as she might be in bed, and she knew she was damned good, performance on the flight deck was equally important right now. Her first interstellar jump had to be absolutely flawless. She would accept nothing less from her watch.

"Miss Jones," the captain rumbled. "Coordinates set for first jump?"

"Aye, sir," she chirped but withheld the smile threatening her lips. "First jump in four minutes, thirty-two seconds. Jump duration will be sixteen hours, twenty-seven minutes, and ten seconds to the Lapella Nebula. All systems nominal for foldspace. Generator at eighty-two percent and increasing nominally."

Mubutai nodded and went about the rest of the ceremony. Satisfied like a gluttonous king on his throne, he finally smiled at the crew and let his eyes linger a fraction of a second on Alicia Jones. "Today, we take the Burton Colony out farther than any known human colony into the inner rings of our galaxy. Today, we add our names to the book of explorers handed down from the time of Columbus, Vespucci, and Drake. May God watch over us and keep us. All sections and all decks, pre-jump protocol in effect. Foldspace jump drives to active. Two minutes to jump. Secure all hatches."

A mild storm of activity took over the bridge of the Haven. Alicia merely strapped herself in to her console and warmed up the foldspace system. *Folding time and space at my whim is great cosmic power*, she thought with a grin. Gravitational fields were set to maximum and the Haven wrapped itself quickly in a field of charged dark matter for protection. Forty-five seconds. She gave the all clear to the captain, who smiled at her approvingly.

A warning light clicked onto her console. <<Obstruction warning. Obstruction warning. Unknown object at two million kilometers.>>

Alicia blinked. "That can't be right. I've run the numbers three times!"

"Is the obstruction moving?" Mubutai growled.

Alicia studied it for a moment. "Yes. Transient course. We will clear the obstruction by two hundred thousand kilometers at passing."

"What is it?" Mubutai asked.

Alicia scanned the target and felt her heart skip. Only certain things in the known galaxy were that big! "Not confirmed yet, sir. It's huge. Likely a Grey mothership."

<<Proximity warning!>> The starship computer chimed and turned the bridge lights to a dull red in response. <<Proximity warning. Multiple unknown contacts in jump path.>>

Mubutai looked at Alicia. "Time to jump?"

"Twenty-six seconds."

"Dampening field to maximum."

Alicia adjusted the dark matter field. Blips began to populate her screen by the dozens. She scanned the nearest one, and then scanned it again. *Oh, my God!* "Captain, I'm tracking over a thousand Grey assault fighters in our orbital plane. They are giving us a wide berth—staying out of our gravity well."

Mubutai nodded. "Comms, relay contact reports planetside."

The communications specialist looked up. "Sir, we're being jammed on all frequencies."

"Options?"

"Sir, we have to jump." Alicia stated the obvious. Once a fold engine started, the only safe way to shut it down was to execute the jump. Sir Isaac Newton would have said it was like falling from a great height. *The fall didn't kill. The sudden deceleration did. Or maybe it was that you couldn't stop a physics problem from unfolding.* "Fifteen seconds."

Mubutai looked at his display, undoubtedly studying the swarming Grey spacecraft above the teal-blue and green horizon of Eden as the Haven emerged from the planet's nightside. Blue-green streams of light began to appear from some of the bigger vessels. A beam shot across the bow of the Haven. "God have mercy on us."

"We're taking fire!"

Alicia consulted her readouts. "Minor fluctuations in the forward quarter, sir."

"Dampening field holding. No damage reported." Another officer on the bridge chirped. Alicia wasn't sure who, but it didn't matter. Hundreds upon hundreds of Grey fighters dove for the surface of the planet like black raindrops falling from the sky. Life as they'd known it on Eden, the premier human developed colony in the Outer Rim, was over. There wasn't time for goodbyes. Alicia ran the last sequencer and initiated the fold engine procedure flawlessly. "Ignition." The viewscreens turned purple, gold and green as the *Haven* folded away. There was silence on the bridge until the captain called for the first watch and stood the rest of the crew down for nominal operations. The vehicle was silent from bow to stern as crewmembers and colonists alike wondered what might come of the Grey assault on Eden.

A warning light pulsated on her screen. "Captain, our fold generator was hit before the jump."

Mubutai looked at her for a long moment. "Engineering? What is the status of the fold generator?"

A voice came back from a speaker above Alicia's head. "The generator is running nominally, Captain. But there are fluctuations in the control algorithms. We'll nail it down, sir."

Alicia sat back in her chair and fought tears. Her first thoughts were of her family on Eden, but she compartmentalized them until there was a chance that she could face her feelings alone. Later during her first watch, the only tears she would cry came. Her family on Eden wouldn't likely survive a full Grey assault. The Greys didn't take prisoners, and they never bothered to trade in humankind. Nothing mattered now but her own survival. There would be no one there if she ever returned. She sniffled for a moment and turned back to the console. *In this business you're rich or dead*, Mubutai'd told her once after their daily exercise. No matter what happened, she would survive, even if it meant sacrificing everything she'd ever known. Emotions buried and resolve strengthened somewhat, she snapped to her duties on the watch. She and her watch would perform to perfection every time she held the bridge. She nodded to herself, looking at the bridge and the detailed screens showing the five-kilometer-long, billion-ton starship. This was her home now. Her only home.

No one was going to take it from her.

* * * * *

Chapter Forty-Six

Rain fell from a bright clear sky, cold and hard as it lashed across Tally's shoulders, stinging impacts like a thousand accusations. Surrounded by azure brightness how could it be raining? And from where? Dancing through a field of golden flowers, her bare feet sliding effortlessly through the soft green stalks and spinning the thick air with sweet pollen, she danced to a song she hummed from the depths of memory. Warm smoky nights surrounded by the layered perfection of a jazz trio. The rain falling harder now, reminding her of every emotion, every touch, every feeling they'd shared. The sun felt like the vacuum of space on her face. The rain fell harder, and she could taste the brine on her lips from the tears that fell from the sky.

I love you Tally. Won't you love me?

Mairin, you know I can't now. You're dead for all I know.

I am always here, cariad. And you know that I will be.

Please, Mairin. I never meant to hurt you. I never meant for this to happen. I wouldn't be here except you couldn't give me a child.

I know, Tally. I know.

The sheets were damp on Tallenaara's side of the bed as she sat up, feeling the cool air bringing gooseflesh to her back. Andrew's side of the bed was dry and cold. Empty. The door to the stateroom was closed with a thin sliver of white light at its base. Not bothering to look for the time or boot up her neural connection, Tally padded to the door and opened it slowly.

"I was trying not to wake you," Andrew said without looking up from a tablet. "But I couldn't sit in the dark without wanting another glass of wine and staring out the viewport." Foldspace melted past the windows in vibrant blues and greens. Supposedly a patient observer could occasionally see a star streak across the view, but they'd not seen one yet. Tally wondered if anyone had ever gone mad from simply staring at the ever-changing, addicting kaleidoscope of foldspace.

"What are you working on?"

Andrew shrugged. "Reports. Trying to keep the North American Territories building vertical farms, that sort of thing."

She walked over to him and placed her hands on his shoulders. "Come back to bed, Andy. That will wait until the morning."

"It is morning." He chuckled and then looked up to the ceiling, his face upside down to hers. His smile faded. "What am I going to find at Libretto, Tally?"

Tally blinked. "What do you mean?"

"I wish I knew." Andrew sighed. "I just cannot shake the feeling that I'm walking into a situation that I'm unprepared for. A situation that Earth itself isn't prepared for. I don't have the slightest clue why the Tueg are adamant that this discussion take place on Libretto, do you?"

"I don't know either, Andy." Tally looked out the portal again. "Have you thought that the Tueg simply want you away from Earth?"

"Then why did we have to meet on the Moon?"

Tally shrugged. "Maybe they tried there but you and the delegation were too distracted."

"Distracted? You mean having to fight a war while convincing one of your key allies to stay in the war?"

There was defensiveness in his voice, an accusation being avoided. "You think this has something to do with me?"

"No," Andrew closed his eyes. "But, what if it has something to do with Styrah?"

"And you think it does?" How much does he know? Or suspect?

"I don't know." Andrew looked up at her. "Damn it, Tally. I don't know what to think anymore. Is there anything that the Tueg and the Styrah don't agree on?"

"Not officially, no."

"What does that mean?" Andrew snapped.

"Easy, Andy." Tally let out a long, slow breath. "Tuegs and Styrahi do not agree on the imprinting of humans. The Tueg say that trying to imprint citizens with past memories and experiences will have a negative effect on our society. They argue that those imprinted values and beliefs will set back our cultural and societal development. Essentially, that those few hundred imprints humans have initiated are abominations who should have remained dead." She thought about Mairin for a split second and almost winced.

"But those imprints are helping us turn the tide of this war."

Tally nodded. "And is that a product of their imprints, or by the application of technology?"

"Both," Andrew nodded. "I see what you're getting at."

"And that is?"

"That human imprints are causing the Tueg issues because imprints are barbarous and uncouth. Something like that?"

"You forgot that they should have stayed dead. The Tueg clearly define the worlds of life and death, Andy."

He laughed. "And the rest of us don't?"

"Not if you count imprinting," Tally said. Styrahi scientists had perfected the memory transfer hundreds of years before, and took the planet from a murderous, war enthralled race to peace in three generations. The idea that humans could be retrained from docile pacifists to hardened warriors simply by imprinting was far-fetched at best. Extreme followers of antiquated religions were capable of violence on behalf of their beliefs. The simple fact was that most of the human race simply wanted to be left alone with whatever particular distraction mattered most. Humans were generally far too lazy and self-absorbed to become brutal warriors in the space of a few generations. If that were the goal of sharing imprinting with humans, Styrahi would have to wait hundreds of years before Earth nearly tore itself apart again.

Andrew closed his eyes for a long moment then looked up and smiled. Tally knew that smile. The conversation was over. "What are you doing up? Another dream?"

Tally nodded. "I was dancing in the rain again."

"Just as lucid and real as the others?" Andrew rotated his head slightly to brush her left forearm.

She snorted. "Surprised I wasn't soaking wet or in the shower when I woke up." She rubbed his shoulders lightly. They'd discussed the dreams over the past few months. Seen psychotherapists and doctors, to no avail. There was nothing wrong with her, or so they said. She knew better. The dreams always centered on something she'd only felt when she'd been with Mairin. As much as she wanted to talk about it, to share the experience and make sense of it, she kept it to herself. No one would understand, especially Andrew. Talking about it would only bring questions that she couldn't fully answer without bringing the Styrahi Council into question.

"You keep rubbing my shoulders and I'll be asleep in a minute."

"Then come to bed." Tally smiled down at him. He smiled back, and her hearts jumped. *I love him*, she thought with conviction, *and as much as I love him, I loved her.* She led her husband-to-be by the hand to their bedroom, without a word. They curled warmly around each other as sleep gently took their hands and led them away, Tally praying for rain.

* * * * *

Chapter Forty-Seven

Sergeant Major Jack Trevayne did not shuffle to attention with the parade ground precision of those around him. Unlike the crowd, he let his eyes follow the Division Commander's entrance with barely contained amusement. *Somebody has watched too many John Wayne movies*, Trevayne thought and cleared his throat to avoid smiling. Never mind that General Talvio was Swedish and could most likely name no more than five movies John Wayne filmed, the shuffling, drawling, spitting cowboy schtick was thickly applied, and for some strange reason, revered by those around him. Talvio could be funny and engaging and aloof and distinctly unprofessional, all at the same time. The last time he'd seen military bearing in the mirror might have been his last day at the Terran Academy some twenty years ago. Since then, well, he'd more than likely regressed to this comical state. *No wonder this division is so fucked up*, Trevayne thought.

"At ease," General Talvio drawled, like he'd been raised somewhere south of Stockholm. Trevayne sat and cleared his throat again. He might have been catching something. "Y'all take your seats now."

For a moment Talvio stood tall in the center of the room and slicked his longer than regulation hair back from his forehead and smiled a loose, gaping grin. "How's everybody doing today? Helluva operation we ran down there on Ashland." There was an enthusiastic chorus of grunts and whistles typical of leaders eager to please their rating official. "Now, we're gonna do something that used to be called an after-action review. We're gonna talk about sections of the battle, what happened, what should've happened, and how we can make it better for next time. 'Cause we know there's gonna be a next time, right? Them damned Greys will make sure of that!"

Talvio sat at the head of the mahogany conference tables arranged, not coincidentally, in a horseshoe-shaped formation, and filled his lip with chewing tobacco. "Y'all can chew if you wanna." All around Trevayne, men reached into their uniforms and gladly followed the lead of the division commander. Trevayne managed to keep a straight face.

"You want some?" A lieutenant Trevayne had never met filled his lip and offered the tin can.

Trevayne shook his head and smiled at the young lieutenant losing the battle to keep his face from turning green. "You go ahead, sir." He turned back to Talvio holding court with his regimental commanders. The engineers, artillery, maneuver, logisticians, and medicos were present. At the far end from Trevayne, a lone woman sat, clearly out of place. Her short brown hair framed her face, blue eyes fixed respectfully on Talvio and her countenance completely blank. The sabers of cavalry glinted on the pointed collar of her uniform tunic. For a reason he couldn't name other than intuition, Sergeant Major Jack Trevayne liked the division cavalry troop commander. He'd heard she was an imprint too, but he'd never been able to talk with her about it. She certainly carried herself like one.

"Let's get started, people." Talvio glared around the room, silencing the lieutenants who covered smiles and tried to act their age. Some of the captains and majors, too, Trevayne thought. *God save me from these assholes.*

"We can say that the action on Ashland was successful. We finally had a battle where we gave a little better than we got. Across the division we lost a total of seventy-four tactical vehicles and roughly two hundred soldiers." Trevayne cleared his throat at the pronunciation of soldiers as "sojers." "We slagged an estimated four hundred thirty Grey vehicles. No telling how many casualties them little grey bastards suffered. That ain't important. We need to talk about a few things, but most importantly...and I want a policy and procedure published on this immediately, you staff weenies...we tried to push out our scouts and perform a passage of lines of Styrahi pathfinders that turned into a huge goatfuck."

Talvio spat loudly into the coffee mug that he'd been drinking out of just a moment before, Trevayne was sure, and glared down the table at Trevayne's commander, Colonel Bob Coffey. "Bob? Why don't you tell me what the fuck happened and why you fucked up my cavalry passing them Barbies through?"

The room tittered at the expressly forbidden derogatory term for the Styrah. Trevayne shook his head and smiled at the stupidity around him. He looked up and saw Captain Shields clinch her jaw shut as a ripple of contained rage crossed her face. Talvio leaned forward to glare at Coffey and continued. "Bob? Tell me what the fuck happened and why you ordered the cav to kill those people without authorization."

Coffey cleared his throat in a very silent room. He looked up at Talvio and began to speak in slow, measured words. "Sir, with respect. The division's intelligence network very clearly identified the four vehicles that approached through the Big Ditch as being targets. Whether they were Grey vehicles or captured allied vehicles was unknown, but the G2 clearly identified them as targets."

Talvio looked back to his staff. "That true, Brooksy?"

A short and stocky full bird colonel stood and shook his head. "Not entirely, sir. Those transmissions were course of action gameplay between my staff and the regimental intelligence officers. We had a confirmation of a Styrahi team operating in our AO and were prepared to pass them through the lines of whatever unit they intersected. In this case, they crossed at the cavalry's forward screen point." Trevayne rubbed his chin. Not knowing the division had the responsibility for an area of operations that essentially encompassed the entire dayside of Ashland had been a blessing at the time. *How in the hell did they honestly expect one division to cover that kind of terrain?*

"Thanks, Colonel Brooks. You just kept your job." Talvio grinned, spat, and turned back to Coffey. "Speculation, Bob? You were listening into the division intelligence net, right?"

"Yes, sir. It's SOP for my subordinate commanders."

"To monitor my operations and intelligence net? For what purpose?" Talvio cupped his chin in a hand and raised his eyebrows. "That's my damn net, Bob. You've got your own."

"We monitor your net to act upon the best possible timely intelligence," Coffey said. "That's part of your guidance, sir. I can quote you the exact reference if you'd like."

Talvio glared. "Not necessary, Colonel. Just tell me why you told Captain Shields and her troopers to engage and destroy those vehicles without better intelligence?"

Coffey glanced at Shields. "Sir, I was concerned Captain Shields and her tanks would attempt to develop the situation to a point that would provide the Grey vehicles an opportunity to penetrate our lines."

"So you jammed the receivers on my vehicles from the Styrahi frequency? So I couldn't attempt to talk to them?" Captain Shields was more professional in her delivery than either of her superiors. Trevayne wondered how many of these assholes caught it.

"I jammed you to keep you from talking to them. A passage of lines is supposed to be a stealthy operation!" Coffey replied.

"Like hell," Shields said. "You blocked my communications and then ordered me to kill those vehicles without developing the situation at all! And by doing so, you cost me eight damned good troopers!"

"Soldiers," Coffey snapped. "Will you stop with this fucking cavalry shit? It's not even recognized by the Terran Defense Force!"

Talvio snapped his fingers. "It's recognized by me, Bob. You got that?"

Score one for Captain Shields, Trevayne thought.

"Yes, sir," Coffey replied. "Sir, my order to Captain Shields was meant to save my regiment from engagement and not give away our position to the enemy in a premature fashion."

Shields snorted. "For God's sake! You were dug in on the wrong side of a slope! The enemy could have seen you from orbit, sir."

Coffey folded his hands on the table. "The element of surprise has long been a friend of the successful commander, sir. I wanted to maintain that as long as possible."

"At the cost of some of our allies?" Shields said.

Talvio raised his palm with fingers splayed. "Stop. Point taken, Bob. Captain Shields, what happened when them vehicles approached your passage point?"

Shields took a breath and replied. "Sir, as the vehicles came to the passage point, I determined the lead vehicle was broadcasting in the clear on friendly frequencies that it was the lone friendly vehicle. The vehicles were too far away to see that the trailing vehicles were firing on the leader until it was too late. The trailing vehicles engaged and destroyed my vehicles at the passage point. Both vehicles were total losses, eight men killed. My Interface confirmed the lead vehicle was friendly just as one of my vehicles destroyed it. I gave the order to dispatch the remaining vehicles, which we did in less than fifteen seconds. At that point, the passage point was compromised, and I fell back to my designated supplemental position to await further orders."

"And did them orders come?" Talvio spat again.

"No, sir. I was unaware that the regimental commander gave a movement order until we determined that two nuclear rounds were inbound to our position." Shields looked at Coffey. "I was to understand later that those rounds were called in by Colonel

Coffey on his position as he pulled the regiment out. A movement order never came to me or my troopers."

"That true, Bob?"

Coffey sputtered. "I transmitted on the cavalry frequency. It's in the mission logs."

"I've consulted those logs," Shields said. "You used a frequency that was six hours old, sir."

"I still gave you the damned order, Captain. Don't you sit there and accuse me of shit I did or didn't do!"

Shields sat forward and raised a finger. "You tried, again, to kill my troopers with your incompetence, sir!"

"That's enough!" Talvio sat forward and pointed at Shields. "Never raise your voice at a superior officer, Shields. You heard the man say he tried to contact you, didn't you?"

"Yes sir, I did."

"A man's word is his bond, Shields. That might be impossible for you to understand, you being a woman and all, but that's the truth. If Bob Coffey says he tried, he tried. The fact you got nuked is sad, clearly, but things tend to happen in war." He glared at Shields for a moment in a test of wills. Shields finally looked down. Defeated.

"Now," Talvio paused and looked around. Trevayne wanted to be sick at the grandstanding asshole ensuring that all eyes were on him. "Communications are vital in this division. Bob, I need you to communicate to me why you felt an emergency move of your regiment was necessary."

Coffey paused for a moment. "Sir, I believed that the Greys would target us because of the successful passage of lines. Rather than expend unnecessary casualties, I moved the battalion and called a nuclear strike on my position as a deterrent. If the Greys had attacked my position, they would've been shit out of luck, so to speak."

"Unnecessary casualties? Like your precious tanks over my troopers?" Shields spat.

"I said that's enough, Captain. Not another word, ya hear?" Talvio spat in his cup but never moved his eyes from her.

"Clearly, sir." Shields sat back in the chair but kept her bearing against the titters and chuckles around her.

Looking at the pretty young woman and the bald gloating regimental commander he was bound to, Trevayne wondered idly just who should be leading the regiment.

Talvio turned to his staff, and they changed the course of the conversation to another portion of the battle of Ashland. The Monday-morning quarterbacking, even in the days beyond football, was still a necessary evil of military action. Trevayne tuned him out but let his neurals record the conversation in case the commander asked him a question. He'd be able to read it and respond quickly. Old dogs could learn new tricks, it turned out.

We moved because Coffey thought we'd be attacked, Trevayne thought. What? We jump away and let a nuke from orbit do the fighting? That kind of doctrinal approach was familiar. Vietnam. Lead from afar and let the troops die. Pawns on a chessboard were all they were, not souls worthy of protecting and nurturing, Trevayne thought. How long would it be before Coffey turned tail and ran? Or had the bright idea that he could better fight a battle from an aircraft? Better yet, how far would the man go to cover his ass?

Trevayne leaned back against the comfortable chair and sighed quietly. He had to clear his throat several times and cough a bit to cover the burst of laughter as his imprinted mind spewed out a random thought that made perfect sense in the absurdity of the moment.

Why in the fuck didn't I join the Air Force?

When the meeting broke, Trevayne moved quickly to the door following the slender cavalry commander. He caught her fifteen meters down the passageway. "Ma'am? Can I have a word with you?"

She looked at him with narrowed eyes and clearly bit her tongue. "What can I do for you Sergeant Major?"

Trevayne looked over his shoulder at the empty passageway. "Keep doing exactly what you're doing."

She squinted. "What do you mean?"

"What you know how to do. From that imprint, right?"

She frowned. "Why should I do that?"

Trevayne smiled. "Takes one to know one, I believe they say. So just keep doing what you're doing, Captain."

"I'll try, Sergeant Major." She nodded, and a little color crept back into her face. "One of these days we'll have to have a chat about these people, huh?"

"Mark it on your calendar, ma'am." Trevayne felt the smile die on his face. "If these assholes don't kill us first."

* * * * *

Chapter Forty-Eight

Spaceflight tended to play hell with the circadian rhythm of a human being. All interstellar starcraft observed artificial night according to Greenwich Mean Time, or Universal Time. Most of the vessels ensured humans couldn't effectively screw themselves by inadvertently triggering banks of artificial lights and jump-starting their neurological and physiological systems. Munsen lay in the darkness of the freighter's hold, bathed in the artificial night and unable to cue any lights in his cabin. Nor could he activate his neural network. The only light in the cabin came from a small diode marking the location of the toilet. Sighing, he rolled up to perch on the edge of the bunk. *Three hours of artificial night to go*, he thought with a grunt. His mind was a jumble of thoughts, theories, and emotions, but no clarity. He pushed aside thoughts of his estranged ex-wife for the millionth time. Francesca would have listened and helped him find the reality in his situation. For moments of true clarity, he never minded waking up at zero three hundred. On nights where his mind wouldn't stop babbling incoherently, he merely wanted to shut up the voices, clear his head and focus on something else for a bit. Meditation never worked, and yoga was for granola crunching hippies, as his grandfather would have said.

Standing slowly, he stripped out of his shirt and shorts and stood in the cool room with his skin drawing up into gooseflesh under the forced air from the ductwork. He breathed deeply, cleansing breaths from the diaphragm, and then sat on the cold metal floor cross-legged. Reaching under his bunk, he withdrew the holster and his most trusted piece of equipment. Sliding the M1911X9 semiautomatic pistol from the holster, its weight reassuring in his hand, Munsen sat it down on the floor in front of him and closed his eyes against the faint light. Hands reaching, searching, cradling, he safed the weapon and cleared the empty chamber. Dropping the magazine and setting it down, his vision of where it lay and its orientation centered his thoughts. Field stripping the Colt came easy. The components were all there, resolute as designed and ready to perform. The weapon would not fail when called upon. Its purpose and intent were clear, as his should be.

He would have a chance to talk to the prelate on Libretto. It might be only a few seconds, but he had to get the prelate's attention. He could not fail. The Tueg would ruin everything given the chance. The Styrahi had apologized for their occupation of Tueg in the second council rule some five hundred years ago, but the Tueg were not shy about holding grudges. Their stance in the Legion of Planets was to ensure that other worlds were not occupied by a hostile force and entire cultures subverted to more "civilized" and "advanced" ones. *Aboriginal hostility. Ask the Australians how that went, or maybe the Maoris.* There was nothing the Tueg would like more than to see the Styrahi dealt an equal blow. Perhaps that was their motivation for entrance into the Legion once the Vemeh made first contact with Earth. *Maybe they'd seen human voraciousness and realized that the Styrahi might be an appropriate target if they steered humans that way? Could they really grow a plan for revenge that long? Certainly not.*

The Tueg didn't trust the Styrahi, which was easy to determine. The why? Well, whatever happened during that occupation sculpted the way this whole damned war was going to go down. The Styrah wanted a very close, interbreeding relationship with Earth. They wanted Earth to move forward and out into the galaxy as an explorational peer. Nothing to the contrary was ever a part of the picture! *Unless...unless there was something that both the Tueg and Styrahi knew that they were keeping from Earth. Something about the Greys? Something about their own relationship beyond the "cold fish" receptions and stilted ideologies?*

There was too much he didn't know. He couldn't even be sure where his intelligence officer was. The last report he'd had from Conyers was nearly six weeks old. The Terran Defense Forces were a joke, and the only real strength Earth could project were the Fleet Battle Platforms and their defensive flotillas. Air assets also were proving to be exceptional in this war, but the ground forces were simply stupid and blind. There were some promising reports from the *Ticonderoga's* division of troops, but nothing extraordinary. This war would be won from the air. Or space, or whatever.

Munsen placed the grip assembly on the floor among the components of the pistol and allowed himself a few breaths before he began to reassemble the pistol by feel. The effort cleared his mind, slowed his respiration, and allowed clarity. Clarity that something was completely amiss on Libretto. *The Tueg want to show the Prelate something. Something they could only do on Libretto. But what? By treaty, the presence of Styrahi on Libretto was limited to the wardens and officials, and the rest of the Legion had a sizable presence across the planet. What could be so damned important?*

Munsen finished the assembly and performed the function check of the weapon. Weapon on safe, does not fire. Work the action, selector switch to fire, the trigger pull results in a click. Place the weapon on safe, load a magazine, but do not chamber a round. Holster the weapon. Munsen opened his eyes and slid the holster back into his luggage by feel before climbing back into the bunk with heavy eyes and a renewed mission. On Libretto, he'd have to get proof something was wrong. If he was wrong, well, this second career had been fun. Seconds chances were rarely fun. While there was much he could not change on Earth, he could still make a difference on the Outer Rim.

The war certainly wouldn't be decided, but the lines would be a little clearer. There might actually be an indication of whom he could trust. As a lifelong intelligence officer in now two lifetimes, trust was the one commodity he couldn't spare to just anyone. And this time, where he placed his trust would be equally important.

* * * * *

Chapter Forty-Nine

Fleet Captain Donovan Garrett wondered what this particular generation would have thought of something like the Challenger explosion or the attacks of September 11th. The loss of Eden appeared to hit all of the younger generations, those whose parents had explored the Outer Rim for the first time, in the gut. In all cases, the identification of the day's events was indelibly written on each person's memory at the time they'd heard the news. Garrett had been sitting in the Combat Information Center going over the latest movement reports of the *Ticonderoga's* battle group when the flash message arrived. The coffee he'd poured went cold as they searched for more information. He'd poured out the coffee next to a sobbing lieutenant who'd lost his entire family on Eden. He'd tried to console the young man, but resorted to simply wrapping his arms around the emotional young officer. Eventually, the young man regained a sense of control and bearing, and walked away. Garrett hadn't known his name and did not attempt to figure it out. For that moment, it was more important to be a human being than a military officer; a concept far beyond the grasp of so many officers in this day and age, to be sure. Whatever the reasoning, officers were tending to be more elitist and distant than Garrett was comfortable being. Had he been on any other vessel but the *Ticonderoga* under Admiral Nather's watchful eye, he'd have been drummed out of the service instead of promoted to Commander Air Group. Actually knowing and caring about those people assigned to his command was regarded as a sign of weakness. Many commanders prided themselves on only knowing a scant few of their troops so as to not feel loss or remorse. There was simply no place in the Fleet for an officer who thought more about those under his command than himself.

For the third night in a row since the fall of Eden, Garrett could not sleep. He wandered the dimly lit passageways of the *Ticonderoga,* convinced the current effort to fight the Greys was incoherent and unable to succeed. There had to be a better answer than resorting to Cold War doctrine. *The Greys were stringently replicating every forecasted Russian attack on the Fulda Gap, only they were attacking the planets of the Outer Rim instead of West Germany. How in the hell did they learn to fight like this?* Echeloned forces, one unit following immediately behind another, devoted to simply punching through defenses using their numbers and mass, without any effort to gain or retain the initiative on a battlefield. Slam against the enemy in the same spot, or hold a key sector of defensive terrain until death. Neither strategy made sense, and the current efforts of the Terran Defense Force and the Fleet were employed in an almost Napoleonic array of forces.

Whatever the enemy can do, we can do better. Garrett pushed the thought aside and checked the time for a fifteenth time. Just past 0300. Giving up on the prospect of sleep, Garrett made his way forward to the Officer's Informal Wardroom and expected to find no one there. All told there were five officers huddled over their individual cups of coffee. A couple of engineers in their dirty shirtsleeves sat in one corner, regarding him with raised eyebrows before resuming a muted discussion on whether trilithium could exist in real life. Two pilots just getting ready to go on Alert Fifteen status waved to him before gathering their trays and making their way to the Flight Deck.

Sitting alone, staring into her own tall steaming cup of coffee, sat Mairin Shields. They'd spoken dozens of times over the radio, but never in person. Studying her file to see what made her different from the other TDF officers had given Garrett the recognition he needed. Her short brown hair touched the shoulders of her coveralls. Garrett looked at her face and saw she was as tired as he was. He poured a tall mug of coffee, added two sugars and a slosh of cream, and made his way to her table.

"Mind if I sit?"

She looked up and then started to stand. "Sir?"

"Sit down, Mairin. I thought we should finally meet. I'm Captain Garrett, the Commander Air Group. You know me as Thunder Six." Garrett slid onto the metal bench opposite her and sat down his coffee mug. "You want to tell me what you're sitting here at 0300 thinking about so hard?"

"Can't sleep." She looked down at her coffee and then back up to him. "I suppose I could ask you the same thing."

She didn't say sir, or Captain, Garrett realized and hid a smile behind a long sip of coffee. Officers that sandwiched their conversations with "sir" or "ma'am" had no place in Garrett's world. First names cut through the bullshit behind so much of military tradition and created respect, as well as opening up younger officers for mentoring while letting them feel as if they were being heard as a person and not a faceless soldier padding a commander's rolls. "You could ask me the same thing, and you'd probably assume that I was thinking about Eden."

"I probably would. Did you know anyone on Eden, sir?"

Garrett nodded. "A few colonists I'd met years ago. They'd tell me not to grieve. They knew the risks of colonization." He watched the young woman nod and look at her coffee again. "Want to talk about it?"

Mairin looked up and Garrett saw the beginnings of tears. "I graduated from the Eden Academy."

"I'm sorry," Garrett said.

"Don't be, sir." She dabbed at her eyes with a napkin. "I shouldn't cry for any of them. They made my life miserable."

Garrett chuckled, and when Mairin's eyes flashed anger, he held up a hand. "Academies are supposed to be colleges or universities, but we know what they really are, right? High school in any form is the closest thing to Hell we can face in life, Mairin.

Don't think you were the only one who had a bad experience in that environment. You wouldn't be here if you hadn't learned a few things."

Mairin shook her head. "All of this is imprinted, sir."

Confirmation of his suspicions didn't bring any satisfaction. "I could say the same thing, Mairin."

Her mouth opened, then closed, and then opened again. "You were at least part of the Fleet before you were imprinted though, right?"

"I was. It's standard procedure."

Mairin snorted. "I was imprinted immediately after graduation from the Eden Academy, sir."

"What?" Garrett gaped. Who would ever think of imprinting someone so young, without any military experience whatsoever? Imprinting was supposed to provide subject matter experts with better skillsets! Not take young girls and make them maneuver commanders! "You're joking, right?"

"No, sir. I met a Colonel Munsen who inbriefed me and then administered the imprint that day. I went immediately to Libretto for something he called walkabout."

Walkabout was supposed to take place on Earth. *Just what in the hell was going on here*? "You had no combat experience before Wolc?"

"No, sir. I'd been an imprint a little more than a month when we dropped on Wolc."

Holy shit. Garrett shook his head. "I don't know what to say. Your situation is obviously not within the normal bounds of the program. All two hundred imprints were supposed to be carefully considered based on experience. Having a young woman straight from high school take on the commission of a captain and lead combat operations is damned irregular. I'd like to talk to this Colonel Munsen—"

"You and me both." Mairin chuckled.

"I'd like to find out why you're here at all."

Mairin looked up at him. "Am I not doing what's expected of me?"

Garrett looked at her for moment before answering. Those wide blue eyes had already seen entirely too much. "No, you're not doing what's expected of you at all. You're exceeding it by leaps and bounds."

"I don't get that feeling from my superior officers, sir."

"They're idiots," he laughed. "That stays between us, understand?"

Mairin grinned. "Yes, sir."

"No, you're doing very well. Don't let Coffey get to you. I doubt that guy could lead his regiment to a bake sale."

Mairin nodded. "The regimental sergeant major is an imprint."

"Really?" Garrett sipped from his mug. "I suppose that makes sense, except that he's too quiet."

"I think beat down is more the description, sir," Mairin said.

His eyebrows rose in reply, but the more he thought about her response, the more it made sense. Coffey is a yes man. He wants to surround himself with yes men. The man already drummed every Styrahi warrior from his regiment and publicly decried the whole imprint concept, why wouldn't his sergeant major stay quiet? Did Coffey even know, suspect, or realize that his own Sergeant Major was an imprint? "Does Coffey know his sergeant major is an imprint?"

"I don't know." Mairin shrugged. "He caught me in a passageway the day before Eden fell and told me he was an imprint too, and that I should keep doing exactly what I'm doing."

"That's good advice," Garrett nodded.

"The trouble, sir, is that I don't know what I'm doing!" Mairin flushed and wiped a stray hair away from her forehead. "We're fighting against an enemy using three-hundred-year-old Soviet tactics and getting our asses handed to us. It's all I can do to keep my troopers from being killed by my own command, much less try to fight the little Grey bastards."

"You seem to be doing all right with that."

Mairin blushed. "Thank you, sir."

"Don't mention it." Garrett nodded. "Now why are you sitting here trying not to sleep?"

"It doesn't make sense."

"Try me," Garrett smiled.

"Not what I'm being all insomniac about. The attack on Eden. It makes no sense other than to breed fear and discontent. It's pure terrorism."

Garrett replied. "Maybe that's their intent?"

"Maybe, but I can't help but think they're chumming the waters. Like they're trying to pick a fight."

"But they've blackened the whole planet. There's nothing really left for us to fight for." Garrett licked his lips. What was she getting at? "If they're chumming the waters, they're attracting their prey, right? We have no need for Eden beyond vengeance really."

Mairin shook her head. "They're chumming because they don't want us out there. They're expecting that we're going to defend Tueg, but that's not their next target at all. They're trying to get us to move in the wrong direction. It's misdirection, sir. I just can't figure out where they'd want to go. There are sixty-seven human colonies in the Outer Rim. Either the Greys want something out there, or they're about to bring this war closer to home."

He hadn't thought of that before. What if she was right? What if the emergency Fleet response to the Eden sector was a move they'd calculated for? The Fleet would arrive with guns blazing and either find the Greys ready to fight, or they'd be looking down on a still burning planet wondering where the Greys were. And the Greys could be anywhere, especially behind them. "You think they're going deeper? Sol-ward?"

"Maybe," Mairin shrugged. "Their targets to this point have all been tactical. The LPOPs, Wolc, even Ashland were designed to take out either resources or intelligence gathering operations. Leave us hurting and blind, if you will. Then they attack Eden. Most likely, they were just trying to scare us and make the Tuegs fully leave the Legion. But I can't help thinking they're chumming us away because they are looking for something specific. Something they didn't find on Eden."

Impressed, Garrett sipped his coffee. This young Captain and her imprint had a clear vision of the big picture, while her immediate commanders complained of fuzzy details and incoherent intelligence. She'd proven fairly decent at tactics as well. *Why not go looking for wisdom from the mouth of babes?* Garrett replied slowly. "I probably shouldn't tell you, but that's exactly why I can't sleep either. Trying to find a way we can fight them and, more importantly, beat them at their own game. They're really good at copying our tactics. Their use of airpower is growing, but not with the precision we have, and they aren't directly working their air and ground assets together. I cannot help thinking that's where to beat them." Garrett thought she wasn't going to reply and take the bait. He watched her take a long sip of coffee and look up at him.

Mairin leaned forward over her folded hands on the table. "Sir, we can't beat them like we're fighting now. You already know that. Stop fishing."

Garrett laughed. "So, more direct, how would you beat them?"

"You're the one that already has an idea, sir. Why don't you tell me about it first?" Mairin smiled. Her confident smile built up his own confidence in the scribbled notes and drawings he'd worked on for months.

"About six months after I received the imprint of a distant cousin who retired as a chief petty officer in the American Navy, I started wondering about how we, the Fleet I mean, were arraying our forces in an attempt to win this war. I didn't get very far. I simply didn't have the knowledge, so I started reading about the time I went through Officer Candidate School. I spent a lot of time on Alfred Thayer Mahan. Heard of him?"

"Should I have, sir?"

"Not as an Army puke," Garrett grinned. "I'll give you the short version. Mahan believed naval conflict would essentially be driven by who had the largest fleet of the largest ships. He believed a lot of other things too, but the whole reason we built battleships was Mahan. When they figured out how to launch and land aircraft from ships we went even bigger with aircraft carriers. Now we have eight thousand crewmembers and four thousand combat troops on a Fleet Battle Platform. We have sixty platforms now. All we are doing is trying to meet a numerically superior force with bigger, more fortified technology. The numbers don't add up, and while we're busy building and building, the Greys are using their simple, massive force to conquer world after world after world. Something has to give."

Mairin nodded. "What are you suggesting?"

"The Greys don't value their own, that's why they simply slag vehicles when a battle doesn't go the way they want it to. I agree with your point that the Greys may be looking for something, but whatever it is, they discard it quickly. They don't value key terrain. They've selected some of the dumbest attack points and defensive positions in recorded history, and the only reason they are successful is their sheer numbers. To make matters worse, they telegraph the punch so badly that we typically have hours of response time when they land an attack."

"Eden didn't have that warning, sir."

Garrett shook his head. "We don't know that. Eden doesn't have a defense grid. The Greys could have landed an advance party weeks before the attack to gather intelligence, or look for something like you suggested. When we can catch them, like Wolc or Ashland, we've mounted a decent response. What if there was a unit created for the sole purpose of defeating those early Grey elements and holding the terrain until reinforcements arrived?"

"What, like special operations forces?" Mairin laughed. "That was the biggest waste of time and effort during every war from Vietnam forward. Our special forces performed missions that small units could have performed with the same intelligence and a lot less resources."

"That's my point, Mairin. I don't think we need special forces. Maybe some Styrahi pathfinders, but not special forces. We need a quick reaction force that's more than ten guys with machine guns in a jeep. A squadron of exocraft and a battalion or so of Slammers would do the trick pretty nicely."

Mairin nodded. "Go back to resources, sir. You're going to need heavy lift to get the vehicles up from the surface. You're going to need supply, command and control, intelligence. This is going to be a bigger unit structure than a squadron and a battalion when all is said and done."

"Point taken." Garrett withdrew a small notebook from a pocket in his coveralls and scribbled a few notes. "So we're looking at two to three hundred folks on the personnel side at a minimum."

"I guess," Mairin said. "Unless you had personnel that could train for two jobs. Say a combat job and an operational job."

"'Everyone fights, no one quits,' right?" Garrett laughed until he saw Mairin squinting at him. "An old movie. Actually, an even older book that every young officer should read. I'll send you a copy." He paused and consulted his notes. "This is my pet project. If push came to shove, I could write the full proposal for a battle group and see what the brass thought of it. Right now, I'm as concerned as you at keeping my folks alive." He fidgeted with the notebook for a moment, then closed the cover and began to put it away.

"You're giving up that easily?"

Garrett met the young woman's eyes. "It's a pipe dream."

"Only if you don't flesh it out."

"What's that supposed to mean?" Garrett snapped. "It is fleshed out."

"No, it's not," Mairin frowned at him. "I'm going to refill my coffee cup and then tell you why you've got the ground forces all wrong. Then, you'll see that it's fleshed out. That it has potential, sir." She gestured to his cup. "You take it black or with cream?"

"A little cream and some sugar, since I can't have whiskey."

Mairin smiled and collected his cup. "We've got about an hour before I have to be on duty. I think we can make a pretty good stab at your notional unit in that amount of time, don't you?"

* * * * *

Chapter Fifty

Andrew Cartner knew the truth of being a politician at the age of fifteen. He'd walked into his father's office one night to find his polished, professional father sitting alone in a darkened room with soft music playing. The ice tinkling in his father's whiskey echoed as Andrew poked his head in and asked if his father was okay. Without turning to his son, George Cartner chuckled and said softly, "Andy, when the time comes for you to sit as the prelate, understand your duty is not a mantle you can don and doff at will. Your duty is a set of shackles. It is unforgiving and relentless, and will break you if you do not understand one single thing—political service is little better than indentured servitude."

Shortly after his father's death, Andrew Cartner became the prelate and learned all too well what his father meant. Now in the ornate meeting room of Consulate of Earth on Libretto, he stood watching the Tueg delegation slowly file past. He smiled automatically for the vids and shook the appendages offered to him with earnest smiles and nods, never letting anyone know that all he wanted was to walk away. As the doors closed and his delegation took stock of the first meeting and the Tueg position, several of his advisors began to speak at the same time. Andrew wasn't listening. There were about three hours before he'd be standing with the Tuegs at a state dinner in his honor, and he didn't want to be there. Didn't want to have all those eyes staring at him like he was a savior. He looked out the window of the meeting room at the artificial sunlight of Libretto City's dome and immediately thought of Tallenaara. In so many ways, this was her city. He could feel her nuances in the architecture when he'd been able to go outside for the press conferences. The calming influence it had was good for him, but here in this gaudy room with its burgundy and gold and hideous carpeting, he felt the shackles around his ankles binding him to the task at hand. There would be no escaping it.

Who says? Andy thought. He turned to the discussion behind him and simply raised a hand. "Please send Darren to see me. I will be taking a private walk in the Promenade Gardens."

There was a rustle of protest that died as soon as his eyebrows rose. He'd have to say something to quell them. "We have worked very hard today and made significant progress. There is much work left to do. Tonight is a State dinner and ball in our honor. My expectations of all of you remain the same—enjoy yourselves, but be ready for work tomorrow. Fun is something not typically included in our work, so take this opportunity. I will see you all this evening."

He left the suite of rooms without another word and walked out of the hotel, pausing only to nod politely at some tourists who recognized him outside. He gestured to the guards to keep their distance as he entered the Promenade Gardens. The efficiency of his people amazed him; they'd been able to essentially clear the entire botanical gardens in a few scant minutes. The afternoon monsoonal storms were past as the seasons began to change. Autumn would be coming soon. He smiled at the thought of seeing the leaves change colors, though nothing would change his idea that the forests of France or the Appalachians were undoubtedly the most gorgeous he'd ever seen. Hopefully they wouldn't be here to see the forests of Libretto turn from green to gold.

"You called for me, sir?"

Andrew shook his head and smiled at his friend. "You know I hate it when you do that."

"One can never be too careful." Darren McMasters grinned and leaned against the railing beside him. "I heard it went well in there today."

Andrew snorted. "Which you've interpreted as?"

"That you're really pissed off the Tuegs are even considering leaving the Coalition, and you feel they are hiding something from us. From what I can see, it's just barely staying below the surface. Not a good way to start negotiations, Andy."

Andrew nodded. *Leave it to Darren to always hit the nail on the head.* "The Tuegs are going to pull out of the Coalition and execute a home world defense. It's only a matter of time."

"Agreed. But why go through the whole production of negotiations here?"

"I've been thinking about that for weeks. Why here? And for that matter, why me?"

"You are the Prelate, Andy." McMasters grinned. "As for the location and the production? Even a state dinner? You've got me without an answer."

Andrew nodded and leaned down on his elbows. They were a long way from Cardiff, and the irony made him sigh. "Am I doing what I need to be doing?"

"Of course you are."

"Don't bullshit me, Darren." Andrew sighed. "I feel like I'm missing something, whether it's something here, something at home, or something in this damned war that I don't know. But it's slowly driving me insane not knowing."

"This war is much bigger than you or any man can understand, Andy. We've got good people around us trying to make sense of this, and we will. It's just going to take time. And I do think you could do one thing better."

"What's that?" Andrew asked.

"Exactly that. Ask more questions. The Tueg are so polite and practiced that even their non-answers can tell us volumes. Have you asked them directly why they wanted you here on Libretto for this? I'd love to see how they don't answer that question."

Of course Darren was right. If they answered the question, there wouldn't be much doubt. If they didn't answer it, then they could speculate and develop a particular line of questioning that could steer the Tueg to a definitive answer. He'd done similar things before, so why not again?

"Any new intelligence?" They'd brought a full diplomatic complement with them, complete with the advance party of "tourists" scouring the planet for information of any significance.

"Nothing yet. We're expecting a full briefing from them tomorrow, but all of the advance materials they've forwarded have been inconclusive. They center a lot of discussion on the Tueg / Styrahi relationship. If the lack of trust and history of deceit is as long and detailed as our intel community says, there are certainly implications we'll have to address."

"Like who to trust." Andrew looked at the hibiscus plant just beyond the railing with its trumpeting flowers of pink and orange. Another example of Earth brought here for a specific reason. Why would the Styrahi go through so much trouble? *It brought you Tally*, he thought with a defeated smile. "Damnit, Darren. What are we going to do now?"

McMasters chuckled. "Same thing we always do."

"Drinking heavily is not an option anymore."

They laughed for a moment, the burdens a little lighter. McMasters spoke softly, "We're going to go to the dinner, and we'll ask some questions. I think I can get a little more information through informal channels."

"You really do have a girl in every port, you sonuvabitch." Andrew chuckled and rested his hand on McMaster's shoulder. "I almost admire you."

"Almost?" McMasters laughed. "We'll see what Lady Tallenaara says about that. Have you asked her about this whole thing?"

Andrew nodded. "She can't shed any light on why we're here on Libretto either, except this planet is designed for all species and is as neutral as Switzerland was."

"Then that's where we start. Switzerland."

"I'm not following you, Darren." Andrew squinted. "What does this have to do with Switzerland?"

"Switzerland was neutral in all things, right? Who's the neutral party here? The Tueg or the Styrahi? We don't know, do we? But now that we're here, we have to assume that everything is on the table, and we have to ask questions. The more questions we ask, the more information we have to make a decision about how to proceed. God forbid there's some piece of information we've been missing all these years. I'd hate to think we'd been dragged into an unwinnable war for all the wrong reasons."

"You think this is an unwinnable war? We seem to be making progress."

McMasters shrugged. "Unless we figure out what we're really fighting for, this could go badly. The Greys exploit any weakness in our tactics no matter what we seem to throw at them. Yes, our forces are having an impact, but the most impacts are with the Fleet assets and not the ground forces the Styrahi convinced us we needed. That concerns me almost as much as not knowing what the Greys want."

Andrew looked at his watch. "I'm supposed to meet Tally for a drink down by the river. Would you care to join us?"

"Absolutely, though I will have to catch up to you. I have the daily staff briefing to attend, and I'm already late for it, though there's something about making underlings wait I find oddly satisfying." McMasters chuckled. "Where will you be down there?"

Andrew checked his neurals. "Little place called 'Terrace.' Apparently you can't miss it. It's on a terrace."

"Smashing," McMasters chuckled. "I'll be along shortly." He turned to walk away. Andrew watched with a small smile on his face as Darren left him alone in the garden.

I am a lucky man, Andrew thought. Best friend and chief of staff in the same person. He left the Promenade Gardens with a long look at Libretto's setting sun, the bright yellow star's warmth radiating its fading light on his skin, the moist air redolent with the smells of flowers and grass, and smiled. His wife-to-be was a brilliant architect, among her other talents. He thought of the comfort of Tally's arms. After a day like this, he needed to see her soft smile. Somehow, being around her would make him feel better. Maybe even good enough to attend the state dinner without complaint.

* * * * *

Chapter Fifty-One

When they designed and built Libretto City, Tallenaara and her associates called it the 'grand illusion.' Fifteen kilometers in diameter and soaring more than six hundred feet from the surface at its apex, the concept of building a domed city on a hospitable planet was laughable to the Styrahi unless they considered several factors. The security of the city was one aspect, as the dome effectively camouflaged the city from orbit. The size of the dome ensured that it had its own weather system, including precipitation. Someone standing in the middle of the dome would likely have no idea they were inside an artificial structure. The illusion, though, was that the dome was built for the humans, a race who'd once explored the stars but now had to be coaxed out of their own atmosphere. Tally and her friends would laugh and wonder whether they were protecting the humans from the environment because of their relative complacency, or were they protecting the environment from the humans?

Many of the Styrahi Council elders openly compared humanity to a bacteriophage, endlessly reproducing and slowly consuming all available resources. If the Vemeh hadn't finally been convinced of humanity's worth, Earth would have provided a unique case study that could have consumed every academy and university in the known galaxy. Earth and humanity certainly had their good points. Humanity had largely adopted democracy, though a sizable portion of the population still clung to organized religion like a tattered security blanket. Peace eventually blossomed, and economic stability improved as humanity left behind the need for fossil fuels, concentrating instead on new energies and living within their means. Cultural shifts from entitlement slowly gave way to true selfless service, but with one critical cost.

Humanity had lost its ability to fight tooth and nail for what it really wanted. Could they learn again to fight for something beautiful and much, much larger than themselves?

Trying to push her thoughts aside, Tally walked along the Little Amazon towards the city center. Among the multi-species throng, she wondered who among the humans she saw here might be on their way to fight and die for the others? *Dulce et decorum et pro patria mori*? Tally shook her head. Mairin didn't fight for king and country.

But Mairin had gone on to fight, hadn't she? If it was truly love she felt for me then why didn't she stay? Tally paused at a railing and watched the farmed trout and carp alert to her presence and hang motionless in the water expecting bread crumbs or the like from her. *What if the grand illusion for Mairin had been me? Dammit, all of this is behind me, isn't it?* She was engaged to Andrew now and in love with him as much or more than a decade before, yet Mairin pervaded her thoughts. Her dreams. And sometimes her memory threatened to derail everything. Like now. A State Dinner in a few hours and she was standing by the river about to cry her eyes out for something fleeting. Something trivial. Something told to old friends over a glass of wine. "Did I ever tell you that I...?"

A small alarm triggered in her neurals that she was due at Terrace in ten minutes. Her best projected time of arrival was eleven minutes, and it would be most wise to hurry. The hungry fish waited for her to throw a morsel, but she turned away. *I'm not like you. Not waiting for my handout for survival. I can move on. I have moved on.*

Looking up at the warm light of Helios, she shrugged off her doubts and thoughts. Yes, they would always remain in some version. The what-ifs shared with friends over a drink with a laugh, the half-hearted regrets she thought she might change if given the chance to do it again but knowing she really wouldn't. She wouldn't be where she was without her experiences. Mairin would always be special, but that would be about it. For now, her life revolved around Andy. The barely concealed security personnel following her every move brought a smile to her face. *Did they really think they were inconspicuous, or were they that confident that most of the species around them were just oblivious? Was the heightened security really necessary here on Libretto?* Not even the Greys knew where it was and if they happened upon it, there would be little evidence beyond the residue from lingering faster-than-light vessels. Otherwise, it looked like a perfect stop for water and oxygen just like at least four hundred planets in this ring of the galaxy.

Apprehension faded as she walked in long graceful strides towards the entertainment district and found her way by consulting the maps she'd scrutinized so hard so many years ago. Her inner compass never failed and brought her through a tunnel and a service entrance to the steps of Terrace with a good four minutes to spare. The media corps were not invited to this event, and thankfully, Terrace was decidedly empty tonight. *A perk of being the Prelate*, Tally thought with a grin. *The best tables are always available when you're traveling in these circles.*

"Good afternoon, Pierre," she spoke French effortlessly as she nodded to the owner of Terrace. She strode through the entrance and easily spotted where they'd be sitting. Her favorite table, alongside Triumphe Falls, brought a smile to her face. She remembered when Emolinna built the six-foot feature with her bare hands. A large bottle of Narrobian red wine sat with fine china place settings. A bouquet of Librettan calla lilies in the center, the best imported silver shining, and some simple one-piano jazz tinkling from across the terrace.

Perfection, she thought and walked to the table. Pierre seated her with the casual grace of a gentleman, his playful repartee making Tally smile as she looked off in the distance. She could see Andy now about two hundred yards away. There was no mistaking him for any other man, with his ambling gait and artfully ruffled suit. His collar was unbuttoned, and his tie was missing, most likely wadded into a pocket for someone else to worry about pressing. He looked relaxed, fit, and more attractive than ever.

He closed the distance at a slow, easy pace, his gaze never leaving hers and the small smile on his face slowly widening. There was a flurry of movement at the entrance, the staff clearing the way for Andy and a few gawking civilians. She smiled at her fiancé and he grinned at her.

I love this man. His eyes flitted from her to the entrance, and his smile vanished. He opened his mouth and looked at Tally—no, past her. A scream left his lips, and she felt strong hands pulling her backward.

"Get down!" A man fell across her. She saw the golden eagles of a Terran Defense Force colonel before a massive explosion slammed her eyelids shut. Heat and debris hit her exposed skin. *What the...?*

"Andy!" She screamed. "Andy!" She couldn't hear anything beyond the rush of blood to her head. She opened her eyes and looked up into the dome. This could not be happening. Not here. Grey ships by the hundreds fired particle beams that stabbed the evening light and evaporated the dome. War descended upon the great illusion. Tears filled her eyes. She pushed against the colonel and he rolled away. "Andy!"

The colonel caught her arm. "He's gone. You need to get out of here."

Gone? Gone where? The realization slapped her in the face. "Andy?"

"Tallenaara, he's dead. The Greys are attacking, and you're about the only person who can escape this goddamned dome before they bring it down. You understand me?"

She smoothed the errant hair from her face and felt the dirt and dust caking her. The route was easy. She could be out of the dome in three to four minutes if she ran the whole way. "What about Andy? The Prelate's diplomatic service?"

The man shook his head. "Without the Prelate, and without your marriage being official, you're nothing to them now. If they try and jump out of here the ship will not wait for you. Now get out of here! Get word to Styrah if you can. Our troops are on the way, but they aren't gonna be here in time to save the city."

She shook her head. It was too much. Get out of the dome? And go where? Do what?

"Listen, Tally! You've got to get out of here. Survive! Mairin still needs you."

She recoiled as if slapped. "What did you say? Who are you?"

"My name's Munsen. I recruited Mairin, you understand? I sent her here in the first place. We were wrong about all of it. She needs you. You have to survive, Tally. What you know about this planet will get you killed! Now get your ass out of this dome!" He touched her neural bracelet and she saw his information feeding in. Along with pictures of Mairin. And her. She saved his information with a thought. *We were pawns*, she thought. *You realized too late that your scheme had actual consequences.*

"Thank you," she said.

"Move!" Munsen drew a pistol and moved away without looking back.

At the speed of thought, her legs jolted into action. The entrance to Terrace was a smoky, bloody massacre. Somewhere in that mess, Andrew Cartner lay dead. She knew it and didn't need any confirmation. Over the railing she vaulted, kicking her shoes off. As she ran, she doffed her tattered jacket and cast it aside. She ran through the entertainment district and its throngs of innocents dying by scores as particle beams tracked them down. She dove into the service corridor and through doors even Libretto City's denizens had no idea were there. She made the outer ring of the dome in four minutes, and it took her two more minutes to get out of the dome on the far side. The Greys hadn't surrounded the city yet. There was a slim opportunity to escape. She ran northwest through the forest as fast as her legs could take her.

There were no flashing messages from McMasters and the Prelate's staffers, so she disconnected her neurals completely. Munsen was right, she knew. The amount of care that anyone on the Prelate's staff, including Darren McMasters, had for her dwindled by the moment. The silence of her neurals comforted her. There was nothing to do now but run, and survive. She wanted to promise herself that Andy would not have died in vain for anything, but she couldn't. The Grey assault ships hovering over Libretto City gave meaning to Andy's death, but there was little solace there.

But what if it hadn't been the Greys? And how did Munsen know?

She thought about those questions as she ran until she could think about them no longer. *Run. Just run.*

Just run.

After four hours of running at the speed of genetic perfection, she burst through the tree line and saw her cabin, the set for her grand illusion with Mairin. Tally sank to the wet grass and sobbed. She fingered the ring on her left hand as she cried for Andy. She would never stop grieving. Her hearts broken twice, she cried until exhaustion threatened to bring her to sleep. Libretto had fallen to the Greys, and she understood beyond measure that whether Munsen had lied to her or not, she had to survive to find out for herself. Legs wobbling and sore from exertion, Tallenaara stumbled to her cabin and her only chance for survival.

* * * * *

Chapter Fifty-Two

The godawful noise brought Mairin out of a deep, dreamless sleep. She slapped at her alarm to no avail, and her anger flared. Opening her eyes, she saw the red cabin lights engaged and knew the braying klaxons were a General Quarters call by how fast Conyers managed to tug herself into a flight suit.

"What's going on?" Mairin yawned and didn't bother keying her neural connections.

"General Quarters!" Conyers was already panting. "We've got to get ready! Emergency Drop action. The ship turned around last night. We're heading into the Rim somewhere."

Mairin slid her legs out of the covers and set her feet on the cold floor. *Another drop*, she thought without much emotion. Her heartbeat barely accelerated at the prospect of combat anymore. Reaching for her coveralls and boots, Mairin allowed her neurals to boot up, only to have the sequence interrupted by Admiral Nather's voice booming on the 1-MC.

"All hands, this is the Admiral. We have been ordered to defend Libretto at all costs. Approximately six hours ago, *Ticonderoga* and her ships jumped secretly toward the Inner Rim of the galaxy in response to a most heinous action. This afternoon, Prelate Andrew Cartner was assassinated on Libretto."

Mairin stood up quickly, slamming her head into Conyers bunk above her. "Goddamnit!" She blinked away the stars and felt tears flow. Tally would be dead too. *Those sons of bitches!*

Nather continued, "In all, there were numerous casualties, and several of his advisors and staff are still missing. Within minutes of the Prelate's death, three large Grey motherships appeared above Libretto. Their attack is well underway. The *Ticonderoga* will arrive at Libretto in approximately seventeen minutes. All combat crews to stations, all gun crews to active, and all offensive and defensive systems to maximum. God help us all. Good hunting."

Conyers looked over her shoulder. "You okay?"

"Fucking bunkbeds!" Mairin rubbed her head and made sure there was no bleeding.

"They killed the Prelate," Conyers had tears in her eyes. "And...they're attacking Libretto!"

Mairin stopped slipping her arms into her coveralls and grabbed Conyers by the arm. "Settle down, Laura."

Conyers was having none of it. "The Prelate! Ohmygod! They got to the Prelate! They can get to anyone! We've got to...got to..."

"Hey!" Mairin stepped into Conyers face. "Knock it off! You're not going to be worth a shit to me or anyone else unless you completely unfuck your mind right now! The prelate and his consort are dead, and there's nothing we can do about it." She paused for breath and felt her heart lurch at the thought of Tally dead. "We're going down there to make those bastards pay, Laura. You've got to get me and my troopers down there perfectly, you got that? Don't think about anything else until we get back here, all right?"

"But it's the prelate!" Conyers pleaded. "He's the voice of Earth."

Mairin nodded. "And he's dead now."

"But...but. . .how can you say it like that?"

"Because nothing is going to change it," Mairin replied and looked away.

Conyers whispered, "When did you get so cold, Mairin? How can you be so detached right now?"

"What? Because I didn't grow up on Earth I'm detached from this whole thing? Bullshit!" Her eyes began to tear, and she let them. *Goddamnit, Tally!* "I'm more emotionally connected than you can possibly imagine right now, Laura. So don't give me that detached shit. It's time to strap on your aircraft and drop me and my troopers down there to give those bastards hell."

"Yeah." Conyers nodded. "Um...okay. You're right."

Mairin smiled tightly. "Damn right I am. Now get your shit together. I'll see you onboard that piece of shit Rhino of yours."

"Screw you," Conyers grinned and stepped out of the stateroom into the controlled chaos of the passageway. Mairin carefully strapped on her boots and zipped up the coveralls. After a stop at the armory for her sidearm, Mairin strode into the drop bay as the last of the first load of Slammers were loaded onto Rhino Four One, her bird. She stepped up onto the front slope of her Slammer and noted it was perfectly slung for the drop. Glancing at the other three Slammers on board, she could tell they were similarly slung, and the rest of her troop would be as well. *Surrounding yourself with the best breeds success*, she pushed the thought down. *Patronize me later, Grandpa.*

"Ma'am?"

Mairin looked at Connors. The young communications specialist was looking at the metal bottle she'd removed from her leg pocket. "It's water, Connors. Want to smell it?"

Connors shook his head. "No, ma'am. Just curious."

"When we get back here Connors, and we're going to be back here after this mission, you get me? When we get back here, I want you to look up a poem called 'Fiddler's Green.' You'll understand then."

"Yes, ma'am."

Mairin nodded as she finished her preparations. She'd woken in the middle of the night two days ago with the words floating in her mind. Written around World War I, the anonymously written poem was the quintessential cavalryman's creed in a sense. When she'd looked up the text in its entirety, she'd been moved enough to go to the maintenance deck and secure a metal canister larger than a flask and about the size of a Thermos, whatever that was. There hadn't been time to push the poem out to her troopers, but she vowed that it would become canon.

"Halfway down the trail to Hell,
In a shady meadow green
Are the Souls of all dead troopers camped,
Near a good old-time canteen.
And this eternal resting place
Is known as Fiddler's Green.
Marching past, straight through to Hell
The Infantry are seen.
Accompanied by the Engineers,
Artillery and Marines,
For none but the shades of Cavalrymen
Dismount at Fiddler's Green.
Though some go curving down the trail
To seek a warmer scene.
No trooper ever gets to Hell
Ere he's emptied his canteen.
And so rides back to drink again
With friends at Fiddler's Green.
And so when man and horse go down
Beneath a saber keen,
Or in a roaring charge of fierce melee
You stop a bullet clean,
And the hostiles come to get your scalp,
Just empty your canteen,
And put your pistol to your head
And go to Fiddler's Green."

Dropping into the hatch, she connected her helmet to the communications cords and smoothed her hair out of the way before slipping it on. Immediately she could hear her crew and the other platoons going through the appropriate pre-combat checks. "Crew report."

"Driver ready."

"Comms ready."

"Gunner ready."

<<Interface ready. Sabot indexed, sabot loaded. All systems nominal, Captain.>>

Mairin nodded and keyed the troop command frequency. "Guidons, guidons, guidons, this is Black Six. Engage all drop protocols at this time. Six out." She rekeyed the radio with her bottom lip and switched to the Rhino's frequency. "What's the plan up there, Laura?"

"Standard drop protocol. Looks like the regiment is dropping about thirty miles to the west of Libretto City. No idea what the mission is, expect a FRAGO on that any minute. I'll push you what I've got."

Icons lit up on Mairin's terminal and she nodded. "Got it. Any idea on our position in this mess?"

"Negative, ma'am."

Mairin blinked. "We're on private channel, right Laura?"

"Yes, ma'am."

"Then knock it off, okay? We're good."

A sigh filled Mairin's ears. "I'm glad to hear that."

"Now, see what you can do to get me some intelligence from the CIC. I'm going to brave the command frequency."

Conyers snorted a laugh. "Good luck with that."

"Maybe he hasn't started drinking yet," Mairin chuckled and made a wind-it-up gesture to Conners, who keyed Mairin's frequencies over to the command net. She listened for a few seconds before calling Bullet Six, to no avail.

Conner replied. "Private transmission inbound from Bullet Nine."

"Give it to me." Mairin glanced at her terminal again.

"Saber Six, Bullet Nine on private. You with me?"

Mairin said, "Loud and clear, Sergeant Major."

"You probably don't need this reminder, but there is an exception to every rule." Trevayne chuckled in her ears. "You understand my meaning?"

You mean to disobey that drunk asshole's orders whenever I see fit? You're damned right I do. "Roger that, Sergeant Major."

"Good. We have no plan right now. I doubt we're going to have one before we drop."

Mairin shook her head. "Don't we have a staff that's supposed to plan shit like this?"

"You and I both know most staff elements above a battalion level can't plan their way out of a wet paper sack." Trevayne sighed. "Besides, what we find on the ground is going to drive how we fight. It always does."

Mairin agreed. "Stay safe out there, Sergeant Major. Be ready to empty that canteen."

Trevayne chuckled. "We end up at the Green today, young Captain, and the first round is on me."

"Deal, Sergeant Major. Saber Six clear."

"Bullet Nine, out."

Mairin saw all of her vehicles were completely ready for drop and allowed herself a momentary pause. *If this ends up being the end of the trail to Hell, it's a good day to die. Wasn't that from a movie?* She shook the thought away. "Interface, what's the weather over our projected drop zone?"

<<Low visibility, temperature of seventeen degrees Celsius, with heavy rain in the area.>>

Mairin almost laughed out loud and then nearly sobbed. Rain. Her heart ached for a long moment, with thoughts of rainy mornings sitting in Tally's arms in the cabin, watching storms roll across the hills and over the lake. Holding hands in the rain. Kissing in the rain. Making love in the—

<<All Saber elements configured for drop. Standing by for Rhino launch order.>>

"Roger, Interface." Mairin sniffled a little and then strapped herself into the commander's chair as tightly as possible. "Time to Libretto?"

<<Ship's time is counting down from one minute forty-one seconds. Mark.>>

Mairin looked at her crew. "Anybody got anything they want to say right now?"

For a moment no one said anything. Then Booker keyed his intercom from the hull. "Ma'am, I have something to say if you don't mind."

"What is it, Booker?"

"Well," he paused as if trying to find words. "Ma'am? Y'all pack any extra clean underwear? I think I might need some in a minute."

Mairin's mouth fell open and then she looked at Conner who began to laugh. The whole crew laughed as one and their tension melted away slightly. The joke took their focus and their stoicism right out the door. Exactly where it needed to go for a fleeting moment. They laughed until tears came from their eyes and their stomachs hurt. As the *Ticonderoga* slid effortlessly from foldspace into orbit around Libretto, they were able to recover themselves enough to prepare the Slammer for drop.

<<Drop sequence abort. Drop sequence abort. *Ticonderoga* reports bay is not clear for drop.>>

Mairin chinned to the command frequency. "Thunder Six, Saber Six. Bay nine abort. Need a status update."

"Roger, Saber Six." Garrett's voice came with a private icon on her helmet visor, "Remember our late-night coffee and napkins exercise?"

Mairin smiled. The man filled five napkins with notes. *He wasn't seriously going to do it, was he?* "Roger, Thunder Six."

"Then be ready for it, Saber Six."

* * * * *

Chapter Fifty-Three

Admiral Nather debated with himself whether or not to go to the bridge and oversee the deployment of forces once the *Ticonderoga* left foldspace and entered orbit. Carefully tugging himself into a combat pressure garment in accordance with general quarters actions, Nather walked from his quarters and entered the bridge with customary fanfare from the officer of the deck.

"Admiral on the bridge!"

Nather looked around quickly. "Carry on." Across the room, the captain of the *Ticonderoga* poured over the planet's data as they approached at multiples of *c*. Where the platform would emerge from foldspace in relation to the planet's rotation seemed to be the critical question, and showed his staff was doing all necessary to support the deployment of the TDF forces in accordance with their battle plan. Nather moved to his chair, sat down, and immediately noticed it was too quiet for the *Ticonderoga* to be less than a few minutes from orbit. Granted, the bridge of a combat vessel should not be chaotic, but quiet and calm just before battle seemed odd. No one twitched with nervous energy. No one seemed to be particularly worried about the big picture. Nather almost smiled to himself at the thought of stirring up his crew and snapped his fingers loud enough that half of the bridge turned to him.

"Ops, I need to know the TDF drop plan. Who are we dropping where?"

The operations officer stood and faced the Admiral. The brassy leaves of a lieutenant commander glinted in the light as he began to speak. "Sir, Lieutenant Commander Porterman. Sir, there is no drop plan from TDF. The only guidance we've received is to drop all forces immediately upon attaining orbit, regardless of position. All combat forces are to secure the immediate terrain and link up. TDF will then develop a plan based on the consolidation of forces on the ground."

Nather felt his mouth drop open involuntarily. "You've got to be shitting me, Commander."

"No, sir. That's the guidance we received from TDF before reaching foldspace, sir."

We're going to kill a lot of troops today for another half-assed operation against a superior enemy force on terrain of their choosing. Jesus Christ! Drop everybody wherever you can? Just like the goddamn gliders of Normandy, Nather thought with a shudder. He looked at the terrain projection of Libretto on the far wall. "Where is the greatest concentration of Grey forces? Are they holding any key terrain or limiting themselves to the cities?" There was silence on the bridge. "Anybody? Do we have any intelligence?"

Nather allowed his eyes to flicker across the room, meeting the expectant gaze of every man and woman in the control center. No one spoke, and Nather felt heat rising from his tunic collar and threatening to take over his face. "Let me state for the record that I am not about to commit any forces without at least a semi-coherent plan from TDF headquarters."

The operations officer shrugged. "Sir, we have no other guidance at this time. TDF Command echelons are still at least an hour out at their maximum *c*. I have drop requests from multiple bays, Admiral."

Like a bunch of dumb rabid dogs, Nather thought. "We don't even know what we're fighting! They have no intel, no information. We're supposed to drop them blind?" Nather fumed for a moment as his mind raced. *I don't like this one bit. If we drop them blind, they're either going to be isolated from other units or we might just drop them right into the proverbial hornets' nest. Even a piss poor plan would be better than this!* He brought a hand to his face and cupped his chin with the flesh between his index finger and thumb. There had to be a way around this with some type of intelligence. "Are we scanning the planet from all available optics on station?"

"We have nothing on any shared intelligence nets, sir. Right now we're operating under the assumption we're going to be the first platform on the scene. Best case scenario is that we'll have our scans and the scans from at least one other platform group in ten minutes," the operations officer replied.

"What's your name again, son?" Nather asked.

"Porterman, sir. Peter Porterman."

Nather nodded, wanting to say something thoughtful. "Give me everything you have when you have it, is that clear?"

"Clear, sir."

Another voice chimed out. "Foldspace termination in five seconds. Three seconds! Now!"

Everything vibrated and Nather bit back a touch of bile in his throat. "Up screens."

Libretto appeared in its Earth-like splendour. The disc of blue and white was seemingly on fire in a dozen places he could see. White plumes of smoke stretched for thousands of miles, like a child's marker across the surface of the planet. He heard the gasps from the bridge crew but ground his teeth together instead of mouthing the horror he felt. Nather snapped. "Time to TDF arrival."

"Fifty-eight minutes, sir," Porterman said. "We're getting repeated calls for drop from TDF commanders, sir. Bays one through eight and bay ten all reporting ready for immediate drop."

Nather snapped his head to Porterman. "Who's in Bay Nine? Why isn't it ready?"

Porterman consulted his screen. "Sir, I'm showing it as Third Tank Regiment's cavalry troop. I have a door malfunction alarm on the lead Rhino."

"I see." Nather looked across the bridge to his Commander Air Group. Garrett didn't smile, but he didn't have to. They held each other's eye contact for a long second. *I hope you know what you're doing, Don.* "Status of aircrews?"

"Sir, all combat air patrols are away. I have recon birds outbound in one minute on polar trajectories. Should have some farside intelligence in sixteen or seventeen minutes," Garrett reported without moving from his console. "All combat squadrons standing by, Admiral."

Nather looked back at Libretto and quietly sighed. *I hope to God this works.* "Drop all bays but bay nine. I want a full status on that bay in two minutes. Relay that status to combat commanders. Drop officer, you have the conn."

The heavy drop bays fell open, and slowly the combat vehicles of the *Ticonderoga* fell towards the dayside of Libretto in a slow-motion ballet. On the grand scale, there was little sense of motion, despite knowing that everything falling toward the planet was moving laterally across the planet's surface at four and a half miles per second.

Nather watched the ballet, grateful that all of the troops dropping from orbit were strapped into vehicles and not in the godawful Heinlein Tube contraptions. A lone human falling through the atmosphere was insane. Dropping from a platform in a vehicle was sane compared to leaping nearly unprotected out of an orbiting spacecraft. *It takes all kinds*, Nather thought before looking back into the bridge.

"Helm, you have the conn," the Drop Officer said. "Drop complete on bays one through eight and bay ten."

Nather looked at Garrett. "CAG, report?"

"Sir, all bays are clear except for bay nine. All drops have PNT and comms at the present time." Position, Navigation, and Timing coordinated from space, courtesy of a few quickly deployed satellites, provided continuous signal updates from the navigation consoles aboard the *Ticonderoga,* and her rapidly approaching sisters gave every single vehicle in the command an exceptionally precise ground location. Direct laser connections between combat vehicles would be dicey depending on the terrain, but their uplinks to the *Ticonderoga* and the TDF command vehicles were clear and unobstructed almost all the time.

"Any reports of jamming?" Nather looked at Garrett and motioned him over.

"Nothing at the present time, sir. We'll see what happens when those units hit the ground."

Nather stood and looked up slightly into Garrett's eyes. "What do you have up your sleeve, Don?"

Garrett's eyes flashed as he pulled up a global projection of Libretto. "We're dropping units along our orbital plane, sir. Most of these units will end up in the temperate zone of the planet, based on their current trajectories. The late bays will fall about two hundred fifty kilometers to the west of Libretto City. Most of those units will face little resistance. My intent is to drop the cavalry troop much closer to Libretto City with significant air cover and develop the battlefield situation. We know there are large encampments of Grey vehicles about one hundred kilometers from Libretto City to the northwest and southeast. My bet is that they've put those vehicles out there to see what we do on the ground. There's little to no air exospheric activity being reported at the present time. I'm betting they're luring us in to determine what we're going to defend."

"And then attack what they think we're defending." Nather finished. "How long can you let the TDF think they've got no regimental cavalry?"

"About another three minutes, sir. TDF policy is that if a unit cannot drop within three minutes of its immediate commander, the nearest commander to the dropped unit retains responsibility. In that case, it will be me."

"How close will Coffey end up being to the cavalry? Is he one of those nearer units?"

Garrett nodded. "Yes, sir. That's another reason to drop Captain Shields in that gap between the Third Tank Regiment and Libretto City."

Nather took a deep breath. "I'm really taking a significant risk, Don."

"We all are, sir. I'm holding back Major Richards and the Fifty-Third squadron along with those newbies, the Seventy-Seventh, in support of this. If we're right, we might give our forces a way to better combat the Greys."

Nather nodded. "Drop the cavalry, but keep them in orbit until you've got the intelligence to drop them in the place they'll make the most significant impact."

"Absolutely, sir," Garrett said and looked back at his staff. "When the bay door clears, drop those Rhinos. Launch the Alert Fifteen fighters now and have them take up a position about thirty nautical miles to the East. We're not going into the nightside without fighters up and fangs out."

*****

Chapter Fifty-Four

Colonel Bob Coffey held the crew handles inside the Intimidator Command Track, forcing himself to keep his eyes open and stare at a small dot on his hatch ring. Closing his eyes, the manual said, would make the inherent feeling of vertigo worse than those typically experienced in a combat drop from orbit. So far, he'd managed not to throw up, a fact that Coffey knew his gunner must appreciate. There was no place to avoid being vomited on. Coffey toggled his status screen and saw a blinking communication from the *Ticonderoga.* From the Admiral himself. He smiled. *Finally talking to the right people.* He chinned the frequency in his command helmet. "Eagle Six, this is Bullet Six. You have traffic for me, over?"

"Bullet Six, affirmative. Maintenance issues prevented Bay Nine from dropping with you. You are still go for combat operations. Recalibrate your command status updates accordingly. Acknowledge."

Coffey looked at the drop status screen and grinned. *Best news I've had in six months!* "Eagle Six, acknowledged. Confirm I am at ninety percent strength and recalibrated. Push command of that unit to the closest available, over."

"Bullet Six, this is Eagle Six. Good copy and good hunting. Out."

Yes! Coffey grinned and thumped his knee in happiness. He chinned over to the regimental frequency. "Bullet Nine, this is Bullet Six. Private Two, over."

A couple of seconds later he heard Trevayne in his ear. "Six, this is Nine over."

"We're short a unit. Drop that cavalry troop off your screens."

"Sir? What happened?"

Coffey gushed like a child. "They didn't drop! Some kind of maintenance issue. So they aren't our problem this time around. Best damned news I've had in six months!"

"Sir, without the cavalry troop, we're going to be blind."

"Nah," he fumbled in the leg pocket of his coveralls. "Push out one of the armor platoons as the lead element. They'll do as good a job, if not better." Curling his fingers around the flask, he brought the specially converted mouth to his helmet, plugged it in, and drank deeply. The whiskey burned just a little, like the first shots always did. *Hell, this was a celebration!* He took another deep swallow before disconnecting the flask and returning it to his pocket.

"Sir, which platoon?"

Goddamnit! "Come on, Sergeant Major! Make a goddamned decision for once! Just pick a goddamn platoon!"

"Roger," Trevayne replied. He didn't say anything more, and the connection terminated.

The Intimidator dropped out of the high cloud cover revealing the immense presence of the Libretto City dome receding to the east. Coffey punched a few buttons on the screen to identify the likely landing zone of his units. A thin, red targeting ellipse settled across a digitized map of the planet below. In the center of the projected landing zone was a long, thin lake surrounded by several good-sized hills. He connected to the interface on his private channel.

"Give me a time on target to that position."

<<All units will arrive in the vicinity of target in two minutes forty-nine seconds.>>

Coffey started to reach for his leg pocket again. "Terrain analysis of the area."

<<The hills surrounding the southern edge of the lake represent the highest terrain in a fifty-kilometer radius. This classifies as key terrain by definition, not by application.>>

I'll decide the application or definition. Without thinking, he reached again for the flask, plugged it in, and had a last swallow before putting it away. Best to save some for the surface. Using a pudgy finger on the touchscreen, he rapidly drew signals to his units in order to effectively deploy them on the hills ringing the southern edge of the lake. "That lake have a name?"

<<I cannot find a name in the limited database onboard.>>

Coffey snorted. What a damned nice place to sit out a battle. No sir, I cannot move to support your attack. I'm holding the key terrain of this sector. He laughed to himself. We'll let some other bastards go to the grinder today. And I don't have that glory-seeking pain in my ass on the ground either! "Identify the lake as Perfection Lake."

<<Identified.>>

Let's see those staff assholes at TDF try to move me off these hills!

<<Bullet Nine is calling on private two.>>

"What do you want, Trevayne?" Coffey growled and finished his crude map of positions. "I'm working on our deployment plan."

"Sir, First Platoon, Second Battalion is our lead element. They'll be on the ground in just over ninety seconds. I was—"

"Fine! Standby for my plan." Coffey stabbed the display and sent the crude drawing to his units before switching to the command frequency. "Bullet Elements, this is Bullet Six. Defensive positions according to the graphics coming your way now. Take up positions looking in all directions and spread out wide in case those bastards lob a few nuke rounds at us this time around. Bullet Six, out."

The repulsor platform of the Intimidator whined to life, and Coffey raised his hatch and stood in the breeze. The air was cool and crisp against his face. He smiled into the wind and looked over the vehicle at the ground. *Just as advertised*, he thought with a grin. Across the narrow lake, maybe two miles distant, he could see a couple of widely spaced buildings of some type. *Most likely vacant and not of concern, unless I need another drink*. He chuckled as the vehicle slowed its descent under power and settled gently into the palette of autumn leaves. "Adjust our camouflage pattern to match. Set up direct laser communications with all team leaders and staff primaries."

<<Confirmed.>>

Coffey nudged the gunner, another sergeant whom he hadn't bothered to meet. "Make sure we've got imagery in all directions. Tie all the vehicle pictures together and get it done before we hit the ground." Of course the gunner wouldn't get it done. That was the point. *Don't get it done and they're out of a job*, his Academy instructors said. The Commander deserves the best of everything, and sub-par performers were *persona non grata* despite the fact that the basic tasks were nearly impossible. *Push, push, push* Coffey told himself.

"The only way men respond to leadership is if they are dehumanized. Do everything in your power to break down your soldiers' ability to think for themselves. If you fail to assert yourself as an officer, as the sole person capable of making any type of informed decision, you will face a degradation of leadership that you cannot overcome. Remember that your soldiers are not people. They are soldiers. They are there for two purposes—to serve you as a duly appointed officer in charge, and to do what the Terran Defense Forces determine they are to do. Nothing else matters. Do not forget your duty." The commandant's nasal voice rang clearly in Coffey's memory despite almost twenty years of service. That final graduation advice served Coffey well as the cornerstone of his leadership. The soldiers themselves couldn't help it, nor could they be expected to do any better. Every movie or holovid they'd ever seen portrayed soldiers as fumbling idiots who were effectively shaped up by the drill sergeants and officers, who showed little emotion and drove them mercilessly.

The foliage was thick enough to conceal the vehicle, but the trees and surrounding exposed rocks would provide little protection. Coffey shook off the thought. The position was perfect. *Every TDF Commander will see I've secured the most influential terrain in this sector by force. They might even give me task force control. Three full regiments!*

Coffey stood in the hatch and used his helmet's binoculars to scan the horizon. The lake appeared the placid gray that defined cold. There was nothing he could see of value. All in all, it was perfectly quiet, like sitting in a duck blind on a day when the ducks would be nowhere in sight. The thought of getting one over, at least for a little while, brought a smile to his face. *Yes, this was going to be a good day to sit out a battle!*

* * * * *

Chapter Fifty-Five

Darren McMasters fancied himself a student of history. For his first two years at Cardiff, he'd lingered for long periods of time in the holosims, experiencing the critical moments of Earth's history. There was no attending the Gettysburg Address, and the experiences of the 9/11 attacks on New York City were two-dimensional news broadcasts at best. *Still, there was significant benefit to the study of history*, as his instructors said. *Humanity is doomed to repeat our mistakes without learning how not to.* Sitting in the Prelate's stateroom aboard the *Executive Platform Kilkenny*, McMasters cradled a glass of cold vodka, no ice, and sat under the only light in the room. He'd sleep in a carefully sterilized bed, but he'd know Andrew Cartner and Tallenaara had been there just days before.

Sitting in the near darkness, McMasters did not think much about his ascension to the role of prelate, nor did he celebrate it. He'd never liked beating Andrew at anything. After winning their first meeting in the intramural tennis tournament, Darren sulked in his suite, electronic music softly playing in the background, drinking a glass of cold vodka. The competitive urge had been too great, and he'd done what others would never consider. Beating the Prelate's son handily could have jeopardized everything Darren's family had worked so hard to have. But that wasn't the case. Andrew Cartner had made it a point to cross over to McMaster's part of the suite, knock on the door and sit in the dark as well. They'd become true friends that night. A night when he'd won something so inconsequential as a tennis match but gained a best friend. Tonight, he'd sacrificed his best friend to his own machinations.

He turned up the music to drown out his thoughts. Ten years hadn't changed his approach to centering himself. Tomorrow he would face his audience for the first time as prelate with a speech being carefully crafted by his writers. *I need to sleep. Wouldn't be a good image to have bags under my eyes for my first press conference, would it?* He would have to be earnest, serious, and compassionate.

And he knew that to appear earnest, serious, and compassionate he would have to banish all thoughts of selling out his planet to become the prelate. He'd certainly sold out his best friend, and Tallenaara was nowhere to be found. *No matter. She'd never suspected anything anyway, besides my ability to drink and leer at women.* He snorted to himself. *The end truly does justify the means*, he thought drolly. *Thank you, Cicero. But now the end is a beginning and I have no idea where to go from here.*

The door chime beeped. *Unfinished business,* McMasters thought before calling up another set of lights. "Enter."

The door slid open, and a tall man with salt and pepper hair marched into the room, standing six paces from McMasters's recliner. "Sir Prelate, Colonel Munsen reports as directed."

"You were supposed to be here two hours ago, Colonel."

The colonel stared at the wall above McMasters. "Sir, docking with a superluminal vessel under fold is quite dangerous and exceptionally complicated. There was a navigational delay that could not be helped."

"Please relax and sit down. May I offer you a drink?"

"No, thank you, sir." The colonel sat in the opposite chair but hardly relaxed. "You wanted to see me, sir?"

"What were you doing at the scene, Colonel?"

"The scene of what, sir?"

McMasters frowned. "Let's cut through the bullshit, Colonel. Why were you at the scene of Prelate Cartner's assassination?"

"I believed that the situation, the Tuegs threatening withdrawal from the Legion and their repeated efforts to get Prelate Cartner off the planet for extended negotiations, represented a danger to him. I was too late."

McMasters steepled his fingers and drummed them for a moment. *Surely this Colonel couldn't suspect?* "You don't like me, do you?"

"Give me a good reason why I should."

"Well, for one thing, your experiment can continue."

Munsen replied, "I have no idea what you're referring to."

"Isn't that what you whispered to Tallenaara before she ran away? Something to that effect? Why she would run away and go...what do your people call it? Yes, off the grid." McMasters smiled. "Your people and their quaint sayings!" He looked at Munsen and let his smile fade slowly. "You are not an imprint, but your deputy is. One of the most senior imprints created. Imprinted by his own great-great grandfather, who led one of the final assaults on Tehran during the last of the religious wars for oil and died in the attack. Mortally wounded by short artillery fire. Do I need to go any further?"

Munsen shook his head. "You obviously are aware of the breadth of the imprinting program to this point."

"Except for why you targeted Tallenaara, my dear, old friend from Cardiff who happened to fall for the son of a prelate. Tallenaara came back to Earth at the direction of the Styrahi Council. She was released from her architectural position to immediately pursue a relationship with Andrew Cartner. Apparently, Tallenaara has a genetic mutation that may allow her to mate successfully with a human."

"I was made aware of her departure, sir."

"And you knew about the mutation?"

Munsen nodded but said nothing.

McMasters sipped vodka and crossed his legs. "Then let's talk about your prospective imprint target. I believe he or she must be an officer in the Terran Defense Forces like yourself, and so would fall under my authority as the Commander-in-Chief, would they not? And as such, I believe I am authorized to inquire as to who they are and what your intentions were with them."

Munsen nodded. "You are certainly authorized to ask, sir. But that doesn't mean that I have to tell you anything based on your need to know."

"Need to know?" McMasters leaned forward. "You're going to see to it that I receive every morsel of information that I ask for, Colonel. If you fail to do so, I will court-martial you and seize all documentation regarding your imprint program. Why did you target Tallenaara?"

Munsen shrugged. "Tallenaara was never the target, sir."

"What?"

"Tallenaara was who the Styrahi Council provided. I knew nothing about her prior to her contact with the target. Captain Mairin Shields is the imprint, based on this particular experiment. Her imprint is a Class Five, the first one of its kind. She can literally remember things from her imprinted subject on an unconscious level. Her acumen for military operations is unheard of for a twenty-two-year-old straight from the Eden Academy. My intention with her imprint was to break from the walkabout protocol. You are familiar with that?"

McMasters shook his head. "Enlighten me."

"All of our imprints, except for Captain Shields, have completed their imprinting and recovery on Earth. A portion of that experience is, the imprinted subjects are given twelve months leave to get their minds together. Literally. They are sent walkabout, meaning they have little supervision but a blank check to essentially go wherever in the world necessary to facilitate the mind grasping the imprint. The program is exceptionally successful. Only one imprint has failed to complete the walkabout experience and enter service with the TDF."

"And what happened to that subject?"

"Committed suicide. Leapt off a mountain in New Mexico."

McMasters chuckled. "So only one of your subjects has failed? Remarkable."

"Thank you." Munsen relaxed slightly. "With Captain Shields, I was trying to do something different based on the completeness of the imprint. I wanted to place her at Libretto for a faster recovery period, and in the hopes that she would bond with something there. I had her under nearly continuous surveillance during her stay on Libretto through one of my operatives. Captain Shields met Tallenaara as planned. We have reason to believe the experiment was successful."

"What are you not telling me?" McMasters squinted. "My earlier threat is still valid."

"I understand that sir, and frankly, your threat doesn't scare me at all. I've served thirty years in the Terran Defense Forces and further back when we were still called the United Earth Armed Forces. I've earned and lost two stars. Did it ever occur to you to ask your questions about Tallenaara ten years ago?"

McMasters waved all the history away. The past never mattered. "What are you getting at? Styrahi students attended universities all over the world."

"And how many of them entered into relationships with human beings in direct disobedience to the Styrahi Council?"

McMasters squinted. "Disobedience?"

"Those Styrahi students received explicit instructions that they were not to become emotionally involved, with one exception."

"So why allow Tallenaara to enter into a relationship? Because she was going to Cardiff? Because of Andrew Cartner?"

Munsen smiled. "Hardly. The Styrahi Council may have known that Andrew Cartner was in school there, along with yourself and other promising young politicians of the time, but they had no idea that Tallenaara would enter a relationship with Cartner. Tallenaara has a genetic mutation never previously seen in a Styrahi. She may be capable of fertilizing a human egg or having her egg fertilized by a human male. For a hermaphroditic species that's a miracle of its own, but the fact typical Styrahi genetic molecules do not even allow for the possibility made Tallenaara an experiment for the Styrahi. They wanted to know if it was possible to breed with a human. Conceivably, Styrahi-Human children could live to an average age of more than one hundred years. Many human diseases would be eradicated with a different physiological make-up than a human, and the capacity of the Styrahi intellect could only serve to broaden human horizons. The possibilities of genetic inter-breeding of our species are endless in theory, for humans and Styrahi alike. We know that Tallenaara had intercourse with both Captain Shields and Prelate Cartner on numerous occasions. There was no evidence that Tallenaara's reproductive system was ever engaged."

McMasters nodded. "I'm aware of all of that, Colonel. The Styrahi Council brought me into confidence at the start of your experiment. I believe we call that redundancy. We have to find Tallenaara."

"No." Munsen shook his head and raised one hand with its palm facing McMasters. "One, I doubt anybody is capable of finding her on a world she helped to build. Two, that woman has been through enough. I am not about to assist you in tracking her down. At this point, if you wish to continue an experimental course of action, we have more than enough genetic material to attempt replication. I doubt our effort will be successful, but like the original series of imprintings completed with Styrahi assistance generated new data sets, further experimentation could certainly have some benefits."

McMasters nodded. "Cloning? You can do this?"

"No, we can attempt it. I have a team in place ready to do just that, sir." Munsen took a deep breath. "Either changing the law or hiding the scope of the project from your own Council is your matter."

"And if it doesn't work? You'll still have the potential to imprint soldiers?"

Munsen nodded. "We have over six million valid DNA samples of American, British, Australian, and Russian soldiers from the twentieth and twenty-first centuries to imprint on genetic descendants."

"Surely some of those samples have no descendants."

"Yes, sir," Munsen nodded. "But that doesn't mean that we might not be able to replicate them if we're successful with Tallenaara's genetic material. We might be able to generate our soldiers without having to compromise the development of human values over the last two centuries. A vast majority of our current imprints will not survive this conflict. Those that do may have difficulties re-integrating into society without further development."

McMasters smiled. Rarely did someone beat him at his own game. He looked away from Munsen and the smile faded. He'd been thinking of history before Munsen arrived, particularly the assassination of John Fitzgerald Kennedy. *What did Lyndon Johnson really feel that night? Was he a part of the greater conspiracy? How must it have felt to pick up the fledgling efforts in Southeast Asia? Sure, he landed men on the moon, but staring at a war he'd really not had more than a tacit understanding of, what did LBJ think that first night? Did he wonder if it was worth it after all? Was he guilty, too? Were their demons in his dreams? Did he feel like me?*

McMasters cleared his throat. "Sorry, I was just thinking about your proposition."

"It's not a proposition, sir. Tallenaara is left alone or I will order the destruction of all imprinting materials, experiments, and data." Munsen sat motionless, his eyes clear and calm.

Keep your enemies closer. Especially a man willing to do what's right at any cost. "Colonels do not set terms with the Prelate," McMasters said through gritted teeth.

Munsen smirked. "You really don't have much choice, sir. I believe the Styrahi Council suspected your intention to have Cartner assassinated."

"You believe it was my intention? I believe the Greys managed to kill Andrew Cartner. Terrible shame, really."

Munsen shook his head and laughed. "You can quit right now. The Styrahi have enough on you, especially your collaboration with the Tueg, to ride you off Earth on a rail, as my imprints would say. You've nearly destroyed their trust in us." Munsen's eyes flashed in the dim room. McMasters found it hard to look away.

"What is it you want, Munsen? To be the Chairman of TDF Forces? Some other position of power?"

"I have all the power I need." Munsen smiled slightly. "What I need now is the proper way of applying that power."

"Beyond imprinting?"

Munsen nodded, but said nothing. His cards were firmly held against his vest.

McMasters drew a long breath. "I will agree to your terms, Colonel Munsen." He paused to let the news sink in. "You will, in turn, avail yourself to me outside of typical channels within the TDF. You will report solely to me regarding imprinting and further experimentation. Is that clear?"

Munsen nodded. "Yes, sir."

"I was going to ask for your resignation." McMasters took a deep breath to say more, but Munsen cut him off.

"You don't have to ask for it." Munsen snorted. "I made my choice when I tried to save Tallenaara, sir. I'm through fucking with people's lives and memories. In one month, I will retire, sir. I've already lost three stars for this project. There are other things I want to do, sir. My deputy can handle this project from here. I have other plans in mind."

"What you've done will save a great many lives."

"No, it will get more killed. We could experiment with memory imprints for a thousand years, and the chances we'd get another imprint like Mairin Shields has would be infinitesimal."

McMasters nodded. "You're certain about your resignation?"

"My retirement. There is a difference, sir." Munsen said. "Thirty-two years is enough."

"And your other plans?" McMasters asked. "What do you have in mind?"

"Right now? Saving Libretto. After I retire, we'll speak again."

"Indeed," McMasters said and watched silently as Munsen turned and walked away. The man's shoulders were straight and strong, not bowed by the weight of his duty. He'd tried to save a woman and her lover, and only been partially successful. McMasters wondered if he could ever be that noble and knew the answer before he could raise the vodka to his lips.

I murdered the only man who was truly my friend. McMasters grimaced at the thought. Was it worth it?

* * * * *

Chapter Fifty-Six

All of the *Ticonderoga's* drop iterations finished on schedule. All combat elements deployed forward with the lead elements passing through atmospheric interface on their way to the ground. All forty-eight Rhinos completed their exospheric deliveries and began to marshall for recovery. Garrett observed the normal flight operations with satisfaction, but could not keep himself from continuing to check the combat scans. "Sir, first drops complete," he reported to Admiral Nather. "Ground forces secure, lead elements are three minutes from landing. No losses at the present time."

Nather nodded but kept his gaze on the curving forward viewscreen. "We have a position fix on their orbital platform yet?"

"We'll pass at conjunction in sixteen minutes. They'll pass about forty kilometers overhead. Tactical engagement time will be limited to seven minutes this pass." Garrett cued the tactical display. "Four CAP squadrons are orbiting us at seventy-five kilometers." The combat air patrol would provide early warning and with luck would take out a few of the Grey fighters before they'd beat feet for the safety of the *Ticonderoga* battle group.

"Just one Jack?" Nather asked. The triple intersecting octahedrons of the Grey attack platforms didn't have an official name, however their resemblance to the childhood toy stuck.

Garrett nodded. "So far. The Greys have too many forces on the ground to have come from one platform. I'd venture to guess they have two more platforms, but not here. They're close enough to reach out and touch us, though."

Nather keyed his console and spoke quietly. "This is the Admiral." The 1-MC rang out across the *Ticonderoga* and to the vessels of the battle group in real time. "Secure for nightside operations. General quarters. Gun crews to stations. Good hunting, and God protect us all."

Garrett relayed commands to his deployed aircraft. "Sir, Bay Nine is clear for operations."

Nather looked up at Garrett with the touch of a smile at the corners of his mouth. "And what do you suggest we do with those troops?"

Garrett cued the ground tactical command visuals. "Sir, TDF forces are still eight minutes away, and we have operational oversight of the forces in Bay Nine. The current situation on the ground is as follows." Garrett cued the display and showed the western edge of the domed remains of Libretto City and roughly one hundred kilometers of the surround terrain. "Sir, the Third Tank Regiment, under the command of Colonel Coffey, has taken up a key terrain position along this ridgeline approximately seventy kilometers from the edge of Libretto City. There are currently significant Grey units to his north and south. The enemy forces to the north are not dug in and appear to be waiting for movement. Their current disposition doesn't hint to a particular target. On the contrary, the forces to the south are clearly intent to attack Coffey's position from the south. If those forces from the south attack Coffey, the most dangerous course of action would be that the forces to Coffey's north would attack as well, leaving Coffey surrounded and most likely surrendering the key terrain."

Nather squinted. "What's so special about the terrain, Don? Just its elevation?"

"Yes, sir. It's the highest terrain in the sector and would provide an excellent firing position for artillery. What I'm more concerned about is there are faint infrared signatures in a line from Libretto City heading southwest immediately under the ridgeline.

Some type of machinery I'd imagine. The sources are scattered roughly every fifty kilometers. There's an exceptionally faint position approximately fifteen kilometers from Libretto City and another more significant position about fifteen hundred meters from Coffey's eastern flank."

"Any information on them from Intel?"

"Most likely pumping stations for an aquifer." Garrett shrugged. "Considering water to be a resource on the surface, it could be part of the Grey's plan to disrupt it and siege the forces attempting to hold Libretto City."

"Deploying the cavalry?"

Garrett pointed to the faint infrared signal. "Right here. Our pathfinders are dropping from the *Harrison* via tubes right now. They'll be on the ground overwatching the station in twelve minutes. We put the cavalry just north of there, overwatching the northern edge of the sector in case of counter attack."

Nather pointed to the display. "There's movement down to the south. The Greys are rolling north."

"That didn't take long," Garrett said with a frown. He turned to his controllers. "Release close air squadrons Sixty-Two and Seventy-One. Drop Bay Nine to grid TT51015086. Give me direct comms with Saber Six on standby." Garrett turned back to Nather. "Your orders, sir?"

"Commit all remaining close air to the fight. We'll hold the ground here with your interceptors and guns." Nather turned his head over his shoulder. "Time to conjunction?"

The officer of the deck called, "Twelve minutes to conjunction, sir. Weapons range in four minutes."

Nather looked at Garrett. "Get all your aircraft off this platform in the next four minutes, Don. Then we'll see about kicking some Grey ass for a change."

Garrett was about to respond when a flash of light in the atmosphere below caught his eye. "What the?"

"Sir, we have multiple contacts. Additional Grey landing craft inbound." Another streak, then another, passed into view as they burned off the plasma of atmospheric interface in long glowing fingers. Garrett's mind drifted for a moment at the thought of a video game...something called...Missile Command... *No way to stop any of them. We'll have to fight them on the ground.* There were hundreds of streaks heading all over the southern hemisphere. "Any of those things headed toward our ground forces?"

"Negative, sir."

"Where did they come from?" Nather demanded.

The officer of the deck looked up. "Sir, they came in on a direct vector from deep space. Current count is at least ten thousand inbound vehicles to all sectors of the planet. Clearly a backing maneuver, they're fortifying their positions across the planet."

Nather frowned, then brightened slightly. "Track them. Calculate the trajectory and launch a recon bird on an intercept. Maybe we can find those missing Jacks."

"Sir, permission to launch a recon mission over the poles? Until the *Viraat* and the *Canberra* arrive on the farside, we've got no eyes over there." Garrett leaned over the display and traced a long line over the pole. "We've got a launch window in one minute that will give max coverage in a highly elliptical orbit. We'll need long dwell time over the northern latitudes to pull this off."

"Get it airborne." He turned to the bridge. "Announce weapons free, all guns loaded and prepared to fire at beyond visual range parameters. Maintain maximum rate of fire through engagement corridor. All damage control crews to standby. Prepare to engage and hold fast. The worst is yet to come."

Alarms rang throughout the fleet at the announcement of weapons free—the ability to engage any confirmed enemy target. Within a minute, the *Ticonderoga* and her entourage of combat vessels were prepared for operations. Garrett ensured that all interceptor aircraft were launched and placed into the proper coverage corridors. All of the Rhinos were recovered and staged for launch. "Sir, all Rhinos are staging. Estimated time to launch supply missions to surface is four minutes. Bay Nine is completely operational and ready for launch."

Nather made a "come here" gesture with his fingers and Garrett approached. "You know what you're doing?"

"I do, sir."

"I realize that hope is not a method, but I seriously hope you do, Don," Nather said. He looked over his shoulder and raised his voice. "Commander Connelly! Front and center."

A ruddy-faced man with a thick mustache came forward from the tactical air console. As the Deputy Commander Air Group, he was responsible for the overall command and control interfaces with every combat aircraft at all times. The perfect person for what Garrett had in mind.

Connelly came to the position of attention and saluted Nather with a forward facing palm. He spoke in a deep lilted Irish brogue. "Aye, sir!"

Nather looked at him and then back to Garrett. "Captain Garrett, by your request you are temporarily relieved of your duties as Commander Air Group. Commander Connelly, you are now the Commander Air Group while Captain Garrett assumes command—"

"Task Force Sixty-Two," Garrett added off the cuff. "It's the only number out there not taken, sir."

"So be it," Nather added.

"You crazy bastards are really going to do this?" Connelly smiled. "It's a damned fine plan, sir. Give 'em hell."

Garrett shook Connelly's outstretched hand. "You keep my wing flying, Seamus."

An alarm klaxon rang behind Nather. "Weapons range. Tracking inbound missiles."

Another operations officer called. "Bullet Six reporting contact from the south, sir! CAS inbound."

Nather snapped, "Full defensive countermeasures! Set all weapons platforms and fire!" He turned to Garrett and Connelly. The light across the bridge from Libretto's sun faded quickly and only the internal lights lit the room until the guns began to silently fire. Hypergolic fuels lit up the surrounding space as the missiles streaked around the curvature of the planet in search of their targets. "Weapons free. Engage all targets."

Garrett watched the receding pulses of light for a moment before approaching his terminal and select crew of operators. "Launch Rhino flight and put them in a hold above Saber Six. Relay to Saber Six that operations are a go and to maintain direct communications. And get Lancer flight vectored in for operations."

Let's see what we can do now.

*****

Chapter Fifty-Seven

The dawning sky above the cabin screamed to life and roused Tally from a restless sleep. Tears no longer came. Her eyes opened bright and clear without a trace of bleariness. The red streaks of blood vessels cleared as she realized what was happening and what she knew she had to do. There were protocols for this, developed as early as the plan to make a nearly dead world into the Paradise of the Outer Rim. *Why didn't I tell Andy about them?* She looked into the sky and saw the flashing descents of a thousand ships streaking over the horizon to the south. The time was obviously now.

She moved quickly, stopping only to discard the smelly, tattered clothes she'd worn during her escape from Libretto City. The day Andy died. However long that had been, it didn't matter. She paused at her closet and eschewed her modern clothing for the *kenaala*, the flowing purple and black garment of the Styrahi in mourning.

Long hair tied at the nape of her neck, she made her way down the wooden stairs without shoes. She would go now, and go barefoot. Echoes of thunder aloft shook the quiet cabin as she crossed through the kitchen into her living room and studio. Wide windows showcased the idyllic purple sky of morning. Thunder rolled, and hundreds of atmospheric contrails ripped across the dawn. She paused at her drawing table and ran a finger across the white surface. All her life she'd dreamed of creating beauty. But nothing lasted. Brick and mortar would crumble with time. Steel would rust and fall to the ground. Stone would erode like the chasms of her heart.

Fingering a piece of charcoal, her thoughts surprised her. She mourned Andrew, but there was a light in the tunnel of her thoughts. *Mairin.* Movement at the corner of her eye caught Tally's attention and she turned. Mairin was sitting in the window sipping a mug of coffee. A whiff of wildflowers filled Tally's nose as the vision faded, Mairin softly smiling. There was parchment on the desk and Tally sat. Taking up the charcoal as she'd done countless times before, she began to write. She wrote with the plodding pace of those either struggling to find the words or those trying not to cry. The pencil stopped as a fresh tear cascaded down her cheek and the thundering skies quieted. Folding the paper, Tally secured it to the desk with two strips of tape then slid out the glass door, leaving it unlocked.

Outside, she opened a locker only she knew about. Hidden flush in the rich redwood decking, she raised the lid and breathed slowly. Lightly oiled rags smelled sweet in the evening air as she hefted the package out to the table. The plasma rifle looked as perfect as the day she'd secured it.

The last line of defense, she thought with a snort. How had it come to this?

She took two bandoliers of ammunition, a total of six hundred rounds, and shouldered them along with the rifle. The air was pungent and moist, yet without a trace of rain. Dusk rose and began to gently turn the countryside dark. The lake was a glimmering silver reflection of the calming sky. She closed her eyes and breathed deeply to steel her nerves. The time had come to say goodbye.

She looked around the deck, the richly appointed cabin, and the surrounding forests with a smile. This was the closest she would ever get to heaven. On her desk, a corner of her note fluttered a goodbye. She'd left a window open somewhere. Maybe it wouldn't rain too much before Mairin came home for good. If she survived this war, this place would be hers. She looked at the flowing script of her calligraphy on the note and read it aloud.

"Cariad."

Tally said it again as a promise that the note would find its way. Turning on her heel, Tally wiped her eyes for the last time and set her jaw. She didn't need her neurals to tell her that the Greys were coming for what they thought was theirs. The bastards had marched across the galaxy for millennia, and it shoud have been obvious. The way they'd eventually attack Styrah, Tueg, and even Earth.

Wherever the oil was.

Wherever they could feed.

The Styrahi mined Libretto for oil with a singular purpose in mind. Chum. Use the rich oil fields of Libretto to create a target the Greys would have to pursue. Maybe the Greys would find the motherlode on Lektia someday. Or maybe the Greys would find Hiallae first, or the fourteen other oil stocked worlds across the Rim.

I'm so sorry, Andy. I didn't realize the Tuegs knew about Libretto. I should have told you about the oil.

Hundreds of trillions of barrels consumed by the human race in a thousand years were perhaps a year or two of sustenance for the Greys. Maybe the Greys would find them eventually. *Maybe the bait would take the Greys away long enough to build a better defense? Maybe the humans could really turn the tide? Humans like Mairin. Where was she? Was she here? Did it matter anymore? As long as oil pumped to the surface of Libretto, the world was an easy target and exactly what the Greys sought. And likely why Andrew died.*

Tally walked with quick, light steps down the path towards the woodline and away from the only home she'd ever really claimed as her own. Today she would help to destroy part of the planet she'd been so privileged and honored to build. Her hearts were light as well, thinking of the note she'd left for Mairin to find. Somehow Tally knew Mairin would find it. Mairin knew of faith, and hope, and she would know that love would last forever.

Helios fully set beyond the mountains of the west as Tallenaara walked into the woodline. She closed her eyes and mouthed a quiet blessing for Andy, then Mairin, before beginning to softly sing the Warrior's Song to herself. Picking up the pace to a light jog, she flew through the waning darkness along a path burned into her mind from years of excursions and inspections. There was much work to do.

Tally chuckled as a line of poetry, from the primitive poets of Earth, of all places, leapt to mind. Yes, there was so much to do. *Kilometers to go before I sleep and all that.*

The first pumping station was twelve kilometers away. She'd not been running or exercising much in Andy's company. She cursed herself for being lazy and used her anger to fuel the pace. Running as fast as she dared in the diminishing darkness, Tally cued her neurals to a basic mode only, just a clock and a compass ring swinging wildly. The Greys were jamming the navigational grid, as expected. The ritual of practice had familiarized her with the ground before she left for Earth. She'd practiced this several times a year. Her last duty. The final line of defense to secure some of the oil reserves and perhaps save Libretto from the Greys. Across the planet, sixteen hundred others were doing this same ritual. Running into the darkness bent on destroying stations the Greys coveted. The Grey's technological superiority didn't allow for a machine or program to destroy the oil supply. So they'd trained and practiced as they built the planet, hoping the day would never come for this, but intent on protecting what made Libretto important to the Legion.

And important to her. Libretto must survive, if not for her, then for Mairin. For the others who loved it, and for those soldiers yet to be created who needed it. Tallenaara darted through the thickening forest and let her eyes adjust to the thin bands of infrared a Styrahi could see in the dark. Within moments, she was reacting by trained instinct and watching the clock slowly ticking.

Thirty-eight minutes at this speed and she'd reach the first station.

Run, eschessa. She chided and sang to herself.

Run.

* * * * *

Chapter Fifty-Eight

The Greys are attacking conveniently at dawn, Coffey thought with a smirk. Like something out of the movies. Dawn or dusk was when the Indians always attacked. Bet old Talvio is having a hoot with this one. Probably even has his cowboy hat on, thought Coffey. Through the extension of his gunner's sight, Coffey saw the inky black shapes of the Greys moving slowly in the distance. Familiar columns began to form. Who taught these guys how to fight? The Greys came in massive numbers using outdated doctrine as a playbook and, until recently, had decimated TDF forces on the ground. The bastards in Fleet air operations fared much better. Why fight a ground battle at all? What is so important on this stinking planet?

"Sir, the Grey CRP has been destroyed. First battalion reports its lead company has no casualties and is green on all resources." The Combat Reconnaissance Patrol was the typical lead element of a Grey movement. *Three to four vehicles moving in a loose diamond formation would travel roughly ten kilometers in front of the next element. The Forward Support Element would be next. The main attack was a half hour away.*

The lead company commander, whoever he was, was going to get a promotion if Coffey had anything to do with it. He'd simply engaged and destroyed the enemy without any grandstanding or trying to win the whole goddamned war himself. *Fucking Shields. Hope she's rotting in that broken drop bay.* Pressing his face to the eyepiece again, Coffey had to use his command control of the turret to locate the Greys again.

"How fast are they moving?" Coffey growled. A typical speed would be about fifteen klicks per hour. If they were deviating from it, the attack would either be later or sooner. "Let me guess. Fifteen? Seventeen?"

<<The lead vehicles of the fire support element are moving in excess of thirty kilometers per hour.>>

Coffey shook his head. "Say that again?"

<<Thirty kilometers per hour. The forward support element will be in firing range of the regimental screen line in approximately three minutes.>> The Interface reported.

"Shit!" Coffey chinned over to the command frequency. "All Bullet Elements, this is Bullet Six. Lock and load all weapons. Kill everything that moves as soon as you've got a weapons lock."

The regiment's operational and intelligence network lit up with frantic conversations and orders to fill the lines, shifting targets and sectors, and adjusting frantic battle plans. Coffey wasn't listening. He scanned the horizon with the infrared optics trying to discern Grey vehicles. The rising sun should be having more of an effect. The whole damned forest was black in his visor. "Interface, where is the main body of the Grey attack?"

<<Unable to determine dispersion between the forward support element and the main body. Probability of attack is eighty percent.>>

Sonuvabitch! Coffey toggled all of the power supply systems for the Intimidator to "on." "Listen up! Prepare to move, I'm unassing this position to move to position Bravo. When the repulsors come up get us to Bravo as fast as you can."

No one said anything among the crew of four. They knew better. The crew engaged their appropriate systems and began to pull the Intimidator back into the tree line and move around to the secondary position. From position Alpha, Coffey had a sweeping view over low scrub oaks of the entire valley to the south of the ridgeline. Below the forests was very little cover and concealment. A killing field. Bravo was certainly more fortified, but would limit even the traverse capability of the main gun.

"Sir, I have one hundred thirty-five degrees of fire control here," the gunner said. "At Bravo, we'll have less than sixty. This is a good position."

Coffey kneed the gunner in the back. "Not good enough. We move to Bravo. That's an order."

"Sir, I—"

"That's a goddamn order!" Coffey roared. "One more comment from any of you and you'll be placed under guard. I make the decisions in this tank and all over this battlefield. Is that clear?"

<<Two minutes to contact,">> the Interface chimed. <<Grey elements are scanning the regiment with targeting pulses.>>

"Driver, move us out now!" Coffey popped open the hatch and cool moist air rushed into the turret. "Command net only," he growled. "This is Six, I'm moving to Bravo now. Bullet Five you have command of the regiment until I can re-post communications."

"Roger, Six. Five out."

The first rounds impacted the ridgeline as Coffey's tank swerved uphill towards position Bravo. The first several rounds fell long and short of most of the regiment's positions. For all their numbers and technological advantage, they still fired ranging shots. Coffey chuckled as he heard the first of the regiment's rail guns open fire.

"Laser communications are down. Working to reacquire on UHF."

Coffey heard static take over the connection on all frequencies but the internal vehicle communications system. "Why can't I talk to anyone?"

"Line of sight," the communications specialist said without turning from the radio.

Coffey bit back a comment about finding someone better for the job as he stood on the commander's seat and looked out of the turret. The Intimidator was nearing the crest of the hill. A thousand simultaneous impacts shook the vehicle. Looking across the front slope, the crest of the hill approached and then fell away. The green fields at the bottom of the valley were black with vehicles. Clouds of dust and smoke rolled up the ridgeline obscuring huge swaths of the field.

"My God," Coffey said to himself.

The radio came to life in his ears. "Bullet Six, this is Bullet Nine. Where are you?"

Madness. This is madness. There's no way to win this fight.

Get down there and fight this battle.

I can't...too many...look at all of them.

Rounds fell near his tank, and still Coffey stood in the hatch mouth agape. The first impact of a round through the front left repulsor nacelle failed to catch his attention. There were hands on his legs trying to pull him down. Someone inside was hurt. *Maybe dead. The driver. Must be. Repulsor failure and the vehicle isn't moving. Nose in the air. Perfect target.* Dirt exploded up around the tank and showered him. Rock fragments tore at his coveralls, his facemask. The other tanks fired into the mass of Greys but there were far too many. He felt his bladder release and scared piss ran down his leg.

Get away.

A round impacted near the turret opposite him and shook the vehicle so hard he toppled out of the hatch onto the top of the tank. Fear took hold. Coffey rolled from the top of the tank to the rocky ground. Pain exploded in his side. *Broken ribs, maybe more. Damned rocks. Get away.*

He crawled behind the tank and crouched to run down the exposed trail to its rear. He felt a rush of heat on his neck. Eardrums ruptured as he felt himself picked up and strewn down the hill, branches and limbs raking him as he flew. His tank exploded violently before he even hit the ground. A fist-sized sapling occupied the place near where his forehead met the ground and he recoiled from the impact clearly seeing stars around his face. He peeled off his cracked combat helmet and tossed it aside. On any previous planet he would not have survived the first attempt to breathe. There was something good about being here.

His neurals were offline. The hill shook with continuous impacts of artillery and tank rounds. The battle raged on the far side. Ears ringing, Coffey sat slowly and cursed his broken ribs. *Need a medic*, he thought. *Screw that.* The division rear headquarters was to the west another ten kilometers. He could make it there. He looked out across the lake and towards the shattered rim of Libretto City. He walked in short pain-ridden strides to the east, away from the battlefield and towards the remnants of the city. The curved dome was visible along the horizon, and black smoke billowed from a thousand fires inside. If he went back to Division, they'd give him another mount and send him back to the un-winnable fight with a smile and pat on the back from that disgusting wannabe cowpoke.

No, I'm injured. A head injury. Something I can fake. The medicos loved that shit. We can blame anything on a lump on your head anymore, he thought with a snort that hurt his head. Find his way into the city. They'd believe him. He was an exemplary field grade officer after all and could do no wrong in this army. There was no choice for anyone but to believe whatever he told them. Holding his left arm tight against his injured chest, Coffey unholstered his sidearm, loaded a round and returned it before limping away. I can always shoot anyone in my way, can't I? No one's gonna miss me in that shit. For all they know right now, I'm dead.

And that sounded good enough as his walk turned to a trot and then into a frantic arms-thrashing sprint towards Libretto City. Impacts rang in his ear. He could feel them. Just behind him. *They're coming. Run faster. Faste*r. He screamed into the brush something unintelligible and nearly inhuman. Chest heaving and throat burning, he crested a hill and ducked behind an exposed rock outcropping. Tears ran over his eyelids and gathered at his dirty chin before falling away. Panic gave way to fear, and fear gave way to certainty. There was no going back now. Going back was death. Down the incline from his position, Coffey heard the unmistakable whirr of machinery. He fumbled the water bottle to his lips with trembling hands. He held it with both hands like a baby and drank between rasps for breath.

Mid-swallow, whatever was down the hill from his position exploded. Coffey sputtered and screamed again, pressing himself into the rocks. When there was no second detonation, Coffey rose to a sitting position. Down the hill, a tall woman in a black outfit ran quickly through the trees on a path to the northwest. She'd destroyed whatever it was. Thick black smoke rose up in a wide column from the site and stained the trees and sky above. He lost track of the woman...*no, Styrahi,* he corrected himself with a sneer. *Goddamned barbies!* He'd never catch her at this pace. But he could follow her. Track her down. Find out what she blew up and then kill her for treason. *Supporting the goddamned Greys!*

Rousting himself with a sore, overexerted groan, Coffey stumbled down the hill and found what he thought was the Styrahi's trail and began to follow. Thoughts of revenge fueled him as much as his panic ever did.

* * * * *

Chapter Fifty-Nine

Human beings are inherently ignorant. Tony Richards chuckled in the cockpit of his Hurricane interceptor seventy-five kilometers ahead of the *Ticonderoga.* The black, starless sky of planetary space dominated his view. The fact that there was a time when human beings assumed every picture of space was a forgery because it didn't show any stars was ludicrous. *People can't see past the sun in their eyes*, he grinned. Heading past the terminator and into the dark side of Libretto, Richards squinted into the sky and could indeed make out a few very faint stars as well as Concerto, the sixth planet of the Helios system some two hundred eight million kilometers away. None of them were bright enough or on the correct orbital plane for what Richards waited for with growing impatience. *Don't get fixated on the target*, he told himself silently as he gripped and regripped the flight control system for the hundredth time in the last two minutes. *Stay loose. Stay...*

The bright spot of the Grey Jack emerged from the thin veil of Libretto's atmosphere in the distance. Richards chinned the command frequency. "Looking Glass this is Lancer One, visual contact time now."

"Roger, Lancer One. Be advised there are multiple birds tracking the target. Maintain present course and speed."

Sure enough, a moving streak of light caught Richard's eye. The first of the outbound missiles rocketed past him on an intercept trajectory with the Jack. Another followed. The barrage of missiles flew past Richards and his wingman on their way towards the Grey platform. Richards grinned with one side of his mouth and keyed the radio. "Looking Glass, permission to rejoin my mates?"

"Lancer One, permission granted. Blackjack Four is twenty kilometers behind you and closing on your station now. You are cleared to divert to briefed holding point and await coordination with Saber Six. Looking Glass out."

Richards pointed the nose of the Hurricane into Libretto's atmosphere and nudged the reaction control system in preparation for a short burn to atmospheric interface. "You can't call this flying," Richards chirped on his direct comm system with Lancer Two off his right wing.

"Falling is more like it." His wingman chuckled.

Richards laughed until his vdar came to life. "I've got multiple targets at two seven zero below us and descending. Looks like six of them. You think the Greys are trying to sneak a few fighters down there for close air?"

"Wouldn't be the first time," his wingman called.

Richards thought Michelle Boyd was right and smart for an Australian. A veteran of the Jabnah campaign several years before, she'd fought more than her fair share of the bastards. The Greys didn't make a habit of sending their Darts into atmosphere. They were hilariously unmaneuverable with turning radii of hundreds of kilometers. The best they could hope for were direct descents as bombing runs. Richards' mouth opened. "Bloody hell." *Did the Greys have nukes?*

"Looking Glass, this is Lancer One preparing to divert. Have multiple contacts in the atmosphere on a descent approach to Libretto City by the look of it. Permission to engage?"

There was a pause of about six seconds and Garrett's voice filled Richards' ears. "What are you thinking, Tony?"

"Sir, do those bastards have nukes?"

"Not that we know," Garrett paused. "It's two against six if you go after them."

"And they can't turn for shit, sir."

He heard Garrett chuckling as he answered. "Permission granted. Good hunting, but get your ass to Saber Six as soon as you can."

Richards clicked his microphone button twice and engaged the twin main thrusters after the Greys. By the vdar, they were moving incredibly fast. He'd have to hustle to even get in weapons range before they dropped whatever they were carrying into the remains of Libretto City. "Let's push it up, Two."

"I'm standing on it, Lead."

Richards chuckled. *I'll never understand that girl.* Off the rounded nacelle of the nose, light wisps of plasma began to curl. Richards waited another fifteen seconds before engaging the atmospheric flight controls. "Got air."

"Two," came the reply. Boyd also had aerodynamic control.

Dogfighting is energy management, Richards thought. He and Boyd had more energy than they knew what to do with. A sweeping turn to the north would dissipate most of it and bring them on an almost perpendicular intercept. Not a textbook application, but the Greys were carrying far too much speed to do any better. With any luck at all, he and Boyd could get off multiple shots as they intercepted and knock the Darts out of the sky. "On my wing, Two."

Richards felt the Hurricane buffeting in the upper atmosphere. The curving horizon of Libretto spread to both sides of the nose and he thought he could see lights from the smaller communities below, then realized he was looking at thousands upon thousands of fires. *They've managed to set fire to most of the planet.* Dipping the Hurricane's wing, Richards started a neural clock and swung the Hurricane in a wide hypersonic turn. Almost like flying the space shuttle, er...orbiter. Richards smiled at the memory. *Why have a spacecraft that nobody knows the correct term for?*

Marking the departing Greys with a cursor in his heads-up display, Richards went through his pre-combat rituals as the Hurricane turned autonomously. "Right, dear." He engaged the Hurricane's interface, "Set inertial gravity to half a gee."

<<Engaged.>>

"Lock harness." He felt the straps over his shoulders tighten and lock down against his shoulder."

<<Locked.>>

"Comm set button one command, button two Saber Six, button three Squadron main."

<<Dialed and locked.>>

Richards smiled. "Tempted to play a little Iron Maiden right now."

<<Would you care for "Aces High", or something else?>>

"No." Richards smiled. "Increase turn rate five percent. Estimated time to intercept?"

<<Fifty-two seconds.>>

Richards flexed his gloved hands a final time. "Okay, dear. Manual control on my mark. Mark." There was a slight wobble, the onboard computer being infinitely more accurate at predicting buffeting and adjusting the control surfaces than even a pilot as experienced as Richards. "Two, follow my lead. This is something called a low yo-yo. You might have heard of it."

"Lead, Two. There's not too much ya can show me, ya know?"

Richards smiled. *Good girl.* "Watch and learn, young one." There were two clicks in his ears. Richards pulled the exocraft into a tighter turn to the right. Airspeed bleeding off slowly, the Hurricane's nose pointed slightly behind the blinking target of the Grey Darts. Sliding across their contrails about twenty kilometers behind the Darts, Richards snapped the Hurricane into a tight left turn and let the nose of the Hurricane dip towards the planet.

<<Fifteen seconds to intercept.>>

"Weapons free. One Streaker per target." The AIM12-X Streaker got its name during its experimental test phase. A technician supposedly told the Prelate's Council the missile packed enough propellant on board to blow someone out of their clothes. Richards just didn't get Luna humor. "Fire."

<<Weapons away.>>

Richards felt nothing as the six missiles fell into the hypersonic slipstream and ignited towards their targets. Swinging the nose of the Hurricane up and to the right, he watched the missiles trailing the six Grey fighters and then three very distinct impacts. The fighters held their tight position. Six more missiles from Boyd were trailing. Another three soundless explosions and the Grey fighters were no more. A bright flash from behind alerted Richards and he leveled the big interceptor's wings.

<<Nuclear detonation. All systems nominal.>>

"Danger from the shockwave?"

<<Not at present course and speed.>>

"EMP?" Richards asked and chided himself. The Hurricane would've succumbed to power failure if there had been any danger. The big interceptor was hardened against EMP and a myriad of other potential problems.

"EMP is affecting approximately one hundred thirty-thousand citizens and TDF personnel on the ground. There are approximately fifty thousand unaffected Grey vehicles in those affected areas.>>

"That's not a good start," Richards said out loud. The Greys were seemingly unaffected by just about anything save armed resistance. An area of electromagnetic pulse rendering electronic systems useless on Libretto meant a significant hole in the newborn TDF attack.

"Lead, Two. I reported the nudet."

And just who the hell came up with nudet? Must we shorten everything? Brevity had its place, but remembering a zillion acronyms and shortened sayings was just too much. "Roger, Two. Level out and prepare to descend. Saber Six is in position six hundred kilometers ahead. Take the lead this time."

"You're joking, right?" Boyd replied.

"I'm not. Rather nice shooting back there. Take us in." Richards retarded the throttle slightly, allowing Boyd to slip into the lead off his right shoulder. Watching Boyd's wing, Richards quieted his mind for a moment and just enjoyed flying again. His imprinted memories of flying ghastly propeller-driven canvas airplanes in the Great War brought a smile to his face. Flying used to be a rather simple thing. None of these computers and gadgets. Just the wind in his face and a stick and throttle. Every little ripple in the air traveled from the wingtips through the fuselage to his hands and feet, not like this inertial-dampening zero gravity environment that made it nearly impossible to get his bearings. *Nothing like this at all*, Richards thought.

Heading east, the curving horizon of Libretto and the dark starless sky of low orbit began to slowly recede. The sun rose in the distance, and Saber Six and her band of miscreants were already enjoying a warm autumn morning. Richards looked up into the sky above to see the *Ticonderoga* receding westward. The bright dot shimmered at one edge, and Richards knew *Ticonderoga* was firing. For a few minutes *Ticonderoga* and her crew would be fighting for their lives until the Greys passed in the opposite direction above them. *Orbital dynamics are quite the bitch*, Richards thought with a smirk.

Turning his head back to the nose of his interceptor, Richards stayed locked on Boyd's wing with barely a thought in his mind except praying *Ticonderoga* survived the next few minutes.

* * * * *

Chapter Sixty

"Class II surface detonation," one of Garrett's crew called. *Captain Porterman*, Garrett remembered. "Sir, I have a Class II surface detonation relayed from Orbital One."

Orbital One was a micro-satellite dispatched from *Ticonderoga* at a stationary orbit above Saber Six's area of operations. Laser burst communications and geospatial intelligence was the primary mission of the device, though having an onboard capability to detect infrared emissions was a distinct benefit. Garrett nodded at Porterman. "I guess that validates your ideas, Porterman."

The young captain grinned. "I'll have a spectral analysis on the explosion in a few minutes. There's a little wind at altitude causing interference. I've relayed the explosion's coordinates to Saber Six. Distance is roughly twenty kilometers north-northwest of their planned drop zone, sir."

Garrett nodded. "Get me what you can on it. Any speculation?"

"Errant round? Something on the ground? Really don't have a clue, sir." Porterman turned back to his screen. "Until I get a spectral, I've got nothing but speculation, sir."

Garrett turned to another operator. "Time to contact with the Jack?"

"Three minutes, sir."

We're not going to have time to run this operation from Ticonderoga when that Jack arrives, Garrett thought. If I had to do this again, I'd find a way to command it either closer in or further away. The thought triggered another one Garrett didn't want to pursue, but found himself scrolling the view to the last known location of the 2nd Armored Regiment. They were taking heavy fire. Sixty-five percent combat effective at the present time. He zoomed in the view and searched for Bullet Six. He found the vehicle. Destroyed? Garrett thought with genuine surprise. Who's in command? What can we do to give that regiment more support? Or a fighting chance?

"Sir, I've got movement north of Bullet Six."

North? Garrett swung the view to the north. "Where?"

"Sixty kilometers to the north, multiple contacts moving south at…a hundred kilometers per hour…now multiple contacts at seventy-five kilometers per hour," Porterman reported. "Looks like a counterattack, sir. That explosion triggered something."

No shit, Garrett thought. "Any birds in the area?"

"Just Lancer Flight, sir."

Garrett looked at the map. Committing Lancer Flight leaves Captain Shields without air cover. Committing Captain Shields' cavalry to intercept the counterattack is moderately risky. They would be outnumbered at least three to one. Combine them with the exo squadron and it might work. There were no guarantees. He reached for the console and triggered a private line to Shields.

"Saber Six, Looking Glass on private. Sending you a drop order now. Intercept a sizeable Grey counterattack on remnants of Bullet Six's position from the north. Bullet Six is down. I'm committing air cover to you. Acknowledge."

"Looking Glass, Saber Six. Drop order confirmed, and Rhinos are at atmospheric interface. Will report on station. Saber Six out."

Garrett clicked his microphone twice in response. In three minutes they'd be on the ground, and he'd be up here watching. Wishing he could do more. He clicked over to Richards' frequency. "Lancer One, Looking Glass. Close air mission order on the way. Acknowledge."

"Roger, Looking Glass, but won't I be leaving my poor ground-hugging charges behind?"

Garrett couldn't help but smile. "Tony, I'm a little more than one minute from engaging the Greys myself. They're coming with you. This is an all or nothing to protect the regiment."

"Right. Well, good hunting, sir. See you in about ninety-six minutes, then?"

"Count on it, you limey bastard."

Richards clicked his microphone twice in response.

"Good luck, Tony," Garrett said to no one.

Turning to his battle captains, he said, "Time to contact?"

"Forty-two seconds, sir. The Greys have commenced firing."

Garrett cinched his restraining belt across his lap and cued the admiral's frequency. "Sir, cavalry is one minute from the ground and the CAS is converging on Grey counterattack. Greys appear to be converging on that Class II detonation site. We're going to defend it and the regiment's position with Task Force Six Two."

"Let me know what you find out," Nather growled. Garrett heard him issuing firing orders before the connection terminated. His console flared again with an inbound transmission from Richards. "Go, Lancer One."

"I've got BVR locks."

"What?" Garrett blinked. "You got locks on Grey aircraft? Beyond visual range? Those fighters are usually stealthed."

"Not their bombers."

Garrett felt a cold sweat stream down his back. *Nukes.* "Fire on all targets. Be prepared for fighter escorts."

"Way ahead of you, Looking Glass," Richards chirped. "Lancer Flight commencing fire."

Porterman looked over. "Sir, we have no way of knowing from this range if those targets are real bombers or drones."

Another operator looked up. "Oh please, Porterman. The Greys don't have drones in their order of battle. If they do, then why haven't they used them in this entire war? Why now?" The operator looked at Garrett. She was young, blonde, and wore pilot's wings on her chest. "Sir, Captain Young. They're not drones, but they might not be bombers."

"What's that supposed to mean?"

"Lambs," Young said.

Garrett was about to respond when the 1-MC rang.

<<All hands brace for impact. Brace, brace, brace!>>

The first impacts were little more than a ripple. Every surface of the *Ticonderoga* rippled as her massive ion cannons returned fire alongside her conventional twelve-inch naval guns. Every impact meant a potential breach in the hull of the *Ticonderoga*. One blast door not secured and the whole damn platform could go up in a heartbeat. Garrett thumbed over to the command net and heard Connelly screaming orders at the fighter and interceptor squadrons to attack.

Let them go, he thought. *Keep your head in your fight.* Connelly was fighting the Greys as best he could. Garrett listened painfully to reports of his men being blown out of the sky through the persistent impacts of Grey rounds on the *Ticonderoga*. Her shields wavered only slightly towards the end of the passing engagement. The fighters and exo suffered badly. As the rate of fire being received by the *Ticonderoga* wavered and then fell to nothing at the end of the four-minute engagement, Garrett realized his hands were cramped against the console. "Damage report," he said automatically, then chastised himself. He wasn't on the command bridge now.

Porterman replied, "All systems are functional. Saber Six is on the ground. I have a preliminary spectral report from the microsat, sir. You're not going to believe it."

Garrett stood up from the console, aware that Nather's eyes were on him from the command bridge. He walked over to Porterman and Young and leaned over the console.

"Try me."

* * * * *

Chapter Sixty-One

At the first sign of a breathable atmosphere, Mairin swung open the commander's hatch on the Slammer and stood. Falling at terminal velocity and stabilized by repulsors on the bottom of the massive tank, the sensation was like floating. She engaged her neurals into the command system of the Slammer by standard operating procedure and then cued a map in her helmet. Additional datamarks pinged, and she blinked them away until she realized what they were.

The big tree she and Tally lunched under every time they hiked. Where they made love. Another site cued from the south shore of the lake where they'd camped one night under the stars. Mairin wanted to blink them away, but she kept them and filed them. They might serve as some tactically important point. She'd have to call artillery on them. Another dagger to her heart that would leave a reeking stench of damnation smeared on her relationship with Tallenaara. Of course, now the prelate was dead, and there was no news about his consort-to-be. Assuming the worst was easy, yet Mairin didn't want to think about it. Now or ever. More data points blinked in her helmet visor, but the terrain below was obscured by a heavy band of mist.

As the Slammer began to track forward and leave the screen of the mists, Mairin saw another marker blink into life exactly where a dark smear of smoke boiled up from the thick forests. *The pumping station*, she thought. *That's the place to start.*

"Guidons, this is Six, rally point is that fire up ahead. Form up in platoon coils approximately three thousand meters to the south east, behind the rolling terrain. We'll group there and see if we can't determine what hit that target. Acknowledge."

One by one her platoon leaders checked in, followed by Ulson in his role as Executive Officer. He sounded as resilient as ever, and Mairin was glad he'd shaken off the Ashland fiasco. She knew he would make an excellent commander one day. Scanning the terrain, Mairin saw no indications of Grey vehicles or assault and all friendly vehicles, and positions were well displayed to her southwest. The regiments there were being hammered. *Is this a CSAR location?* She cued the command frequency. "Looking Glass, this is Saber Six. Identify all CSAR missions in my AO, over."

Fifteen agonizing seconds passed. "Negative on all, Six." The transmission was filled with static and shouting voices in the background. *How badly had the* Ticonderoga *been hit?*

"Ma'am, I've got an infrared signature. Lone biped leaving that fire to the north-northwest. Interface confirms. I think we've identified the culprit."

Mairin looked at the slowly moving figure for several moments and then backed the tactical view out to a much broader field. The Greys were moving towards the fire. "Interface, analysis of Grey movement."

<<There is a sixty percent probability that the Greys are counterattacking the site of that fire. If that is the case, the regiment will be pinched between sizable Grey forces and would likely be destroyed in place.>>

Why would the Greys want the pumping station? It's just an oil station. Mairin felt her mouth open. They want the oil. Tally said that, didn't she? For what? Oh shit. What if that is the target? "Interface on private."

The private connection clicked. <<Yes, Captain.>>

"I need a combat intelligence query. Flash priority. Do you have substantial connection to the *Ticonderoga?*"

<<The connection is marginal.>>

Mairin chewed her lower lip for a moment. *What the hell?* "Known fossil fuel deposits on planets that have been attacked by the Greys in the last five years."

<<Probability is ninety-two point six percent that all planets attacked had some type of fossil fuel resources. The terraformed worlds of Eden, Narrob, and Shelby make up the remainder.>>

Holy shit. "Relay that to Thunder Six. The Greys are likely targeting petroleum and fossil fuel deposits. Libretto has a significant oil resource." Mairin punched another few buttons. "Trace all of the known pumping stations connected to the burning one in front of us."

<<General map downloading now.>> The image burned into Mairin's visor.

"Overlay all of the known Grey positions to this image." Immediately, Mairin could see that the Greys had good intelligence, but were misplaced around the planet in areas. Or were they? What if they were waiting for something to cue their attacks? She looked up at the smoldering fire and grinned. "They need the oil and they're waiting for something to catch fire to track it down."

<<Your conclusion is likely, Captain Shields. Shall I relay it?>>

"Relay everything we've talked about." Mairin watched the tops of the trees reaching up to the Slammer as they hovered in mid-air. "Location of our lone target?"

<<Six hundred meters to the north-northwest.>>

Mairin dispatched First Platoon to close with and identify the target. As they did she drew up a hasty plan to defend the destroyed pumping station. Scrolling the map, she noticed for the first time how close the cabin was, merely ten kilometers away across the lake. She looked up in the direction of the cabin and directed Booker to bring the Slammer to treetop level. The lone white dot on the distant shore made her eyes well with tears. *What if the Greys destroy it?*

That's not going to happen, Mairin.

She blinked. What's that supposed to mean?

You're not going to let that happen. Are you?

No, Mairin said silently and wiped her screen. They'd assault across the lake and take up a defensive position on the far side in the craggy hills to the north. Where Tally said she'd seen a stag as big as an autocar. *Tally*. Mairin blinked away the tear.

"Black Six, this is White One, over?"

The transmission brought Mairin back to reality. "Go ahead, White One."

"Um, ma'am, you're going to want to come up here."

"You've got that lone target?" No response.

"Ma'am, get up here. Please."

Shit! Mairin chinned to the Ulson's private channel. "You hold everyone here. I'll go up there and see what's the problem."

"Roger, ma'am."

Mairin leaned down into the tank. "Booker, get us to ground level and navigate to White One. Gunner, index sabot."

"Sabot indexed and loaded."

The Slammer settled through the tree limbs to the moist floor and began to slide forward through the trees. Mairin stood in the hatch and could see the Slammers of First Platoon in the distance. As her tank approached, Mairin was aware of screaming coming from the vehicles ahead. They were arranged in a tight coil with their guntubes out on the perimeter. Looking into the space between the Slammers, Mairin saw the dirty and torn coveralls of a Terran Defense Force officer. His slick bald skull gleamed in a stream of morning sunlight.

What in the hell is he doing here? Mairin climbed up out of the hatch. "Conner, alert command that I have sighting on Colonel Coffey at this location and he appears to be either lost or injured. Call for immediate retrieval."

Conners nodded. "Right away, ma'am."

Mairin unplugged the helmet and felt the cool morning Libretto air on her face. She dismounted the tank and attached her shoulder holster and map case by regimental policy before walking into the perimeter. The platoon leader shrugged from the top of his tank as Mairin walked past and into the circle formation. Immediately the screaming stopped, and she stood facing Coffey about ten feet away. "Sir, are you lost?"

Coffey sneered. "Give me your vehicle, Shields."

"Sir, I asked you a question. Are you lost? Do you need assistance back to your unit? The regiment is being—"

"I don't give a fuck about my regiment! Give me your vehicle, Captain! That's a direct order!"

Mairin took a breath. "Sir, I believe you are injured. I have requested immediate medical retrieval. I will not comply with your order on the grounds that I find your condition questionable and your order to be unlawful at the present time, sir."

Coffey stomped forward to cover her face with his whiskey-singed breath. "Now see here, Captain. You are an insubordinate, Styrahi-loving bitch! I want your vehicle! You're not going to keep me from going after that Stryahi terrorist that destroyed whatever that was back there! You understand me?"

Styrahi terrorist? "You saw someone, sir?"

"Black dress, dark hair. Had to be a fucking Styrahi. She's headed that way." He gestured to the northwest.

Mairin's mind flashed and the world tilted a little. "I'm sure that's not the case—" She rocked backward from a blow she hadn't seen and felt the wet fern leaves tickling her face. Her jaw throbbed.

"Treason, you bitch! You're covering for some terrorist!" Coffey loomed over her. "Now give me your vehicle!"

Mairin stood slowly and gave herself some space from Coffey. "No."

"I told you, I'm chasing a terrorist."

Mairin nodded. "Why are you not in command of your regiment twelve kilometers from here?"

Coffey blustered. "My regiment is not your concern!"

"Sir, did you desert your regiment?"

"My tank got shot out from under me. I came this way and discovered this terrorist. I'm going to gut her abomination of a body in the ground and put her head on a pike! You're not going to stop me!"

The wet smear down the leg of his combat suit said differently. Mairin unholstered her sidearm and leveled it at Coffey. "Sir, you're under arrest for desertion and cowardice in the face of the enemy. Place your hands behind your back and prepare to be subdued. Sergeant Mason!"

A deep voice from one of the Slammers boomed. "Yes, ma'am."

"Bring a kit and subdue the regimental commander."

"Moving, ma'am." The enormous man gracefully bounded down from a tank and closed the distance.

Coffey sneered. "You think you can stop me, Shields? You really think you can hold a gun on me? When I tell command that you let a fucking terrorist that I was trying to capture go free, you'll be drummed out of the TDF faster than shit through a goose! Not me." He laughed like a hyena. "I'm gonna be the hero, just like before. There's nothing you or your unit can do. So what if I ran from an unwinnable fight? They'll make me a general because I had the presence of mind to take care of myself! To get out alive! That's more than you can say! And now you're the one holding the bag full of shit, Shields. You stopped me and gave me this bullshit arrest in the middle of a pursuit! What can you say about that?"

Mairin squinted. "You're a deserter, sir."

"Fuck you, Shields! There ain't a damned thing you can do about it!" Coffey laughed and raised his sidearm.

Mairin squeezed the trigger on her forty-caliber pistol three quick times in succession and holstered the weapon even before Coffey fell completely to the ground, mouth slack and eyes staring uncomprehendingly into the forest canopy. Mairin looked up at Lieutenant Thornton. "You heard what he said, right?"

"Every word, ma'am."

Mairin looked up into the collected faces of the tank commanders and loaders who were watching. "Anybody have anything to say?"

There was no response. Thornton cleared his throat. "Ma'am, the Grey counterattack is accelerating. They'll reach the north shore of the lake in about six minutes."

Mairin nodded and looked a last time at Coffey's pale face. "We're going to give those bastards the fight they should have had from him. Mount up." She stomped through the brush back to her Slammer and climbed aboard. "Interface, recall the troop to this location. Assault Plan Bravo. Prepare to attack."

She chinned over to the command frequency. "Looking Glass, this is Saber Six, did you copy my query transmission, over?"

Garrett's voice came over the substantially better signal. "Roger, all. You really think that's the target?"

"Yes, sir." Mairin looked at the icons of the advancing Grey column. "We've got a massive attack about to bear down on this location, sir. If it looks like a duck and quacks like a duck...."

"Roger," Garrett chuckled. "I'm committing all squadron assets to you."

"Thank you, sir." Mairin swallowed. "Sir, I called a retrieval down for the regimental commander."

"I heard that."

"It won't be needed, sir."

"Why not?" Garrett asked.

"Sir, Colonel Coffey is dead. He admitted to cowardice in combat and then tried to shoot me. I shot him, sir."

"Okay, stop." Garrett said. "Say nothing more about this until retrieval. You understand me? I can't afford to relieve you in the middle of a battle, Shields."

"But, sir, I said that he tried to—"

"And you shot him. Until this is reviewed by legal you are not to discuss it. Now lead your troop, Captain Shields. We'll discuss the rest of it when the time comes."

"Understand, sir," Mairin choked. *Didn't I do the right thing?*

Have faith, Mairin.

She nodded and looked in the direction of the cabin. *It's Tally.* Her heart leapt. None of this shit would matter if she could have Tallenaara again. Chinning the command frequency, she ordered, "Guidons, this is Six. Move out. Good hunting. If we make it all the way across that lake, take up positions in the hills above those buildings."

As the Slammers broke through the woodline and crossed the thin ribbon of shore to the lake, Mairin reached into her leg pocket and brought the cold metal bottle out. With great ceremony she unscrewed the lid of the bottle and dumped the canteen's contents into the lake. She looked across and saw Ulson standing in his cupola doing the same.

If I die here, I die happy, she thought as Ulson chimed into the command frequency.

"Guidons, Black Five. Sound the charge!"

Mairin wasn't listening. Across the lake, she saw a black clothed figure running down the shore towards the cabin. From two thousand meters or more and at the limits of her enhanced eyesight, Mairin knew it was Tally. The stride was hers. They'd run along that beach for hours. Mairin commanded Booker to the far right flank of the assault. She opened the faceplate of her helmet and screamed.

"Tally" And again. And again, but the figure on the beach ran harder towards the cabin.

<<Contact front!>> The Interface chimed and Mairin felt the air around them fill with projectiles. She dropped into the tank and engaged her visor. All of her vehicles were firing now. She looked again for Tally, but the beach was empty. Her heart

fell and then jolted with anger. *These bastards will not take her from me today. Not here! Not ever!*

Mairin chinned the command frequency. "Looking Glass, I'm committing forces now. Give me everything that you can. Kill everything that moves!" The Slammer reared up on its repulsors. Mairin swept her tanks from the trees and directed the volume of fire into the broadside of the Grey attack.

* * * * *

Chapter Sixty-Two

Sergeant Major Jack Trevayne focused on the assaulting Grey tanks and walked thousands upon thousands of machine gun rounds into the swarming black vehicles below his position on the ridgeline. He felt an impact on his shoulder but continued firing. *Center mass of target, squeeze. Center mass of target, squeeze. Traverse to the right.* Over and over again, Trevayne squeezed off bursts until the gun was out of ammunition. Reloading meant dropping into the turret for another case. He reared up through the cupola with a new box and saw his commo specialist, Specialist Dossett, staring off the back deck.

"Dossett!" Trevayne called and then looked where the loader was looking. The force to the front of their position appeared positively tiny compared to the boiling column of Grey vehicles descending the ridgelines and crossing the shore of the lake below in his general direction. To his right, Trevayne saw a company-sized element of Slammers burst from the trees in counterattack. *There's too many Greys, Shields! What are you doing?*

A slowly rising column of black smoke caught his eye, and Trevayne knew they were holding the wrong ground. "All Bullet elements, this is Bullet Nine. Prepare to move. We're backing down off this ridgeline. There's a counterattack coming from the north. We're going to give up this position for one that can put fire on those bastards." Trevayne sketched a quick graph on the console and sent it to the regiment. "You've got it. Move out!"

Trevayne chinned over to the command frequency from the *Ticonderoga.* "Looking Glass, this is Bullet Nine. I'm in command of the regiment at this time. We're moving to secure a position in support of Saber Six. Drop every orbital gun platform you can on my position in about sixty seconds. Acknowledge?"

A static-filled transmission met his ears. "Roger, Bullet Nine. Copy all. Good luck."

Trevayne backed his Intimidator down from the ridgeline and swung to the center of the line as his vehicles dropped quickly towards the lake and pivoted towards the smoking target. *Whatever it is, it's important.* A tank round passed close enough that he could see it. "Contact left! Match bearings and return fire!" he roared into the regimental channel.

A massive shockwave broke over Trevayne from behind. Orbital gunfire began to fall on the top of the ridgeline and the destroyed remnants of the regiment. Trevayne saw a flash in the sky as fighters converged over the lake and began to engage the Greys.

God help us, Trevayne thought as he felt his own tank begin to return fire on the advancing Greys. *Help us die well.*

* * * * *

Chapter Sixty-Three

Richards dropped his Hurricane out of the clouds and saw the unfolding battle clearly. The Greys were attacking something smoking in the forest. The cavalry was counterattacking from the east into the broadside of the Greys while the tank regiment who'd been holding the high ground gave up their position to defend whatever was smoking. *What in the hell do they expect us to do?* he thought even as his plan formed.

"Lancers, engage all targets of opportunity. Coordinate attacks with follow-on squadrons." Richards looked across his shoulder at his wingman, or would it be wingwoman? *Bah!* "Boyd, you're taking charge of the inbounds. Three squadrons are inbound now. Stay up here and coordinate attack runs. Hit the Greys center mass and keep right on hitting! Are we clear?"

"Roger, all. Good hunting, sir." Boyd replied.

How can someone so competent sound so unfazed by all of this? Richards swung the Hurricane in a descending turn and saw that all of his Hurricanes, except for Boyd's, followed him. "Combat spread," he called over the radio. Immediately the four remaining fighters spread out to about two hundred meters apart and opened their weapons bays. "Time to targets is ten seconds. Do me proud, lads."

"Looking Glass, this is Lancer One. Confirm no atmospheric air-to-air?"

In the static Richards clearly heard Garrett reply. "Negative in this area, Lancer One. SITREP?"

Richards chuckled. "Now's not the time." He grunted and dropped a salvo of armor piercing bomblets into the Grey advance. "Will coordinate a full SITREP when it's over."

He cycled another salvo and dropped it before flashing over what appeared to be the tail of the Grey column. Bringing the nose up, Richards looked over his shoulder in the loop. Blossoming explosions filled his view. He could see more than a dozen exocraft and interceptors rallying on the Grey attack with everything in the inventory.

The cavalry vehicles were about to reach the north side of the lake. Without air support, they'd be overwhelmed. "Lancers, Lancer One! On me!" A wide swath of Greys broke off from the main column and moved east down a deserted autocar path on a perfect intercept for the cavalry. "On me, lads!"

They might just make it. "Looking Glass, Lancer One. Got a bit of a situation you might say. I'm breaking away to get some Greys trying to flank the cavalry. We're going to need more support."

* * * * *

Chapter Sixty-Four

The urge to hit something inanimate overwhelmed Garrett enough that he nearly lost both his bearing and composure. Radio transmissions were static-filled bursts of partial information barely relaying an accurate picture of the ground. The *Ticonderoga* herself was too far away and moving farther in her static orbit. Three different types of forces and however many types of combat vehicles were trying to coordinate a complicated fight on a very dynamic battlefield, and there was nothing Garrett could do about it.

"Communications are boosted, sir. We cannot take any more bandwidth from the *Canberra* without failing their systems," Porterman said. "Sir, without a direct lock on laser communications, we're going to lose their signal in less than six minutes. We can expect the loss of signal to last at least ten minutes based on our position."

Garrett walked over to Nather. "Sir, I've got to have more bandwidth."

"You know I can't give it to you, Don." Nather grunted and turned to a Terran Defense Force colonel that hadn't been on the bridge during the initial engagement with the Jack. "You have any assets, Colonel?"

The colonel looked at Nather and then at Garrett. "My name is Munsen, Captain Garrett. I'd suggest a simple approach. Take a multi-band communications node and provide an airborne command and control platform."

Munsen? Why is that familiar? Garrett shook his head. "Our multi-bands are either already deployed to the surface or were destroyed when the Greys targeted the communications decks. We don't have one aboard."

Munsen smiled. "Good thing I happened to bring one aboard on my shuttle. By your leave, Admiral?"

"Of course, Thom." Nather looked at Garrett for a long moment and extended a hand. "Good luck, Don."

"Thank you, sir."

Nather turned his attention to the horizon of Libretto as they neared the midpoint of their trek across the planet's nightside. "We'll see you on the other side."

Garrett ordered his officers to the flight deck and broke into a jog behind Munsen. "So, just who are you, and when did you get aboard this platform?"

Munsen slowed slightly allowing Garrett to join up on his shoulder. "I just came back from briefing the Prelate. I was in the city until about three minutes after the Greys landed. I was on the ground during the initial attack and sat out for a couple of days in the bowels of Libretto City waiting for the TDF to come in and get me. That obviously never happened."

Garrett noted the man looked more than a few years older than himself, but given his impressive physical conditioning and the fact he'd not even started breathing hard in spite of the pace they ran to the flight deck, the answer was obvious. And then it hit Garrett between the eyes. "You're the officer from imprinting. You were a general, weren't you?"

"Long story," Munsen replied. "About time you remembered me, Garrett."

This wasn't the man who'd interviewed Garrett for the process, but he'd been there in the background. Watching. Observing. Learning. "You take over the program from Evan Richards?"

"Years ago. There are more than two hundred active imprints now. And at least one down on the surface that's special enough to merit my trying to save her ass."

They entered the flight deck and Garrett saw the *Spectre*-class shuttle sitting undamaged in the midst of the chaotic deck. "Nice ride," Garrett said. "You're talking about Mairin Shields, right?"

Munsen nodded and slowed to a fast walk. "She's a Class Five imprint, Garrett. She can literally remember things her imprint did, not just instincts and flashes of feelings. This is a whole new ballgame. She's worth protecting."

"There's something more you aren't telling me."

Munsen glanced his way. "You have no idea how important she is, Garrett."

"Then you're not going to like this." Garrett stopped Munsen with a hand on his arm. "She reported to me that she shot and killed Colonel Coffey for cowardice in the face of the enemy."

"What?"

"She said he confessed to it and that she has witnesses—"

Munsen's face contorted. "That's not the best news you could give me."

"You need to know."

"Yeah I do." Munsen shrugged and began to climb aboard the shuttle. "Get aboard, Garrett. Let's see if we can make a difference in this fight."

Garrett whistled. The beautiful shuttle was unlike anything in the Fleet. "Where did you get this?"

"I stole it," Munsen grunted. "Come on."

"We're not gonna make it in time."

Munsen just smiled as they strapped into their seats and the engines began to spool. Garrett was quite sure he'd never heard anything like them, and as he thought about it, the shuttle glided effortlessly from the flight deck and into space. A split second later, Garrett was sure they'd exploded as acceleration pushed him into the cushioned seat. When he realized the truth, Garrett smiled and watched the planet turning quickly underneath them with the daylight terminator approaching.

"Still think we don't have enough time?"

"How in the—"

"There's no time to explain, Don. What's your plan?"

A thousand clichés ran through his mind. *When in charge, take charge. Secure the high ground. Lead from the front. Put steel on target.* All of them worthless, seeming like platitudes of false motivation. "I'm making this up as I go."

"What's the mission then?"

"Get our people out alive," Garrett said.

"Isn't that what it's all about?" Munsen asked as the shuttle's nose dipped into the atmosphere for the first time. "How we do that will never be the same way twice. That's the first thing you've got to remember about a command like the one you tried to put together."

Garrett nodded. "And what's the second thing I need to remember about a command like this?"

"Two hundred years of polarization of forces and missions means they are naturally not going to work together. That's what you've got to do. You've got about two minutes to figure out how you're going to do it."

* * * * *

Chapter Sixty-Five

As she broke from the woodline, Tallenaara saw the Greys rolling down the autocar easement towards the rear of her cabin and the exposed flank of the vehicles to the southwest. Shouldering her rifle, Tally moved to the east of the cabin and stood her ground. The narrow entrance to the cabin was flanked with rock formations on either side. If she could channelize them, stop them even for a moment, the attacking friendly vehicles could react and protect themselves, and turn back the Greys. The first Grey vehicle moved into the gap between the crags of sandstone and began a pivot turn. Tallenaara squeezed the trigger on the plasma rifle and dispatched the Grey tank with one round.

Another tank appeared behind the smoldering first victim and began to push it through the gap towards Tally. The wind freshened, and the smoke swirled just enough that she released a second round and tore the turret off the Grey vehicle.

A Grey tank appeared fifteen meters to the east of the crags through the heavy brush. Tally fired again, this tank taking three rounds before exploding. As she loaded a new magazine into the rifle, another tank tore out of the forest to the west of the crags, followed by another. And then a third.

Tally ran towards the lake, squeezing off several blind shots as she did. She fired a round across the formation of friendly tanks screaming across the lake. The presence of a plasma round got their attention. She turned back to the advancing Greys and engaged them as calmly as she'd been in training all those years ago. *Center, breathe, squeeze.* Each report of the rifle came as a surprise as she sighted the tanks and fired. Four of them turned their tubes in her direction and she felt her knees tremble.

"*Da bo ti,* cariad," she whispered as light drops of rain began to fall. *I love you.* She saw the muzzles of all of the Grey tanks flash. She'd stood here with Mairin watching a sunset and holding the young girl tight against her chest. Their breasts touching, a playful grin on her lover's face. She'd sworn the memory would stay with her. As death took her, Tallenaara felt no pain, remembering the warmth of her lover's arms and the gentle touch of their lips.

* * *

M*y God*, Richards thought as he watched the Greys execute whoever that had been on the shoreline. We're about to lose this fight. He dropped a final salvo of bomblets into the Grey's column and whipped the Hurricane around for a strafing run. The white clam-shelled cabin swung under his canopy as he turned into the Greys, descended to just above the water's height, and began to fire.

"Lancer One, this is Looking Glass. You read me?" Garrett sounded as clear as if he was in the next room. How'd they done that?

"Roger, Looking Glass, copy you loud and very clear. Not sure how you did it."

"Look up." Richards looked straight up and saw the silhouette of a gunship skimming the underside of the low clouds some two thousand meters overhead. "I've got command of this attack. You and your Lancers regroup and prepare to cut off that avenue of approach to the north of the cabin. You know what I mean?"

"Roger, quite." Richards swung around and initiated a recall of his squadron. "We'll take care of the whole easement there. Bomb everything to the Stone Age nicely."

Garrett interrupted. "Not the cabin. No collateral damage, Tony."

Bloody hell? "Acknowledged, Looking Glass."

"Just cut off that corridor, Lancer One. And do not hit that cabin. Priority One order."

"On it, boss," Richards quipped and dove with his flight of Hurricanes into the breech once again.

* * *

Trevayne watched Shields' counterattack from his position and knew it was destined to fail unless he did something. The regiment had been decimated, down to thirty percent combat effectiveness. Vehicles listed and smoked in their defensive positions. None of that mattered now. Their brothers needed help, and a bunch of airplanes weren't enough to get it done. Billy Mitchell was only half right, Trevayne thought, and wondered who Billy Mitchell was before chinning up the regimental frequency.

"Bullet elements, this is Bullet Nine. Follow me."

Gliding down the slope, the regiment reached the water in less than a minute. The repulsors kicked in and kept the vehicle at a one-meter altitude above the glassy lake. Trevayne forced his stomach to calm down. Throwing up wouldn't be the best idea. "Interface, as soon as you have a solution on the nearest Grey vehicle, target it. Gunner, take all firing commands from the Interface."

Dossett looked over to him as he stood up in the hatch and charged the machine gun. "What are you going to do, Sergeant Major?"

"Same thing you're going to do. Get up here and on that machine gun." Trevayne grinned. "We're gonna bust some caps, Dossett. Teach those little grey bastards not to fuck with us."

*****

Chapter Sixty-Six

Nather watched the countdown clock aboard the *Ticonderoga* ticking down to four minutes. The Grey platform's previous engagement with the *Ticonderoga* had nearly destroyed the pride of the fleet. Her containment shields were only performing at forty-five percent and fires still raged on several decks. The guns were silent and useless, pointing aimlessly over the right rear of the platform as daylight approached. The litany of pre-combat checks did little to settle Nather the way routines seemed to settle everyone else. *Maybe I'm finally getting too old for this shit.*

"Sir, HICAP reports no visual on the Jack."

What? "Orbital analysis? High, low, geo?"

"Nothing, sir. The Jack is gone." The officer of the deck looked at Nather and smiled briefly before getting a third confirmation that the HICAP wasn't delusional or compromised. "Sir, all forward scans are clear. Ground units in line of sight to us are reporting Grey vehicles are slagging in place."

Nather leaned forward in his chair. "Get me in contact with all platforms. Confirm the situation and prepare to recover our troops." For a moment, he did nothing but wonder what it meant. *In no way is this over. The Greys are too resilient for that.* The very real feeling that things were just getting started was enough to get Nather out of his chair and leading the recovery effort for everyone on Libretto, including his soldiers and airmen. *We need every man and woman we can rescue.*

"Any contact with that shuttle dispatched earlier?" Nather asked.

"Sir, I have positive lock on the shuttle near Libretto City. No damage."

Nather smiled at the communications officer and leaned back in the chair. *Don Garrett and Thom Munsen live to fight another day. Maybe we can win this war after all.* "Status of troops?"

"Heavy losses across the board, sir."

Nather sighed. "Saber Six?"

"Saber elements are less than sixty percent combat effective. I cannot raise their leader."

Nather took a deep breath, held it for ten seconds, and let it go slowly. *Have faith*, he told himself. Looking down on the scarred, burning planet of Libretto, he tried not to imagine it being Earth. And failed. *If we don't figure out our enemy, this fight will go all the way to our doorstep.*

*****

Chapter Sixty-Seven

Far-off explosions rumbled down the hillsides and across the lake. Mairin tore off her helmet and vaulted out of the hatch. Stomach clenching and her throat tingling as if her stomach would betray her, she leaped off the tank and blinked through heavy tears as she came upon Tallenaara's body. Her lover lay in bloody, charred pieces on the ground. She raised her arms, silently giving her troopers the command to form a coil around her. The heavy tanks moved to their positions, gun tubes facing out, as Mairin fell to her knees and pressed her fingers deep into the dirt.

The ground trembled slightly as Mairin dug. The eyes of her troopers and officers watching her every move weighed heavy on her shoulders. Sweat ran into her eyes and mixed with hot, rolling tears. Her mind numbed and shocked at Tally's violent death, Mairin closed her eyes and worked as if trying to remove the guilt. *I was too late. If only I'd known.* Hands aching and arms burning from the effort, she dug Tallenaara's shallow grave. Only the roars of exocraft caught her attention. She watched them circling the slagged Greys waiting for any movement to pounce and deliver more ordnance on target. She wished she were there in a cockpit instead of here. Anywhere but here.

She buried Tallenaara above the shoreline, where the sandy soil was loose and dry. Her tears mixed with sweat and ran in rivers down her face, taking the grime of war with them. *Too late. I was too late. I'm so sorry. Please.* There was no comfort from the wind. Mairin stared into the hole she'd dug. Cheeks burning with shame, she wanted to be there instead of Tally. Her lover deserved so much better. So much more. *Oh god, Tally.*

She took too long, much too long, to gather up her lover's remains and gently place them into the grave. Dragging Tallenaara's dismembered body racked Mairin's body. "Tally," she said over and over again. She laid Tallenaara out in the grave and gently reached in to caress the cold, gray flesh of her lover's peaceful face. Mairin spoke softly, the wind carrying her words no farther than the graveside.

The tattered ceremonial dress Tallenaara wore became a shroud. Mairin knelt at the side of the grave and wanted to pray. But to whom? *Who could possibly take away this pain?*

A cool drop of rain fell from the clouds, joined by another, and then many more until Mairin couldn't see the ridges and the lake no longer mirrored itself against the sky. Rain fell, and her memories swirled like windblown pictures. Fleeting, vivid moments in time that she would never have again. Water ran down her neck, soaking her jumpsuit thoroughly, like the night she'd gone home with Tally for the first time. To this place. To this forever sacred place.

Ulson called to her, something about a counterattack. Artillery started to fall to the west. The magtanks spooled their engines, and two of them fired in quick succession. The battle wasn't over. Mairin looked at the grave and felt her chest hitch as the tightness in her throat gathered. She covered her lover's shallow grave with sandy soil, oblivious to the physical pain as she opened sores on her palms.

Her task was done. She looked at the oblong mound and swore she would make it better. She would return to their home and make it better. Leaving now did not feel right, turning away without saying something more. She could not, would not, say goodbye. She wouldn't pray over Tallenaara either. Eyes closed, she raised her chin to the rain. *Always the rain.* She smiled through her tears.

"I love you, Tallenaara. Every day, I will pray for rain."

* * * * *

Chapter Sixty-Eight

Three months later…

Inside the shattered dome of Libretto City there were three levels of security, each more stringent than the first. Mairin got out of the autocar at the second checkpoint, slung her combat rucksack over her shoulders, and carried her duffle bags in both hands to the third checkpoint, eight hundred meters inside the final ring. The dome was coming down, being removed now that the great illusion of the planet was sullied by the Grey attack. There was no point in doming the city anymore. The Greys knew where it was, and should they return, they could wipe it off the face of the planet in a matter of minutes. Crews of all species worked to clear debris continuously. The shattered remains of the hotel where Mairin had spent her first nights still remained, though standing only to the sixth floor in most places, the higher floors now strewn in all directions. The entertainment district still smoldered in places more than three months after the attack that killed Andrew Cartner.

Her cavalry troop remained out in the northern continent more than four thousand kilometers to the west. The oil-pumping network was more complicated than anyone had known, and after following the destroyed pipeline, all hell broke loose. Earth's closest allies had kept a vital secret. Something that Earth needed almost as badly as the Greys, even as they moved past fossil fuel dependency. Humans always wanted more.

The Styrahi and the humans were now on tenuous ground. The oily secrets of Libretto were known to the galaxy, and the Greys were nowhere to be seen. The promise of oil, the driver of Earth's history, brought new excursions into deep space. The

Greys were going to come back, of that Mairin was certain. Yet, she'd been recalled into the smoldering city in the midst of their investigations for a reason no one seemed able to state.

As she approached the final checkpoint to the Terran Defense Force headquarters, the level of security present caught her attention. Armed guards patrolled inside a perimeter of concertina wire more than three meters tall. Several cy-dogs patrolled as well, robotic eyes scanning in all areas of the spectrum. At the checkpoint, Mairin dropped her bags and presented her identification.

"Captain Mairin Shields?" the guard asked.

"That's me."

The guard's pistol came up and pointed at her chest. "Ma'am, you are under arrest—"

Mairin blinked and brought her arms up showing empty palms. "I have orders to report to the commanding general."

"Under Article Thirty-Two of the Reformed Code of Military Justice, you are placed under arrest until such time as a hearing can be convened in your legal matters."

"Legal matters?" Mairin shook her head. "I have no idea what you're talking about!" Try as she might, her imprint said nothing except to be calm, that things would sort themselves out. "Take me to the commanding general, Sergeant."

The guard shook his head and kept his weapon trained to her chest. His eyes scanned across retinal displays. "A detachment is on the way to collect you, Captain Shields. If you run, I am instructed to shoot to kill. Do you understand?"

Fucking MPs, Mairin thought. "You can put the gun down, Sergeant. I'm unarmed and no threat to you."

The sergeant smiled with the corner of his mouth. "Anyone suspected of murdering a superior officer is hardly someone I'd trust, Captain."

So that's what this is about. Shit. Mairin shook her head. "Not a superior officer, Sergeant. Merely a higher-ranking one who deserted his regiment in the face of the enemy. I'd like to think, given the circumstances, that you would consider doing the same thing."

The reaction force arrived with a half-dozen vehicles. A dozen armed men surrounded Mairin in a matter of seconds. She kept her eyes on the guard she'd first spoken to. His eyes never left hers, but he nodded slightly before lowering his weapon and directing the guard force to take Mairin away. A large man put Mairin in handcuffs and sat her in the transport vehicle. Mairin let her anger boil up, even as it threatened to bring tears to her eyes. *They want blood, do they?* Mairin sat with her hands in her lap, waiting, as the vehicle drove to the converted barracks serving as the TDF headquarters on Libretto. The flags of a dozen species flew over the building, though all Mairin saw in any direction were humans. Many of them would be staring when she exited the transport. Some would whisper about her, like in the halls of Eden Academy.

This is different, Mairin, she thought. This time, what they're going to say is partially true. You killed a higher ranking officer for desertion and being drunk on duty. You were justified, and no military court in their right mind would find you guilty. She took a breath and held it, letting it out as she wondered if she was a scapegoat. The transport stopped, and Mairin stepped out with as much dignity as she could muster with her wrists bound in front of her. There were plenty of stares as she walked quickly, head up and shoulders back, through the entrance to TDF headquarters. After a few turns past disjointed and spastic staff sections working to extend the reach of the commander, Mairin stepped into a dark, cool room. As her eyes adjusted, there was a single chair in the center of the room facing a raised dais with six chairs.

This would be what a court-martial feels like, she thought with gallows humor. If they kick me out, maybe I can retake the Civil Consideration examination.

A short, thin lieutenant with dark skin walked towards her. His arms hardly moved as he walked and when he spoke, Mairin strained to hear him. "Ma'am, please have a seat. The Council of Colonels will begin shortly."

"This isn't a court martial?"

The lieutenant looked briefly at her and then away again. "No, ma'am," he slunk away quietly, so much that the heavy wooden door hardly made a sound as he walked out behind Mairin. The chair looked hard and unforgiving. There was no point in sitting down before the proceedings began. Mairin closed her eyes and took a deep breath. Whatever was coming would never be as hard as where she'd been. What she'd seen.

Tally firing that damned plasma rifle and disappearing in a cloud of red mist. Her burial mask peaceful and serene while Mairin collected appendages and pieces to bury.

No court will ever compare, Mairin. Aware that she was flushed and angry, Mairin let the emotion wash over her. If they want to question her and her actions, fine. The truth wasn't going to set her free. *It's all a show,* Mairin sighed to herself. A door behind the dais opened and Mairin snapped to the position of attention.

The first figure appeared in the door, and Mairin sucked in a breath. This wasn't a Council of Colonels. The balding, fat man wore the two stars of a major general. Every one of the council bore at least two stars, with the President of the Council's shoulders bearing the four stars of a general. She'd never seen a four-star up close and knew that she should be impressed, but she wasn't. The likelihood that he was another TDF idiot who'd managed to get promoted on the backs of others and was just better at politics than the rest of his peers was likely what set him apart.

Allowing her eyes to quickly glance at the rest of the board, she recognized a familiar face. His uniform bore two shiny new stars and Mairin wanted to grin as he set a spittoon on the desk before he sat. *If Talvio is here, maybe I have a chance after all.*

"Captain Mairin Shields," the presiding general looked at her. "This proceeding is in accordance with Article Thirty-Two of the Reformed Uniform Code of Military Justice. As an investigative hearing, you are granted the assistance of legal counsel, if you so choose. Do you wish legal counsel?"

Mairin wanted to look at Talvio's face as she said, "No, sir." Her voice sounded more confident and self-assured than she felt inside.

The general blinked but said nothing for a long moment. "Be seated, Captain."

"Thank you, sir." The seat was as hard as she'd imagined it would be.

The general looked at the officers on the dais before speaking. "Captain Shields, this hearing is to investigate your actions starting on or about twenty-five July of this year on the planet Rayu-4 through your recent conducts at the Battle of Libretto. At any point in time, the officers of the council are allowed to ask you anything, and you are required to respond in accordance with your rights as a witness. I will start the questioning on twenty-five July of this year. At that time, what was your duty position?"

"Sir, I had no duty position. Upon the verbal order of the ground force commander, then-Lieutenant Colonel Robert Coffey, I assumed command of a detachment of six Slammer magtanks and their crews, totaling twenty-three personnel and myself."

A lieutenant general with salt and pepper hair and the uniform of a quartermaster asked, "That is not a doctrinal deployment of the Slammer magtank. Were you aware of that, Captain?"

"Yes, sir." Mairin said. "I'm also aware that a combat commander is not bound to doctrine in the accomplishment of the mission, sir."

"We do not need a lecture from you, Captain. You are to cooperate with this investigation into your actions on Libretto. Are we clear on this, Captain?" The President of the Board clenched his jaw.

This wasn't starting well. "Yes, sir."

A pregnant pause followed her response until a female Major General with the tunic of a Terran Defense Force nurse asked. "How long had you been a captain when you took command of these six vehicles and dropped on Rayu-4."

Mairin thought for a moment. "Roughly three and a half months, ma'am."

"And how long had you been an officer at the time of this action?"

"The exact same amount of time, ma'am." Several members of the council gasped. The president rapped the gavel twice to gain everyone's attention. He nodded for the nurse to continue.

"What were you doing four months before your first combat drop, Captain Shields?"

"Ma'am, I was an upperclassman at the Eden Academy."

A murmur rose, and the President rapped the gavel again. "Any more interruptions and I will place all members on report."

The nurse ran a hand through her short blonde hair. "You were a student at Eden Academy four months before this operation?"

"Yes, ma'am."

"Then how in the hell did you become an officer, Captain? Our officers undergo years of undergraduate training as cadets or serve with distinction as members of the non-commissioned officers corps before accepting a commission as a Terran Defense Force officer! How did you come to be an officer?"

Mairin looked at the president of the council. "Sir, I respectfully request a security verification of the Board privately under Terran Defense Force regulation fourteen dash four. I have reason to believe my answer in this court could release classified information."

The president of the board shook his head. "Captain Shields, the board is aware of your status as a test subject for imprinting. Now answer the question for the record."

Mairin tried not to smile. "I was a student at Eden Academy, and on the day of Civil Consideration, I met a Terran Defense Force officer by the name of Colonel Thomas Munsen."

Major General Talvio cleared his throat and leaned forward. "Sir, why don't we cut to the chase? I'd like to get to the meat of this proceeding and discuss Captain Shields' actions here and the engagements prior to the Battle of Libretto. As you are aware, I do have some knowledge of the captain's conduct and performance prior to her alleged crime."

The president of the council scowled for a moment. "You do at that, general. In an effort to speed this process, how would you characterize Captain Shields' performance as an officer?"

Talvio spat into his spittoon and his face became hard and serious. "Outstanding, sir. Captain Shields is one of the finest tactical commanders in the Terran Defense Forces. I would put her in front of every graduate of the Academy I've ever known."

The nurse spoke again, "But that behavior and performance is more in line with her imprint, than her own actions."

"Bullshit," a major general with fleet aviator's wings on his shoulders replied. "You cannot teach a leader how to care for soldiers and how to effectively fight the enemy. Warriors are born with that."

The president looked at Mairin. "Would you consider yourself a warrior, Captain Shields?"

"Sir, I hate that term. I am a soldier. I do what I'm told and accomplish the mission to the best of my ability within the guidance of regulations and the orders of my superiors." Mairin licked her lips. "Even if that means holding a commander to a higher standard present in the regulation versus their conduct."

Talvio leaned forward again. "Sir, Captain Shields was recommended for the Silver Star for her actions at the Hoffman

Colony. The award is currently on hold pending the results of this investigation, in accordance with regulation. Captain Shields is presently flagged and unable to receive that award and others she is due."

"Others?"

"Captain Shields," Talvio nodded at her, his eyes twinkling, "will receive two Bronze Stars for her actions on Ashland and Waters City. For the Battle of Libretto, the intent of my command is to recommend her for the Medal of Earth."

Mairin blinked. She'd never imagined being nominated for the highest award in the Terran Defense Force. The blustering quartermaster general brought her back to reality quickly.

"Absolutely not! She killed a superior officer!" His pudgy hand pointed at Mairin. "Do you deny killing Colonel Coffey during the Battle of Libretto?"

Silence fell quickly. Mairin spoke as clear as she could. "Sir, I shot and killed Colonel Coffey for desertion in the face of the enemy and drunkenness on duty. I would also clearly put to the record all testimonies of my soldiers regarding Colonel Coffey's intent to shoot me for attempting to arrest him."

The quartermaster leaned back in his chair and smiled toward the president of the council. "She admits it, sir. Can we go about getting her out of the Terran Defense Force now? She's a disgrace to the uniform!"

The president of the council glanced at Talvio, then Mairin, and then to the quartermaster. "That will be enough, General. Your personal views are not part of this hearing."

The quartermaster crossed his arms. "She was fucking the late Prelate's Consort for God's sake! Her dalliance with a Styrahi is highly suspect to her motives!"

"That will be all!" The president of the board roared. "Captain Shields, you are instructed to disregard the General's comments."

Mairin shook her head. "No, sir. I will not. My personal relationship with Tallenaara was before she became the Prelate's

Consort, and besides that fact, my personal relationships are outside of the bounds of the Terran Defense Forces at all times. I will not be insulted by a rear—" Mairin paused. Calling the general a "rear-echelon mother fucker" wouldn't help her case at all. "By a higher ranking officer whose personal beliefs contradict my own."

Several voices spoke at once, with Talvio covering all of them in a bellow. "I think we've heard enough, General." The man looked over the collection of generals and back to Mairin. His left eye blinked rapidly and Mairin felt her heart soar.

The president of the council nodded his head. "Captain Shields, you are dismissed. Until further notice, you are on administrative leave without pay. Benefits will be available at any military treatment facility. Until such time as you are cleared for a return to active duty, you will not discuss these proceedings with anyone. Is that clear?"

They're letting me go? "Yes, sir."

The President stared at her a moment and consulted his notes. "You are excused, Captain Shields. May the record state that executive privilege is afforded to the next witness."

Mairin moved to the door as it swung open and stopped. Behind her, Mairin heard the president say, "The Council calls Colonel Thomas Munsen, retired."

* * * * *

Requiem

The *nahalla* came early for Mairin's last night on Libretto. Standing in the warm summer rain, light gently fading in the gray skies, she settled onto the cool wet grass where her love lay forever at rest. The tears still came easily, and her aching chest reminded her that she would never let Tallenaara go. Running a hand through the grass, Mairin smiled. *So many people longed only for sunny warm days.* Every drop of rain held memories for Mairin of her time with Tally. *Our first kiss, coming here to the cabin for the first time, making love*—Mairin felt the tears coming and could not stop them. She'd been unable to stop the Greys from murdering Tallenaara not far from here. Burying her lover in the rain, with bleeding hands, while her troopers watched. Some of them cried for her loss, some of them pitied her, and she knew that some of them would never understand.

Mairin turned her face up to wash her tears away, cool her burning cheeks, and bring back her happiness. "Tally," she whispered to the rain. "I miss you so much. You know I have to go. But I will be back, love."

The rain quickened as if to answer.

"I'm leaving in the morning. We're forming a quick reaction force to defend colony worlds more effectively in case the Greys come back." Mairin wanted to spit. "Little bastards. They roll into the Rim and destroy everything in their path without giving us a clue to what they wanted. Then you destroy an oil pumping station." Mairin laughed. "Now we all know that's what they eat. I wish you'd have told me that."

Tears flowed. "I couldn't...." The sob choked her, and the words wouldn't come easily. "Oh Tally, I'm so sorry. I couldn't get there in time. I wanted to kill them all, but the little bastards slagged themselves and left the system."

The air was turning colder now. The short autumn of Libretto was coming, and the damp cold seeped into Mairin's skin. *Oh* cariad, *how I miss you.* Lowering her head to the grass, Mairin wished the rain would take away her pain as it soaked her clothes, and rivers ran down her cheeks mixing with her tears.

After a significant effort to compose herself, Mairin raised her head and sniffled. A familiar weight hung from her neck. Eyes closed, her hand clasped around it and she smiled. Wiping her tears, she said, "Yes, this is where I went. All the way back to Rayu-4. Took me two days to find it in the grass. Wouldn't have taken me so long, but the recovery teams had already removed Two."

The smell of the burning Slammer still came to her as pungent as death itself. Her stomach flopped, and bile touched her tongue. The memory of kneeling in the grass to vomit washed over her. Her gut twisted. *Stop it, Mairin. You did everything you could have done. It was their time, and they went down fighting.* Pulling in a deep breath, she said, "I went back for the necklace and to pay my respects. I didn't even really know them when we dropped. But they were my troopers. I don't expect you to understand, Tally. But those four young men died under my command. The first four I lost. Nothing is ever going to take that away."

The necklace was warm in her grip. "And I shouldn't have left this there. I should have had more faith in you. In me. But I didn't."

Lowering her head to the grass, Mairin whispered, "Please forgive me, Tally."

There was no answer. Then again, there seldom was.

The rain tapered off after a while, and Mairin shivered against the coming chill of night. The warmth of the cabin beckoned, however hollow it might be. *No*, she thought, *that is our home.*

Standing slowly, she caressed the grass a final time, then touched her fingers to her lips and laid them on the cold ground.

"If I do not come home, then I will be with you forever. No matter where I go, you are with me. I love you, Tally." With her fingers, she bored a small hole in the ground and slipped her captain's bars inside. "It's not much, but my future should have been with you and not with the TDF. At least I can say I made that decision, *cariad. Da bo ti.*"

Mairin made it a point to not look back. Shoulders square and back straight, she walked to the cabin to pack her belongings. The cabin would be hers as long as she wanted it. The Styrahi Council assured her of that. Their doting over her was welcome after the Terran Defense Force had all but turned her out on her ass.

Colonel-retired Munson would arrive within the hour. There was time enough for a shower and a fresh change of clothes before she'd head out into the void. Munson wanted to find the Greys at all costs, and no one would officially back him. The TDF and the Fleet would sponsor the effort, but it would take place outside the bounds of military operations. Being a mercenary did not sound right to Mairin, but in the end, it didn't matter. There, she would make a difference. And have a last full measure of revenge.

<<<< >>>>

About Kevin Ikenberry

Kevin's head has been in the clouds since he was old enough to read. Ask him and he'll tell you that he still wants to be an astronaut. A retired Army officer, Kevin has a diverse background in space and space science education. A former manager of the world-renowned U.S. Space Camp program in Huntsville, Alabama and a former executive of two Challenger Learning Centers, Kevin works with space every day and lives in Colorado with his family.

Kevin's bestselling debut science fiction novel, ***Sleeper Protocol***, was released by Red Adept Publishing in January 2016 and was a Finalist for the 2017 Colorado Book Award. Publisher's Weekly called it "an emotionally powerful debut." The sequel, ***Vendetta Protocol***, was released in 2017. His bestselling military science fiction novel ***Peacemaker*** was released in late 2017.

Kevin is an Active Member of the Science Fiction Writers of America and he is member of Pikes Peak Writers and the Rocky Mountain Fiction Writers. He is an alumna of the Superstars Writing Seminar.

* * * * *

Connect with Kevin Ikenberry Online

Learn more about Kevin Ikenberry at:

http://www.kevinikenberry.com/

Facebook: https://www.facebook.com/authorkevinikenberry/

Twitter: @thewriterike

* * * * *

Titles by Kevin Ikenberry

"Sleeper Protocol" – Available Now

"A Fistful of Credits" – Available Now

"Peacemaker" – Available Now

"Vendetta Protocol" – Available Now

"Lancer One" – Available Now

"Runs in the Family" – Available Now

* * * * *

Acknowledgements

Runs In The Family was originally published in January 2016 by Strigidae Publishing and my longtime friends Henry and Hollie Snider. Later that summer, Henry underwent heart surgery and they were forced to shutter the fledgling press just as this novel was really gaining steam. While this was an unfortunate development for everyone, I'd rather have my friend alive and well. I can report that Henry is doing just fine and that he always knew this book would find another home.

I'm exceedingly grateful to Chris Kennedy for agreeing to bring this book to Theogony Press as a Second Edition. I've been very fortunate to work with Chris and fellow creator Mark Wandrey in the bestselling Four Horsemen Universe books, and when I told Chris about this book, he agreed to look it over and eventually gave the approval to bring it back into print. As we pushed it to publication, editor Tiffany Reynolds climbed on board and helped to tweak the manuscript into what you've read and hopefully enjoyed.

I'd be remiss without thanking my family and my team for all the work they've put in and put up with over the course of the last six years. I wrote the original draft for this novel in 2011 and it's been through lots of ups and downs ever since. The future of The Imprint War is uncertain right now, and it's not because of the ending you just read. (Note: I know it's not a happy ending – war doesn't end happily for everyone.) I do look forward to following the continuing adventures of Mairin Shields, but it's going to take some time because of other projects in front of me. But, I can assure you that we haven't seen the last of her.

And, if you're wanting a little more Imprint War right now, check out a prequel novella to this book called Lancer One – available only through Amazon.

Colorado Springs, Colorado
December 2017

The following is an

Excerpt from Book Six of the Revelations Cycle:

Peacemaker

Kevin Ikenberry

Available Now from Seventh Seal Press

eBook, Paperback, and Audio Book

Excerpt from "Peacemaker:"

"Well, shit," She laughed. "This isn't going to be easy."

Her earpiece clicked. "Bulldog, Hex. Over."

"Go ahead, Hex."

There was a pause. "It's bad. Kei is dead along with three other Angels. I mean, we're assuming she's dead. We can't find a body. It's like her CASPer detonated instead of the camera system. There's at least 40 Altar dead, maybe more. The server compound is gone. It shouldn't have detonated like that. I don't…no idea, Jess."

Jessica paused. She needed to calm him down. "Hex? What about Altar casualties?"

"Um...yeah, there's about a 100 wounded and the central air defense system was damaged. Klatk is getting a damage report now."

"I need you to take charge up there."

Hex sighed. "How am I supposed to do that?"

Jessica shook her head. "Find out what happened, Hex. What's the situation down below?"

"Klatk lost contact with her team. There's been a cave-in on at least one of the lower levels. I'll send a team down there as soon as I can."

"Gotcha. Keep security up and don't let your guard down."

"Roger, Jess."

She studied the control console and decided it was worth trying to climb. "Keep the faith, Hex."

"Roger, Bulldog. Will advise of changes. Out."

Jessica turned and looked around the slightly curving wall with the light for anything usable. She snapped the light's cylindrical shaft into a 90-degree bend and nested it into a bunch of cables and wires so it pointed up at the target console. Wiping her hands on her coveralls, she reached out to an open panel on the control console and found a solid handhold for both hands. Swinging her left leg up as she vaulted to the console, she found purchase on the side of the control station, pulled her full weight up, and scrambled for a higher grip. Right foot placed on her initial handhold, Jessica tested her weight on the console and found it stable. Able to rest, she looked up into the cockpit at the systems station and froze. One entire panel was gone, revealing the inner workings and board systems within. The interior gold board reflected the flashlight and showed row upon row of silver connections and black chipsets. Most of them were square, but a few were round. In the depth of the console, there was a board of rectangular shaped ones just like...

Oh, shit!

An icy bolt of electricity shot down her spine and she reached into her pocket—

WHAMM!

<<Airstrike!>> Lucille called. Jessica bent over the control console and grabbed for anything as the Raknar shook around her. <<The Raknar has been hit by incoming aircraft.>>

No shit!

The Raknar bucked from side to side as multiple detonations hit the mech's body. From the feel of it, several hit the Raknar's back, and the vibrations threatened to throw her off the console completely. Whole body frantically grabbing the console, Jessica barked at her earpiece. "Hex! Report!"

Outside, she heard the Altar batteries open fire with a deafening whoosh. "Returning fire on red air. Six bandits. They're making another run. Hang on, Jess!"

A series of detonations rippled along the spine of the Raknar. The first few were lower down, near the Raknar's hips. They traveled up the imaginary spine of the beast, and Jessica realized it wasn't any type of collateral damage. The Raknar, and she, were the targets. This wasn't about the Altar colony at all. The Raknar and whatever was below the surface were the problems. *What if it's all connected? Klatk's people are simply in the way and—*

Jessica didn't have time to finish that train of thought. A large explosion threw her from the control console and toward the cockpit door. Pain shot through her for a millisecond before her head glanced off the cockpit rail. She slid down the wall and came to rest in a pile of cables and filth as the cockpit door clanged shut above her.

* * * * *

The following is an

Excerpt from Book One of the Revelations Cycle:

Cartwright's Cavaliers

Mark Wandrey

Available Now from Seventh Seal Press

eBook, Paperback, and Audio Book

Excerpt from "Cartwright's Cavaliers:"

The last two operational tanks were trapped on their chosen path. Faced with destroyed vehicles front and back, they cut sideways to the edge of the dry river bed they'd been moving along and found several large boulders to maneuver around that allowed them to present a hull-down defensive position. Their troopers rallied on that position. It was starting to look like they'd dig in when Phoenix 1 screamed over and strafed them with dual streams of railgun rounds. A split second later, Phoenix 2 followed on a parallel path. Jim was just cheering the air attack when he saw it. The sixth damned tank, and it was a heavy.

"I got that last tank," Jim said over the command net.

"Observe and stand by," Murdock said.

"We'll have these in hand shortly," Buddha agreed, his transmission interspersed with the thudding of his CASPer firing its magnet accelerator. "We can be there in a few minutes."

Jim examined his battlespace. The tank was massive. It had to be one of the fusion-powered beasts he'd read about. Which meant shields and energy weapons. It was heading down the same gap the APC had taken, so it was heading toward Second Squad, and fast.

"Shit," he said.

"Jim," Hargrave said, "we're in position. What are you doing?"

"Leading," Jim said as he jumped out from the rock wall.

*****

Get "Cartwright's Cavaliers" now at: https://www.amazon.com/dp/B01MRZKM95/.

The following is an
Excerpt from Book One of The Kin Wars Saga:

Wraithkin

Jason Cordova

Available Now from Theogony Books

eBook, Paperback, and Audio Book

Excerpt from "Wraithkin:"

Prologue

The lifeless body of his fellow agent on the bed confirmed the undercover operation was thoroughly busted.

"Crap," Agent Andrew Espinoza, Dominion Intelligence Bureau, said as he stepped fully into the dimly lit room and carefully made his way to the filthy bed in which his fellow agent lay. He turned away from the ruined body of his friend and scanned the room for any sign of danger. Seeing none, he quickly walked back out of the room to where the slaves he had rescued earlier were waiting.

"Okay, let's keep quiet now," he reminded them. "I'll go first, and you follow me. I don't think there are any more slavers in the warehouse. Understand?"

They all nodded. He offered them a smile of confidence, though he had lied. He knew there was one more slaver in the warehouse, hiding near the side exit they were about to use. He had a plan to deal with that person, however. First he had to get the slaves to safety.

He led the way, his pistol up and ready as he guided the women through the dank and musty halls of the old, rundown building. It had been abandoned years before, and the slaver ring had managed to get it for a song. In fact, they had even qualified for a tax-exempt purchase due to the condition of the neighborhood around it. The local constable had wanted the property sold, and the slaver ring had stepped in and offered him a cut if he gave it to them. The constable had readily agreed, and the slavers had turned the warehouse into the processing plant for the sex slaves they sold throughout the Dominion. Andrew knew all this because he had been the one to help set up the purchase in the first place.

Now, though, he wished he had chosen another locale.

He stopped the following slaves as he came to the opening which led into one of the warehouse's spacious storage areas. Beyond that lay their final destination, and he was dreading the confrontation with the last slaver. He checked his gun and grunted in surprise as he saw he had two fewer rounds left than he had thought. He shook his head and charged the pistol.

"Stay here and wait for my signal," he told the rescued slaves. They nodded in unison.

He took a deep, calming breath. No matter what happened, he had to get the slaves to safety. He owed them that much. His sworn duty was to protect the Dominion from people like the slavers, and someone along the way had failed these poor women. He exhaled slowly, crossed himself and prayed to God, the Emperor and any other person who might have been paying attention.

He charged into the room, his footsteps loud on the concrete flooring. He had his gun up as he ducked behind a small, empty crate. He peeked over the top and snarled; he had been hoping against hope the slaver was facing the other direction.

Apparently Murphy is still a stronger presence in my life than God, he thought as he locked eyes with the last slaver. The woman's eyes widened in recognition and shock, and he knew he would only have one chance before she killed them all.

He dove to the right of the crate and rolled, letting his momentum drag him out of the slaver's immediate line of fire. He struggled to his feet as her gun swung up and began to track him, but he was already moving, sprinting back to the left while closing in on her. She fired twice, both shots ricocheting off the floor and embedding themselves in the wall behind him.

Andrew skid to a stop and took careful aim. It was a race, the slaver bringing her gun around as his own came to bear upon her. The muzzles of both guns flashed simultaneously, and Andrew grunted as pain flared in his shoulder.

A second shot punched him in the gut and he fell, shocked the woman had managed to get him. He lifted his head and saw that while he had hit her, her wound wasn't nearly as bad as his. He had merely clipped her collarbone and, while it would smart, it was in no way fatal. She took aim on him and smiled coldly.

Andrew swiftly brought his gun up with his working arm and fired one final time. The round struck true, burrowing itself right between the slaver's eyes. She fell backwards and lay still, dead. He groaned and dropped the gun, pain blossoming in his stomach. He rolled onto his back and stared at the old warehouse's ceiling.

That sucked, he groused. He closed his eyes and let out a long, painful breath.

*****

Find out more about Jason Cordova and "Wraithkin" at:
http://chriskennedypublishing.com/imprints-authors/jason-cordova/

*****

Made in the USA
Monee, IL
26 June 2025

20073062R00252